## THE GREY FALLS . . .

"Ruby, put the scissors down."

I turned, saw Mark in the doorway. "I can't," I told him. "I have work to do."

"No, you don't. We're going canoeing, remember?"

"I can't go anywhere now. I have clients. Grace can't handle this alone." I looked around. "Where's my notebook? I need my notebook."

"I don't know about the notebook," Mark said. "But I do know that Grace is doing okay on her own."

"Okay? Okay? Mark, look around. She's made a mockery of everything." I turned to the woman in the chair. "What's your name?"

"Ruby, it's me," she said. "Joannie from Algonquin Island."

"Of course you are." I swung around to the women on the couch. "The rest of you . . . I don't know. I'll figure something out. But right now I need my goddamn notebook."

Mark put his hands on my shoulders. "Ruby, give me the scissors."

Maybe it was the way the silence suddenly pressed in on me or the looks on the faces all around me. I don't think I'll ever know what stopped me, what made me come back to the moment. But for some reason, I was acutely aware of what I had just done.

My daughter was outside, crying. My best friend was on the verge of it herself, and my clients, women I'd known for years, women I considered friends, were staring at me as though they'd never seen me before. They were right. They hadn't. This was the new Ruby. Big Al's girl. And she was down by more than a few points.

# ISLAND GIRL

LYNDA SIMMONS

BERKLEY BOOKS, NEW YORK

**THE BERKLEY PUBLISHING GROUP**
**Published by the Penguin Group**
**Penguin Group (USA) Inc.**
**375 Hudson Street, New York, New York 10014, USA**
Penguin Group (Canada), 90 Eglinton Avenue East, Suite 700, Toronto, Ontario M4P 2Y3, Canada
(a division of Pearson Penguin Canada Inc.)
Penguin Books Ltd., 80 Strand, London WC2R 0RL, England
Penguin Group Ireland, 25 St. Stephen's Green, Dublin 2, Ireland (a division of Penguin Books Ltd.)
Penguin Group (Australia), 250 Camberwell Road, Camberwell, Victoria 3124, Australia
(a division of Pearson Australia Group Pty. Ltd.)
Penguin Books India Pvt. Ltd., 11 Community Centre, Panchsheel Park, New Delhi—110 017, India
Penguin Group (NZ), 67 Apollo Drive, Rosedale, North Shore 0632, New Zealand
(a division of Pearson New Zealand Ltd.)
Penguin Books (South Africa) (Pty.) Ltd., 24 Sturdee Avenue, Rosebank, Johannesburg 2196,
South Africa

Penguin Books Ltd., Registered Offices: 80 Strand, London WC2R 0RL, England

This book is an original publication of The Berkley Publishing Group.

This is a work of fiction. Names, characters, places, and incidents either are the product of the author's imagination or are used fictitiously, and any resemblance to actual persons, living or dead, business establishments, events, or locales is entirely coincidental. The publisher does not have any control over and does not assume any responsibility for author or third-party websites or their content.

PRINTING HISTORY
Berkley trade paperback edition / December 2010

Library of Congress Cataloging-in-Publication Data

Simmons, Lynda, 1954–
    Island girl / Lynda Simmons. — Berkley trade pbk. ed.
        p.   cm.
    ISBN: 978-0-425-23724-3 (trade pbk.)
    1. Alzheimer's disease—Fiction. 2. Mothers and daughters—Fiction. 3. Domestic fiction. I. Title.
    PR9199.4.S547I85    2010
    813'.6—dc22                                                                    2010027941

PRINTED IN THE UNITED STATES OF AMERICA

10   9   8   7   6   5   4   3   2   1

*For Hedy,*
*with love from the troll*

# acknowledgments

While I was working on this book, people who weren't familiar with the Island would often ask, "Is this a real place?" I was always delighted to tell them yes, the Island is real, and magical, and truly unique. A place where farm animals and Ferris wheels blend easily with parkland, bird sanctuaries, and a neighborhood of homes that only survived because of the dedication of those who stood together to stop the destruction of everything that had once been. As a result, history on the Island isn't merely a reenactment or a collection of empty buildings and commemorative plaques. History here is part of a living and vital community. And the Island is the only place I know of where it doesn't matter who you are or how much money you have. If you want to own a little piece of this paradise, you have to get in line and wait like everyone else—and I hope that never changes.

I'd like to thank the many Islanders who shared their time and their stories with me, including Peter Holt, who answered questions about the smallest details with a patience that was always appreciated. Elizabeth Amer, who served me tea and gave me wonderful insights into the fight to save the Island homes. David, Ellen, and Eric Smiley, who allowed me a glimpse into everyday life on the Island. And, of course, Albert Fulton, who not only opened the archives to me but also helped me navigate through the volumes of information he lovingly gathered and painstakingly maintained for so many years. And finally, I would be remiss if I didn't give a tip of the hat to Toronto Island Connection, the online group who welcomed me into their discussions of Island lore, and made an outsider feel like one of the gang.

I also owe a debt of gratitude to the families and patients who were so generous in sharing their experiences with Alzheimer's. And a kiss to Lorraine and Edna, whose lives have touched me deeply.

# RUBY

If I were a teenager, this would be a coming-of-age story. But having celebrated my fifty-fifth birthday yesterday—complete with champagne, cake, and more candles than anyone wants to see in one place—I suppose this is more a coming-of-old-age story. The tale of a woman well aware that the best is no longer yet to come. Proud that all the years of canoeing and weight training and green tea have given her firm arms, a straight back, and a heart so strong the little darling will probably beat for years and years to come. Yet knowing with aching clarity that none of these things will stop, or even slow, the inevitable decline before her.

Fortunately, it's not all bad news. As those thoughtful cards from the Humorous Birthday section of the Hallmark store pointed out, I may be "Over the Hill" and "Past My Best Before Date," but I am also officially a "Junior Senior" now, entitling me to a free coffee refill at Donut King and a 10 percent discount on power tools this week at the hardware store on Sherbourne. Pity I swore off coffee twenty years ago and already have a shed full of tools courtesy of Jack Hoyle—the man who finished renovating my second-floor bedroom yesterday and shared it with me last night after the party.

While I never expected my handyman to hang around for the long good-bye, a kiss on the cheek or even an elbow in the ribs would have been better than waking up to find an empty pillow on my right and a few words scrawled on the back of an envelope stuck to the fridge. *Catching early flight from Hanlan's. Tools in shed for safekeeping. Good luck, Jack.*

I couldn't believe it. After everything I'd explained, after everything he'd read, the idiot had still booked a flight out of the Island Airport. Another blatant example of self-interest trumping reason. Then again, what else could I expect from a man with broad shoulders and a narrow mind?

"Good luck to you too, Jack," I whispered, dropping the note into the garbage and smiling as I went to plug in the kettle. I'd always meant to tell him that the old shed leaks like a sieve, see if he wanted to stick around a while longer, maybe fix it for me. But like so many things these days, it must have slipped through a crack in my Junior Senior mind, and I can't imagine I'll remember to add that repair to one of my lists any time soon.

The lists are everywhere now. Grocery lists, address lists, lists telling me where to go and when and why. I write them to keep myself on track, to stem the flow of details through those damn cracks. For the most part they work, which is why I am dressed in my best trousers and jacket with my hair freshly highlighted and sprayed into submission. The next ferry leaves at 8:30 A.M. and I plan to be on it, because the first line on today's to-do list reads, *Find Liz*, and the city is as good a place to start as any.

Of course as my Grandma Lucy used to say, *The best laid schemes o' mice an' men gang aft a-gley*, which roughly translates into *Shit happens*, and while I was dropping tea bags into the pot, one of those Junior Senior cracks opened wide and in danced Mary Anne Biggs, my closest neighbor, my best friend, and my first Tuesday morning appointment—something I would have remembered had I checked my appointment book before climbing the stairs with Jack last night.

"Wonderful news," she announced, waltzing herself over to the barber's chair that takes up far too much room in this tiny house but has enormous sentimental value. "I have decided to have both a trim *and* a permanent wave. But you're not to cut my bangs. If you so much as brush my bangs with your nasty great shears, I shall be utterly wretched for weeks." She sat down and started pulling pins from her hair, slowly unleashing miles and miles of frizzy salt-and-pepper tresses upon a hapless world. "Now, I must know. Did you get your secret paramour out before Grace woke up, or is the poor boy still hiding upstairs?"

Mary Anne is the only person I know who is ever *utterly wretched* or refers to men as *paramours*. I put it down to too many years teaching Jane Austen at the University of Toronto. If she had taken a sabbatical now and then as I suggested, or perhaps taught contemporary lit for a few years, she might have something in her closet now besides long skirts and straw hats—and she might even let me update her hairstyle by at least a century.

"Jack is hardly a boy," I said, writing *Check appointment book* at the top of the next page in my notebook and underlining it. Twice. "And he was already gone when I woke up."

She squinted at the page. "Was that planned?"

I closed the book. "No, but it's for the best. And Grace will never be the wiser." I poured boiling water into the teapot, went to the table for the cozy, and glanced out the kitchen window, thinking I'd see Grace on her bike, certain she should be home by now.

While I like to start my day with a paddle around the lagoons, my younger daughter prefers a morning ride, pedaling the five kilometers from our house here on the eastern tip of Ward's Island, all the way across Centre Island to the dock at the western end of Hanlan's Point. I like to think she pauses there, giving a finger to the Island Airport before starting back, arriving home while the air is still cool and the ferries have yet to start bringing the hordes across the bay from the city.

Hundreds of years ago the hordes could have come on foot because the Island was nothing more than a peninsula of sandbars protecting Toronto Harbour from attack. All that changed in April 1858 when a storm severed the peninsula once and for all. Decades of dredging and remodeling since have created five major landmasses all connected by paved paths and foot bridges and collectively known as the Island—the city's oasis in the lake.

A ten-minute ferry ride is now the only way over, and from mid-April to October three of them ply the water between the Island and Toronto Harbour every half hour. During the summer months, sweltering city dwellers jam those boats every day, coming across to enjoy the parks, the rides, and Toronto's only nude beaches. Don't misunderstand me, I know I'm lucky to live with the parks and the beaches, and the hordes would be fine if they stuck to Centre and Hanlan's. But inevitably they find their way here, to the narrow shaded lanes of Ward's and Algonquin.

They wander our streets and peer at our homes, taking pictures and passing judgment—*My God, these places are small. Why are they cheek by jowl like that? And honestly, look at that garden*—acting as though they're visiting a zoo, as though we can't understand what they're saying or doing. Most of them are okay, but there are always those who knock on our doors, demanding to know how much it costs to rent a place on the Island for the summer. It never fails to amaze me. They live ten minutes across the bay yet have no idea that we're here year-round and have been for generations.

"Ruby?" Mary Anne called. "Ruby, are you all right?"

I turned to find her watching me intently. "Of course. Why wouldn't I be?"

"Because you've been staring out that window for the last five minutes." She sat back, massaging her scalp with her fingers. "Tell me the truth. Are you unhappy that Jack left?"

I laughed and put the cozy back on the table. "Not at all. I just didn't think he'd do it on a flight out of the bloody Island Airport. But on the plus side, I scored a shed full of tools. Know anyone looking to buy a miter saw?"

She went back to pulling out pins. "They say a vengeful heart is usually a broken one."

"And sometimes it just wants to make a buck. Would you like tea?"

Without waiting for an answer, I poured a cup and set it in front of her, hoping to avoid another rant about the inseparability of love and sex in the female constitution. Because no matter what I said—or how loudly—Mary Anne would smile and nod knowingly, confident I was covering up. Lying to avoid confessing to a shattered heart, a splintered soul, or something equally ridiculous when the truth is that I have never been even a little bit in love with most of the men I have known, including Jack Hoyle. It was sheer coincidence that he was the first one to stay under my roof in close to eighteen years.

With two daughters in the house, discretion was always my first concern. Even when they lived in the city I was vigilant, keeping sex and home separate, knowing it would matter when Grace came back again. Jack Hoyle had been a slipup. Someone tall and strong, and standing in the right place at the right time when I hit a low ebb. He didn't question why I was waiting on the stairs wearing nothing but high heels and a frosty bottle of his favorite beer when he came back from lunch. He just went along. Swept me off my feet and carried me up those stairs. Allowing me to believe, if only for a while, that I still had something to offer, that I wasn't already finished.

It was a scene Mary Anne would have appreciated if I'd told her about it, which I hadn't because I was still embarrassed by my own reaction. Who knew he'd pick that moment to pull a Clark Gable on me? And who knew I'd like it? But I would never mistake lust for love.

"Ruby!" Mary Anne said too sharply. I looked over. She was watching me again, obviously waiting for an answer, but I had no idea what the question had been. "Ruby, what is going on with you?" she asked, and I could not have been more grateful when Grace came up the stairs calling, "I'm home," saving me from a discussion I was not yet ready to have.

"You'll never guess what I saw," Grace sang, shedding sandals, notebook, and binoculars on her way to the fridge.

My younger daughter may be an adult, but she's as carefree as any ten-year-old. Her hair is usually caught up in a ponytail, she wears jeans or cutoffs, and her T-shirts invariably have a slogan: Walk for the Cure. I'm with Stupid. The list goes on and on. She picks them up at the Bridge Boutique, our local clothing swap at the foot of the Algonquin Island Bridge.

This morning she's sporting an electric blue number that is far too large and reads It's Good to Be Queen. As always, I am struck by how beautiful she is. Tall and willowy with white blond hair, pale blue eyes, and a misty, far away look, just like her father. Eric Kaufman. Now there is a man I have loved. One who will never know he has a daughter who looks just like him.

"I saw a Cooper's hawk," Grace said, her head in the fridge, her hands routing through jars and plastic containers. "That's really rare, and since I don't have any customers till ten, I—"

"Grace, I'm sorry." Her hands stilled and I took a step toward her. "I know this is short notice for both of you, but I have to go into the city, so you'll have to take care of Mary Anne."

"Fine by me," Mary Anne said. But I didn't breathe until Grace said, "Okeydokey. Just don't ask me to cut those bangs."

Mary Anne pointed a triumphant finger at her. "There's a girl who knows a thing or two about hair. I shall trust you to give me both a trim *and* a permanent wave."

Grace laughed, a sweet, rippling sound that had my shoulders relaxing, my breath returning to normal. "Anybody want eggs?" she asked, holding the carton aloft like a prize.

Like the morning ride, eggs are also part of her new routine—two over easy with two slices of toast and two cups of tea. At lunch she'll have a sandwich, usually grilled cheese, and for dinner she likes chicken or beef with potatoes and any vegetable that isn't brussels sprouts. She only likes surprises at dessert, so I try to make sure she doesn't have to deal with them at any other time. But Mary Anne had been a surprise even to me this morning, and I was lucky things had gone so smoothly with Grace.

"She likes her perms tight," I reminded her.

"And her tea with milk and sugar. I remember."

I glanced over at Mary Anne. Her tea was still untouched. I had served it clear. Damn.

Grace slipped bread into the toaster, then carried milk and sugar over to Mary Anne and lifted a few strands of that salt-and-pepper hair. "You need conditioning."

Mary Anne nodded and poured milk into her cup while Grace went back to her eggs. They were settled and happy. I could leave, confident things would go well. Grace loves Mary Anne and she was born to do hair. When she was little, she was always with me at my shop in the city, Chez Ruby on Queen, playing with dolls in the waiting room, coloring pictures by the shampoo sinks. Unlike Liz, she loved being at Chez Ruby and she loved being with me.

Some people think I was wrong to start training her when she was only thirteen, but the girl was going to need a trade and time to learn it. Why pretend? Why put off the inevitable? And look at her now. She's a good hairdresser and the clients love her, especially the seniors.

I always thought Grace and I would work together at Chez Ruby on Queen forever. But after that trouble with Liz a few years back, I moved the shop here instead, bringing the barber's chair and some of the other equipment with me. I lost a handful of customers at first. But when I lowered the prices to reflect the savings in overhead, more and more of them started coming across the bay in all but the very worst weather to join us at Chez Ruby on the Island. As I say to Grace all the time, that's what comes of good service.

The horn blast from the dock reminded me that I had five minutes before the ferry left. Grabbing my notebook, I read *Find Liz* again, then stashed the book in my purse. "I'm off," I said, giving Grace a hug on my way out the door.

The morning was already hot, the air close. In the garden, the lilac still needed pruning, the rich purple faded to brown weeks ago and waiting patiently for me to get busy with a different kind of shears. My grandmother planted that lilac bush in 1943, the year she built our home. It's now fifteen feet tall and the pride of a property that has been nurtured by Donaldson women ever since. On any other morning, I'd pause to inspect the daylilies, the climbing roses, the pots of geraniums. Taking time to breathe in the perfume that is unique to this garden, this Island. But not today. Today I have to find Liz.

Kicking back the stand on my bike, I gave Grace a quick wave as I pulled away, still grateful to see her at the window, to have my girl home again.

I pedaled carefully along the narrow lanes, dodging cats and kids, giving way to the bikes moving faster than mine. With the exception of emergency crews and park staff, motorized vehicles are prohibited on the Island. No cars, no Vespas. Definitely no golf cars. Bicycles get us where we need to go, with carts on the back and baskets on the front to help us carry groceries, liquor, tired kids, and anything else we need from the city because there are also no stores on the Island. Life can be hard in the winter when the wind cuts your face and heavy snow makes the going impossible on two wheels. But Islanders have always been a different breed. Urban misfits the lot of us, happy to sacrifice a few comforts for a life apart from the push and shove of the city.

There used to be five thousand of us here, with houses and businesses spreading from Hanlan's Point to Ward's Island. Everything from hotels to corner stores and a milkman who came to our doors every morning. Life was good until the late fifties when the city decided the Island should be a park. Year after year they came with their sheriff and their bulldozers, pushing us back farther and farther until we finally took a stand in July 1980. Banded together and said no more. We would not be moved.

There are only seven hundred of us left, but instead of chasing us away, the hardships make us stronger, more determined to hold on to the homes and the life we love. Which is why another blast from the ferry had me pedaling faster. I could not afford to miss that boat.

My bike is a black 1946 Schwinn. Brand-new when my grandmother brought it over after the war and in its prime when my mother claimed it as her own in the fifties. But now, just like me, the poor thing is well past its best before date. There won't be anything worth passing on, so I never bother with the lock when I leave the bike at the ferry dock. If some kid pitches it over the wall into the eastern channel, I won't mind. In fact, I can't think of a more fitting tribute for the old girl than to be laid to rest among the other bikes at the bottom of the gap.

Jamming the Schwinn into the last available spot, I raced aboard the *Ongiara*, the small ferry that trundles back and forth between Toronto and Ward's year-round—the one meant for Islanders. The 8:30 A.M. serves mostly commuters, and I moved through the crowd as I used to every morning, calling hello to people I knew, nodding to those I only recognized. There was a time when I missed my daily commute. Missed the small talk, the gossip updates, and the money that came with working in the city. But like Grandma Lucy, I've come to prefer the pace and freedom of working from home. And I have always known how to stretch a buck until it screams—something Liz's father used to admire about me.

"Ruby, darlin'," he'd say. "There is nothing sexier than watching you clip those coupons. Gets me all hot and bothered just sittin' here." That much was true. Doubtless because I was building a healthy sum in the coffee tin we were filling for our future together.

His name was Gideon, he hailed from Oklahoma, and he was just another draft dodger who found his way to the Island during the sixties and seventies. I was no child when he arrived in 1974. No breathless virgin waiting to be wakened to the joys of sex, but the day that man stepped off the ferry, I stood perfectly still on the dock, barely breathing while I watched him come down the ramp.

Gideon may have been a hayseed back home, but to me he was a dark and exotic mystery. A man who smiled easily, knew every sensitive spot on a woman's body, and played a mean guitar. Grandma Lucy warned me about him from the start, but I fell in love anyway. Made us a nest in my room and gave birth to his daughter a year later. I even thought about marriage every time I clipped a coupon or stashed another bill in that tin.

Liz was almost two years old when Jimmy Carter granted amnesty to all the artful dodgers in January 1977. I left Chez Ruby early that day, heading home to celebrate. Mary Anne met me at my front door, told me Gideon and my money had hopped on the ferry an hour earlier, bound for the city and a train to warmer climes. She knew because she caught him packing the coffee tin into a duffel bag when she dropped by to check on Grandma Lucy.

"I have spent long enough on this godforsaken spit of land," he'd said. "And I am sick to death of leaving my balls at the dock."

She tried to stop him, ending up on her backside in a snowbank for her trouble. I haven't heard from him since and don't care to either. He was just another man I have loved. Another man who has a daughter who looks just like him. And Grandma Lucy was right again.

I made my way to the front of the *Ongiara* where old Benny Barnes had taken up his position at the railing. Benny's family has lived on the Island as long as mine, maybe longer, but I don't remember him aging. As far as I can tell, he has always been old, which must have been easier than coming to it the way I did—head on and without warning.

He nodded and moved his bike over so we could stand together, watching the harbor come closer and closer. The skyline has changed dramatically over the past few years. More office towers, more condos—nothing that means anything to me. I prefer the view at night when the lake reflects the lights and the city looks like a fairyland from my bedroom window.

"Gonna be a hot one," Benny said.

I smiled and turned my back on the city, watching the Island recede while he made small talk. Special on pork chops at Sobeys. Another damn rock festival coming. And finally, "Poor Mike lost another bicycle. Kids dumped it in the Eastern Gap. Someone ought to do something."

"Indeed," I said, not mentioning my thoughts about my own bike and the watery graveyard at the bottom of the gap. Some things you kept to yourself on the Island.

The *Ongiara* began to slow. The deckhands readied the ropes for docking and Benny raised the kickstand on his bike. "You shopping today?"

"Not today." I left it at that, joining the pack heading down the ramp before he got his bike rolling. No one needed to know why I was in the city. Not even me.

I stood for a moment at the traffic lights on Front Street, checking my notebook, reading again the first few lines. *Find Liz. Go to 100 King Street. Look up Mark Bernier.*

King Street wasn't far from the harbor and I found the address in under fifteen minutes. But since when were community legal clinics located in bank towers? Worried I'd taken down the address wrong, I ventured over to the directory and breathed a sigh of relief when I saw the sign for Fleming, Hitchcock, Romney and Bernier, Barristers and Solicitors. Thirtieth floor.

So much for community legal work. And I couldn't help smiling as I walked into the elevator, wondering if Mark ever missed his principles.

I met Mark in 1979 at a Save the Island Homes rally. I was with Eric then, the one with the blue eyes who would be Grace's father in a year but never know it. Mark was big—six foot four—with a handshake that made my teeth rattle and an openness that took me off guard. Both Eric and I liked him right away, and Liz adored him, but she was only four and based her judgment solely on the fact that he always brought treats, so hers was not a fair assessment.

Even then, he spoiled that girl, but I was pleased when he kept coming to the meetings, grateful he was there the day Eric took the ferry into the city for the last time, and shocked he didn't run for the next one after I confessed in a drunken slur that I was pregnant.

Mark stayed with me through everything. The pregnancy, the birth, those first horrible weeks, trying to keep Liz from lugging that baby around like it was her own. I was surprised to find him still with us when Grace turned one. I'm not sure when we decided we were officially living together, but if you were to ask Mark, he'd say it was the day Grace was born.

A pretty redhead looked up from the reception desk and smiled. "Can I help you?"

"I'm looking for Mark Bernier."

"Do you have an appointment?" She frowned when I shook my head. "I'm afraid Mr. Bernier is tied up in meetings for the day—"

"Tell him his ex-wife is here. And tell him she's pissed."

She was on her feet at once. "I'll be right back."

I have never been anyone's wife, but I knew the line would work better than, "A situation has come up and I could use his advice because I'm very confused right now, but I can't afford a lawyer and I'm hoping he'll be a sweetie and help me out, you know?"

Sure enough, she was back within minutes, escorting me along gleaming hardwood to an office furnished with leather chairs, a rosewood desk, and modern art, undoubtedly expensive, on the walls.

Mark looked up from that desk as I stepped past the secretary. "Ruby, good to see you."

I paused, suddenly flustered. "It's good to see you too."

He rose and approached, hand outstretched, face collapsing into a minefield of wrinkles when he smiled. My God, but the man had aged. I couldn't help wondering if he was thinking the same thing as he took my hand. *My God, Ruby's looking old.*

But he said, "You look fabulous," and I smiled back, wanting to believe him. He may have been older, but his handshake hadn't changed and my teeth were still rattling when he said, "Have a seat," and led me to the desk.

"I assume you're no longer in the legal aid business," I said, taking in the floor-to-ceiling view of the city before sitting down. "What made you change your mind?"

"Debt mostly. Drink?" he asked, indicating a bar on the far side of the room.

I was still curious about his leap into the world of big law, but nothing about him indicated a willingness to chat about that chapter in his life. So I said, "Not right now," and stashed my purse under the chair. "Thanks for seeing me."

"I always make a point of seeing a pissed-off ex." He sat down and folded his hands. "What can I do for you, Ruby?"

And suddenly I had no idea. Not a clue as to why I was there.

"I need to talk to you," I said, because it made sense.

"About what?"

"It's hard to explain," I said, and waited, hoping it would get easier. Or at least clearer.

He tipped his head to one side. "Do you want to try?"

"I hardly know where to start." I rose and walked around to his side of the desk because it felt like the natural thing to do. The picture in the frame by the phone made me pause. Mark and a little girl in a tree house. Same brown hair, same green eyes. His daughter? Possibly, but where was the mother? Why no shots of her?

"Ruby? Are you okay?"

"Yes, of course." I smiled harder and did the only thing that came to mind. I moved in closer, making him roll his chair back to accommodate me. Those green eyes flicked up and down my body. He let out a long controlled breath, inched his chair back a little farther, and I could have cried. The child's mother aside, he still found the ex tempting.

I perched myself on the corner of his desk. "I've been thinking about you a lot lately," I said, which was probably true. Why else would I be there? "And I'm happy to see that life has been good to you."

He rolled his chair back farther still. "What do you want?"

"A chance to get reacquainted? Let bygones be bygones?"

"Ruby, you can't—"

"Can't what?" I leaned forward slightly. "Stoke an old flame? See what flares up?"

He leapt up, knocking over his chair, and flattening himself against the wall. "For God's sake, what are you doing?"

"Trying to stir up some memories," I said, which was definitely true. I moved closer, pressed myself against him, ran my hands over his chest. "I see it's working."

"It's not working."

"You never could lie to me. Not about this." Cupping his face in my hands, I brought his mouth down to mine, kissed him lightly, once, twice. Third time and he was on me, dragging my mouth closer, covering my lips with his and trying to get his tongue inside. He might have been older and out of shape, but he was hard in a hurry and he still wanted me.

"Oh, Mark," I said, feigning breathlessness, hoping the real thing would overtake me while I tried to pull him to the floor.

Halfway there, he stopped, dragged me back to my feet, and stepped away from me. "What the hell are you doing? What is this about?"

"Reconciliation?" He looked doubtful and my shoulders slumped. "All right fine, I don't know what it's about right now. Let's assume it's about sex. Let's just do it and I'll leave."

He held a hand over his belt buckle. "Ruby, stop. I'm not going to let you screw up my life again."

"I screwed up your life?"

"For years and years to come." He moved me around to the other side of the desk, sat me in the chair. "I need a drink. Do you want one?"

"Something red. Something I wouldn't buy for myself." I flopped back in the chair, told myself to concentrate. There was a reason I was there. I was sure of it. I crossed my legs and my foot nudged a purse under the chair. My purse. The one with my notebook inside.

While Mark poured us both a glass of something red, I took out the notebook, read the first line. *Find Liz.* Of course. Find Liz. I gave myself a mental slap. *Stay on track, Ruby.*

He set a glass on the desk in front of me. I raised it and sniffed. Pomegranate juice. Definitely red. Definitely something I wouldn't buy for myself. I should have known.

He carried his own glass around to his side of the desk. "Okay, be honest. What has gotten into you today?"

"Today, nothing. But last week . . ." I closed the notebook and set it on my lap. "Last week was another story completely."

"Go on," he said more gently than I'd expected. But then he had always been gentle, hadn't he? Even on the day I threw him out. If only I could remember why I'd done that.

"Ruby," he said. "Tell me what happened last week."

"Last week. Yes. That's why I'm here." I drew in a quick breath and said the words out loud for the first time since the diagnosis. "I have early onset Alzheimer's."

If I'd hoped for a feeling of relief, a lightening of the load perhaps, I was sorely disappointed. The telling had only made it more real, more frightening, more final. It didn't help that Mark's face drained of color. Or that he shook his head and moistened his lips. I watched the horror leave his eyes, saw comprehension take its place, and in a flash, I became something new in those eyes, something dreadful. An object of pity.

He tried to say something, but his first attempt failed. He couldn't find the words, sounding much like I imagine I'll sound in a year or two. "Are you sure?" he managed at last. "Have you been tested?"

"Extensively. The actual diagnosis was a year ago. I've been on medication since and it seemed to be working fine until a few weeks ago. So I went back for a checkup, thinking all I needed was an adjustment on the meds. It hadn't been that long, after all. But apparently I have the form that progresses rapidly. This time next year, I probably won't know you."

"This makes no sense. You're too young."

"Like I said, it's early onset."

"But no one in your family had it."

"My mother died young. Who knows what might have happened later? And I'm sure now that Grandma Lucy had it, but no one knew. We just thought she was old and doddery."

He reached across the desk to take my hand. "Ruby, I'm sorry."

"Me too." I looked down at our hands. His were huge, paws really, made for working outside, for cutting wood and tilling soil, not for pushing papers around on a desk. He'd always dreamed of going north, as far as Alaska, to work on the land and see justice done. But he'd been tied to the city in his youth. Tied by an un-accountable love for me and my daughters, and I couldn't bring myself to pull away just yet. "As much as I appreciate your sympathy, you don't have to worry about me, because I don't plan to stick it out."

"I don't understand."

I smiled and ran my thumb across his. "Don't play dumb, Mark. You know how I feel about this, how I've always felt."

"Ruby, if you expect me to take you out and shoot you—"

"I don't, so you can relax." I sighed and took my hand back, knowing I shouldn't be weak, shouldn't lean, and more important, I shouldn't feel sorry for myself. "Just because I don't want to hang around for the long good-bye doesn't mean I'd ask you or anyone else to do it for me. I'll take care of that end of things while I still can."

"You're being hasty. You need to explore alternatives. There are new treatments all the time. New drugs, therapies—"

"Nothing permanent, nothing guaranteed to stop the progression. All roads eventually lead to a nursing home, and I've styled enough hair in those places to know that I don't want it and I won't have it. End of discussion."

"Ruby, I can't let you kill yourself."

"Fortunately, you don't have a say in this."

"You're being selfish."

"I'm being practical."

"And what about Grace? Have you thought about her at all?"

I laughed, I couldn't help it. "All I ever do is think about Grace, you know that."

"Have you told her you're sick? Does she know about your plan?"

"I have no intention of telling her about my plan." I raised the glass, finished the juice, and pushed the empty toward him for a refill. "I'll tell her about Big Al once I have everything in place. Which is why I'm here. I need you to help me prepare."

Thankfully, he didn't argue. Just carried my glass to the bar and opened the bottle. "You'll need a new will. Power of attorney—"

"Eventually, yes. But first I need Liz to come home. You have to help me find her."

He started to protest and I held up a hand. "Don't tell me you don't know where she is because it wouldn't make sense, not even to my mind."

He refilled my glass. "I can't betray—"

"A confidence? Come on, Mark. Stop thinking like a lawyer and think like a parent instead." I walked over to the bar, waited until he stopped pouring. "It's time for Liz grow up and come home, take her proper place in the family again. I don't expect you to tell me where she is. Just set up a meeting and I'll take it from there. Can you do that for me?"

He sighed and set the bottle down, slid my glass toward me. "Fine."

I let my breath out slowly. "I appreciate it, Mark."

He didn't answer. Simply walked back to the desk and sat down.

I turned the bottle around, examined the label. Hadn't I read somewhere that pomegranate juice is good for the brain? I chugged the stuff like water then went back to the desk. Opened my notebook and took a pen from his holder. Wrote *Meet Liz* on the second line. *MEET LIZ*. I wrote again and underlined it. But where? When?

"Tomorrow at Fran's on College Street. Six o'clock." I scribbled that too and glanced over at Mark. Saw fear, frustration, everything I felt myself clearly written on that sweet, ravaged face.

"Ruby," he said softly, "you can't do this alone."

I wasn't ready for the sudden tightness in my throat, the threat of useless tears, the heightened emotions of Alzheimer's. I picked up my purse. Walked briskly to the door. "Like I said, don't worry about me. Just make sure Liz is at Fran's on Wednesday." I paused with my hand on the knob, but couldn't risk looking back. "And Mark. Tell her not to be late."

# LIZ

So I was standing outside Fran's, talking to Mark on my cell phone, when the question came to me. Do you have to forgive someone just because they're sick?

"Your mother's not just sick," he said. "She has Alzheimer's."

A streetcar arrived at the stop behind me, the driver ringing the bell to summon the last of the rush hour crowd aboard. *Ding, ding.* Next stop, one block west. *Ding, ding.* Come one, come all. *Ding, ding.* Plenty of room in the back. *Ding, ding, ding.*

"Irritating prick," I muttered, and pressed the phone closer to my ear. "No, not you," I assured Mark. "But I'm curious. How exactly does Ruby having Alzheimer's change anything?"

The streetcar moved off and I stepped closer to the glass, watching my mother through the restaurant window. I'm pretty sure Fran's has been around forever—a landmark for apple pie—and I swear I could smell apples and cinnamon out there on the street while Ruby tossed her jacket into the booth and smiled at the hostess before sliding into her seat.

I hadn't seen my mother in over two years yet she looked as normal as she ever had: body fit, back rigid, red hair skillfully colored and cut. Nothing about her suggested confusion or anxiety, and I admit I was vaguely disappointed, hoping I'd catch her talking to herself or flirting with the coatrack. Something that would get her carted off to a safe place with coded doors and bath chairs, giving me a good story for the pub. *So my mother went crazy at Fran's.*

"Liz?" Mark said. "Are you still there?"

"Where else would I be?"

"Inside with Ruby, perhaps?"

"Dream on," I said, paying close attention to the way she opened the menu and studied the pages, biting her lower lip and shaking her head as she moved through the choices. Pretending she was tempted by everything she saw when I knew damn well she was merely avoiding eye contact with me. Trying to make us both believe she had no idea I was standing on the other side of the glass in my orange and white Donut King uniform—complete with flattering hairnet—while Mark pleaded her case and the streetcars rumbled past. *Ding, ding. Ding, ding.* Assholes.

My boss at the Donut King two doors down knew I was there. I was already late for my shift when I'd walked into the place earlier, and I should have ignored the voice in my pocket hollering *Answer your goddamn phone!* The phone was new, an update from Mark, and I'd been playing with it at the pub the night before, snapping pictures and sending them to my buddies at the next table. I took one of the bartender and she said, "Hey, let me program that for you." So I handed her my phone.

I should have known better—that woman has always had a twisted sense of humor. But I kind of like the obnoxious tone, and who ever calls me anyway? Only Mark. And only if it's important. So I'd ignored the Donut King's dirty look and answered my goddamn phone, hoping it wasn't bad news. Hoping harder it wasn't about Grace.

I almost hung up when Mark said he was calling about Ruby. But when he mentioned Alzheimer's and suicide, and told me she was at Fran's at that very moment hoping to meet with me, morbid curiosity had me walking away from my post behind the crullers and down the street to Fran's with the King himself, Mr. Lau, right behind me. "Hey, you. Where you going?"

"I'll be back," I said. I even smiled and waved, but he didn't smile back. Just shook his pointed head and went inside. Chances were good that I was already fired, which was just as well. This was my third week on the job, and boredom had set in after the first. But I was going to miss the free day-olds at the end of the shift— Mr. Lau's idea of a benefit plan.

"What's your mother doing now?" Mark asked.

"Ordering tea."

"How can you tell?"

"Because she's doing that embarrassing pantomime. The one where she shows the waitress that she wants the tea bag *in* the pot, *not* on the side."

I could hear the smile in his voice when he said, "I remember," and I felt genuinely sorry for him. To be Ruby's child was a cruel twist of fate, but to be in love with her was a curse, one not easily lifted.

"Liz," he said. "Will you please go inside? Just say hello."

Just say hello. He made it sound so easy. But what to do after hello, that was the hard part because she would say hello too. Then she'd probably invite me to sit down, join her for dinner, maybe even try to hug me, and then what? Hug her back? Order a burger? Or simply be honest and throw the tea at her. Hope it burned. Or melted her. Either one would be appreciated.

"I don't have time," I said, glancing along the street to the Donut King. "In fact, I should be at work right now."

If I got there and discovered I no longer had a job, so what? The good people at the Mucky Duck would love to see me walk in early. The Duck is my hangout, my local, my Cheers. It isn't much, just a little dive near Spadina, but the bartender knows how to make a decent Car Bomb, and I know enough to drink it fast. *Take one for the team, Donaldson?* No problem. After that, I'll drink whatever I can afford—vodka if I'm flush—or whatever anyone will buy for me if I'm not. The day I go home sober will probably be the day I kill myself. Like mother, like daughter, I suppose.

"What's she doing now?" Mark asked.

"Ordering something else." I watched Ruby hand the waitress her menu. "Twenty bucks says it's a grilled cheese."

"You're wrong."

The waitress grabbed a bottle of ketchup from a neighboring table and set it down beside the teacup. I smiled. "You want to take that bet?"

"Can you afford to lose?"

He knew damn well I couldn't. Payday was Friday, and my worldly wealth now amounted to what was in my pocket—five bucks and a streetcar token. But Ruby had always loved Fran's and since she had named the meeting place, I figured she was taking a stroll down memory lane while she still could, and that would definitely include a grilled cheese sandwich.

"Okay, you're on," I said. "What's she ordering?"

"Avocado and sprouts on whole wheat."

I had to laugh. "Mark, if you want to give me money, it's easier to send me a check."

"I'll send you a check if you come with me to an AA meeting."

And there it was. Mr. Bernier's Monthly Meeting Reminder. He meant well, and he'd always been good to me, even after Ruby packed his bags and left them at the ferry dock while he was at work. I was seventeen and Mark was the closest thing I'd ever had to a father, so of course I lugged those bags straight back to the house. Started unpacking his stuff while she was down the street putting streaks in a neighbor's hair.

I was almost finished, just his stick deodorant left to put in the medicine cabinet, when she came back. Ruby likes to tell people she never hit us as kids, but I assure you she couldn't hit me hard enough that day. Mary Anne had to come and pull her off.

An hour later, every trace of Mark was gone—Ruby's declaration fulfilled. But he never lost touch with Grace and me. He even put me through law school and gave me a place to crash whenever I missed the last ferry, which was most of the time. But honestly, who decided the last ferry should leave the city at 11:30 P.M.? What do they think we are over there? Pumpkins?

To this day, Mark buys me dinner once a week, pays my annual fees to the law society, and keeps my cell phone turned on. If he would stop nagging about AA, he'd be the perfect father figure, but he can't help himself. The poor guy still thinks I have potential, and it bothers him that my law degree is sitting in the bottom of a drawer. I know he sees it as a personal affront, but my decision had nothing to do with him. After everything that happened to Grace, I don't have the stomach for law anymore. Don't believe in right and justice or truth and fairness because there was nothing right or just or true or fair in what happened to my sister. The law failed her, failed me, failed us all, and I am done. It's just a pity I can't sell the degree on eBay.

But Mark is right. I should stop drinking. Clean myself up. Get a full-time job. Be a contributing member of society again. But the thing is, I like to drink. And I like who I am when I'm tipsy. I'm more jovial, more fun to be around. I'm also sexier. Men tell me that all the time. Man, you are one sexy bitch. Let's dance. Let's kiss. Hell, let's fuck.

Okay by me, only not at my place because I don't want you to know where I live. I just want to close my eyes and let the world spin while you take care of business, understand? And I don't want you to call me later, and I'm sure as hell not going to call you because honestly, honey, I don't want to know you. I just want to screw you and take that streetcar home. *Ding, ding. Ding, ding.*

Things were easier when I was married. Sex was there all the time whether I wanted it or not. Mostly I wanted it. Like mother like daughter again. Once Mark was gone, Ruby's libido became legend across the Island. I honestly don't remember a time when there wasn't a man in my mother's life. Young, old, even someone else's, it didn't matter to Ruby as long as she was getting what she wanted. The way I see it, I'm just carrying on a family tradition.

"What do you say?" Mark asked, his voice soft—not pleading, but close. "Will you come to the meeting? The church is just around the corner. I can pick you up after you talk to Ruby."

I should go, if only to humor him, but there's been enough coffee and donuts in my life lately. And I doubt I'd be popular at AA. *Hi my name is Liz. I drink and I'm happy, so leave me the fuck alone.* Better to let Mark keep thinking better of me.

"As tempted as I am," I said. "I'm really not dressed for the occasion. Maybe next time, but for now keep your wallet handy because the waitress is coming back."

Sure enough, she set a grilled cheese sandwich in front of Ruby and another in the spot across from her. For me, no doubt because any minute now I was going to break down and go inside. Admit I'd been a horrible daughter and accept her goddamn grilled cheese offering.

"She hasn't changed at all," I told Mark, and turned my back on her. Watched another streetcar rumble past and wanted nothing more than to be on it. Heading west toward the Duck and a Car Bomb and anything else anybody wanted to buy for me. Except the waiter. I think his name is Grant or Greg or maybe it's Steve. At any rate, he's around my age, he's okay to look at, and we both know he'd take me home if I let him. But I won't because he's a nice guy.

He'll think he can help me, change me, even fall in love and want to marry me, and I won't be able to say no. I can never say no, and I refuse to show up at the pawn shop with wedding ring number three. The last thing I need is a customer appreciation card from Fast Eddie's.

I was surprised to see Mr. Lau coming out of the Donut King again, motioning me to come back this minute. I gave him the finger. "Fuck you, Mr. Lau. And your day-old crullers." I turned my back on him too. "I just lost my job," I told Mark. "And you owe me twenty bucks."

"I'm on my way. Stay there and keep an eye on your mother. What's she doing now?"

I pressed closer to the glass, cupped my fingers around my eyes. "Dipping her sandwich into the ketchup. Dabbing her mouth with the napkin. I'd forgotten how prissy she can be."

"Liz, I'll give you a hundred dollars if you go in and sit with her."

Now he was playing dirty. "I'm hanging up."

"Okay, okay, I'm sorry. I'm almost there. Don't leave, all right?"

My mother put her napkin down and turned her head. Looked straight into my eyes, I swear. I couldn't move, couldn't think. Just stood there. Face pressed to the window. Unable to turn away. Waiting for God knew what while my heart beat too hard, too fast.

She went back to her tea and suddenly I was walking, getting as far as the Donut King and then heading back to Fran's. Making my way to the King again and then turning around. I did it twice more before I finally parked myself outside Fran's once and for all and put my back to that bloody window. Perhaps I couldn't leave, but I'd be damned if I'd go inside. Let her come to me if it was that important.

I jumped when the door beside me opened. Two men stepped through. The door closed. Ruby was still at her table. Had I really expected anything else?

"Liz? What's going on?" Mark asked.

"Nothing," I said into the phone. "But you know what I hate most about this? I hate the way people think Alzheimer's grants a person immunity. A kind of moral 'get out of jail free' card, relieving them of all responsibility for the mess they've created."

"Your mother isn't relieved of the mess. She just needs your help to fix it."

"Why should I?"

"Because she's your mother."

"Not good enough."

"She's losing her mind, for God's sake. She doesn't deserve this."

"Yes she does. If you ask me, this Alzheimer's thing is divine justice. A cosmic 'Up your ass, Ruby Donaldson.' The only tragedy in all of this is that no matter what Ruby does, Grace will be screwed."

"I was going to talk to you about Grace . . ."

"I'm sure you were, so let me save you some time. I know Grace won't be able to handle Ruby, but if my mother is hoping I'll move back and be the next Donaldson chatelaine, then she has deteriorated faster than I would have imagined possible. I promised myself that I would never again set foot in that rat hole on Ward's Island. Since I have no intention of disappointing myself any more than I already have, there is nothing further to discuss. When the time comes, I'll figure out what to do about Grace. And you still owe me twenty bucks."

I pushed End, but the stupid thing started hollering a moment later. *Answer your goddamn phone!* This time I switched it off and glanced over my shoulder into the restaurant. Ruby had finished her sandwich and mine was now wearing a silver cover to keep it warm. The loving mom looking out for her wayward daughter.

The waitress brought apple pie and more hot water. Dinner was almost over. Night would soon be upon us, bringing music and dancing and enough alcohol to keep any woman happy. Suddenly I was so thirsty I couldn't wait a moment longer.

Another streetcar rumbled to a stop behind me. *Ding, ding.* All aboard for the Mucky Duck. *Ding, ding. Ding, ding.* I yanked off the hairnet and lowered the zipper at the front of my uniform. Then I walked across the road to the streetcar and climbed the stairs. Dropped my token into the box and went straight to the back door, ready to hop off when the moment was right. Car Bombs awaited. Men were out in force. And I had no intention of spending tonight alone.

# GRACE

My mom would have a fit if she knew I was here. I don't do it to make her life miserable, I just like to watch the planes. Love to see them charging down the runway like they're going to fall in the water for sure, and then suddenly *whoosh*, they're up in the air and gone to Halifax or Montreal or even New York City. When I was little, I asked my mother where they were going and she said, "Straight to hell, Grace, straight to hell," but I knew she was lying. Even then, I knew those planes were taking people someplace good. And one day I could be on one.

Of course, my mother would be happy if no one ever got on those planes. And she'd be even happier if one of them *did* fall into the water because like most people on the Island, she hates the airport. She's what Liz calls a diehard and she still goes to the protests all the time.

I know enough to keep quiet when she starts going on about noise levels and bird sanctuaries and all the other reasons why the airport should be closed. I just listen and nod because I never could talk the way she does. Never could explain properly why I think she's wrong. And when she asks me for a *cogent argument*, I get confused and say stupid things like "Oh yeah?" and "That's just dumb" and she tells me that isn't a *cogent argument*, that's just yelling. "You need to know what you're talking about, Grace. You need a *cogent argument* if you're going to take a stand like that."

So I keep my mouth shut because I probably don't know what I'm talking about. I just like to watch the planes. And if they were to suddenly stop flying, I'd probably cry because it would mean the ferries are the only way out of here, and I'll never get to the city again.

I used to live over there with Liz. She had a condominium at Bloor and St. George. A really small place. My mom never saw it, but she said she could imagine it. "Those places are all the same, Grace. Just shoe boxes. Cramped and tacky shoe boxes."

But Liz called her condo a *jewel box* and it was. A little jewel box with a ruby red sofa and black tables. I missed that place when I moved in with Bobby Daniels. Missed the Downy-fresh smell of Liz's sheets and the way my head would sink into her pillows that were too soft to be good for me. I missed Liz when I was with Bobby, and I missed my mom all the time. And even though it's been two years since I came back to the Island, I still miss the baby.

But I'm seeing Liz this very morning. She's coming on the 10:00 A.M. ferry to Hanlan's Point. And I'm going to meet her here by the statue of Ned Hanlan, the rower who beat everyone in the world, even the smug Americans and the well-trained British.

Most people don't know it, but there was this one time when Ned was rowing against this big American champion and the gun went off, and Ned rowed out so fast he left the champion way behind. So he came back and rowed with him for a while, then he took off again. Then he stopped and waited for the American to catch up, and he still beat him by three lengths. Drove the other guy crazy.

He was really something, that Ned Hanlan. Just a little guy, but he was a genuine hero here on the Island. That's why when I had to come back home two years ago, Liz made me promise that as soon as I could ride my bike again, we'd meet at Ned's statue every Thursday from April to October and she would always bring a bucket of KFC.

I really like KFC, but my mother won't have it in the house. "That stuff will kill you, Grace." But like Liz says, "We're all gonna die someday. Might as well go with eleven different herbs and spices in your belly."

The ferry docked, the ramp came down, and there was my sister at the front of the line like always, strutting down the ramp in a short skirt and platform shoes, picnic basket in one hand, beach bag and chicken in the other. People flowed around her like water. Men laughing and walking close together. Mothers with little kids in strollers and bigger kids running ahead. But Liz never once took her eyes off me.

"How's my baby sister?" she called once her shoes hit dry land.

My mother always tells people I'm the pretty one, but I don't know how she can say that. For as long as I can remember, I've wanted to look like Liz. Wanted to be a beautiful gypsy with black, black hair and eyes to match. Wanted to wear red lipstick and throw my head back and laugh the way she did, and give my mother the finger every time she said "You do realize you sound like a hyena." I never thought Liz sounded like a hyena. I thought she sounded happy. But sometimes she was just drunk.

"I'm fine," I called, and jammed my bike into the rack and started running because Liz was going to need a hand. Not only does she bring the chicken, she also brings the blanket and the salads and the drinks because I can never bring anything. If I left the house with more than my binoculars and my bird book, my mom would know I was up to something. And if she found out that something was Liz, she wouldn't let me have Thursdays off anymore.

She thinks I spend the day bird-watching. That was Liz's idea. When I was finally allowed to ride my bike again, she told me to tell my mom I wanted to try bird-watching. Called it the perfect excuse for spending Thursday's on my own. My mom was happy I was taking up a hobby, and when she handed me *The ROM Field Guide to Birds of Ontario* and a pair of binoculars, I felt a little guilty. But Liz said, "Don't be ridiculous. She brought this on herself."

I started riding my bike on the first day of July—exactly one year ago today. And that very afternoon, Liz and I sat on the beach together for the first time in years, laughing and eating chicken and deciding which bird I'd seen that day.

It was the same every Thursday after that. "How about the green-winged teal?" Liz might say. Or "The black vulture sounds good to me." Then I'd write down the name of our bird of the day in my notebook and tell my mom all about my adventure when I got home.

At first I was nervous because she liked to ask questions, liked to *make me think*. "Are you sure, Grace, because I don't think the yellow-throated swallow comes this far north."

Of course I wasn't sure so I started reading that book. Every day and every night, I read about birds. Then I found these websites where you can listen to what they sound like and see videos of them walking around and sitting in their nests. I spent so much time reading and listening that soon my mom stopped questioning me because we both knew she couldn't make a *cogent argument* about whether or not I'd seen a blackpoll warbler, even if she wanted to.

And that fall, when the ferry stopped running and Liz couldn't get to Hanlan's anymore, I started to really look for the birds, and now I find them all the time. Big ones, little ones, some that only come in the spring, and some that hardly come at all. You just never know what's out there!

Like this morning, when I was passing the lighthouse on my way to the airport and I heard a bird I'd never heard before singing and singing and singing I knew the 6:55 A.M. to Montreal would be taking off soon, but that bird was so loud I had to have a look. So I hopped off my bike and grabbed my binoculars.

I spotted a couple of phoebes and a nuthatch, and even a Lincoln sparrow I'd been looking for since Monday, but no matter how hard I searched, I could not spot that one noisy bird. So I wrote *Lincoln sparrow* in my notebook—because it's not a find until you see it—then I got back on my bike and made it to the fence just in time to see the Montreal flight lifting off.

That noisy bird was still singing when I was on my way home and again when I was coming back to meet Liz. I couldn't stop then, so I was hoping I could talk her into having a look with me after our picnic.

"Nice T-shirt," she said, setting down her beach bag and pulling me in for a one-armed hug. She smelled of coconut sunscreen and fried chicken—the two scents that mean summer to me now. She stepped back and studied my shirt, that big smile returning to her face. "Looks like vintage Greenpeace. Is it new?"

"New for me," I said, pulling the shirt away to look down at the baby seals lined up across the front. I only shop at the Bridge Boutique, the little wagon at the foot of the Algonquin Island Bridge. All the clothes are donated, so I don't have to pay for them and people like to see their T-shirts walking around again. *I always loved that one*, they'll say. Or *Grace, you do me proud in that*, and I like that they're still smiling when I leave.

"I found this one last night," I told Liz. "It's the first time I've had anything like it. I can keep an eye out for one for you if you like."

"I don't do seals. But if you see a skull and crossbones, be sure to grab it." She picked up her bag, handed the basket to me. "Did Ruby tell you she tried to meet with me the other day?"

Liz tried for a long time to get me to call my mom Ruby too, but I think it would make her unhappy, so I don't. It makes me sad that they're still fighting, and that it's all because of me, but I can't make them stop. I've tried, but they both say the same thing, 'It's not your fault, Grace, it's hers,' and they won't hear anything else.

"Did you talk to her?" I asked, not surprised that my mom hadn't told me about her plans. She tells me all the old stories, the tales about Great-Grandma Lucy from Edinburgh and how she met my great-grandfather when she was only sixteen and told her family she was going to marry him no matter what and didn't care when they disowned her. And then, after he died in a coal mining accident and she was only seventeen and pregnant and all alone, she still didn't go home. She came to Canada and found her way to Ward's Island and built a house and stayed here the rest of her life, just like every Donaldson woman since. My mom says that we are strong and capable women, just like Great-Grandma Lucy, and I am never ever to forget that.

My mom also talks to me about the customers and the perms and the roller sets that the seniors always want. Or the airport and the city and how lucky we are to live on the Island and how we must always be vigilant because there are still those who want to see us gone. But she never talks about where she's heading when she gets on the ferry or what she does when she's on the other side of the bay, even though I know there's usually a man involved.

"Why would I talk to her?" Liz said. "She's an idiot. I just thought she'd tell you. Anything to make me look bad, after all." She grabbed my elbow and pulled me along to the bike rack. "Get your stuff quick. It's going to be hot today, which means the crowds will be huge, the naked men will be out in droves, and we will need a good spot on the beach."

She wiggled her eyebrows at me and I laughed and took my stuff out of the basket on my bike; looping the binoculars around my neck and jamming the field guide and notebook into the beach bag. We walked along the main road, talking about everything except why my mom wanted to see her, until we reached the cutoff for the nude beaches. Then Liz said, "Okay, go!" and we started running, racing each other to the first path that would take us down to the lake. I never go to the nude beaches on my own, but I love to go with Liz.

At the end of the path, we stopped and kicked off our shoes. The sky was clear, the sun sparkled on the water and the sand was warm under my feet. Liz was right. This was a perfect beach day and we weren't the first to arrive. Six other groups had already marked their territory with blankets, coolers, and umbrellas attached to folding chairs. No children here. Just adults, mostly men, a few of them already naked and strolling along the water's edge, displaying what God gave them and eager to share.

While Liz searched for a spot of our own, I finally asked. "Do you know what mom wanted to talk to you about?"

"Who cares?" she said, shading her eyes with a hand, surveying the possibilities. "Look at that one," she whispered, and sighed. "Why do gay men always look better than the straight ones?" She pointed farther along the beach. "I see it. The perfect spot. Right there."

I hurried to keep up. "But didn't you wonder why she wanted to see you?"

"I know why. Mark told me. He says hi, by the way. Wants to know if you'll do lunch with him on Centre Island on Sunday."

I smiled. "I love lunch on Centre, especially with Mark."

"That's why I told him you'd meet him at the Swan Ride." We slapped hands above our heads because I also love the Swan Ride and she knows it. "He'll be there at eleven. Probably best not to tell Ruby."

As if I didn't already know.

My mom always said it was silly for us to see Mark. He wasn't either of our real fathers after all. She says our real dads were both jerks, and we wouldn't want to see them even if we could, but Mark wasn't a jerk. And he was like a real dad for so long that I never did understand why she wanted to keep us apart after he left. But like the airport, I don't say anything. I just keep my mouth shut, and meet Mark whenever he can come to the Island.

"Speaking of Mark," Liz said, claiming our spot by setting the basket down. "Did you hear the news this morning? The court overturned another wrongful conviction. Another miscarriage of justice made right."

"That's nice." I reached into the beach bag and pulled out my field guide and notebook. "I heard a strange bird by the lighthouse, and I thought we could look for it after lunch."

She set our bucket of chicken in the sand—something that would have made my mom crazy—and came toward me. "Grace, this is important."

I kept my head down and flipped through the field guide. "But in case you don't want to, we can use the Lincoln sparrow for our bird of the day."

"You need to think about launching an appeal of your own."

I held out the book. "See? This is the sparrow. He's not really exciting. Kind of drab—"

"Will you stop? We need to talk about this."

"I don't want to talk about it." I closed the book and turned away. "There's no point dredging up the past when the future is all we have."

"Listen to yourself! You sound just like Ruby."

"Well, maybe she's right."

"Grace, honey, trust me." Liz took hold of my shoulders and turned me around to face her. "She's not right. She never was. You know Mark will handle everything for you. All you need to do is say yes."

And that was just one more thing I couldn't do.

"Maybe we could go to the lighthouse after lunch," I said, and squeezed my eyes shut so I wouldn't have to see the disappointment in hers. "Maybe we can find that other bird together."

"Maybe we can," she said softly, and rubbed her hands up and down my arms before letting me go. "But right now, let's get this party started."

I opened my eyes. She winked at me, letting me know it was over, we were on safe ground again. Then she opened the picnic basket and hauled out the blanket. "Take this end."

I felt my shoulders start to relax as I walked backward with my end, slowly unfolding the red and black plaid that has seen more picnics than I could count. "Did Mark tell you what Mom wanted to talk to you about?" I asked as we gave the blanket a shake.

"Nothing we all haven't heard before." The blanket lifted into the air between us, once, twice, three times—a secret signal that the Donaldson girls were together again. "She wanted me to come back. Take my rightful place in the family home, blah, blah, blah."

We let the blanket down slowly, spreading it over the sand and marking our territory. Then Liz took off her shirt, revealing breasts that are bigger than mine by a country mile and a belly button with a diamond in it. I don't have piercings anymore. I took out all the plugs and rings when I found out I was pregnant. It didn't seem right, somehow, for a mother to have so many holes in her body.

"You going to join me today? Add some color to that porcelain skin?"

I shook my head. She shrugged and pulled sunglasses, a straw hat, and a tube of sunscreen from her beach bag. "You never used to be a prude."

"I never used to have stretch marks."

She laughed and pulled another pair of sunglasses from her Mary Poppins bag. Handed them to me, then shucked off her skirt but left her underwear on. Good manners dictated that she wear them until after lunch. She stretched out on the blanket and closed her eyes while I applied sunscreen to my face and arms then went about setting up our picnic. Taking the bucket of chicken out of the sand and placing it squarely in the center of the blanket.

Following it up with a tub of potato salad, rolls already buttered, and two cans of iced tea. I weighed down the paper plates with the cans, set out plastic forks, and said, "Lunch is ready," after positioning myself close to the potato salad.

Liz went straight for the bucket. Tore off the lid and shoved a hand inside, searching for the biggest piece as usual. "I am starving. Haven't eaten since lunch yesterday."

I didn't want to know what she did last night besides not eat, so I dug into the potato salad and shook a forkful of the sticky yellow mush onto my plate.

"Maybe Mom didn't tell Mark everything," I said, because just like Liz, there were some things I can't let go of. I wanted to know what my mother had been up to in the city, why she'd been making more and more trips lately and why she'd think Liz would talk to her after all this time. "Maybe if you'd seen her, you would have found out more."

"I found out enough. She wants me to come home because she's sick." Her hand stilled in the bucket. "You knew that, didn't you?"

I said no and tried to ignore the sudden buzzing inside my brain. "How sick?"

Liz hesitated. She didn't say, "Hardly at all" or "Don't worry about it." She hesitated and I knew right there that it was bad.

"How sick is she?" I asked again, and tried hard to hear the voice of my mother, the voice of reason saying, *Calm down, Grace. Calm down and listen.* But all I could hear was the buzzing and the buzzing, and my own voice rising, harsh and ugly and scary even to me. "What is wrong with her?"

"Grace, I'm sorry." Liz pulled her hand out of the bucket, a thick and crusty drumstick dangling from her fingertips. "I didn't realize she hadn't told you."

I knocked that chicken right out of her hand. "You wouldn't have told me either, would you? You would have kept me in the dark, treated me just like she does. 'Don't say anything to Grace.

Don't upset Grace.' I'm not stupid you know. I'm not some fuck-ing retard who can't figure out what's going on all around her!"

Liz held up her hands in a gesture so like my mother I wanted to smack her. "I know you're not stupid. I've never treated you like that, and you know it."

"Do I, Liz?" I followed as she scrambled back, trying to stay out of reach. "*Do I?* You come here and tell me what I should do for my own good, just like she does. And then you keep me in the dark about the really important things, just like she does."

"Grace, honey—"

I put my hands over my ears. "Don't talk. Unless you're going to tell me the truth, just don't talk!" *Stop it, stop it*, I told myself, but the buzzing inside my head kept rising and the words kept coming out, louder and louder all the time. "Tell me what's wrong with my mother!"

People were starting to look. I could see them from the corner of my eye. Naked men cutting their stroll short. Bathing beauties roused from sleep by the crazy girl.

"Grace, it's not that easy," Liz said.

I saw a can of iced tea hit her square in the forehead. Saw the drop of blood, the welt already starting to rise. I couldn't think, couldn't focus. The buzz was gone, replaced by a single phrase. *Your mother is sick. Your mother is sick.* Dear God, what would I do now? Now that my mother was sick.

I grabbed Liz by the shoulders and shook her hard. "What is wrong with my mother? What have you done to her this time?"

# RUBY

I used to be a marathon canoe racer. Discovered the sport the summer after Grace left, and by that fall I was hooked. Even in winter, I'd be out on some river with the rest of the team, breaking ice jams on the Speed, battling early snow on the Humber, and running with that damn canoe to the next checkpoint. Fools with parkas and paddles and only one thing in common—a love of life on the water. We called ourselves the T.O. Terrors and we were, growling and snapping as we passed the competition, howling our pain if we lost and shamelessly congratulating ourselves when we won, which we did—often.

I dropped out last year after the diagnosis, citing age and joints to my teammates when really it was nothing more than ego and vanity. Better to bow out early while I was still doing the talking, instead of waiting until Big Al gave me away, betrayed my dirty little secret.

I sat around for a month afterward, eating everything in sight and posing the inevitable "why me?" questions to a God I didn't believe in, until I was as bored with myself as he must have been. Finally one night, the cookies were gone, Grace was eating the last of the ice cream, and I had two choices—raid Mary Anne's fridge or find something else to do. As luck would have it, Mary Anne wasn't home, so I wandered down to the beach instead, hauled someone's canoe into the water, and set off by myself.

I didn't cover anything close to the thirty- and forty-kilometer distances that were common for canoe marathons. But I was on the water long enough to realize what I'd been missing and convince myself that I still belonged there. By the time I arrived back home I was tired, sore, and the proud owner of a used canoe.

I didn't miss a day until freeze-up after that and was back out again once the ice was gone. Every morning since, all the lamps in my room switch on at 5:45 A.M., a marching band starts into a particularly rousing version of "Anchors Aweigh," and I am instantly awake, heart pounding while I stare, wide-eyed at the sign on my bedroom ceiling. *Go canoeing.* A note stuck to the alarm says the same thing: *Go canoeing.* As does the one in the bathroom: *Go canoeing, you stupid cow.*

The music might keep me awake, but the notes are what keep me moving.

"Go canoeing," I whispered this morning while pulling on shorts and a T-shirt. "Go canoeing," I said again as I tied my hair back in a scrunchie. "Go canoeing, you stupid cow," I told the pale and puffy face in the bathroom mirror, then grabbed my notebook from the bedside table before dashing down the stairs.

In the kitchen, I opened my notebook and read the first lines on the page. *Take meds. Check appointment book.* The doctor had given me a brand-new medication box—a big clunky affair with separate boxes for each day of the week as well as time of day: morning, afternoon, evening, and night. A DYMO label across the bottom read, Flip up the next closed lid. Do not close it after taking medication. I lifted the last closed lid. Tonight, I would need to refill the container for the next week.

After jotting that down in my notebook, I poured a glass of water and shook the pills into my hand. Grace thinks they're hormones—the benefits of which we have discussed at length. Just as we have discussed the memory cards the doctor gave me, as well as the reasons why I need to get lots of sleep and drink at least eight glasses of water a day. Preventive measures, I told her. To keep me healthy and help stave off old age—a luxury I won't have anymore.

Pills swallowed, I poured more water and sat at the table, sipping slowly while doing Mindfulness Exercises. Breathing deeply, in and out. Focusing on the breath, holding firm to the breath before opening the memory box and picking a card, any card. *Who is the prime minister? Where are you? What day is it?* Silly little questions that were both telling and reassuring.

This morning, everything was wonderfully clear. No fog and no hesitation. It was Friday, I was in my kitchen and only too well aware of who was still in power. I was having a good day. I didn't even need to check the appointment book. Every Friday, Betty Jane Parker came at nine for me, and June McKnight came for Grace. One point for Ruby.

Grabbing a couple more memory cards, I slid them into my pocket with the notebook and glanced over at Grace's bedroom door. We usually ran into each other here in the morning, grunting a greeting, kissing a cheek before setting off in different directions. But I hadn't heard any movement in her room since I came down the stairs.

I tiptoed over and rapped lightly. "Grace, you up?" No response. I knocked louder. "Grace?" That was when I noticed her binoculars weren't hanging by the back door. Her shoes were gone too. I wandered over to the window. As was her bike. She always says the birding is best at dawn—or maybe she still wasn't talking to me.

It still amazed me how quickly Grace took to bird-watching. She'd spend hours with that little bird book if I let her. Committing every fact, every statistic, to memory and throwing them out at the oddest times. Like the tidbit about Canada geese at the birthday party. Honestly, who cares that the dirty things poop every six minutes? And who was paid to find that out anyway?

But there were no tidbits for me when she came home yesterday afternoon. No interesting facts to ponder, no picture to look at. Just a tube of sunscreen slapped on the counter and a grumpy "You should use this," when I asked her what was new.

She was still angry and restless when we sat down for dinner, which was unsettling enough. But then she wouldn't tell me what was wrong, wouldn't talk to me at all while we washed the dishes, which was doubly unsettling because we talked about everything. From sex to politics, there was nothing Grace and I couldn't discuss, nothing we weren't perfectly open about. Except the Alzheimer's. That remained private.

Mark, and presumably now Liz, were the only ones who knew, and that was how I intended to keep it for a while yet. Mary Anne would be annoyed for days when I finally told her, but the truth is that Alzheimer's scares people—Lord knows it terrifies me daily—and I cannot imagine being gracious if I am ever on the receiving end of one of those false bright smiles people reserve for poor unfortunates like myself. They say Alzheimer's patients are given to violent outbursts, and is it any wonder?

I'll have to tell Grace eventually, but for now it was more important that I went canoeing. I'd find out later what was on her mind. To make sure that happened, I scribbled, *What's wrong with Grace?* into my notebook and stuffed it back into my pocket. Then I grabbed a life jacket from the hook by the door, my paddle from the shelf above, and headed outside.

The sky was clear, the air warm. I pedaled slowly, watching for Grace on the narrow streets and playing the memory game again. *What did you have for dinner last night? What time is it? What color is a five-dollar bill?* I had pork chops, the time was 6:21 A.M., and a five-dollar bill has always been green. Or was it pink? Maybe it was blue. I sighed. One point for Big Al.

The memory blanks have been coming more frequently lately, lasting longer. Before the diagnosis, I'd shrug and put it down to menopause or overwork. Convince myself that losing my keys a half dozen times a day was perfectly normal. And hadn't everyone put the toaster in the freezer at least once? Now, of course, I knew the truth. The sad and ugly truth. And the color of that bill would haunt me until I got home. Or until I forgot, whichever came first.

Grace was still nowhere in sight when I reached the boat launch by Algonquin bridge. Just me and two young men carrying their canoes down to the water. I was fairly sure they weren't Islanders. Someone's guests perhaps or members of the yacht club. Whoever they were, they were blond, tanned, and equally fit. If not for an eyebrow ring on the one on the right, it would have been hard to tell them apart. They stood on the shore, stretching triceps, loosening hamstrings, getting ready for a real workout I'd say. With luck, they wouldn't be making a habit of it. "You're out early," I called.

"Have to be if we want to beat the rush," the one with the ring called back.

"I hear you." I hauled my canoe off the rack, tossed the paddle inside, and dragged her down to the edge of the lagoon. "You training for something?"

"We're planning a corporate canoe challenge," the other one said. "Laying out the course for a mini-marathon. Nice boat, by the way."

"Thanks," I said, and smiled because it was true. She was a nice boat. After a season in that old used canoe, I figured I owed myself something a little nicer. Something in lipstick red with a carbon fusion shell. And this baby was perfect. Lightweight and tough, much like myself.

"You do a lot of canoeing?" the boy without the ring asked.

"Every day," I said, and should have left it at that, but I couldn't resist. "In fact it's funny you should mention marathon canoeing. I used to do a little of that myself."

"Hey that's great." He held out a hand. "I'm Jason, and this is Jonah."

Jason and Jonah. Of course. I shook their hands. "I'm Ruby."

"Ruby," Jonah said, "I hope this doesn't come off wrong, but could we use you for a little while? Just to help us set up the course, see how long it will take, level of difficulty, that sort of thing. You probably represent the top end of the ages we'll encounter, so it will be good to see how it works for you." He gave me a quick grin that might have been endearing if I hadn't wanted to slap him so badly. "That didn't come out right. What I meant is—"

"I know what you meant and I'd be happy to help. Are you planning a portage or is it strictly a water race?"

"Strictly water," Jason said. "We don't want to lose anyone on this thing."

"I understand. Bad for business." I nudged the canoe into the water and followed her in. "It's about eight kilometers from here to Lighthouse Pond and back. Sound good?"

"Sounds far," Jonah said.

"For whom?" I asked as I fastened my life jacket.

"The suits," he said with that same charming smile. "Half that would be better. Let's end at the lighthouse." He dipped his paddle into the water and nodded at mine. "Bent shaft, eh?"

I shrugged and settled into the Lipstick Queen. "Once a marathoner . . ."

He chuckled. "I'm just surprised is all."

And rightly so. The Island waterway isn't exactly a raging river. Just a winding series of lagoons that take you from Ward's Island to Hanlan's Point at whatever pace you want to set. A straight paddle would definitely have been easier to use in these waters, especially since I was canoeing solo these days. But I was used to a racer's paddle and a racer's stroke and couldn't bring myself to abandon either.

I aimed my canoe at the bridge. "How long do you want this race to take?"

"As long as you need," Jason said, and I like to think he didn't mean to be rude.

"Tell you what. Why don't we make this a little more interesting?" I looked from one to the other. "Ten bucks says I beat you both to the lighthouse."

Jason bit first. "Make it twenty and you're on."

"Twenty it is." I wrapped my fingers around the paddle. "You might want to get in line."

They laughed and shook their heads but got themselves into position nonetheless—canoes even, paddles out of the water. "From a dead stop?" I asked.

"Is there another way?" Jonah answered.

I sat up straighter. "Which one of you wants to get us started?"

"On your mark," Jason said.

I flexed my fingers, eyed the route ahead. I wasn't facing white water and there wouldn't be a decent ice jam for months, but still my heart started beating faster, warming my skin and turning my stomach just a little, just enough. Prerace jitters. God, how I'd missed them.

"Get set."

I raised the paddle.

"Go!"

They weren't expecting much, so it wasn't hard to shoot ahead right off the mark.

But they figured out quickly enough that I wasn't kidding and both of them rose up on one knee, assuming a sprint racer's stance and pulling ahead as we passed Snake Island.

"Nice start," Jason said on his way by. "Too bad the race wasn't over back there."

I laughed and held to a steady pace because a marathon isn't only about speed. It's also about stamina, breath control, and negotiating the twists and turns while maintaining a constant pace. Not an easy task in a racing stance.

I was sure Jason was going over on the first turn past the church. He managed to right himself and hold on a while longer, but by the time we reached Far Enough Farm, they were both sitting lower and they were both starting to slow. There's a reason sprint races are short. Not many people can keep up that kind of pace for long.

While the two Js continued to flag, the Lipstick Queen and I powered on, catching up to them as we rounded the curve by the Carousel Café, and nosing ahead as all three canoes burst into the Regatta Course. I whooped as I pulled into the lead, my back, my arms, every muscle in my body working, pulling, stretching. I felt strong again, more like myself, or who I used to be. Adventurous, fun. Free.

I was reaching my stride on the straightaway past the grandstand and knew I could have kept going for miles. Paddling until the moon came up, and pushing on until the sun returned, just as I had on so many rivers for so many years. But the end of this race was around the next bend, and I didn't look back until I reached Lighthouse Pond.

The Js arrived a minute later, wiping their faces with their T-shirts as they pulled up alongside my canoe. "You should have warned us," Jason said, taking his wallet from his backpack and digging out a crisp twenty-dollar bill. It was green.

I snapped the money out of his fingers. "Not bad for my age level, I guess."

Jonah groaned and went for his wallet, handing me two wilted tens. Both purple. If only he'd handed me fives.

"Nice race," he said.

"You too," I said, and shook their hands, because I'd mellowed and was now gracious in victory. But that didn't mean I'd be returning their money. "If your suits enjoy themselves half as much as I did, you will have a definite hit on your hands."

"We're going out to explore the inner harbor a little," Jason said. "See if there's something we can do out there as well. Want to come along?"

A year ago, I wouldn't have hesitated. I would have been right there beside them, talking paddles and canoes, races and strategies. But not only has Big Al made me mellow, he's also made me fearful. I no longer leap before I look, no longer fly by the seat of my pants. Every move, every decision is carefully weighed and measured, examined for dangers and possible traps. The lagoons were safe, the shore always within easy reach. But the harbor was a different story, with heavy boat traffic and water cold enough to steal your breath, even this time of year. As much as I longed to go with them, open water was no longer safe for me.

Clutching the bills and my small victory tightly, I smiled and waved them away. "You go ahead. I should be getting back."

"Nice meeting you," Jason said.

"Good luck with the suits," I told them, and split off, leisurely making my way back to the regatta course without once looking back. What was the point, after all? As Grandma Lucy used to say, *The foolish woman dwells on what's gone by her. The wise one looks ahead at what's to come.* Even when what's to come is hard to imagine.

Contrary to what Mark might think, putting an end to myself is not something I take lightly. I've always wanted to live forever, become the wise old woman of the Island, the keeper of history, the teller of tales, respected by all for her honesty and wit. That's why I hope for miracles daily. The sheer number of pills in my cupboard are testament to that. As well as the prescribed medications, I have ginkgo biloba, Siberian ginseng, and St. John's wort or blister or whatever it was the poor man had, all sold to me as Guaranteed Memory Enhancers.

When I get home, I'll swallow those pills and think positively about miracle cures. But because I'm a realist, I'll also sit down at the computer and type "painless poisons" into the search engine. Does that make me selfish? Perhaps, but the alternative is too grim to consider. I refuse to spend the rest of my life warming the bench. If I can't play, I'll take my ball and go home. Wherever that may be.

Rounding the bend near the farm, I lifted my paddle out of the water and drifted for a moment, hoping I might see Grace pedaling along the paths or peering through her binoculars, watching for birds. While I am honestly pleased she's found a distraction, something to keep her mind off other, unpleasant things, I'm more grateful she hasn't started bringing any of her feathered friends home—Lord knows we had enough of that with Grandma Lucy. And I doubt that even I'll manage to forget the night they found my grandmother trying to liberate the Silkie chickens at Far Enough Farm. Stupid things just flapped about refusing to move, to comprehend the gift she was giving them. She didn't mean to kill any of them, I'm sure of it. Accidents just happen. Especially in this family.

With no sign of Grace anywhere, I put my paddle back in the water and pulled out another memory card. *What is your mother's name? What month is it? What year were you born?* My mother's name was Rose. It was July, no June, and I was born in 1955. I still couldn't remember what color a five-dollar bill was, but took comfort in knowing I hadn't forgotten the question. Another point for me.

By the time the Lipstick Queen and I made it back to the bridge, I'd completed two more cards and the score was now Ruby, 3, and Big Al, 1—a good morning indeed.

Hauling the canoe out of the water, I couldn't wait to tell Grace about the race. Hand her the forty dollars and tell her to order something for herself on the Internet. Another bird book. A T-shirt that hadn't been someone else's first. Anything that would make her happy, make her start talking to me again. But there was still no sign of her when I arrived back at the house fifteen minutes later.

What was going on? Did she want to make me worry? Was she punishing me for something? I glanced over at her bedroom door. There was only one way to find out.

I opened the door, checked the kitchen window for any sign of her in the yard, then stepped into her room. Her bed was unmade, her clothes all over the dresser, but that was fine. This was her domain. The one place in the world that was hers to control. And she would never know I'd been there.

Her computer sat on the desk by the window. An old model but fast enough to get whatever she needed from the net. I eased the chair back and pressed the space bar. Sat down and watched the monitor come to life, the icons slowly lining themselves up on the screen. "Come on," I whispered, listening for the gate to close, a bike to drop—any sign that Grace was back while the screen settled and the hourglass finally disappeared. I put my fingers on the keyboard and a box came up demanding a password. I sighed. Not this again.

I tried *1234*, then *birds*, then *Grace*, then *Wards*, then *Hanlans*. None of those worked so I tried her birthday, my birthday, the current year, still nothing. I looked around the room for clues and typed in *paperweight*, *mouse*, *Angelinajolie*, and *bikingworld*. That did it. I was in.

I checked the browser history first. Nothing interesting there. Then I punched around in her e-mail, checking the sent files, the deleted files. Again, nothing out of the ordinary: a birding website sending an update, another inviting her to join its chat group. Fortunately she had declined, making life easier for both of us. You never knew who was creeping around those sites.

A new message popped up. A note from some beauty college thanking her for her interest in their online aesthetics courses. A brochure was attached. I hit Reply and asked them to remove me from their mailing list. Then I deleted the original message as well as my response and logged out of her e-mail. I don't know how many times I've told her that Chez Ruby was not now and never would be in the aesthetics business. But at least we'd avoid the discussion today.

I waited for her computer to resume hibernation, then rolled her desk chair back in and closed the door when I left. Taking my notebook out of my pocket, I wrote, *Reminder: Grace's password bikingworld,* and jumped when I heard her coming up the stairs.

"Morning, Mary Anne," she called as she opened the door.

I shoved the notebook back in my pocket and stepped in front of her before she could drop the binoculars and the bird book. Before she could make her way to the kettle, the fridge, the eggs over easy. "Where have you been?" I demanded.

"Birding," she said, and gave me a kiss on the cheek. "You use the sunscreen?"

I lied and said, "Yes," because it was easiest.

"Good." She dumped her book and binoculars on the table, headed for the fridge. "When's my first appointment?"

"June McKnight at nine."

I watched her put eggs in the pan. Bread in the toaster. Click on the kettle. "You eaten?" she asked. I shook my head and she broke two more eggs into the pan, slipped two more slices of bread into the toaster. "How was your paddle?"

"I won forty dollars," I told her, still trying to figure out the kiss. And the sunscreen. "So is it over?"

"Is what over?"

"Your snit. Is it over?"

"I wasn't in a snit, I was just . . ." She paused, obviously searching for a word. "I was preoccupied."

I crossed my arms. "Grace, who told you to say that? What have you been up to? If you've been talking to the park workers again, I will be so annoyed. I've told you time and again what those men are like—"

"I haven't been talking to anyone. I've been thinking, that's all." She smiled and flipped the eggs. "How did you win forty dollars?"

While I told her about the race, she took mugs from the cupboard, silver from the drawer, and the morning chugged on as usual. Except she was still in no hurry to tell me where she'd been or what she'd found. Kiss and sunscreen aside, something was definitely wrong.

When her back was to me, I took out my notebook, scribbled *Follow Grace* under her password, and jumped again at the sound of footsteps and voices bickering outside.

Grace was already smiling by the time someone knocked on the door. I glanced at the clock, then over at the appointment book. Whoever was out there was early. But whoever it was didn't wait for me to answer the knock. Simply turned the handle and walked into my life.

"Hey," he said, and grinned at Grace. "You making coffee this morning?"

"You're here!" She raced over and hugged him hard while I slipped the notebook back into my pocket. That's when I noticed the girl slouching against the doorframe behind him.

I'd seen her before. In the picture on his desk. She was a little older now. Maybe twelve but definitely the type that stood out in a crowd. Tall and thin with bloodred hair, a stark white face, and black eyeliner that not only circled her eyes but also dotted her cheeks with tear drops. She wore a black T-shirt, black boots, and a short black skirt with Hated printed across the hem.

A baby Goth. How precious. But underneath it all she was a pretty girl. Prettier than she'd been in the picture at least, which was a blessing. No girl should look like Mark.

He drew her forward. "Ruby, Grace. This is my daughter, Jocelyn."

"This is gay," she said in that bored tone that only adolescents do well. "Can we go?"

"Anytime you like," I told her, and turned to Mark. "What are you doing here?"

"Paying a call on our new neighbors." He produced a cup from behind his back. "Can we borrow some sugar?"

Grace was already on her way to the pantry, but I stopped her midstride. "No, you cannot borrow sugar and what are you talking about? Whose neighbors?"

"Yours." He carried the empty cup over to Grace. "Fill it with coffee instead."

She smiled and returned to the stove, flipping our eggs onto a plate before taking the coffee from the cupboard and the French press from the shelf, acting as if nothing was wrong. As though having him here was a dandy thing.

For her, it probably was. They'd been close when she was little. But she hadn't seen him in years. Not since she moved back to the Island at least.

"What's going on here?" I demanded.

"I'm moving back," he said.

I stared at him. "Moving back where?"

"I can't stand this," Jocelyn said. "I'm going outside."

"Young lady, you sit down and be polite." He pointed to my barber's chair. She rolled her eyes and dragged her heels on her way to the chair, but she sat. Of course if looks could kill and all of that, but I was still impressed. I could never get Liz to do anything at that age.

"Hi," Grace said, and grinned at her. "I'm Grace. Would you like tea?"

Jocelyn turned to her dad. "Who *is* this person?"

"Your new nanny." He smiled at Grace. "If you're up for the job."

Jocelyn was out of the chair and in his face so fast I swear those boots didn't touch the floor along the way. "I don't need a nanny."

"She's right," Grace said. "But maybe she could use a friend."

Jocelyn laughed. "What is this? An after-school special? Or maybe one of those gotcha shows with hidden cameras and geeks like her trying to make a fool of you."

"I'm not making a fool of anyone," Grace said. "I'm making breakfast. Want some?"

Jocelyn turned to her father. "You can't make me stay here."

He sighed. "Jocelyn, you're twelve and I'm your father, which means I can indeed make you stay here. Why not give it a chance? You might like it."

"I hate it already, and I hate you too. I do *not* want to live here."

"I wouldn't worry about that if I were you," I said. "You can't just live on the Island because you feel like it. You have to be on the list. Takes years to get a house."

"Only if you're buying, which I'm not," Mark said. "I'm renting. Actually, I'm house-sitting for a buddy."

"What buddy?"

Grace handed him a cup of coffee with cream in it. I couldn't believe she remembered after all this time. "You want toast with that?" she asked.

"If you're having some."

"We just frigging ate," Jocelyn said.

"I had a bagel." He turned back to Grace. "If you're having toast, I'll join you."

I held up my hands. "Can we focus for a moment? What buddy are you talking about?"

"Seth Harrison. You know Seth. Tall, dark, used to be handsome."

"Of course I know Seth. I see him all the time. And he's still handsome. Are you telling me the two of you are friends?"

"Beer and wings every Friday night. Our twentieth anniversary is coming up soon. I should get him something nice."

I was completely confused and it had nothing to do with Big Al. "I need a straight answer. What are you doing on the Island?"

"He paid some guy to let us live in his house for the summer," Jocelyn said. "He thinks it will be good for me. And for some reason he brought you a gift. It's outside on the step."

"Ooooooh, what is it?" Grace asked, already opening the door and bringing in a box wrapped in red paper. "It's heavy." She held the box out to me. "Heavy is good."

I shook my head. "I can't accept it whatever it is."

"Of course you can," Mark said. "Grace, open it for her."

She was on the floor, ripping off paper before I could say "Don't you dare."

"It's a bottle of pomegranate juice and a box of magazines." She glanced up at Mark. "What are they?"

"What do you mean what are they? Can't you read?" Jocelyn snatched a handful of magazines out of the box. "We've got crossword puzzles, brainteasers, connect-the-frigging dots." She handed them all back to Grace. "Nothing but boring crap."

"They're not boring," Mark said. "And they're not for you anyway."

"Thank God." She slumped against the door and gave me a once over. "Who are you anyway?"

"An old friend," Mark and I said together.

"They used to be lovers," Grace whispered.

Jocelyn winced. "That is so gross. Can I leave now?"

"Absolutely," I told her. "Mark, will you join me outside a moment?"

"Sure." He set his empty cup on the table and pointed a finger. "Jocelyn, you be nice."

The girl dropped her head back, muttered something about hell on the water, then smacked the puzzle book Grace was holding out to her, sending it flying across the floor.

"Pick that up," Mark said on his way out the door. I followed, hoping that daughter of his didn't decide to pitch coffee or hair dye or anything else that would make me have to kill her.

Mark walked across the yard to the birdbath. I followed and smiled up at him. "Your daughter seems like a nice girl. Who does her hair?"

He sighed and looked back at the house. "She did that when I told her about Seth's place. I don't think she's completely comfortable with her new look, but I'm going to buy her some fishnets this afternoon, let her know I'm okay with it."

"Will you take her for piercings too?"

"Fortunately, she's still too young. No one will do it." He glanced over at me. "You probably find my parenting methods odd, but her mother died when she was six, so it's been just the two of us for a long time now."

"I'm sorry to hear that. It's hard to lose your mother when you're young."

He shrugged. "We're doing okay. And I find that the best way to diffuse a rebellion is to embrace it. Find out all I can about the movement or the phase and then encourage it. Last summer, I developed a real appreciation for gangsta rap, but now she refuses to listen to it."

"Mission accomplished?"

"And I'm hoping the fishnets will work as quickly. Once she adjusts, I think Island life will be good for her. Let her be a kid a while longer. She starts junior high in the fall, and to be honest, I'm worried."

"As you should be. But be honest, are you really here because of me?"

"Maybe a little. Okay maybe a lot." He gave me a sheepish grin and for a moment I caught a glimpse of the young man he used to be. The one who taught me how to laugh again after Eric left. "You scared the shit out of me the other day, okay? I couldn't get you off my mind. Couldn't say, Oh well she's going to kill herself, what's for dinner? Life is precious, Rube. You can't throw it away like that."

"I'm not throwing anything away. I'm merely helping nature along. Speeding up an inevitable process, thereby saving us all a lot of time, money, and heartache. And I don't need interference from you."

I looked back at the kitchen door, saw Grace watching us and started walking, leading him away from the house and the possibility that she might hear. Heading out the gate and down toward the bay. Nodding to neighbors and picking up speed as I went, making him hurry if he wanted to keep up. He was out of breath in seconds. "If I'd known you'd go this far, I wouldn't have come to see you in the first place," I said. "All I wanted you to do was talk to Liz. But you can forget that too. I'll find another way. Maybe hire a hit man. Get him to wing her and bring her home in a sack."

"That's crazy talk and you know it," he said between breaths.

"So what? I am crazy and *you* know it."

He took my arm, tried to make me slow down, but I shook him off and kept going. "This is exactly why I'm here," he called after me. "You're not thinking clearly. You need me."

I took a quick look around and then hurried back to where he stood. "Keep your voice down. I don't need this all over the Island. And I don't need you."

"But you could have years ahead of you," he said.

I started walking again, heading back the way we came. Going slower so he could keep up this time. "Years of what?"

"Life."

"No, Mark. What I'll have is years of existing, not life, not living."

"But there are always advances. That's why I brought the crosswords and brainteasers. Studies show—"

"That crosswords can combat loss of memory and improve brain function. I do keep up. But the fact is that there is no cure. My brain is deteriorating, rusting over as we speak."

"So until they find a cure, there are people who love you, who will take care of you—"

"Please. I refuse to be *tended to*, or *lovingly cared for*, or anything else in the Alzheimer's handbook. I want to take care of myself. When I can no longer do that, I want out. End of story."

When we reached Channel Avenue, a blast from the ferry had me turning around, heading back to the house. My clients would be at the dock. It didn't matter that I couldn't remember who was coming anymore. With luck, I'd remember when I saw them.

Mark was still beside me when I reached my gate. "So you're saying that any day now I could come over and find your body on the floor."

"Don't be dramatic. It's not like I'm going to off myself tomorrow. The neurologist changed my medication and I think it's working, slowing things down a little. As long as that's happening, I'll be around. But once the illness starts progressing again, then I'm out of here."

I opened the gate, but he took hold of my shoulders again, turned me to face him, and this time, I couldn't shake him off. "Ruby, you have to give me time. You have to let me try and change your mind."

"Why?"

"Because I love you. I always have."

I pushed at him. "Don't be ridiculous."

"I'm not ridiculous, I'm pathetic. There's a subtle but important difference. And I can't let you go without trying to help. It's not in me and you know it."

He was right. I did know that about him. He was the man who ran legal aid clinics, volunteered at food banks, and held free ESL classes on his lunch hour. Mark was a helper, a do-gooder, a man who believed in the greater good and never could leave well enough alone.

"I should never have contacted you."

"But you did, knowing full well that I'd fight you. Which means you don't really want to die. You want someone to stop you, and here I am."

He looked so happy, like he actually believed what he was saying. Like *I* should believe what he was saying. Proving once again that there is no saving some people from themselves.

I patted his hands and gently removed them from my shoulders. Turned away and was relieved that I did indeed recognize my clients when I saw them.

"See those two women coming toward us?" I said to him. "The one on the left is Betty Jane Parker and the other is her daughter Chloe. I've been doing Betty's hair every Friday for thirty years. She likes lots of back-combing and lots of hairspray. I'm the only one who can do her hair the way she likes it, only she doesn't know that anymore because she has Alzheimer's. She doesn't know who I am or where she is or why she's here. See how she's clinging to her daughter's arm? See how her daughter is talking to her, showing her the flowers and the birdies and the cat that has come out to greet them? She wasn't always like this. Betty was a teacher with a wicked sense of humor, the kind that comes from insight and wisdom and cuts straight to the core of the matter. She's traveled extensively and was passionate about children and learning. It was a privilege to know her. And now her daughter points out the birdies to her."

"Looks to me like she's enjoying them."

"Enjoying them? Mark, she's not even seeing them because she's not there anymore. Her body is just a shell going through the motions, and that is what I am determined to avoid. I do not want anyone to take me for a walk and show me the flowers, the cats, or the goddamn birdies. I just want to go while I'm still me. Is that so hard to understand?"

"Suicide is a sin, Ruby."

"So is inflicting suffering and torture."

Betty and Chloe continued toward us. Chloe waved and

pointed, but Betty kept her eyes on the ground, her feet shuffling forward, no idea where she was going or why. An hour from now her hair would be shampooed and back-combed, and she'd be on her way home for another week. And my heart broke for her.

"I won't give up," Mark said softly. "I'm determined to change your mind."

"Then you're going to need a miracle," I said, and stepped forward to greet my 9:00 A.M.

# LIZ

It was a familiar sight—my mother and her cronies lined up along a patch of grass across from the airport ferry terminal, banging a drum and waving signs at passing cars and taxis.

### Close the Island Airport
### People Not Planes

And my all time favorite,

### Honk If You're With Us!

Watching Ruby give the finger to a driver who clearly wasn't, I knew I was in for a treat. Just a few more steps and I'd have a front-row seat for this afternoon's performance of Close the Island Airport, the city's longest-running protest, brought to you by Ruby and the Diehards—those fun-loving rascals who still believe they can stop the planes, make a difference, even change the world if they just keep on picketing.

Maybe one day, someone will tell them that the war has been over for a while. But until then you can catch all the action every Friday right here at the foot of Bathurst Street, where the land meets the lake and the airport ferry leaves every fifteen minutes. Admission is free, so bring the kids, the dog, the whole fam damily! It's tons of fun for everyone!

I hadn't intended to be here today. But when I finally rolled out of bed at noon, my room was already hot and stuffy with the weatherman promising more heat as the afternoon wore on—the kind of day Great-Grandma Lucy would have called a *bloody scorcher.* My bumping head and sour stomach insisted on fresh air—or at least air that smelled better—so I went for walk.

It's always cooler by the water and that's where I ended up, heading west on Queen's Quay. When I hit Bathurst Street I thought, what the heck. Why not have a look? It would be good for a laugh if nothing else. Now, creeping closer through the trees, staying out of sight, I was glad I'd made the stop and more than pleased with my seating choice. I knew from experience how hot it would be on that sorry patch of grass across the road. But here among the poplars and the scratchy scrubby bushes, it was shady and cool and only a little buggy.

Swatting a mosquito out of the way, I hunkered down with my backpack and parted the branches. Other than the protesters there wasn't much to see. Just a warehouse, the terminal, and a long line of taxis waiting for the next flight to arrive. Behind me, a baseball game was getting under way in Little Norway Park—red shirts versus blue. If you didn't know, you'd never guess that this quiet, unassuming area housed the approach to an international airport.

Mind you, we're not talking about a major transportation hub here. On the contrary, the focus of Ruby's protest is nothing more than three short runways on the western tip of Hanlan's Point, a mere 397 feet from the mainland. There are no jumbo jets, no flights after 11:00 P.M., and no bridge between here and there. Just a fleet of turboprop planes and a dedicated ferry trundling passengers back and forth across the Western Gap.

For all I know, it might be nothing but armed guards and sniffer dogs on the other side of that gap. But things have always been more casual here at the end of Bathurst, and no one minds a few protesters banging a drum within pitching distance of those runways. I love that about this city. But it still surprises me that no one has insisted on removing the copse of trees that shields the baseball diamond from the rest of the street, given that it makes a perfect hiding spot for someone like myself. Someone who wants to watch all the action without being seen.

"Close the airport," Ruby hollered, and the Diehards took up the chant. "Close. The. Airport." Drumbeat.

Their staging was the same as I remembered—a table with a banner, a petition, and a box full of flyers—as were the dozen or so marchers. Islanders all, people I've known my whole life, plus the two Bobs from Mississauga, friends of the family since the bathhouse protests of 1981.

Faithful Mary Anne was there too, occupying the spot on Ruby's right now that Grace didn't come anymore. Benny was on her left, where I used to be, the three of us competing to see who could get the most taxis to honk. Grace usually won, which wasn't surprising. She was like a little kid out there, pressing an imaginary horn, begging the drivers to please, please press theirs. There was nothing political about it for Grace. She was just having fun. And the delight on that girl's face whenever one of them honked was always enough to make another join in, just to see it again. And if it meant more attention for the cause, then Ruby was happy.

Watching her bang that drum, I tried to think of a time when we hadn't been protesting something. A birthday party that hadn't included an antipoverty petition. A Christmas when we weren't kicked out of Eaton's for handing out child-labor flyers in the toy department. But no matter how far back I went, I kept coming up empty. As far as I knew, the Donaldsons had always been rabble-rousers. Great-Grandma Lucy marching for women's rights when Ruby was little. The two of them marching to stop the Spadina Expressway when Ruby was grown. And finally Grace and me marching arm in arm with Ruby and Mark to stop police brutality or save the manatees or ban the ban against altar girls.

There have never been manatees in Toronto, and since my mother never took us to church, I didn't understand the problem with the altar girls. But as Ruby always said, having a social conscience meant seeing the larger picture, looking beyond our own front door.

"It's our responsibility, our duty, to act for social change," she'd say. "To hold those in power accountable. To always question authority." Unless it was her authority. That was to be honored at all times because who knew what you needed better than your own mother? No one, that's who.

"Lizzie, you need to listen carefully," she said when I was five years old. "What we're learning here is called civil disobedience, and it's exactly what we need if we want to hold on to our homes. The time for polite conversation is over. Do you understand?"

I was a little kid, for chrissakes. What did I understand about civil disobedience? All I knew was that some man with a beard and hunchy shoulders was going to help us put together an elite group of freedom fighters. And all I saw was my pregnant mother's hand shoot up in the air, waving and begging *pick me, pick me,* when that same man asked if anyone was willing to go to jail for the cause. "Don't be silly," Ruby said when I objected. "Everything will be fine. Now go sit with the other kids. The grown-ups have things to discuss."

Long after the other kids grew bored and went in search of something more exciting, I was still there, a fixture at every meeting. Sitting on the floor, breathing in the language, the mood, the very pulse of the struggle. I was still too young to grasp much of anything that was going on, but still I wrote *Save Our Homes* on everything I touched. Surrounding the words with flowers and smiley faces while the adults said things like *passive resistance* and *police brutality*. Finally understanding that the baby and I were the reason my mother was there, the reason she wanted to get arrested, because we were the future of the Island.

When they started practice drills with make-believe policemen taking people to make-believe jail, Ruby would put an arm around me and whisper, "Whatever happens, remember that I love you very much," scaring the shit out of me even as my skin prickled with pride.

That summer, Ruby's pregnancy and the fight to Save the Island Homes came down to the wire. The Islanders were ready, Ruby was ready, and I knew exactly where I would be the day the sheriff finally came—at the front of the pack with the other kids, blocking the way.

On Monday morning July 29, 1980, as soon as everyone who worked in the city had left for the day, the siren on top of the clubhouse went off, the phone chain started up, and the calls went out all over the Island and across the water into the city.

*The sheriff is on his way. Eviction day is here. Come stand with us.*

I remember watching the first boats come across the bay. The dinghies and the water taxis, the canoes and the motorboats, and of course the old barge that was the flagship of the Island navy. All of them speeding toward us, bringing the believers, the curious, and more important, the press, to witness the standoff we had promised.

We gathered by the hundreds at the foot of Algonquin bridge that day, our banner pleading SAVE US BILL DAVIS while television and newspaper cameras stood ready. It had come down to this—the last of the Islanders waiting in the rain for the final showdown. Sure enough, out of the gloom came two cars. Eviction on wheels.

My mother went into labor right there, falling heavily against Mark. He picked her up and started carrying her away. "Keep Liz with you," she called to Mary Anne. Then she blew me a kiss. "Do me proud, Lizzie. Do me proud."

Ruby and Mark disappeared from sight, but I stayed behind with Mary Anne. Pushed my way to the front of the pack with the other kids and stood my ground. When a girl younger than me started to cry, I took her hand, told her to stop being a baby and sing, just sing with everyone else. "Like a tree standing by the water, we shall not be moved."

But inside, just to myself so no one else could hear, I prayed that the real sheriff and the real evictors were coming another way. That they would hammer their notices on our doors and everything would be over before we knew it, and my mother and the baby would not go to jail the way she wanted to so badly.

As it turned out, no one went to jail that day. Mark took my mother to a hospital in the city, the sheriff agreed to delay the evictions, and the Islanders declared a victory. Two days later, we won the right to appeal the city's decision to get rid of us. At long last, the tide had turned.

When my mother came home with Grace, she put the baby in my arms and Mark took pictures of the three of us. I never told anyone about my secret prayer. I just wanted to forget all about civil disobedience with its threat of police and jail and let everything go back to the way it used to be. I was too young to recognize the change in my mother, to understand the difference between a mere rabble-rouser and an activist, but I've always been a quick learner. By the time we hit the streets for the bathhouse protests in 1981, I was six years old and making my mother proud as her own little agent for change.

"Stop those planes!" Ruby yelled.

"We have to make a living," one of the taxi drivers called.

"And we have to bird," she yelled, and we both froze. A simple slip of the tongue or had Alzheimer's dropped by to say hello? She moistened her lips. Tried again. "We have to breathe," she yelled, and the taxi driver shook his head and rolled up his window.

"Nice save, Mom," I whispered while she laughed it off with the Diehards. "Nice fucking save."

It's funny, but I always thought Ruby was invincible, that she'd live forever just to piss me off. Even now, even knowing the truth, it was hard to imagine her without words or opinions. The shit disturber silenced, no longer rallying the troops and fighting for the underdog. Incapable of doing the one thing she'd always been good at. The one thing I'd liked about her, the one thing we'd had in common until she turned her back on Grace. Refused to join the very fight that should have been instinctive, unquestioned, a natural for any mother whose child is falsely accused. Any mother except our own.

"Save the birds," she yelled.

"Fuck the birds. And fuck you too," I muttered, and got to my feet, suddenly hot and itchy, unable to breathe among those god-damn prickly bushes. I snatched up my backpack, pushed through the branches, and went straight to the drinking fountain. Splashed water on my face, my neck, the visible pulse at my wrists. But it wasn't enough to cool my skin, or slow my heart, or let me catch a breath. What I needed was a drink. And it had to be happy hour somewhere.

On the baseball diamond, the red team was up to bat. A woman with huge boobs swung the bat, hitting a pop fly into the air above the pitcher. But all eyes were on those boobs as she ran to first base, giving me enough time to pull a vodka cooler out of my backpack unseen. I don't like coolers much, but they were on special—six for six dollars—and I never could resist a sale. It's a weakness in my character.

The pitcher fumbled the catch and the boobs headed for second. The guys on the blue team had to be giving her this one, which meant all heads were still turned that way, which suited me just fine. With my back to the game, I unscrewed the lid and took a long swallow. Nearly gagged on the sweet, fizzy shit. Should have spat it out then and there. Drank water instead. But who could get happy on water?

So I soldiered on for the cause. Polished off the rest and dropped the empty into my backpack. Pulled out a second and was getting ready to enjoy another refreshing beverage when a muffled voice behind me said, "I told you she was drinking beer."

I jerked around. Two little boys with matching freckles and Blue Jays hats stood watching me with wide, brown eyes.

"What's that on her face?" the younger one whispered.

"It think it's the mark of the devil," the older one replied.

More the mark of a liar. A scabby half-moon in the middle of my forehead, a reminder of the dangers of canned iced tea and the lie I'd told my sister to save my own ass—to keep her from following up with a handful of macaroni salad.

*Ruby has cancer,* I'd said. *Nothing serious. Just a basal cell. Came off with a laser.* Making up the story as I went along. Knowing Grace would believe whatever I told her, wishing I had the courage to tell her the truth.

I'd forgotten about the scab but recognized an opportunity when I saw it. "What nice little boys," I said, walking slowly toward them. "Would you like some candy?" I held up my backpack. "I have lots and lots of candy."

The older one grabbed the younger one's hand and backed him up a step.

I hunched my shoulders and crooked my finger, beckoning them closer. "Don't be afraid. I like little boys. I like them a lot."

"Aaron, run!" the older one shouted, and took off in the other direction, hauling the whimpering little one behind him.

"See you later, boys," I called, and headed back into the trees while the boobs ran for home.

The bottle was empty before I reached my spot, so I opened

a third, chugged it, belched twice, and then leaned back against a tree, watching Ruby, red-faced and sweating, still beating that stupid drum. "Stop. Those. Planes."

"Crazy bitch," I muttered. "Go ahead and off yourself. Who gives a shit anyway?"

The fourth cooler didn't go down as well as the other three—chugging will do that sometimes—and I was thinking about taking a break, maybe going for walk, until Mark's black SUV pulled into the curb across the road and I knew I wasn't going anywhere.

"What the hell are you doing here?" I whispered, dropping the empty into the bag and giving the fifth bottle a pass for the moment.

He stepped out of the van and went around to open the back hatch while a young man moved over into the driver's seat. "I come bearing gifts for a great cause," Mark called to the Diehards. "But I'll need some help getting them out."

They were on him in seconds, hugging him, slapping his back, welcoming him back into the fold. If they ever found out he'd been catching flights out of that airport for years, there would be nowhere for that man to hide. The only one holding back was Ruby. "Stop. Those. Planes." Drumbeat.

"What is wrong with you?" I said. "The man has gifts, for chrissakes."

He called her name, but she only beat that drum louder. She was obviously ignoring him, but why? What had he done to her? Surely she didn't blame him because I wouldn't go into Fran's?

"Stupid cow," I hollered, then ducked and lowered my voice. "It's not his fault."

"What are you doing in there?" a woman demanded.

I turned too quickly. Caught my balance on a tree, belched once, and giggled. Who knew fizzy booze packed such a punch? I held on to the tree and waited for the world to settle. Saw a face I recognized watching me from the path. A strawberry blonde so short she bordered on circus freak, which was probably why she was also hard-nosed and a little twisted and didn't take shit from anyone. I could tell by the way her brow unfurrowed and her shoulders relaxed that Brenda the Bartender recognized me too.

I smiled and waved. "Hey, Brenda. What brings you here?"

"My kids." She came toward me through the trees. "They said there's a witch in here drinking beer." She smiled at my forehead. "I've never seen the mark of the devil before, but it explains a lot." She took a quick look around. "What are you doing in here anyway?"

I pointed over my shoulder. "Watching the show."

"You're spying on the protest? You really need to get cable."

"I'm not spying, I'm observing." I parted the branches for her. "See the sweaty redhead ranting at a taxi driver? That's my dear old mom."

She leaned closer. "Doesn't look like she's ranting. Looks more like she knows the taxi driver. Maybe they're even flirting." She glanced up at me. "Your mom's got a great smile."

"But she bites." Most of the protesters were back on the line, wiping their brows and fanning their faces while they marched. But a few were setting up a canopy and a circle of chairs on the grass. Mark had brought the gift of shade. How clever.

"Anybody else think it's break time?" he called, dragging a cooler out of the back of the SUV and waving the driver away. More protesters broke ranks and went to join him in the shade of the canopy. But Ruby kept banging that drum and poor Mary Anne and Benny kept slogging along behind her. "Save. The. Birds." Drumbeat.

"Self-righteous bitch," I yelled. "The world will be better off without you."

"Liz," Brenda said softly. "What's really going on here?"

"My mother has Alzheimer's," I said, and instantly regretted it, wishing I'd kept my big mouth shut. As my great-grandma used to say, *You don't owe a thing to a bugger*, including bartenders, bar buddies, and best friends—not that I had any of those these days.

They'd all screwed off after I refused to sit through their ridiculous intervention. As though it was my fault I'd walked into our regular Friday night get-together, expecting dinner and drinks with the girls, only to get hand wringing and coffee instead. *We love you, Liz. We want to help you, Liz.* Who the hell did they think they were anyway?

I told them all to fuck off and leave me alone, and they had, for over a year now. Not so much as a phone call from any of them. And who cared? As Great-Grandma Lucy used to say, *I dinna need you or yer shite.* No wonder people were afraid of the old bat.

"I don't know why I told you that." I pulled out the fifth cooler and waved Brenda away. "Don't you have kids to watch or something?"

"Two wonderful boys." She parted the branches again. "But your mother looks too young for Alzheimer's."

I ignored her. Focused on my fizzy booze instead. Downed half the bottle and belched loudly. If only the stuff wasn't so gassy.

"Can't be more than fifty, fifty-one—"

"She's fifty-five. And yes, that sounds too young." I belched again and checked on the Diehards. Mark's group was drinking bottled water under the canopy while Mary Anne and Benny stood watching them from the curb, and Ruby kept on drumming.

"Are you sure that's what she has?" Brenda asked.

"Positive." I swirled what was left in the bottle, watching it go round and round. "It's called early onset because it usually hits people in their fifties, but it can happen younger. And the good news is that it's often genetic, which means that shit may be happening in my own brain as we speak."

"You seem to know a lot about it."

"In the last few days, I have become a fucking encyclopedia on all things Alzheimer's. Causes, signs, treatments, you name it, I know it."

Brenda eyed my bottle. I offered her some, but she shook her head. Who could read people these days?

"But why are you spying on her? Why not just go over and talk to her?"

"Because we don't speak, which has been working well for both of us. Except now she's changed her mind. Decided we should talk after all."

"Understandable."

"You might think so, but you'd be wrong because I don't care what happens to that woman. Grace, yes. Ruby, never." The end of my nose began to burn. "Enough of this crap. I have better things to do."

I took another pull on the bottle, hoping to swallow that stupid ache. But Brenda laid a hand on my arm before I could go for another, her touch as soft, as compelling as her voice when she asked, "Who's Grace?" and that ache kept right on building.

"My sister," I said, my voice sounding strangled and weak, leaving me pissed off with Brenda, with Ruby, but mostly with myself for making happy hour too small. Honestly, six coolers? What the hell was I thinking?

"Is your sister protesting too?" Brenda asked.

"Of course not. She's at home on the Island. Terrified to leave the goddamn place anymore, which suited my mother just fine until the Alzheimer's thing happened. Now she expects me to come home and be Ruby the Second, devoted to all things Island, including that fucking protest." I pointed my bottle at the airport. "Well you know what, Brenda? I love those planes. If I had the money, I'd fly in one every day and I'd have the pilot pull a sign behind it that says 'Up your ass, bitch. We are here to stay.' " I took another pull on the bottle. "I don't know why I'm telling you all this. It's not as if you care."

"You're right, I don't care," she said, which I appreciated. Then she blew it by adding, "But I will take that bottle." She held out a hand when I hesitated. "Now."

I shrugged and handed it to her. The stuff had no taste anymore anyway, so why not move on? Think about what I'd like next instead. Real vodka, Car Bombs, the choices were vast, but the destination always the same. "You working at the Duck tonight?"

"It's Friday isn't it?" She poured out the last of my fizzy booze. "Have you eaten dinner?"

Dinner? I wasn't even sure I'd had lunch. Fact is, I rarely think about food these days. I figure it's nature's way of helping a drinker keep her girlish figure.

"I'm going to assume the answer is no." Brenda bent to pick up my backpack. "Come on. I have sandwiches and cold drinks. Not the kind you like, but you're welcome to one."

I shouldn't have been surprised. Brenda was the kind of person who spoke her mind and never judged anyone. Not even me on the many occasions when I'd passed out, facedown, on one of the Duck's tables. She didn't dump me on the sidewalk or slap me into consciousness or even call the police as a more prudent bartender might have. Just poured me into a taxi, paid the driver to make sure I got through my front door safely, and put it on my tab.

"What else was I supposed to do?" she'd asked when I finally had the nerve to go back after the first time. "Let one of those jerks take you home? It's your business if you walk out with them under your own steam but not when you're out cold. Not on my watch."

Like I said, I shouldn't have been surprised that she wanted to take care of me here too, and yet I was. Surprised and pleased and more than a little sick. I held my stomach and belched again. "Goddamn fizzy drinks."

Brenda took hold of my arm. "You need to eat. And the boys will be wondering what's happened to me."

"I don't know," I said, but her fingers were strong, her hold firm. "Maybe for a moment then," I said, and tried not to stumble on my way out of the trees.

# GRACE

Everyone always thinks that people on the Island are friends with everyone else, but it's not true. We're just like people anywhere—we recognize the faces we see every day. The ones on our street or on the ferry or at the Bridge Boutique, but there are seven hundred of us here, for goodness' sake—as many as you'd find in a small town or a condominium building—and no one expects all those people to be friends.

But the thing about Islanders is that while we don't necessarily know all the *people*, we definitely know all their *houses* because each one is different. We'll say things like, "You know the house with the pink and purple door," and everyone will nod and say they do. And then we'll talk about the renovation or the paint job or the landscaping or whatever's going on for hours. But that doesn't mean we've ever been past the front door because we might not be friends—which is why I had no idea that the house Mark was renting was so nice or so big inside.

The houses on Ward's were all built on the old camping sites, so there's not enough room to add anything to the sides or the back. But Mark's house was on Algonquin and those lots were bigger, so his house had a room out the back *plus* two extra storys! It looked like one of those beach houses in a magazine, with white walls and red tile floors and the kind of furniture my mom said was supposed to look antique but wasn't really. I didn't care what it was supposed to be. I liked it.

And lucky Jocelyn got the third floor all to herself with her own bathroom and a bedroom that didn't double as anything else, and there were windows on both ends of the hall and a ceiling fan that kept everything cool.

The red tiles looked nice up here too, but after a while they got really hard on the butt. I knew because I'd been sitting on the floor outside that girl's room for almost an hour, trying to get her to open the stupid door.

When I first came up the stairs, I wasn't even sure she was still in there. I thought she probably climbed out the window and made a run for the ferry the moment Mark and my mom left for the protest. It's what Liz would have done when she was twelve, and if I had it to do over again, I would have climbed out right behind her. But after a few minutes of knocking on her door and calling, "Jocelyn? Are you in there?" I heard a low thump, thump, thump, like she was banging her head against the wall, and I knew she hadn't gone anywhere. It was the third floor after all. That probably made a difference.

Still, it was Friday night and for the first time since they made me come back to the Island, I had somewhere to go and something to do. But Mark had asked me to keep an eye on Jocelyn while he was gone, so I couldn't very well leave the house without her, and since she wouldn't come out no matter how nice I asked, I finally sat down and said, "Okay then, I'll keep you company right here."

Until this morning, I hadn't seen Jocelyn since she was six years old. Her mom never wanted her daughter to know about us or about Mark's life on the Island, so we used to meet him every week for lunch and we'd talk on the phone whenever my mom wasn't around. It wasn't like we were little kids who were hurt by this arrangement. I was eighteen when Jocelyn was born, and Liz was twenty-three, so we really didn't care one way or the other.

After her mother died, Mark finally brought Jocelyn to Fran's to meet us. He didn't explain who we were in advance, just said he had a surprise for her. But I guess she was still missing her mom, and seeing two women give her dad a hug was too much. She had a really big voice for a little girl and made sure everyone knew she was not sharing her dad with anyone. Mark took her right back home and said it would be best if we kept things as they were until she was older. But I'm pretty sure he must have been thinking much older when he said that, because being twelve hadn't made her any friendlier than she'd been at six.

And since the sound of my voice seemed to bug her as much as being stuck in the hall bugged me, I started talking. And I was going to keep right on talking until she finally came out screaming, "No more! No more!" Then I'd work on getting her to hop on a bike and come with me to the lighthouse because that was where I had to be.

I started by telling her all about the scalp massage I gave Mrs. Jackson this morning, going over it step by step, describing the bumps on her head and the horrible tarry smell of the shampoo she always brought with her. Then I moved on to Sandra Morris's color job, giving her the formula that I mixed and carefully explaining how one part opened the hair shaft and the other part added the color.

When I'd exhausted all my clients, I started listing the birds I'd seen that morning, saying the names nice and slow in case Jocelyn wanted to take notes. I didn't really see all that many and I was afraid that when I ran out of birds, I'd have to start talking about my dreams or something. But just before I reached the end of the list, I heard that same low thump, thump, thump, and I smiled, knowing it wouldn't be long now.

"Did I tell you I pished in the woods this morning?" I said.

I love that word, *pish*. People always think it means something rude, but it doesn't. It's a perfectly nice word used by birders all over the world for an almost-acceptable way of getting a bird's attention. But I didn't think Jocelyn would know that so I leaned closer to the door, hoping this would do the trick.

"I've never pished in the woods," I continued, "because it's not really a good thing to do. But even the best people say that sometimes when you're out there, and you've been waiting forever and you really have to go, but you still haven't seen the bird you're looking for, that's when they say it's okay to pish. And I really did want to see that bird."

I waited and listened. Still the low thump, thump, thump but nothing more. Not even a *shut up* or an *f you*. So I kept right on going.

"I admit I was a little nervous. But I kept hearing this bird singing and singing, and it was really strange because sometimes he didn't even sound like a bird. Sometimes he sounded like a cat or a dog, and once he sounded like a truck backing up, so of course I wanted to find it."

All of a sudden I heard her shuffling around in there. Moving things, probably wishing she'd taken her iPod and cell phone in with her, or at least a pair of earplugs. But all of her stuff was sitting on the counter in the kitchen, and I wasn't about to go down there and get any of it for her. Not when she was being so rude.

When my mom left for the protest earlier, I came over to see Mark's new house, and he was giving me a tour when Jocelyn came inside, asking if she could go into the city to see her friends.

"You want to take the ferry alone?" he asked. And she said, "Well, duh," and he said, "No, I'm sorry," and she said, "You're holding me against my will?" and he said, "Don't be silly," and that's when she started talking about the Charter of Rights and something about liberties.

Mark held up his hands and said, "Jocelyn, don't try to out-lawyer me. You're twelve. You don't know the Island or the ferry docks, and I don't want you going over alone yet. Why don't you come with me to the protest? It'll give you a chance to get used to the ferry as well as an understanding of what we're up against with that airport."

Instead of saying okay, she shoved her fists into her hips so her arms looked like wings and said, "You want me to join your stupid protest? Are you kidding? I *love* that airport. If I could, I'd get on one of those planes and get the hell off this Island right now!" Then she ran upstairs and locked the door, leaving all of her stuff behind.

I'd watched her go, still not believing she felt the same way I did about something, and I was still thinking about that when Mark asked if I'd mind keeping an eye on her while he was at the protest. "You can use my laptop while you're here if you like." He held out the phone. "Mary Anne has a cell phone. You can call and ask to talk to your mom. See what she thinks."

I knew she wouldn't care, but what could I say to Mark? I can't stay here because I have plans? If I told him that, then he wouldn't go to the protest. And if he said anything to my mom after, she'd want to know where I went and with who and for how long, and I knew better than to start a Charter of Rights fight with my mother.

So I said sure, I'd stay with Jocelyn. And Mark wasn't gone two minutes when her phone started buzzing and vibrating itself all over the counter. I called up the stairs, "Jocelyn, your phone's buzzing," but she didn't come down so I ignored it too. Sat on the sofa with Mark's laptop and checked my e-mail, hoping for something more from Liz.

She'd sent me a dirty cartoon that morning, just like she did every day, so I figured she wasn't mad about the whole iced-tea-in-the-head thing yesterday. I'd have liked a real e-mail too, just to be sure, but my mailbox was empty. So I'd gone upstairs and parked myself outside Jocelyn's door, purposely leaving her phone behind. If she wanted it, she could go and get it.

"I'd been looking for that bird for an hour," I continued. "And it was getting later and later, and my first customer was coming at nine and I was almost ready to give up when Benny came over to see what I was doing. You don't know Benny, but he's lived on the Island forever I think, and he's told me stories about my Great-Grandma Lucy that even my mom doesn't know. Like how she wasn't afraid to go swimming in the ponds at Hanlan's Point even during the polio scare. And how the two of them used to have a special spot where they'd sit and watch the fireworks every summer when the exhibition was on. I think he really liked my great-grandma, and when I told him I was looking for a bird I'd never heard before, he listened for a minute and you'll never guess what he told me."

"That the sound of your voice made him want to kill himself?" Jocelyn hollered.

"No, silly. He said it was a mockingbird."

"Who gives a shit?"

"He said he could tell by the strange sounds it made and the way it kept singing and singing."

"It was probably telling you to fuck off, just like I am!"

"I don't think that was it at all. Benny said that a male mockingbird looking for a mate will sing night and day like that until a lady mockingbird answers back. They're the only birds who never shut up."

"Kind of like you?"

"I'm not looking for a mate."

"Oh my God."

"That's when I decided it was time to pish or go home. So I clenched my teeth together really tight, and then I whispered nice and loud, "Pish, pish, pish," and I waited. The mockingbird stopped singing, but he didn't come out like the other birds, he just stayed still. I thought about pishing a second time, but I was a little afraid he might attack. Benny said that happens sometimes with mockingbirds, and I know it's true because I read about it on my favorite birding website when I got home."

"God save me from birding websites." The door swung back and Jocelyn stepped into the hall at last. "Has anyone ever told you how irritating you are?"

She was still wearing her black T-shirt, but she'd traded the Hated skirt for a pair of shorts and the boots for flip-flops. She looked like a kid again, one who'd gotten into her mother's black eyeliner. Now if I could just change the color of that hair.

"I guess it depends on what you think is irritating," I said.

"I don't believe this," she muttered, and walked past me and down the stairs.

Hurray for the mockingbird! Hurray for pishing!

I followed her down and went straight to Mark's laptop to check my e-mail again, but there was still nothing from Liz, which was weird because she usually sends me a bunch of e-mails every day. But today, she'd been as silent as Jocelyn.

"A person could starve to death in this place."

Jocelyn was standing in front of the fridge with the door open, staring at the shelves. There wasn't much in there—a loaf of bread, a carton of milk, and a small jar of peanut butter. Mark must have forgotten what the shopping is like on the Island.

"This is gay," Jocelyn muttered, and slammed the door. "What am I supposed to eat?"

"Your dad left a lasagne in the freezer, or I have this." I held up the money he gave me before he left—five twenty-dollar bills all rolled up nice and neat and held together with an elastic. "He said we could go out for dinner if you like."

"Of course I'd like." She tried to snatch the roll from me, but I shoved it down the front of my T-shirt, tucking it into my bra so it wouldn't fall out on the floor.

Jocelyn's eyes narrowed. "I thought retards were supposed to be kind and gentle."

"I am kind. And I'm smart enough to know that I have to hold on to the money if I want to be sure my dinner is paid for." I headed for the door. "Let's go. There are plenty of restaurants on Centre Island."

"There's two."

"And that's twice as many as we have on Ward's." I looked back. "You coming?"

She didn't move and I was afraid she might call my bluff and head back to the bedroom. But hunger must have won out because she grabbed her cell phone and her iPod and pushed past me out the door. "How far is it?"

"About a ten-minute ride." I kicked back the stand on my own bike and pointed to a blue Raleigh by the porch. "Your dad had that one brought over for you."

She glanced over at the bike, then bent her head over her phone and pressed some numbers. "This is so lame. Why aren't there at least buses?"

"Because the Island is a park, and parks don't have buses or subways or cars."

"Well, they should," she said and put the phone to her ear.

Across the road, a couple of girls about her age came around the side of the house, walking on stilts and laughing. The Watts twins, Brianne and Kiley. Nice girls but a little rambunctious. At least that's what their mom said the last time my mom did her hair.

I waved and the twins waved back. "You're really good on those," I said. "Are you going to be in the show this year?"

"Yup," Kiley said. "How about you?"

"Not this year." I pointed to Jocelyn. "This is Jocelyn. She's living here for the summer."

"I'm not living here, I'm a prisoner."

The girls looked at me funny and I felt my face warm. "She's not really a prisoner. Not in that way."

Kiley nodded and then smiled at Jocelyn. "You want to try the stilts?"

Jocelyn scowled. "You won't believe what they're doing," she said into the phone.

"It's not that hard," Brianne said. "And it's kind of an Island tradition. Most of the kids who live here learn."

"Like I said, I do not live here, and I do not want to try your lame stilts."

I shrugged my shoulders at the twins and they shrugged back and stilt-walked across the lawn and down the other side of the house to the backyard.

"That was rude," I said when they were gone.

"It was honest." Jocelyn hung up the phone, hooked her iPod into her ears, and threw a leg over the bike. "I want to go to the Carousel restaurant. And just so you know, you are *not* eating with me when we get there. My friends are coming over on the next ferry. I'm having dinner with them."

"That's okay. But I still have the money."

"You'll have to give me half when we get there."

"I don't have to do anything."

"Listen, Short Bus . . ."

"No, you listen. I'm not retarded and if you say that one more time—"

"You'll what? Tell on me? Beat me up?" She pointed to her chin. "Go ahead. Right here. My father's a lawyer. I dare you to hit me."

I knew it was wrong, but if I'd had a can of iced tea right then, I'd have pitched it at her and not because I couldn't help it either. And I wouldn't have felt a bit bad about it after. "You're not a nice person."

"And you're an idiot."

"I'm not giving you the money."

She came a step closer. "Wanna bet?"

I was really glad when Jocelyn's phone started ringing because it meant I didn't have to bet her about the money. And I didn't care when she flipped me the bird and said into the phone, "Don't worry, I'm on my way." Or when she turned her back and started talking like I couldn't hear her, saying things like "Everyone here is making me crazy" and "I can't believe they live like this." But when she looked right at me over her shoulder and said, "And the blond retard is the worst," my skin got all hot, and I could hear that horrible buzzing inside my head again.

I was worried because this would be the second time in less than a week, and I'd been doing so good for months and months, even my mom said so. "Those breathing techniques are really working for you," she'd said more than a few times now.

I knew Liz wouldn't tell anyone what happened on the beach, but Jocelyn would tell everybody everywhere, and nothing good could come of that. Nothing good for me anyway.

So I tried to breathe it all away, tried to stay calm and focus like my mom always said to do, but it wasn't working, it never did, in spite of what she wanted to think. And when I closed my eyes, stupid Jocelyn said, "Oh my God, now she's doing some kind of meditating thing. Wait, I'll take a picture and send it to you," and I opened my eyes in time to hear the click.

"This is too good," she said into the phone, and the buzzing got louder.

"Not now," I whispered and closed my eyes again. "Not now, please."

This time I gritted my teeth and concentrated harder. Kept breathing slowly, in and out, in and out, while the buzzing got louder and louder.

"She's talking to herself too," Jocelyn said, and when I peeked, I saw that she was smiling for the first time since she got here. "Hold on," she said, then raised her phone and took another picture. "She is such a freak," she said to her friend, and I watched my hand reach down and pick up a rock.

"No!" I yelled. "Not now!"

"Grace?" someone said. I jerked my head around. Kiley and Brianne were by the gate on their stilts. "Are you okay?" Kiley asked.

"She's fucking nuts," Jocelyn said to them. "Want to see the pictures?"

I saw the twins shake their heads and back away from Jocelyn's pictures. They really were getting good on those stilts. And when I realized the buzzing had quieted, I told myself not to think about the buzzing anymore. To think about the mockingbird instead and Benny and how I was glad he'd been there to tell me what kind of bird it was. And how I was going to go back and find that bird and how I hoped he was making the truck noise again. And then I made my fingers release that rock.

"I'm fine," I said to Kiley, probably too loudly if the look on her face was anything to go by, and I knew I had to get away. Had to get back into the house as fast as I could, but Jocelyn took another picture and that was it.

I snatched the phone right out of her hand and I told her friend, "Jocelyn can't talk right now," and then I snapped that phone shut right in her face. She didn't say anything, just stood there with her mouth open.

And suddenly the buzzing in my head stopped altogether, like it was as surprised as Jocelyn, and didn't know what to do next. So I kept on not thinking about it and I hopped on my bike instead, and I could hear Kiley and Brianne cheering as I took off.

Jocelyn didn't move for three full seconds, which gave me a decent head start. Then she hollered, "Give me back my phone, you fucking retard," and I knew she was coming after me.

She wasn't very good on a bike, so she probably wouldn't have ever caught up to me, but I was afraid I'd lose her and then Mark would worry and I'd be in trouble. So I stopped when I got close to the ferry dock and I waited. The next ferry wasn't due for a half hour so I was the only one there right now, but soon the people would start coming and even though I had no idea what I was going to do, I really hoped Jocelyn got there before they did so I could find out.

I saw her come around the corner and start pedaling faster when she spotted me. When she pulled up close to me, I did the only thing I could think of. I dropped my bike and ran to the railing at the end of the dock. And *that's* when the idea hit me.

"Stop right there," I said, and held her phone out over the water.

Her bike clattered to the ground and she came toward me. "What the hell do you think you're doing? Give me back my phone."

"I'll drop it," I said, letting the phone dangle between my thumb and first finger. "And no one will blame me because I'm a retard, remember?"

Her eyes narrowed to nasty slits and her face went as red as her hair. She looked kind of like a cartoon only it would have been better with steam coming out of her ears. "Give me back my phone right now."

"Why? So you can take more pictures and call me more names?"

Her eyes followed the phone as I swung it back and forth between my fingers. "Okay, you win. No more pictures, no more names. Just give me the phone."

I laughed and held the phone still. "You really do think I'm stupid. As soon as I give it back you'll just say it again."

"I won't, I promise."

"You'll have to do better than that." I lifted her phone, opened it, and then glanced over at her. "Who will I get if I push redial?"

"Don't you dare."

I smiled. "Or you'll what? Tell on me? Beat me up?"

It was her turn to close her eyes and take a deep breath, and if I'd known how to take a picture, I would have done it right then.

"Look," she said. "I won't call you retard anymore. I give you my word."

"You'll have to give me something else too."

"What else?"

"Something important. Like your iPod. Give me that and if you don't call me names for two full weeks, I'll give it back."

"Forget it."

I shrugged. "Have it your way," I said, and stuck my arm out over the railing again. "Bombs away—"

"Wait!" she called, and I could see that she really wanted to add something else, something worse than anything she'd said yet, but she didn't. She just took her iPod out of her pocket, unlooped the earplugs from around her neck and held the whole thing out to me. "Two weeks," she said. "And I know where to find you."

I wanted to punch a fist in the air and cheer the way Kiley and Brianne had, but that would have been rude, so I just took the iPod with one hand and gave her the phone with the other. The moment she had it, she flipped that thing open, hit a button, and turned away from me.

I told her, "I'm right behind you," and I stayed there too, turning the wheel on the iPod and trying to get the earplugs to stay in my ears while she talked to her friend about the ferry schedule and when were they coming and how she wished she could get off this f-ing Island.

But she didn't once call me a retard or anything else and that felt really good because I'd won, all on my own, without the breathing or the focusing or any of that other stuff that never worked anyway.

Even if she told on me later, even if my mom grounded me for a week, I knew I wouldn't care, and I wouldn't give back the iPod either. It was mine for two whole weeks, fair and square, and I was going to use it. All I had to do was figure out how turn it on.

# RUBY

Another flight touched down on the other side of the gap just as Dean Martin's voice floated by me on a breeze too hot to be refreshing, asking that time-honored question, "Ain't that a kick in the head?" The taxi driver with the Rat Pack taste snickered. Another grinned and a little boy on the passing shuttle turned in his seat to stare at me—the lone protester on the grassy knoll.

"Fine," I called to the traitors under Mark's canopy. "We'll take a break. But don't get too comfortable. We reassemble in fifteen minutes."

Mark saluted me with a bottle of water and Mary Anne had the grace to look guilty, but the rest were too busy checking out what Mark had in his cooler to even hear me. "Fifteen minutes," I muttered, and carried the drum back to the table. Laid it carefully on the grass and used the edge of my sleeve to wipe the sweat from my face. Pretended not to notice Mary Anne fanning her face with her straw hat as she crossed the no-man's land between the two camps.

"Ruby, don't take it personally," she said, holding out a peace offering as she drew up beside me—one of those bloody bottles of water. "The sun is brutal and a few minutes' rest won't hurt a thing."

"It's not the rest I object to, it's Mark." I eyed the offering. "And doesn't it strike you odd that we're marching in the name of air quality yet you're drinking water from a plastic bottle that arrived in an SUV?"

"Not for an instant." She plunked the bottle on the table and her hat back on her head. "Now stop being hateful and come sit in the shade. There's fresh fruit in that cooler. And a box of the most wonderful little pastries."

"I'm fine right here. I have eco-friendly water, chocolate granola bars, and a perfectly good hat to keep the sun off my head." To prove the point, I dragged my bag out from under the table and withdrew a stainless steel water bottle, a box of bars, and one hot-pink baseball cap with Foxy embroidered across the front.

Mary Anne laughed and picked up the cap. "You have to be kidding."

I sighed. If only.

Mary Anne and I have always agreed that no thinking adult should ever wear a baseball cap. They're unflattering, highly impractical in terms of real sun protection, and they lower your perceived IQ by ten points the moment you pull one on—turn it backward and you can make that twenty or more. Which is why she wears wide-brimmed straw, and I wear a Tilley. One made of sturdy cotton duck with brass grommets and a brim that protects my face *and* my neck.

That hat is timeless, easy to care for, and has seen me through more canoe races and protest marches than I can count. It is absolutely perfect for days like this, and I'd have been wearing it right then if I'd been able to find it. But it wasn't on the hook by the door where I always left it, or in the bathroom or any of the bedrooms. And I couldn't think where else it might be with Grace shoving her damn tube of sunscreen under my nose every two seconds.

"You need protection," she kept saying, as though there hadn't been sunscreen in every jar of cream I'd bought since I turned thirty. But who needed to reapply the stuff ten times a day?

I tried reasoning with her, but she only covered her ears and kept shouting, "Use it, use it, use it," until I finally gave in and dabbed more on my nose. I didn't argue when she slipped the tube into my bag either, hoping that would be the end of it. But when I still couldn't locate my Tilley, she dropped the pink baseball cap in there as well, insisting, "You'll need this too."

Sadly, she was right. The heat was unbearable and the sun a torture. It was either run into Mark's shade before I melted or break down and wear the damn cap.

"I rarely kid," I said, snatching the thing back from Mary Anne and jamming it on my head. "Besides, I can use an image update." I turned the cap backward. "See? Instantly hip."

She laughed again. "Whatever you say, Foxy." But she couldn't resist turning my hat around the right way. "Are you coming or not?"

"Not." I sat down and tugged the bill lower on my forehead, grateful there were no mirrors around, that I could only imagine how ridiculous I looked. "One of us should be here in case someone stops by to sign the petition." I smiled up at her. "You can join me if you want."

"No one is going to stop by, and you know it." She sat down beside me anyway and pulled the box of granola bars toward her. "Why are you so annoyed with Mark anyway?"

I flicked up the lid on my water bottle. "Because he's pushy. First he moves back to the Island without so much as a heads-up. Then he roars in here bearing pastries and shade and everyone acts like it's perfectly okay."

"Because it is okay. Mark's a wonderful man and everyone likes him." She waited while I took a few gulps of my guilt-free water, then handed me a bar and took one for herself. "While I don't for an instant believe his story about returning to the Island for his daughter's sake, having seen the girl, I'm sure it can't hurt. But judging by the way he looks at you when he thinks no one else is watching, I'd say he's come to his senses at last and has returned to win fair lady's heart once more. And how can he do that if he's not pushy?"

She screwed up her nose at the melting chocolate mess beneath the granola wrapper and dropped the whole thing into the garbage bag beside the table. "Like it or not, that canopy was meant for you, to protect you from the sun, and that is easily the most romantic gesture I've seen in years." She poured water onto her fingers and shook them dry over the grass. "I'm telling you, that man is a knight in shining armor."

"Well, you know what they say. One woman's white knight is another woman's stalker."

She frowned at me and I was tempted to set the record straight. To tell her everything, starting with Big Al's invasion into my life and ending with Mark's objections to my plan for a graceful exit. Point out that a real white knight would have helped me research painless poisons or, at the very least, kept his opinions to himself. But this was neither the time nor the place for such a discussion, so instead I said, "Trust me, Mark's not here to win anyone's heart." But couldn't resist turning my head just a little, to see what he was up to now.

Telling a story by the look of it, and doing a fine job if the smiles on the faces around him were any kind of gauge. Then again, Mark had always told a good story, turning the simplest bedtime tale into something wonderfully funny and silly. Reading them backward, upside down, changing the endings, the beginnings, sometimes the whole thing, and always with a different voice for each character. That man could get my girls laughing so hard I'd have to go in and threaten to ground all three if they didn't settle down. He just didn't understand that bedtime stories were supposed be boring. How else could you get a kid to go to sleep? And it always hurt just a little that they never wanted me to read those books to them.

Mary Anne got to her feet again. "Say what you want, I still think he's here for you. And you can sit in the sun and eat melting granola if you want to, but I'm going back to the shade to get myself something cool and cream-filled."

"You've got ten more minutes," I called after her, then picked up my own bar. Gave it a squeeze and put it back down. Went for more water instead, discovering there was barely a mouthful left. I'd have to walk over to the water fountain to fill it, which was fine. Perfect in fact. I could use the exercise. And so could Mark. Life in the city had not been kind to his health. Although I noticed he wasn't eating any of his own pastries. I had to smile when he bit into an apple instead. Having to depend on a bike again must have been a rude awakening for a man accustomed to driving everywhere now.

Still with all the money he must have these days, he hadn't pulled up in a Hummer. His nod to air quality, I suppose, which was significant given the love he'd had for all things motorized. The day we met, he and Eric had talked nonstop about Mark's 1965 Shelby GT350. I had no idea what that was, but according to Eric, it was the gas-guzzling, ear-blasting, drag-race-winning marvel that had transformed the Mustang from a secretary's car to a street racer's dream. Eric could not have been more jealous if Mark had said he wanted to sleep with me—probably less, in fact.

Mark loved that car, but on the day Grace was born he went out and bought a baby seat for the back of his bike and came back with a receipt for long-term storage of his Shelby as well. It was his way of letting me know that he'd be around for a while yet, and it is still the most romantic gesture I have ever known.

He looked over and caught me watching him. Held up the pastry box and signaled for me to come join him. I shook my head

and saluted him with the granola bar, even took off the wr̶.
and bit into the warm gooey mess. We both knew I was being
petty, but that will happen when someone pokes his nose into
things that don't concern him—and I was not about to encourage
more canopies.

With that in mind, I decided to devote this forced break time
to other, more urgent matters. I smiled at him again, even gave
him a little wave, then discreetly dropped the rest of the bar into
the garbage, wiped my fingers on a flyer, and took my notebook
and a pen from the bag. Wrote *more research on painless poisons*
under Grace's password and underlined it. Three times.

I wasn't completely convinced that poisons were the way to
go, so to speak, but in a year of looking I'd failed to find a suitable
alternative. It's not like you can ask your friends for suggestions,
casually drop the subject into dinner conversation and not expect
them to watch your every move for a month afterward. And apparently librarians have suicide hotline numbers—or maybe it
was just the one I spoke to—but I was not about to test that route
again.

So eventually I turned to the Internet and was shocked the first
time I encountered an alphabetical list of tried and true methods
on Wikipedia, covering everything from asphyxiation to venom.
And I was frankly appalled to find as many websites dedicated
to helping me achieve my goal as those dedicated to helping me
change my mind. There was a world of whackos out there, but
they had nothing to do with me.

My choice was clinical, not emotional. I wouldn't be leaving
a note or citing a cause or putting the whole thing on tape for
posterity, and I certainly wouldn't be taking anyone else with me. I
would just be gone, and it would look like an accident because that
was the only way to be certain the insurance would pay. And once
Chez Ruby closed, Grace was going to need the money.

Discretion was my top priority, which meant toasters in the
bathtub were off the list, along with closet hanging and anything

to do with razors and messy cleanup. *CSI* was making it harder and harder to believe that there were any poisons left that couldn't be traced, so the choices were narrowing quickly. A heart attack while parachuting would be ideal but difficult to guarantee, which brought me right back to *painless poisons*, with *untraceable* printed beside it.

"I'm curious," a man said, and I jumped. Slapped the notebook closed and jerked my head around. Mark smiled and held out a bunch of red grapes. "Like I said, I'm curious. How late are we marching these days?"

"You're being polite," I said, ignoring his latest olive branch. "What you really mean is why are we still doing this?"

"That's harsh." He plunked the grapes and a bottle of water on the table, then sat down and mopped his brow with the back of his hand. "It's just that it's after five, I'm getting hungry and thought we could grab some dinner when it's over." He smiled hopefully. "So is it almost over?"

"Almost," I said, and had to smile myself when he merely nodded, pretending not to be overjoyed.

"Then would you like to have dinner in the city?" he asked.

"I don't see why not." I picked up his water bottle, pressed it to the back of my neck, and gasped at the sudden shock of cold against my skin. I let it rest there a moment longer, savoring the shiver that ran through my body, before setting the offending plastic back on the table. "I think the Bobs would really enjoy it."

"I wasn't going to invite them. Or anyone else." He flipped up the lid on my steel bottle, emptied the plastic one into it, and set it down in front of me again. "Let me take you to dinner, Ruby. Just the two of us."

"Definitely not." But I did take a welcome sip of water. "Having dinner together would make it look like I've forgiven you, and I haven't."

"How long before you do?"

"Hard to say." I put the container down, picked up the pen

instead. "First I have to get Liz to come home, and then I have to figure out my exit route. Once I've completed both of those tasks, I'm sure I'll forgive you everything." I opened the notebook and tapped the pen on the page. "As you can see, I'm still researching poisons, although I'm also considering bungee jumping, parachuting, and hiring a hit man. A hit man could work, but it would be expensive. Cars, however, offer a variety of alternatives." I glanced over at him. "Was that your SUV earlier?"

"Forget it. I'm not going to let you wreck my car."

"And it would be rude of me to ask. Besides, an accident isn't always fatal. What I have in mind requires a garage. And a hose. Do you happen to have either of those?"

"Ruby, stop."

"Why? Does it make you uncomfortable? Then perhaps you should get back to the party because this is what I'll be working on for the rest of the break. But thanks for these." I snapped a grape off the bunch and popped it into my mouth. "They're delicious."

"If you think those are good, you should try the pineapple. And just so you know, your notes don't make me uncomfortable at all."

"That's wonderful." I went back to my list. Wrote *CARBON MONOXIDE* in letters big enough for him to read from where he sat. "Perhaps you can help me out then, offer some suggestions, something I might have missed."

"Not off the top of my head. But a hit man does make sense, plus it adds a bit of fun to the plan. When will he strike? How will he do it? Could be exciting, and I could help out with expenses if you need it."

I put the pen down. "Are you serious?"

"Are you kidding?" He picked up my pen and slipped it into the pocket of his polo shirt. "The whole idea is ridiculous. But now that you've put the pen down, let's call a truce for the five minutes that are left." He rose and held out a hand. "Come sit in the shade with me."

"Not a chance." I snatched the pen back and underlined _CAR-BON MONOXIDE_. "In fact, I'm not speaking to you at all now."

"Suit yourself." He sat down again and popped a grape into his mouth. "I'll just sit here and watch. Point out spelling errors. Like that one there—"

"Don't you dare. And don't speak to me either."

"Okay. Just one last thing and then I'll shut up." He poked a finger in my ribs and grinned. "Gotcha last."

_Gotcha last_. I hadn't thought of that game in ages. Certainly hadn't played it since he left. But I remembered it well enough now. I bent my head over my list. "I'm not playing."

"Even better, because that means I win."

"You can't win if no one else is playing."

"Says who?"

"Says everyone. Now stop talking so I can think."

"Sure." He poked me again. "But I definitely win."

Mary Anne and the Bobs walked past the table. "We're going to the ladies' room," she said. "Well, some of us are." She paused, looking from me to Mark and back again. "What are you two up to over here, anyway?"

"Gotcha last," he said, at the same time as I said, "Nothing."

Mary Anne and the Bobs smiled. "Who's winning?" she asked.

"I am," Mark said.

"He is not," I insisted. He poked me again and I slapped at his hand.

"He's definitely winning," the Bobs agreed as the three of them walked away.

"This is silly," I said.

Mark smiled. "So why don't you just admit defeat and the whole thing will all be over."

"I am not admitting defeat." He poked me again. "Fine." I reached over and punched him on the arm. "Got you—"

He poked me again. "Last," he said.

"Oh no you don't." I punched him and jumped up, staying out of reach. "I got you last and now it's over." He stood up and I took another step back, knocking over the chair. "Mark, I mean it. The game is over."

He came a step closer. "Says who?"

"Says me." I took another step back, a smile coming to my lips. Every cell in my body suddenly alert, awake.

"I don't think so." He lunged and I leapt to the right. He lunged again, got me this time. "Dammit, Mark."

"Gotcha last," he said, and started to stroll away, back to the canopy.

"Not bloody likely," I yelled, and darted after him. Jumped up, tapped him on the head, and kept on running. "Gotcha last!" I called over my shoulder and felt my stomach leap when he came after me. "Stop it!" I hollered, and kept running, around the canopy, back to the table. Around the table, back to the canopy, with Mark on my heels the whole way.

I started to laugh, I couldn't help it. "Stop him," I called to the canopy party, but they only laughed as we went round the chairs a third time. Then he stopped abruptly, picked up a chair, and came straight through the middle. "No fair!" I yelled, and dashed out into the line of taxis. I was still laughing, needing to stop, to catch my breath, but that would mean he'd get me last and I couldn't let that happen.

Round the taxis, round the limos, the two of us laughing, stumbling, finally stopping, one car apart. Bending over, sides aching. "Admit I won," I gasped. "Admit it."

"Never," he roared, and this time I was too slow off the mark. He had me before I knew it. Picked me right up off the ground and threw me over his shoulder. Carried me back to the grass. Taxi drivers honked, the canopy party cheered, and I was still laughing when he finally sat me down on the table. He put one hand on either side of me, trying to catch his breath as he pressed his nose against mine and announced, "Gotcha last. Game over. I win."

"Okay, okay, you win," I said, giggling and gasping for air while my hands searched for water. He handed me the bottle. I knocked back three fast gulps and hiccuped.

He laughed and shoved the flyers over, sat down beside me. Close but not touching. "One more lap and I'd have been dead."

"I'll remember that next time." I didn't move over, didn't need more space between us. Just wiped my mouth and handed him the bottle. "I saved you some."

He nodded his thanks and drank it slowly, wisely. No hiccups from that side of the table. He always did have impeccable manners. He handed me back the water. "I haven't run that hard in years."

"Same here," I said, feeling lighter, calmer than I had in a very long time.

"Don't let it go to your head, but nobody ever played that game the way you do."

I fluttered my lashes at him. "Well, you do bring out the idiot in me."

"I'll take that as a compliment. I like your hat, by the way."

I'd forgotten about the hat. I lowered my chin, looked at him from underneath the bill. "It does have a certain *je ne sais quoi*. I'll get you one if you like."

He laughed and leaned back on his hands. "All kidding aside, you look great. A protest always did bring out the best in you."

"It's not the protest," I said, closing my eyes and leaning back with him. "I'm just having a good day. No fog, no confusion. Just me and the hat, having some fun."

"Are you having fun?"

"I really think I am."

He went quiet for a moment, and then asked. "Is this an official truce, then?"

"It must be."

"Good." He sat up again, his breathing normal at last. "So you're still rabble-rousing, I see."

"Not much anymore." I sighed as yet another turboprop plane flew over my head. "In fact this is the only protest I come to these days."

"The Bobs mentioned something about that. What happened?"

"Nothing earth-shattering. Once Grace went to live with Liz, I just lost interest. For the first time since she was born, my life was my own with no one else to think about, no one else to take care of. I had all this time on my hands and I could have gone anywhere. Europe, Africa, the choices were endless, but I didn't have the heart anymore, and eventually I couldn't fake it either."

"I can't imagine you even trying."

"I did for a while. I thought that if I went through the motions, the feeling would come back, but it didn't. So I stopped."

I sat up and pulled the bunch of grapes closer. Snapped off a handful and popped one into his mouth, another into mine. "I felt a little guilty at first. All those years telling people it was their duty to get involved, to take a stand, and there I was, sitting at home, staring at the television."

"You did more than most for a long time. You had nothing to feel guilty about."

"Took me a while to figure that out." More grapes—one for me, one for him. The fruit was warmer now. Sweeter, more satisfying. "But eventually I realized I wasn't as important as I thought I was. That the world was chugging along quite nicely without me, and the guilt eventually went away. So I got up off the couch and joined a marathon canoe club."

He smiled at me. "Isn't marathon canoeing for crazy people?"

"That's why I liked it. Plus it was demanding and exhausting, and after a few hours in the canoe, there was nothing in my mind but the next stroke. Not Grace or Liz or what they might be going through on the other side of the bay. Just the next stroke."

Over at the canopy, Mary Anne and the Bobs were back, the three of them clapping their hands and getting the rest of the protesters on their feet. "Break time must be over," I said.

"Must be." Mark groaned as he slid off the table.

"Don't worry, we won't be much longer." I stood beside him, watching the others assemble at the curb, waiting for me. Waiting for the drum, at least. "Funny isn't it, that of all the causes out there, this is the one that keeps me coming back, even though it's never gone particularly well."

"What are you talking about? They didn't get a bridge, did they?" I looked over at him and he shrugged. "Seems like a victory to me."

I smiled. "Thanks. I think I needed that."

He turned away, looked out over the row of taxis. "I hate to say it, but I've missed you, Ruby."

"I've missed you too," I said, watching the taxis with him, because it was easier. "But it doesn't change anything."

"We could have dinner. Then I wouldn't be hungry anymore. That would change something." He turned back to me. "What do you say? Can I take you to dinner when this is over?"

I'd almost forgotten the way his eyes tip down at the corners, making him look sad even when he's smiling. And the way his head tilts slowly to the right when he's waiting for an answer and not at all sure it's going to be the one he wants. But standing there watching him shuffle his feet as that smile twitched and threatened to fade, I suddenly remembered everything. The softness of his lips on my throat, the tickle of his breath in my ear, the gentleness of those big, ham hands in the dark. And I heard myself saying, "Yes, I'd like that."

His smile came back. "Great, you pick the place," he said. And as I walked to the curb with the drum, I told myself not to worry, everything would be fine.

It was only dinner, after all.

# LIZ

"What happened to your head?" Brenda's younger son, Aaron, asked.

"Don't be rude," Brenda said, but I waved it off.

Since her kids had finally accepted that I wasn't a witch, and had even helped set me up with my own section of blanket, an egg salad sandwich, and a drink box, I owed them something in return. So I smiled and said, "My sister threw a can of iced tea at me."

Ethan, the older one, stared at me wide-eyed. "Did your mom get mad?"

I leaned closer, whispering, "I didn't tell her because I didn't want to get my sister in trouble."

"Does it hurt?" Aaron asked.

"Not right now," I said, which wasn't surprising considering I couldn't feel anything anywhere. I stretched out my legs, bounced them up and down, even sucked in my cheeks, hoping for a little sensation somewhere, but came up with nothing. Happy hour was still upon me.

"Stop pestering Liz and eat," Brenda said, but Ethan asked, "Does your sister always throw things?"

"Not as often as she used to." I leaned back on my elbows and squinted at the baseball field. "Which team are we rooting for anyway?"

"The blue shirts, who else?" Aaron said, and the two boys rolled their eyes at each other.

"Give her a break, fellas," Brenda said, and flashed me the kind of grin I had only seen once or twice at the Duck—full and un-guarded, the kind that made you want to grin right back. "You have to cheer for blue," she said, "because Mitch plays first base and my brother Gary's the shortstop." She dug a couple of carrot sticks and some celery out of a Tupperware container and laid them on my plate beside the sandwich. "Do you remember Gary?"

I closed one eye and focused on the shortstop. "I do now," I said, and sat up a little straighter.

Brenda's husband, Mitch, was short and solid-looking, square really, like a stump with buzzed blond hair. He was probably a nice guy but definitely not my type. Gary, on the other hand, was tall and dark with a wiry, athletic build and a slouchy, loose-jointed walk. The kind of guy who would probably be paunchy and round-shouldered later in life but looked good now, when it mattered.

I had seen him at the Duck a few times over the past couple of weeks. He never stayed long. Just came in to talk to Brenda and then left. He didn't look anything like her, which had made a few of the regulars question the whole brother/sister thing. But Grace and I were nothing alike either, so you never could tell with families. Besides, Brenda didn't seem like the type to cheat on her husband. Smack him a good one if he needed it? Definitely. But run around behind his back? I'd have to vote no.

"You should have introduced us," I said, watching Gary roll his shoulders, adjust his cap. "What's he do for a living?"

"Electrician, but don't get any ideas. He's already recovering from a bad relationship."

"You're saying I'd be a bad relationship?"

"Yes. You like pickles?"

I nodded and turned back to the field. "Who's winning?"

"Red," Ethan said.

"But it doesn't matter because it's all for fun and charity," Brenda said in a voice that told me this wasn't the first time she'd made that little reminder. She nudged my plate closer. "Eat."

I maneuvered half the sandwich to my mouth, took a bite, and tasted nothing. "This is great," I said, taking another bite anyway because Brenda was right. I needed to eat.

"You don't have to be polite."

"No, really. This whole thing is great. The sandwich, the game, inviting me to join your family. You're much nicer than you let on."

"We all have weak moments." Brenda picked up the drink box and held it out to me. "Drink this."

"Apple juice? Never touch the stuff." She raised a brow. "Fine," I said, and stabbed at the stupid little hole with the stupid little straw more times than I could count before handing the whole thing back to her. "Not thirsty."

Brenda inserted the straw and put the box back in my hand. "Now try."

"Smart-ass," I said and was sucking back that juice like it was world-class wine when Aaron said, "Mommy, this could be strike three. Blue could be up soon."

We all turned to watch as the pitcher wound up. Threw the ball. And whack—the hitter was on his way to first. The bench cheered, the boys groaned, and Gary moved back farther and farther—still watching the ball while the hitter kept running. And Ethan and Aaron weren't the only ones on their feet screaming, "Catch it! Catch it!" when that ball started its descent.

The runner was closing in on third. Gary raised his glove. The boys held their breath. Brenda stopped fussing with the food. All eyes were on that ball when it hit Gary's glove and stayed put.

"He's out!" Ethan hollered, and the boys were off and running to greet the conquering heroes as both teams left the field to join family and friends for their picnics. "Third inning stretch," Brenda explained to me. "You have to love friendly baseball."

As Gary came closer, I pushed at my hair, brushed the crumbs off my shirt, my lap, the blanket all around me, remembering why I didn't usually eat when I was drinking.

"Nice catch," Brenda said when Mitch and her brother reached the blanket.

"Now it's up to Mitch to bring up the score," Gary said, hitting another high-five with the boys.

"Don't count it. I'm really off tonight." Mitch smiled at me and reached into the cooler. "Who's our guest?"

"This is my friend, Liz."

Her friend? I suppose it would be hard to explain the truth with the kids around. *This is one of the drunks I talk about all the time. The one with no morals, remember?* So we'd have it her way.

"Nice to meet you both," I said, holding out a hand to each in turn, figuring it was safer than trying to stand up.

Mitch grabbed a sandwich and sat down with Brenda and the boys, while Gary took a seat next to me. Up close, he looked even better. Plenty of thick dark hair, angular jaw, brown eyes. I have always had a thing for brown eyes.

"You look familiar," he said as he bit into egg salad. "Have I seen you at a game before? Or maybe the Duck?" He snapped his fingers. "That's it. You were at the Duck last Friday, dancing the Highland fling."

Brenda laughed. "She'll do that sometimes."

I looked down at my sandwich. "Usually after someone has suggested tequila shooters."

"I've never seen such creative use of coasters." Gary leaned back with his sandwich. "It was very impressive."

"It's a skill I'm proud of, plus it looks great on a résumé."

Gary laughed. "Must open a lot of doors."

"More than you can imagine." I raised my head, met those brown eyes again, and that's when I saw the family resemblance. The smile. Open, unguarded, the kind that made me smile back. Too bad it had been declared out of bounds.

"Hopefully I'll get to see another performance. What have you got to drink in here?" Gary asked, lifting the lid on the cooler. But he didn't take anything out. He closed it and got to his feet instead.

"Are you up to bat next, Daddy?" Aaron asked. "Daddy? Are you listening?"

"Sure, buddy," he said as he rose and went to stand beside Gary.

Brenda looked up from her plate. "What's wrong?" she asked, and we both turned around to find four men standing no more than five feet from the edge of the blanket.

Two of them were medium, one was large, and the one with the aluminum baseball bat was an extra-large. All four wore sunglasses, steel-toed boots, and more than a couple of interesting tattoos, but not one of them wore a blue or red T-shirt. Baseball bat aside, these men clearly weren't here to play games.

Brenda's face went white, but she recovered quickly, jumping to her feet with a broad smile on her face. "Hi, Hal," she said, stepping in front of Mitch. "What brings you here?"

The feeling came back to my legs in a sudden rush, so I rose and took a casual step to the left. A quick getaway would be easier without the cooler in my path.

"Hi, Brenda," the man said. "Having a picnic?"

"Just the usual." Brenda's voice was high and bubbly, not at all like her own. She turned to her children. "Boys, why don't you go and kick the soccer ball around a little? Just stay close." Oblivious to the stupidity of adults, the boys were running with that ball within seconds. I could not have been more envious.

"You and Liz should go with the boys," Mitch said, moving her around behind him.

I was ready, but Brenda shook her head. "Now, Mitch, that would just be rude," she said, still smiling as she put herself between the two men again—like a little dog who doesn't know when she's in danger, or doesn't care. "So how's Debby?" she asked. "I haven't seen her in ages. And the kids? Are they with you?"

"Brenda," Mitch said, his voice low and warning as he moved her around behind him more firmly this time. I was tempted to reach out and grab her, haul her back where she belonged, but the determination on that little smiling face kept me in my place.

"Speaking of rude," she said, stepping right back into position, "where are my manners? Hal, you remember my brother Gary, of course, but this is my friend Liz."

I smiled and nodded—wondered if this was the perfect time for that getaway.

"Hal has worked with Mitch for years," Brenda continued, then turned that smile back on him. "How long exactly has it been now, Hal?"

"Five years," Mitch said, stepping around her. "He's worked with me for five years. And like I told him this afternoon, we'll talk at the shop on Monday."

Hal thumped the bat against his palm. "I want to talk now."

Gary held Brenda back and said, "We should take this somewhere else."

A couple of blue shirts stopped by the blanket. "Hey, Mitch, everything okay?" one of them asked.

"Everything's fine. These men were just leaving."

Another blue shirt showed up and another. Then a player from the red team and her boyfriend wandered over. Soon it was eight to four and our little corner of the park had the full attention of all players.

Hal may have looked dumb, but at least he could count. "That's right," he said, lowering the bat. "We were just leaving."

He pointed a finger at Mitch. "I'll see you on Monday morning. Nine o'clock sharp."

The band of men strolled off and both teams went back to the business of having fun. Only Mitch and Gary kept watch until Hal and his buddies disappeared beyond the bathrooms.

"What the hell is going on?" Brenda finally asked.

"We need to take a walk." Mitch turned to Gary. "Will you watch the boys?"

He waved them away. "Sure, go ahead."

"Thanks." Mitch started walking, heading for the path with Brenda hurrying along beside him. "There are brownies in the cooler," she called over her shoulder. "Make sure Liz eats a couple."

"I'm good," I said when Gary opened the cooler. "In fact, I should be going. Places to go, people to see and all of that."

"Plus you're worried that those guys might come back."

I picked up my backpack. "With guns or something worse." I glanced over to where the boys were kicking around the soccer ball, then knelt down beside Gary and lowered my voice. "What kind of trouble is Mitch in anyway? Because if it's something illegal, you need to get Brenda and the kids out of that situation as soon as—"

"It's nothing illegal. Mitch is squeaky clean."

"Really? Then why was that guy threatening him with bodily harm in a public park?"

"Because Mitch owes him money and Hal's a hothead. He doesn't think before he acts."

"So this was all about money, yet you expect me to believe there's nothing dirty going on?" I rose and hoisted my backpack onto my shoulders. "The arrogance of men astounds me."

Gary got to his feet. "I'm telling you the truth. Mitch runs a legitimate business, but he's having financial difficulty right now, just like everyone else."

"Everyone else doesn't have guys with bats after them."

"Everyone else doesn't know Hal Meaney."

Brenda and Mitch were over by the water fountain, standing close together. He was doing most of the talking, but every once in a while she'd nod and reach out. Touch him, lightly, briefly, as though saying, *It's okay, I'm here*. I hoped that wouldn't prove to be a mistake and turned back at Gary. "What happened to Mitch?"

He shook his head and sat down again. "In a nutshell, he took on a big job, the customer won't pay, and now he's left holding the bag."

I remained on my feet. "Won't pay? Why? Did Mitch screw something up?"

"No, and you really ought to stop beating on him like that. Mitch is the only one who isn't being an asshole in this whole thing." Gary opened the cooler, dug around inside. "What I wouldn't give for a beer right now."

"You and me both." Mitch and Brenda were still talking, but now Mitch was pacing back and forth, running a hand over his face, through his hair. To be fair, he didn't look like a bad guy, and Brenda was probably too smart to hang around if he turned into one. So I dropped my bag and sat down again. "Okay, I'm willing to reconsider. Give me the details."

Gary took out the container of brownies and let the lid fall on the cooler. "Mitch is a millwright. Specializes in moving and installing heavy equipment." He plunked two brownies on a plate and set it on my lap,  held up his hands when I balked. "You can take it up with Brenda later, but I know better than to disobey a direct order. Besides, you should try one. She makes the best brownies."

"Fine," I said, taking a bite and discovering he was right. Brenda's brownies were fabulous. Chewy and fudgy with pecans, not walnuts. I popped the last mouthful and went for the second.

"Told you," Gary said, putting two on a plate for himself. "So Mitch coordinated the moving and rebuilding of three shot peening machines as well as the installation of two new dust collectors.

It was the biggest single job he'd ever undertaken, and he came in on time and under budget. But the company refuses to pay the last third, which is well over a hundred thousand dollars."

I had no idea what a shot peening machine was, and the only dust collectors I knew were the Royal Doulton figurines Great-Grandma Lucy brought with her from the old country and that Ruby regularly threatened to leave to me one day. But the details of the equipment didn't matter because I could already see where this was going to end.

"I'm guessing the company that hired him is big, giving Mitch a lot of comfort while he was climbing out on a limb to make the job come together."

"They even showed him a letter of credit from the bank, proving they had the financing for the move."

"And based on that, he probably maxed his line of credit plus every one of his credit cards. Maybe even reached out to family and friends to get this job done."

"We all helped out, yes."

"Then there's something you all need to know. I guarantee that Mitch is never going to see the rest of the money."

Gary stared at me. "What are you talking about? He has a signed contract. The equipment is up and running."

"Doesn't matter." I finished the rest of the brownie and wiped my fingers on a napkin. "They're gambling that he'll go bankrupt before they're forced to pay."

"But how can they do that?"

"Unfortunately, all too easily. If Mitch's company doesn't survive, then the debt is wiped out and the money stays in the other guy's pocket. It's dirty, but it happens more often than you'd think."

Gary put his plate down, his appetite clearly gone. "How do you know all this?"

I smiled. "Because I'm more than a fabulous Highland dancer. I'm also a lawyer. At least I was a lawyer." And it amazed me how quickly the blocks had fallen into place. Like Mark said when I cleared out my desk: *You can take the girl out of the courtroom, but you can't take the—*

"Were you disbarred or something?"

"Nothing that exciting. I just got tired and quit."

"What are you doing now?"

"Pursuing my options."

"At the Duck?"

I started to get up. "I should go."

He laid a hand on my arm. "I'm sorry, it just seems like a waste, that's all. You obviously know your stuff, and Mitch could use someone like that right now."

"Doesn't he have a lawyer?" Gary nodded. "And what's he done for him so far?" I asked.

"Lots of letters. He says the next step is a lawsuit."

"Which will be expensive, with the costs due up front, of course. He's probably explained that it will take at least two years to get to court and by then Mitch's company will be bankrupt anyway so what's the point. And for this he's already charged him an arm and a leg."

"Two legs, I believe."

I shook my head. Goddamn lazy lawyers. No wonder people hated us.

Hated them.

"Well, Gary, I can tell you with every confidence that the lawyer is wrong. There is indeed something else that he can do."

I opened my backpack, hunted around until I found a pen and a scrap of paper. A receipt from the liquor store, what else? I turned it over, printed on the back *petition into bankruptcy*, and handed it to Gary. "The lawyer won't want to do this, so Mitch will have to insist."

"What if he still won't?"

I zipped up my backpack. "Then he needs a better lawyer."

"Gary," Mitch called, and waved a hand when we both turned. "We're up."

"Be right there," Gary said, then turned back to me. "You going to the Duck afterward?"

"There's a good chance of that, yes."

He tucked the note into his pocket and gave me another of those smiles. "See you there then. I'll talk to Mitch about this. You talk to Brenda."

"Will do," I said, watching him jog back to the baseball field and wishing he were anyone's brother but Brenda's.

She sat down next to me. "Stay away from him," she whispered, as though reading my mind.

"I'm just looking." Gary took his spot on the bench next to Mitch. Raised a hand and waved to me. I waved back and tried not to think about brown eyes, or full lips, or a wiry naked body moving over me—

"I mean it," Brenda said, taking her cell phone out of her purse and punching in a number. "He is off limits." She rose and spoke into the phone. "Hi Marty. It's Brenda."

Marty West was the owner of the Duck. He rarely came into the pub, leaving Brenda in charge on a day-to-day basis, but his was the number they called in case of emergency.

"I can't come in tonight," she said. "You'll have to call Stevie." She shook her head. "Don't give me a hard time on this, Marty." She walked away from the blanket and I couldn't hear what was being said anymore. But I could see her spine stiffening and her hand clenching at her side.

"Then screw you, Marty!" she finally yelled. "I quit."

She closed the phone and came back to the blanket, sank down on her knees, and stared at the cooler a moment. Then she started picking up plates, napkins, empty drink boxes. Her movements brisk and efficient, almost masking the shaking of her hands.

I screwed the lid on the pickle jar and crawled with it over to the cooler. "Brenda, I know how hard this must be, and it's really none of my business—"

She snatched the jar out of my hand. "You're right, so drop it."

"It's just that Gary told me what's going on and—"

"And he should have kept his mouth shut."

She kept her head down, her lips pinched tightly together while she wrapped the sandwiches, snapped the lid on the brownies. Proving she was tough and strong—and breathing deeply enough to keep the tears from giving her away.

"Brenda, you need a plan—"

She raised her head and glared at me. "I suppose you have a plan. And I should take advice from a drunk who hides in the trees because she can't talk to her own mother?" She picked up the last Tupperware container, dropped it into the cooler. "You need to leave. I have to see to the boys."

"Mitch is never going to see that money," I said softly.

Her hands stilled, her eyes met mine. "Leave me alone."

"You have to talk to your lawyer."

She got to her feet. Kept her voice low, her tone level. "And you have to drop it."

I rose and picked up my backpack. "Fine. Just promise me—"

She shoved me hard enough to get the attention of the families around us. "Are you fucking deaf? I said drop it."

I felt the eyes of her neighbors taking my measure, assessing her risk. I swung the backpack over my shoulder. Nothing to see here, folks. Move along, move along. "Take care of yourself, Brenda."

She said nothing, just glared at me, lip curled, fists clenched at her sides. All she wanted right now was to smack me a couple of good ones. Pow. That's for Hal. Pow. That's for my husband. Pow, pow, pow. And that's for the asshole lawyer who should have come up with a plan before the fucking drunk.

Instead she snatched up the garbage bag, tied the top, and walked away, leaving me alone, a visitor no longer welcome at her party.

What else had I expected? Brenda wasn't a sorry, sloppy drunk with no one else to talk to. Her family was close, her circle of friends probably still intact, and she didn't need the likes of me for advice.

The beat of Ruby's drum was suddenly all around me, steady and low, like a heartbeat. Walking back toward the trees, doing my best to avoid the stares from the sidelines, I glanced over at the diamond. Gary was up to bat. I couldn't resist pausing a moment, watching the windup, the pitch, and every player on the bench leaping to their feet when he drove that ball right out of the park. "Off limits," I whispered. "Way off."

He started running the bases and I started walking again, heading for my hideout in the trees. I was sober enough to feel a little foolish taking those first few steps off the path, but the drum drew me on and I promised myself I would only stay a couple of minutes. Just long enough to shake off this shit mood and get ready for a night at the all new Brenda-free Duck. Yes indeed, good times were on the way.

By the time I was in position, act II was already in progress: Ruby marching, Mark following, and everyone chanting something about birds again. The only difference was Ruby's hot-pink baseball cap. How about that? Back for less than a minute, and I was already smiling, wondering when she'd forgotten how much she hated those things.

I parted the leaves for a better view but must have made more movement than I intended because suddenly Mary Anne turned and looked straight into my eyes. She raised a hand and pointed. I shook my head. "No, no, please." But Mary Anne was indeed faithful and Ruby was her friend.

"Ruby!" she called. And again, louder. "Ruby!"

Mark looked over. Dropped his sign and started toward me, coming through the taxis and limos while Ruby kept beating that drum and marching. I gripped my pack and backed away from the hiding spot, reaching the path as a car screeched to a stop and Ruby's drum fell silent.

"Mark!" she screamed.

My whole body went hot and then cold. I couldn't feel my legs, but I didn't need them. My feet were taking me around the trees all on their own. I saw people running, Mary Anne fretting, and Ruby leaning over Mark, who lay on the ground in front of a taxi.

"Call 911! Call 911!" someone hollered, and suddenly baseball players and little kids were all around me.

"Don't bother," Mark said. "I'm fine," He put a hand on the grill of the taxi and tried to pull himself up. "Just a little winded is all." He made it to his knees and paused. Looked around. Spotted me. "Liz. Stay there."

Not a chance.

Telling myself he was okay, I turned and pushed my way through the crowd. Sprinted along the path toward the bathrooms. I had a good fifty-foot head start when Ruby hollered. "Liz, please. Just talk to me."

Maybe it was the way she said please or maybe it was just too much trouble to keep running. Either way, I stopped and turned around. Watched my mother walk toward me for the first time in more than two years.

She was flushed and sweating as I must have been, and we both made a discreet ladylike dab at the line of sweat on our upper lips at exactly the same moment. Funny, the habits you pick up from your mother and cannot shake for the life of you. I did not, however, tip my head to the right and fold my arms over my chest once she was standing in front of me. That pose was all Ruby's.

"You look terrible," she said.

"Nice to see you too, Mom."

"Liz, I'm sorry. But I haven't seen you in a while, and you're so pale and thin . . ." She lowered her arms on a sigh. "It was a bit of a shock, that's all."

Couldn't be any worse than the view from this end. She looked good from a distance, but up close her skin was dry and there seemed to be too much of it for her face. The tiny lines around her eyes had deepened into a full-blown web that was starting to reach down as well as out. My mother was getting old—just not old enough for Alzheimer's.

"Were you equally shocked when you saw me outside Fran's the other day?" I asked.

She had the grace to look away. "I only had a glimpse of you. And then you were gone." Her eyes flicked back to mine. "I ordered you a grilled cheese sandwich."

"And apple pie. Yes, I saw."

"But you didn't come in."

"And you didn't come out."

She took a few steps away. Turned and came back. Pacing as she always did when she was trying to think, to pull her story together. I could only imagine what great shape she'd be in soon, now that she had Alzheimer's.

"I wanted you to make the next move," she said. "Prove that you're as interested in getting past this nonsense as I am."

This nonsense? Is that what she was calling it now? Like everything had been a silly misunderstanding. Another tale of the Donaldsons to be trotted out whenever one of us had too much to drink. *Remember the time Mom took out a restraining order against me?*

She smiled. "But what happened at Fran's or anywhere else doesn't matter any more. The important thing is that you're here and we're talking."

I wanted to hit her so badly. Make a real impression on my mother for once. But I didn't. I merely moved in closer and closer until she either had to back up or rub noses with me. It was almost funny the way the very idea had her moving away, putting space between us again.

"Liz, you have to work with me. For Grace's sake. You've spoken to Mark. You know the challenges I'm facing."

"The Alzheimer's, yes. Bad bit of karma there."

"Karma has nothing to do with it."

"They say suicide only makes things worse. You may come back as a rock on Uranus." I didn't know much about karma or reincarnation. I just knew it would piss Ruby off to hear it.

She glanced out at the street, the crowd still gathered for Mark. "I don't have time to get into this with you. I need to get back to Mark and you need to come to the house. I have to make plans. Ensure that Grace is taken care of and the house is secured for the next generation."

I leaned in close, lowered my voice to a whisper. "But what if there is no next generation, Mom? What if you, me, and Grace are the end of the line?"

She looked back at me. "You'd do that, wouldn't you? Deny yourself the joy of a child just to spite me."

She was trying her best to be patient, to keep the fight from starting. But the button was right there, and someone needed to push it. "You don't have to worry too much, Mom. Grace is young. She might have another baby one day."

"I can't imagine she'd ever want to go through that again."

I smiled and pushed that button a little harder. "You never know. There may be another man waiting right around the corner."

"Let's hope not. We've already seen where that leads, haven't we?" She wrapped her arms around herself again, stared across the field at the flashing lights of an approaching ambulance. "I always knew there'd be trouble the moment men came sniffing around. What that boy did to her was tantamount to rape."

I almost laughed. Pretty Bobby Daniels had been many things—vain, cowardly, dumb as dirt, to name a few—but sexually abusive? Hardly. Grace met him at the coffee shop on the main floor of my building shortly after she moved in with me. He was the new barista, she was new to espresso. He taught her all about lattes and the importance of milk texturing—and he always poured a teddy bear face on top of her coffee.

After a few weeks, Grace started borrowing my makeup and

humming while she was getting dressed, and I knew Bobby was teaching her about more than lattes. But she was twenty-five for chrissakes. And every movement, every smile told me she was having fun. So we had "the talk" because I was sure Ruby had never told her anything about birth control, and I let her go, I let her grow up.

Bobby told her from the beginning that he was only passing through, that he was traveling cross-country to find himself. I expected Grace would cry when he left, even miss him for a while, but I wasn't ready when she bought herself a backpack and said she was going to join him on the hunt. "You need to find yourself first," I told her. But she only laughed and said she already knew where she was, and she wanted to be somewhere else. What could I do? Tell her I'd lied about the importance of travel and freedom? Become my mother and hold her back? Of course not. So I gave her my telephone card and made her promise to call me—and Ruby—every Sunday to let us know she was okay.

I made sure I was in a public place when I told Ruby, but that still didn't stop her from shoving my face against a bus shelter. That was when we officially stopped talking.

She tried everything to get Grace back. Private investigator, social services, even told police she'd been kidnapped, but nothing worked. Grace was an adult in everyone's eyes but hers, and there was nothing she could do but wait for those weekly calls.

Being Grace, she kept her word. No matter where they were—Winnipeg, Calgary, Galiano Island—my phone rang precisely at noon every Sunday. She always sounded happy. Said Bobby was taking good care of her. She was gone for seven months. Then one day, the phone rang on a Saturday. A local call. Grace trying not to cry. "I'm downstairs," was all she said. "And I can't find my key."

"Bobby didn't rape Grace," I said evenly. "She wanted him. She loved him."

Ruby turned her head slowly, like an owl. Looked at me like I was the slow child, the one who didn't grasp everything the first

time around. "She loved the idea of him," she said. "Like any little girl loves the idea of Prince Charming and happily ever after.
But there was no happily ever after for Grace and her baby, was
there?"

"His name was William, Mom."

She held up her hands and walked away. "I am not getting into
this with you again. Everyone knew I would have gladly looked
after both Grace *and* that little boy—"

I was right behind her. "You can't even say his name can you."

She rounded on me. "I would have gladly looked after *William*.
Loved him and raised him as my own. All you had to do was let
her come home."

"She didn't want you to raise him. All she wanted you to do
was help her learn how to be a mother herself."

"Grace was never equipped to be a mother. It still shocks me
that social services allowed her to take that infant home."

"If you'd been there, you'd know that they were happy to see
her take her son home. She was a fabulous mother, completely
devoted—"

"And yet she killed him."

The breath caught in my throat. "You can't honestly believe
that."

"It doesn't matter what I believe." Her shoulders slumped and
she turned away. "He died in her care. That's all that matters."

"And when you found out, you weren't sad for an instant, were
you? Your own grandson and you didn't feel a goddamn thing."

She shook her head, hand fluttering at her throat. "You have
no idea what I felt."

"Devastated, I'm sure." I took a step toward her, crowding her,
stalking her. "But now she's back on the Island. That should make
you happy."

She backed up a step. "I'm happy she's safe. And you don't
know it, but she's flourished since she's been home. She's working
again, she bikes every day. She even has a hobby."

I laughed and closed the space. "You are so oblivious."

She shoved me backward, reclaiming her ground. "What is that supposed to mean?"

"Don't worry about it. Just know that I applaud your decision to take yourself out of the picture now that you have Alzheimer's. And rest assured that once you're gone, I will do everything in my power to get Grace on a ferry and off that island for good. Until then, you keep telling yourself she's fine."

I turned and started walking away, heading east to the Duck and a fresh start to happy hour.

Ruby followed me for a few steps. "Where are you going? Liz, come back here." She stopped and made her final stand. "Elizabeth Lucille Donaldson, how dare you walk away when your family needs you."

I laughed and kept going. "I learned from the best, Mom. The very best."

# GRACE

Jocelyn's friends didn't arrive on the next ferry or the one after. In fact, they didn't come at all because some boy named Josh sent a message inviting everyone to his house. I was still spinning the wheel on that iPod, trying to get it to come on without having to ask her how, when her phone made that funny half ring that meant she had a message, not a call.

She was so mad when that message came in, she said, "Shit! Shit! Shit!" Then she got on the phone with someone named Maddison and it sounded like Josh's parents were going out and that meant a party. Not a birthday party or a dinner party, but the kind of party my mom used to warn me about. The kind with beer and boys and God knew what else, and Jocelyn wanted to be there so bad I was afraid she'd say to heck with what her dad wanted and get on that ferry anyway.

But just like she didn't climb out the window earlier, she didn't get on the ferry then either. She just yelled and said the f-word a lot and told this Maddison that she hated her dad, but I didn't think that was true. I've seen what hate looks like, and that wasn't it.

"We can still go to the Carousel," I said when she hung up.

"With you?" She curled her lip. "Nice try," she said, and started walking back to her house.

"You forgot your bike," I called, but she gave me the finger and kept going. So I put the iPod in my pocket, picked up both bikes and followed. It wasn't easy walking two bikes at once, but if I went nice and slow and made sure they didn't get too far apart, I could manage. The hard part was getting them up over the Algonquin bridge and then keeping them from running away on the other side. That was a killer.

When I reached her gate, I pushed the bikes through one by one, and left them next to the front porch stairs. Jocelyn was already inside, sitting on the couch, eating bread and peanut butter. I took the lasagne out of the freezer anyway and turned on the oven. "It's good you're having something now," I said. "Because this will take a while."

"Like I give a shit." She pointed the remote at the television. I couldn't see the screen, but I could hear the theme from *CSI: Miami*, which changed to the song from *The Simpsons*. She kept clicking the remote while she punched numbers into her cell phone again. A commercial for cheese with chanting monks was quickly interrupted by a trailer for a new Angelina Jolie movie. "It's me," she said to whoever answered.

I would have liked to watch the movie trailer, but Jocelyn kept flipping channels while she talked. *CSI. Law & Order. Two and a Half Men.* The cheese monks again. She was back at *The Simpsons* when my mom banged open the front door and hollered, "Mark's hurt. I need you now!"

That brought Jocelyn to her feet, the phone and remote still on the couch while we both raced to the door. "What happened?" she demanded.

"Liz happened," my mom said as Mark limped through the door.

Jocelyn looked at me. "Who's Liz?"

"My sister."

"She was at the protest," my mom said.

"Why?" I asked.

My mom threw up her hands. "Who knows why she does anything? But when Mark spotted her, she ran off like some sort of criminal. He went after her, a taxi came out of nowhere, and the next thing I know, he's on the ground. Did Liz care? Of course not. That girl is so—"

"Why aren't you in a hospital?" Jocelyn cut in.

"Because even the paramedics agreed that I'm fine." He looked over at my mom. "And Liz didn't run like a criminal. She ran because she was scared."

"Of what?" my mom asked.

"You, mostly." He tried to smile at Jocelyn. "Hi, honey. Have you had dinner?"

"I don't care about dinner. Where exactly did the taxi hit you?"

Before he could answer, Mary Anne and the rest of the protesters came through the door, everyone talking at the same time about Liz and her friends and how lucky Mark had been with that taxi. On the television, Homer Simpson chased a dog with a fluffy tail.

When no one was looking, Jocelyn shoved me against the wall. "Is your whole family whacked?"

I shoved her back. "We're not whacked. My sister just doesn't get along with my mom."

"Your sister doesn't get along with anyone," my mom said. "And if I ever hear of you speaking to her, if she ever tries to contact you—"

"Ruby, relax," Mary Anne said, putting an arm around her shoulder, trying to lead her away from me, to keep my secret safe. "Why don't you sit down? In fact, why doesn't everybody sit down. Grace and I will make a pot of tea."

"What we need is ice." My mom brushed Mary Anne's arm aside and pointed a finger at me. "I meant it, Grace. If Liz ever contacts you, I want you to tell me right away."

"Ruby, let it go," Mark said. "And I don't need ice."

But my mom already had the fridge open and ice cube trays in her hands and we both knew there was no point arguing. While Jocelyn sat with her dad and the protesters found spots on the floor, I put on the kettle and tried to make sense of what was going on, tried to put the pieces together, but nothing fit right. I needed to talk to Liz, find out what was going on, why she'd been at the protest.

I knew she had a cell phone, but I never called because lately my mom had started checking the history on our phone all the time. Writing down what came in, what went out. "I'm on the phone so much every day," she'd say. "I can't be expected to remember everything."

I didn't really get what she was talking about, but I understood that there could be no more secret calls made from our house. But if I could sneak out for a minute, I could use Mary Anne's phone. All I needed was for my mom to stop watching me.

She held the ice pack out to Mark. "Put that on your knee. Jocelyn, don't let him take it off for ten minutes."

Mark closed his eyes. "Does anyone have an aspirin?"

"I have Advil," one of the Bobs said and brought him the bottle with a glass of water.

Jocelyn crouched down on the floor in front of him. "Will you finally admit that this whole Island thing was a horrible mistake so we can go home?"

He reached out to touch her hair. "Honey, please," was all he said, but everyone could tell what was coming next, including Jocelyn.

"I don't believe this." She ran up the stairs to her room and slammed the door. This time, she took her cell phone.

"She'll be fine," Mark said.

"But what about you?" my mom asked.

On the other side of the room, Homer Simpson cheered, Lisa blew her saxophone, and my mom looked confused. "What the hell is that?"

"*The Simpsons*," Mary Anne said. "It's that episode where—"

My mom put her hands to her ears and squeezed her eyes shut. "I don't care what it is. Someone turn off the noise!"

Mary Anne grabbed the controller and pressed the button. The room fell suddenly, scarily quiet. "Ruby," she asked, "are you okay?"

My mom lowered her hands and opened her eyes. "Of course I'm okay. It's just been a long day." She looked around. "Everybody needs to leave. Mark has to get some rest."

She didn't say good-bye to any of them, not even Mary Anne. Just turned to me and said, "You need to go home and cancel all of tomorrow's appointments. Tell everyone we'll be closed for the day." Both Mark and I started to argue, to tell her that wasn't necessary, but she held up a hand. "There are no buts. Mark, you're probably still in shock, so I'm staying here tonight to keep an eye on you. I won't argue with you about this, but it means I won't be in any shape to work tomorrow and Grace needs to make those calls. It's summer so there aren't many anyway."

That wasn't the point. My mother always said, *Cancel an appointment, lose a client. That's the only thing you can count on in this business, Grace.*

Our client list was already shrinking. She never said anything, but I could tell all the same and we couldn't afford to lose any more. "I can do the work," I said.

She rose and went into the kitchen. "Don't be ridiculous. Just do as I say. I'm going to make tea."

I looked over at Mark. "I can do it," I whispered to him.

"I know you can."

"What's in this oven?" my mother called.

"Lasagne," I said. "It needs another thirty minutes."

"Then what good is it." She opened the fridge. "Is that all you brought?" She closed the fridge and said, "I'll get some groceries in for you tomorrow."

"Your mom's a little tense right now," Mark whispered to me. "It's probably easier to make the calls."

He was right, as always. I sat down on the arm of the couch beside him and lowered my voice. "Can you do me a favor? Can you lend me your cell phone? I want to call Liz."

He pulled the phone from his pocket and handed it to me. That was what I had always loved about Mark. I didn't have to explain myself, or answer a million questions. He just trusted me.

"Make sure you tell her I'm not hurt and I'm not mad. But I am worried about her, and I'd like her to call."

I nodded and slipped the phone into my pocket.

"One more thing." He paused and checked on my mom's whereabouts. "I want you to keep the phone for yourself."

I couldn't help smiling. "Are you sure?"

"Positive. I use my BlackBerry for everything. This number was strictly for Jocelyn, in case of an emergency. But she's older now and refuses to call it anymore, so what's the point carrying around an extra phone? Plus, it's time you had one of your own."

"Thank you!" I hugged him and kissed him on the cheek.

"Just remember to tell Liz to call me."

"I will." I rose and headed for the door. "I'll go home and start making those calls," I said to my mom on my way by.

"Come back as soon as you're done. I want to keep an eye on Mark tonight, and I'm sure he won't mind if you sleep on the couch."

"Plenty of room," he said.

"I don't really have to," I said. "I'll be okay alone."

My mother's hands came down hard on the counter. "Grace, will you please stop arguing every little thing. Just come back here when you're done."

I lowered my head and walked out the door, got on my bike, and rode home. When I was inside, I went straight to my room for my bird book and flipped it open to the page where I kept Liz's number. Then I opened the cell phone the way I'd watched other people do it and I pressed the numbers but the line just rang and rang and finally her voice mail came on, *What the hell do you want now?* followed by a beep.

"Liz? It's me, your sister, Grace. I have to talk to you. I have Mark's phone. I don't know the number. Call me as soon as you can."

I closed the phone and slipped it back into my pocket and then I checked my e-mail. An offer for a credit card and a Nigerian prince wanting to send me money. Nothing interesting. I signed into Hotmail and checked my secret e-mail account, the one Liz opened for me. More junk, but nothing from Liz. I logged out and deleted the history in the browser, then went back into the kitchen. The sun was starting to set and the house was quiet with just me in it. No radio, no TV. Just the crickets outside the window, making their own kind of music.

I thought about that. About crickets making music and hoping to find a mate in the dark. Then I thought about the mockingbird and wondered if Benny was right—if he really would be out there all night, singing in the dark until a lady mockingbird came to find him. I wanted to know more than anything, but I didn't dare go to the lighthouse because right now I had calls to make.

The appointment book was on the counter by the phone. I flipped it open to Saturday and stared at the names. Six calls were all I had to make. Four for my mom and two for me. A couple of my mom's clients would be okay with changing the date, but Marla Cohen was mine and she wasn't the kind to let her roots go an extra week. *Cancel an appointment, lose a client.* I didn't want to lose Marla. She was funny and she always gave me a tip even though my mom told everyone not to. "Just come back, that's tip enough for us," she liked to say. Maybe it was for her, but I never said no to Marla's money.

I didn't want to make the call, but I picked up the phone anyway and pushed Marla's buttons. Let it ring once, twice. On the third one I hung up and stared at the phone. It wasn't like I needed help to do Marla's hair. My mom always said the final result was fine and Marla never complained. It was just dumb to cancel that appointment.

I moved on to the next name on the list, Audrey DeSanto, my mom's ten o'clock. Cut and blow-dry, exactly the same way every time. I punched in the number and hung up again after two rings. This whole thing was dumb. Six appointments just weren't that many. I could do this.

I closed the book. I wouldn't tell my mom, I'd just come home early in the morning and show her she was wrong. I could so do the work.

I pushed the book away, drummed my fingers on the counter. If I went back to Mark's now she'd ask me about the calls, and I needed time to think about what I was going to say. So I could sit here and think, or I could go look for the mockingbird and think. I drummed my fingers again. It wouldn't take long to get to the lighthouse and back. The bird was either singing or he wasn't, and if he wasn't I'd just come straight back and go to Mark's. But if he was . . .

I walked over to the fridge, took out the brick of cheese, made myself a sandwich, and ate it while I tried to figure out what to do. I looked up at the clock above the table. It was almost nine. By the time I got to the lighthouse, looked for the bird, and came back it would be after ten. It wouldn't take that long to make six phone calls. So what would I tell my mother when she asked what I'd been doing all that time?

Maybe that I went for a walk on the beach. It was a nice night, it would make sense. Only she didn't like me to go walking in the dark on the beach. *Who knows who's out there, Grace? You need to be careful. Stay away from strangers.*

Stay away from men is what she meant. Strange men, park men, men I'd known since I was little. Stay away from them all, is what she meant. *No good can come of it, Grace. You know that as well as I do.*

I suppose I did, but I never went looking for men anymore anyway. I only went looking for planes and birds, and what was wrong with trying to find a bird at night? Nothing, that's what. And if I was lucky, Liz would call before I got back and she could tell me what to say to my mom. But if I wasn't lucky? I'd think about that on the way home.

I grabbed my bird book and my binoculars and the flashlight my mom kept plugged into the wall beside the kitchen table, and I went back outside. I rolled my bike to the gate and lifted the latch as quietly as I could. We might not be friends with all the neighbors, but that wouldn't stop a few of them from reporting every move I made anyway.

Once I was clear of the narrow streets, I pedaled full out, going as fast as I could past the ferry dock and the playing field and the sailboats returning for the night. When I rolled by Algonquin bridge my heart was beating so loudly I was sure my mom would hear it all the way over at Mark's house. But I kept my head down and my feet moving and by the time I reached the dock at Centre Island, my heart was doing just fine, and I wasn't thinking about my mom or Marla or anything but finding that mockingbird.

The rides and the parks on Centre were closed for the night, so the road past the dock was almost deserted. Just a few stragglers sitting by the fountains and a couple of artists carrying easels and paint boxes back to the retreat at Gibraltar Point. I was the only one going farther, and even before I reached the lighthouse I could already hear that bird singing and singing.

It was a little weird, hearing a bird at night. Like I was hearing something private, something special, and I couldn't stop smiling as I rolled my bike across the grass to the big front door of the lighthouse.

I grabbed the flashlight, but I didn't turn it on yet because I didn't want to attract attention, and besides, I knew this place pretty well. Liz and I used to come here for midnight picnics in the summer. Once our mom and Mark were asleep, Liz would wake me up and we'd climb out her window and walk our bikes to the end of the street so no one would hear us.

Then we'd ride as fast as we could to the lighthouse, taking our bikes around the back and through the trees to the clearing by the lagoon. Then Liz would prop the flashlight against a rock so the light went up into the air. And we'd sit on our sweaters and eat squashed cheese sandwiches, and she'd put the flashlight under her chin and tell stories about zombies in motorboats or vampires who lived in the woods. Sometimes, if it was raining and we couldn't go to the lighthouse, we'd eat our sandwiches in her room and she'd tell the same kind of stories, but they were always scarier here because everyone knew that the lighthouse was haunted.

The plaque outside says that in 1815 John Rademuller, the lighthouse keeper, disappeared. But the truth is that Mr. Rademuller was also a bootlegger and he was murdered by three drunken sailors who tossed him off the top of the lighthouse when he wouldn't give them any more rum. When they realized he was dead, they cut his body into pieces and buried them all over the Island so they wouldn't get caught. Ever since, people say they can hear thumping and moaning from inside the lighthouse, and other people have seen him walking around, looking for his bits.

Liz always said she didn't believe in ghosts, but I think she was disappointed that we never heard a thing in all the times we came here—something I was truly grateful for. And as I walked around behind the lighthouse with my flashlight, I was grateful all over again that the only things I heard were a million crickets and one lonely mockingbird.

His singing didn't stop even when I flicked on the light. Then again, it's not a big beam. Not like those million-candle ones you see in the Canadian Tire flyers. "More like a birthday candle," Liz said one time when we were here, and the two of us were searching for the underwear she lost by accident the night before.

We could have used a million candles that night for sure, but tonight the light was just enough to check the branches without scaring the bird away. After Benny told me earlier it was a mockingbird making all the noise, I checked my book as soon as I got home, and now I knew I was looking for a bird about the size of a robin with smoky grey feathers. They weren't beautiful like indigo buntings or cardinals, but none of those other birds sang at night. And they couldn't imitate things the way the mockingbird did either!

I'd never head a bird that sounded like a dog before, or a cat, or another kind of bird altogether, and standing there in the dark, I thought it was the neatest thing ever. But Benny said it could backfire sometimes because a lady mockingbird picked her mate based on how well he sang. And if his singing sounded like a chain saw or a truck backing up, he was probably going to wait a long time to be picked.

But that wasn't a problem for my mockingbird. He was singing beautifully, just like the recording on the website, with a little barking and meowing every now and then, so any ladies going by would know how talented he was. That didn't make him easy for me to find, of course. Every time I saw a movement in the branches, by the time I focused my light on the spot, he was gone, teasing me from another branch somewhere in that same tree. I knew I couldn't stay long, my mom would be looking for me soon, so I had no choice. I clamped my teeth together and I pished in the woods for the second time that day.

This time it worked. That bird came right out, in fact he flew down to see what all the bother was, and he sat on a branch not six feet away from me. We stayed like that for almost a full minute, just looking at each other, until he flew away and started up all over again.

I couldn't believe it! I'd found the night singer! I punched a fist in the air and I whooped and I spun in a circle so the light made crazy patterns on the trees.

"Oh my Gawd, you are such a geek."

I froze and stuck the flashlight out in front of me. Jocelyn lifted a hand in front of her face. "Put that down," she said, and I said, "What are you doing here?" and she said, "Watching you be a loser."

She walked toward me. "Does your mom know you're out here?" I didn't answer and she laughed. "I didn't think so." She walked in a little circle around me. "This is going to cost you."

"I don't have any money."

She stopped in front of me and poked a finger in my chest. "You still have the cash my father gave you. We can start with that and see where we go from there. All the way to my iPod, I'll wager." She looked up at the trees. "Doesn't that bird ever stop?"

"He's looking for a mate. He's singing so a lady mockingbird can find him."

"A lady mockingbird? What's wrong with you anyway? You're like a little kid in an adult's body."

"Nothing's wrong with me. And we're lucky we heard him because if she comes tonight, he won't sing in the dark anymore. They'll start working on a nest and he won't have time." I looked up into the tree. "I kind of hope this is the night. I like the idea of a lady mockingbird hearing his love song and setting out to find him. Flying all by herself in the dark, following only the sound of his voice."

"Are you always this weird?"

I put the flashlight under my chin. "Sometimes I'm worse," I said in my best Dracula voice. Then I walked around the base of the tree, watching the branches, hoping to spot him again. "Of course, she'd have to come from the city because Benny was pretty sure this is the only mockingbird on the Island this year." I lowered the light and looked over at Jocelyn. "But what if his song doesn't travel that far? What if none of the lady mockingbirds in the city can hear him singing? What if no one ever comes for him?"

"You're ridiculous. Unless he's as weird as you, he'll figure out there's no action here and take his song somewhere else." She smiled and strolled toward me. "Now, about that money."

The mockingbird kept on singing and I felt kind of sorry for him because sometimes it takes me a while to figure things out too. But maybe it would be a lucky night for both of us, because I already knew what I had to do! I shone the light in Jocelyn's face. "We can talk about the money later. But what I'd like to know is how come *you're* here. And if your dad knows where *you* are?"

"He knows I'm with you. I couldn't help where you took me. I'm just the little twelve-year-old who was led into the darkness by the crazy woman." She smiled again. "So where's the money?"

"Mark sent you to follow me?"

She shrugged. "Not so much sent. Your mother was bugging the crap out of me, ordering me around and writing everything down in a notebook. Has your family always been nuts or is it something you caught by living here?"

"We're not nuts and my mother writes everything down because she's had a lot on her mind lately and she doesn't want to forget anything."

"If you ask me, she's losing her mind."

It was my turn to poke a finger in *her* chest. "Lay off my mom, okay? She had cancer, but she didn't tell me because she didn't want me to worry. She's okay now, but it took a lot out of her and that's why she makes notes." I poked her once more, just because. Then I turned around and shone my light up into the tree again. "You still haven't told me how you found me here."

She came up beside me, her eyes following the light as it moved slowly across the branches. "I couldn't stand your mother another minute, so my dad said I should go and keep you company. Then he said it might be best if we both stayed the night at your house instead of coming back to mine."

I stared at her. "And my mom agreed?"

"She didn't say no. So I was on my way to tell you what was

going on, and I saw you riding past the bridge. That meant I could either go to your house alone, which had a certain appeal, or I could follow and find out what you were up to. If I'd known you were looking for a bird, I would have stayed back and checked out your room instead. I bet there's all kinds of secrets in there." She pointed at a branch to my right. "Is that it?"

I moved the flashlight over the area, but it was just a clump of leaves.

"Stupid bird," she said, and moved a little to the left, still checking the branches. "How long are you going to keep looking?"

"My mom is probably calling the house already. We should go." I aimed my light at the path and was heading back to the front of the lighthouse when another bird began to sing. I stopped and told Jocelyn to be quiet. That other bird sang again, and this time my mockingbird answered. I grabbed Jocelyn's arm. "She's here! The lady mockingbird is here!"

Sure enough, she started to sing again on the other side of the lighthouse. The male was already on his way, flying past us to meet the lady who had come for him. Jocelyn and I were running to catch up when a cat went by really fast, like something up ahead was about to become dinner.

"Oh no you don't," Jocelyn said, and ran faster, but we were too late. By the time we rounded the lighthouse, that cat already had a bird in its mouth. "Wings to go," Liz would have said, and laughed.

"Drop it!" Jocelyn yelled, clapping her hands as she ran toward the cat. "I said drop it!"

Another bird dive-bombed the cat, Jocelyn kept clapping her hands, and pretty soon the poor thing gave up. Just dropped that bird and ran. But she didn't go far. I could see her sitting in the bushes, waiting.

"That is so gross," Jocelyn said, creeping slowly toward the fluttering bird in the grass.

It wasn't gross, it was nature. There were lots of feral cats on the Island and they had to eat too. But that didn't stop my stomach from flipping over as we crept a few steps closer.

"Please don't let it be a mockingbird," I whispered. "Please don't let it be a mockingbird." But I knew even before I shone the light on those soft grey feathers that it was going to be one of them.

I knelt down in the grass while the other mockingbird flew from branch to branch and called to the one on the ground. "She's still moving," I said. "Not a lot, but at least a little."

Jocelyn crouched beside me. "How do you know that's the lady . . ." She started again. "How do you know that's the female?"

The male started barking, like he'd heard the question and wanted us to know the answer. "It's her all right," I said. "And she came all this way just to find him."

The poor lady mockingbird fluttered again, trying to fly. Above my head, the male started singing his song again, loud and clear, so she'd know he was still there. I couldn't just leave her there, so I said, "Stay here and watch for the cat," and I ran behind the lighthouse.

"Don't tell me, let me guess. You're pishing in the woods again."

"That would be silly. But I do need something to wrap the bird in, so I'm using these." I came back around and held up my underwear. Good thing I never started wearing those thongs that Liz gave me. I couldn't have wrapped a sparrow in one of those.

Jocelyn closed her eyes. "That is truly disgusting."

"No, it's necessary."

I laid the underwear on the grass and smoothed it out. As gently as I could, I rolled the bird into my hands and set her on the soft cloth while the male kept singing and singing.

"You're taking her home?" Jocelyn asked.

"If I don't, the cat will come back and finish the job for sure."

I folded the edges of my panties up and over the brave lady

mockingbird, keeping her still and warm. Then I took off my T-shirt, folded it into the basket on the front of my bike, and gently laid the bird in the center. When she was settled, I threw my leg over the bike and looked back at Jocelyn.

"You coming?" I asked.

She nodded and the mockingbird called from the tree beside her.

And I knew they were both right behind me as we raced back to the house.

# RUBY

The moment I opened my eyes, I knew this was not going to be a good day. Outside the bedroom window, the sun was shining, the birds were singing, and the familiar drone of the ferry horn assured me I was still on the Island. I just had no idea *where* on the Island.

A bedroom, yes, since I was in a bed, but a quick look around begged the question, whose bed? Naturally, my heart leapt into action, beating harder and faster, ready to take me from concerned to panicked in ten seconds flat.

"Stop it," I muttered, and sat up straighter. Drew in a long, calming breath and took another, slower, look around. White walls and pine furniture. Ruffled curtains and a dresser lined with photographs of people I didn't know and places I had never been. No sign on the ceiling, no notes to myself anywhere. My shoulders sagged. Where the hell was I? And who was that lying beside me?

That's when Big Al stepped into the game, encouraging me and my silly heart to leap up and run, run! Get out of there as fast as I could, screaming all the way for his added enjoyment. Instead, I lay back down and told myself to shut up and stay put. That bugger might be in the driver's seat, but as long as I could still reach the brake I would not make things easy for him. Right now that meant controlling the panic, giving my heart a chance to slow and my stupid Swiss-cheese brain a moment to clear.

As always, I started by focusing on my breath. *In*, two, three, four. *Out*, two, three, four. *In*, two three four. *Out*, two, three . . . Oh, forget that. I had to know whose head was on the other pillow.

My bed mate's back was to me, forming a white mountain under the sheet. With shoulders like that, it could have been a female wrestler, but I was pretty sure it was a man. I lifted myself up and peeked over those shoulders. Moved the pillow enough to reveal the back of his head. Then I lay back down and stared at the ceiling. I was in bed with Mark? How could that be?

I ran my hands over my legs, my chest. I wasn't naked. In fact, I was still wearing jeans and a T-shirt. I must have crashed here with him, but why? And where was here? This couldn't be his house. He didn't live on the Island. He lived in the city somewhere. So whose house was this?

I sat up and took a closer look around for clues. Portable phone and digital alarm on the nightstand. A man's shirt on the closet doorknob. Large jeans on the floor in front of it. I peeked under the sheet. He was still wearing boxers. Definitely a night without fun for anyone, which struck me as sad.

I drew in another, deeper breath and continued my survey of the room. Huge running shoes by the dresser, a suitcase on the floor beside them . . . That was when a hole opened up in the fog and I knew that this *was* his house. For the summer at least. I remembered him telling me that yesterday. He came to my door. Announced that he was renting a house on the Island and he was going to change my mind about taking care of Big Al.

Hah! One point for Ruby.

*Now we know why he's here*, Big Al whispered in my ear. *But do you know why* you're *here?*

I waited, hoping the fog would clear a little more, but sadly the answer was still clouded and out of reach. One point for the bad guy. Damn.

I could have reached over and poked Mark, asked him straight out what was going on, but I wasn't ready to do that yet. Yes, he knew about Big Al and the "situation," but I wasn't ready to let him or anyone else start remembering my life for me. I wasn't there yet. And if things went according to plan, I never would be.

I continued my study of the room, looking for clues, anything that might lift the fog a little more. I saw my shoes under the window, my sweater on the back of a wooden chair, and a small canvas carryall tucked underneath. Bright yellow, no zipper, just white handles and a line of black ants snaking up from the bottom, zigzagging across the front and then disappearing over the edge, into the bag.

I hadn't seen that bag in a very long time, couldn't even have said with any confidence where I'd stored it. But I would have recognized it anywhere.

I eased out of bed and walked toward the chair. Sank down on the floor and drew the bag into my lap. Ran my fingers over the canvas, the handles, the long line of ants, and remembered everything.

Liz made this bag for me when she was ten. For my birthday. I'd been using my mother's paisley carryall for years—a perfectly serviceable bag with a skate lace filling in for the drawstring that had snapped long ago. I never thought much about the bag one way or another. Just tossed it over my shoulder and went. I didn't think anyone even noticed until the day Liz declared it old and disgusting and announced that it was high time I had one of my own.

She was wriggling like a puppy when she presented me with the new one. We immediately dubbed it "the ant bag" and took it everywhere with us after that. Grocery shopping, protest marches, picnics, day trips. There was nowhere that bag didn't go, including the many sleepovers that Liz attended once she started making friends in the city. Back then, she'd liked having a bit of me around and wasn't afraid to admit it.

If I hung around long enough, Big Al would make sure I forgot everything about that bag. But on the bright side, I'd also forget the day she no longer wanted anything to do with me or that bag, so he had his good points too, I suppose.

Following the row of ants with my finger again, I traveled with them to the top of the bag and finally took a look inside. My hairbrush, my wallet, a pair of underwear, a knot of socks, and a plastic toiletries bag—black with cherries on it. One of those gifts with purchase for some makeup I bought last year.

Feeling myself relax a little more with each new discovery, each small recognizable item, I set the clothes and socks on the floor and reached in again, hauling out a pink nightgown followed by the navy blue U of T sweatshirt I'd stolen from Mark way back when we were together. I laid the nightgown on the chair and pulled on the sweatshirt, wondering who had packed this bag anyway.

"Good morning," Mark said softly.

I turned and smiled at him over my shoulder, "Good morning to you," I said, but wasn't ready when he groaned and struggled to get himself into a sitting position on the side of the bed. Something was wrong, but since I had no idea what that was or even why I was there, the day still officially belonged to Big Al.

Over the past year, I'd become quite adept at ducking and weaving, finding ways to keep my inadequacies to myself for as long as possible. In the same way that a clever child who can't read finds ways to fool everyone for a while, even herself.

I smiled again and said, "How are you feeling?" and hoped Mark would fill in the blanks without knowing it.

"Better," he said, gingerly touching his left knee. "Still a little tender, but I'll live." He grimaced and propped the pillows behind his back. "How are you doing?"

Gripping the bag tighter, like a charm or an amulet, I said, "Good," and watched him closely. Hoping his actions might trigger an image, a memory, something to hold on to. Something I could point to and say with certainty, *That's right, that's what happened, that's why I'm here*. But all I had were vague and shifting images, momentary flashes that wouldn't bind together to form any kind of meaningful whole. Nothing that would bring back the warm glow of confidence the way the ant bag had.

"You're not tired are you?" he asked.

"Why would I be tired?"

"Because you hardly slept. You kept waking up with nightmares."

I stared at him. Nightmares and no sleep? It all made perfect sense now. No wonder I was having a bad morning.

*Meds. Exercise. Sleep.* My neurologist's mantra. *The illness is progressing faster than we'd hoped for, Ruby,* she'd said the last time I was in her office.

Dr. Mistry. Pretty little thing. Impossibly young. But she seemed to know what she was doing and for the most part I liked her.

"You hungry?" Mark asked, picking up the phone on the nightstand. "I'm starving."

*Hopefully this new medication will slow things down*, Dr. Mistry had said.

That was the dream, wasn't it. Pop the pills and bam! Clarity restored. Big Al sidelined. Somewhat. For a while anyway. We both knew my future was predictable. We both knew the truth.

"I'll phone over and see how Jocelyn and Grace are doing," Mark said.

Grace. Wasn't she here somewhere?

"I'm sure they had a great time at your place last night," he said. "Jocelyn would have loved being anywhere I wasn't."

My place. They were at my place alone? I'd allowed that?

"I'm sure they're fine," he went on. "I just want to say good morning. See if Jocelyn is speaking to me yet. She wasn't when they dropped off that bag for you."

The ant bag. If the girls had dropped it off, that meant that Grace had dug it up from God knew where and packed it. But why bother? Why not just toss everything into the bag I usually used?

He pressed buttons on the phone, put the receiver to his ear. "Once we talk to them, we can pick up some breakfast at the café in the clubhouse. They're open this early, aren't they?"

*Try to avoid stress and noise as much as possible*, Dr. Mistry had said. *You'll find a calm environment helps.*

I remember I'd laughed. How do you manage a calm environment in a beauty parlor?

*You close it*, she said softly, and patted me on the back.

"Hey, Jocelyn, how's it going . . ."

*You simply cannot go on much longer on your own*, La Mistry had said, taking that firm, parental tone that always made me want to smack her. *You're going to need a caregiver sooner rather than later. Someone to help out at home, prepare meals, make sure you take your medications at the right times.*

Someone to remember my life for me.

*Have you given any thought to who that might be?*

Why would I when I wasn't going to be around long enough for it to matter? I didn't tell her that, of course. She'd have had me locked up and thrown away the key. It was her job to save lives, after all. Even those that weren't worth living.

"How's Grace . . ."

*I can put you in touch with a support group. People who—*

*Not interested*, I'd said, adding, *Not yet anyway*, when she frowned at the interruption. She was the doctor after all, and I was the one with half a brain.

*About the caregiver*, she'd said.

*I'm looking into solutions*, is what I told her. She didn't know I meant poisons.

She'd smiled and opened the door. *See you in six months.*

"Do you and Grace want anything from the café . . ."

Six months. Half a year. When exactly would that be over? When exactly was that last appointment?

"Sounds like you're having fun . . ."

I'd have to check my calendar, my notebook. Where was my notebook?

I always kept the notebook handy. So I could write things down. Important things like meds, exercise, sleep. My neurologist's mantra. See you in six months.

How long is six months?

"Ruby?" Mark had a hand over the receiver and was smiling at me funny. "What are you searching for so intently?"

I looked down, saw my hand inside the bag. "Nothing," I said, and curled my fingers into my palm, slowly drew my hand out. "I was just seeing what's in here."

Wrong answer. I could see it on his face. Six months might have ended yesterday.

"I mean, I packed in such a hurry, I wasn't sure. . ." Wrong again. The girls brought it. Remember that, remember that. I picked up the underwear and socks, stuffed them back in the bag. "I need to go."

"I'll call you back," Mark said into the phone. "Ruby, where are you going?"

"Canoeing."

I hadn't known that before I said it, but it made sense. A nice long paddle always set things straight, set *me* straight.

Mark threw back the sheet. "You're going out this early?"

"It's not early. It's late." I stuffed in the toiletries and the hairbrush. Pulled on my shoes.

"A nice long paddle," I said, and got to my feet, swung the bag up onto my shoulder. It felt good there, as it always had. I walked with it to the door, wondering why I hadn't used it in such a long time. And where it had been. And how Grace had known exactly what to put inside.

Except for the pills. Where were my pills?

In the bathroom. Secret pills. Shhhh. Don't tell Grace.

"Ruby, wait," Mark said.

I stood perfectly still in the doorway, studying the hall in front of me. Three doors, a potted plant, and a window with pretty ruffled curtains.

"I'll go canoeing with you," he said.

I could hear him dragging on jeans and zipping them up while I searched for the way out. Door number one, door number two, door number . . .

"Wait for me downstairs," he called.

Stairs. Of course. Right there at the end of the hall. Idiot.

I headed over with renewed purpose. If I could just get outside, then I could find my way home, I was sure of it. And when I got home I would swallow my pills, grab my paddle, and go canoeing. And all would be well again. Meds and exercise. Meds and exercise.

I went down the stairs.

"Ruby."

Mark was only a few steps behind when I reached the bottom. I stopped again. More doors, more furniture, more pictures that meant nothing. The burning question: How to get out?

"Over there," Mark said softly, pointing to a big wooden door with a brass handle.

The front door.

"I knew that," I said, marching across the foreign living room with its red tile floors and slippery area rugs. I grabbed the brass handle and pulled. Stepped out into a yard smelling of cinnamon and overrun with Russian olive and honeysuckle. "Needs pruning," I muttered, and followed the stone path to the gate.

As soon as I was on the other side of that gate, things started to come together again. The city was to my left. Home was the other way, over the bridge. I looked back at the house. I recognized it now. It belonged to someone I knew. But why was Mark sleeping there?

I heard the ferry horn, bringing the hordes over again. Soon, the lagoons would be too crowded for a good fast paddle, and that was what the doctor ordered today.

"Ruby, wait up," Mark called. "I'm coming with you."

"Coming where?"

"Canoeing, of course."

"You hate canoeing."

He smiled and closed the gate behind him. "I used to hate canoeing. Today, I'm ready to love it."

I started walking. "If you think I need company, you can think again."

He managed to keep up, but was limping slightly and breathing heavily. "My desire to pick up a paddle has nothing to do with you. If last night taught me anything, it's that I'm out of shape."

That much was true. He had never been fat and flabby when he lived with me. It was good to know he was trying to do something about the problem. But what had happened last night? Why was he limping?

I walked faster. Over the bridge, turn left. Heading for familiar territory. I needed the peace of the water and the work of the paddle. And meds. Mustn't forget the meds.

Once I had all of those, I would try again to think, to remember what had happened. I just needed to hold on a while longer.

Turning the corner onto my street, I broke into a run. Not a jog, a run that left Mark far behind and shouting my name. I didn't stop. He'd catch up. He always did.

I drew up short at my gate, flipped the latch, and walked into a garden party. Not a big one. Just three women with towels on their heads sitting around my birdbath sipping coffee from my mugs and eating muffins. I recognized most as clients.

A horrible heat moved through my entire body, right down to my fingertips. Dear God. I'd forgotten all about them.

"Ruby, darling, how are you?" Audrey DeSanto called, and twiddled her fingertips at me over the rim of her cup. "Didn't expect to see you today."

I walked toward them. "I'm as surprised as you are."

To Audrey's left, Marla Cohen laughed and said, "You are such a card. By the way, Grace is doing a great job." She shucked off the towel and ran her fingers through her hair. "And that bird she saved? No one can believe it survived the night. She's definitely got the touch."

What bird? What touch? What was she talking about?

To her left sat Judy Vanlith—a scowl on her face and a muffin bottom in her hand. "Ruby, you know I don't like to complain."

"But you will," Marla said, and got to her feet. "I need more coffee."

When Marla was halfway to the front door, Judy started again. "I don't like to complain, but if I'd known you wouldn't be working today, I wouldn't have come. I have to be out by noon and she hasn't even started the cut yet."

"I understand," I said. "I'll have you on your way as soon as possible."

Laughter, music, and women's voices came at me from inside the house. Behind me, Audrey DeSanto started telling knock-knock jokes, trying to jolly Judy out of her bad mood. Knock-knock. Who's there? How should I know? I couldn't even think with all this racket. And somewhere in the yard a bird was singing and singing and singing.

"Ruby," Mark called. He was at the gate, saying hello to my clients, making his way to where I stood, lost.

"You poor dear," Audrey said to him. "We heard all about what happened. I can't believe Liz would do such a thing."

Liz? What did she have to do with anything? I hadn't seen her in over two years. Not since Grace came home after the trial.

A girl with stop-sign red hair burst through my front door. "Daddy," she called. "You should see what Grace and I found at the lighthouse!"

That yanked me out of my stupor. What had they found? And was it inside my house?

"Over here," she said to him. "See? We found a cage and made a nest inside a box."

Cage, box. What the hell was going on? I pushed past her to the stairs, swung back the door, and tried to make sense of the scene in my kitchen at least.

Two women on my couch, reading magazines and eating more of those muffins. Another leaning back over the sink and a third finishing her coffee at my workstation while Grace cut her hair. And everywhere at once, it seemed, was Mary Anne in one of her long skirts and ridiculous off-the-shoulder blouses, pouring coffee, serving muffins, and flapping her hands like a bird.

The women called out hello one after the other. Hi. How are you? Welcome, welcome. As though I was the unexpected surprise and not them.

"Mom," Grace said. "Where's Mark?"

Music came at me again from somewhere. The CD player on the shelf. But it was the wrong music. Too loud, too fast. Completely, utterly wrong.

"Ruby, sweetie," Mary Anne said. "Good to see you. How are you feeling?"

She kissed me on the cheek and held out a cup. "I saw you at the gate, so I made a cup of tea."

I ignored her and went straight to Grace. "What's going on? Why didn't you call me?"

She looked confused. "You said you didn't want to work today."

I shook my head. "I would never say such a thing. Never. What are you trying to pull?"

Grace's cheeks pinkened and the women hushed, and somewhere outside that bloody bird kept on singing and singing.

"You told me last night," Grace insisted. "You said you were going to stay and take care of Mark and that you'd be too tired to work this morning."

That was why I was at his house, in his bed. To look after him and his aching knee. That made some sense, but the rest of Grace's story was impossible. "Did I also tell you to handle everything on your own today?"

She looked down at the floor. "No. You told me to cancel the appointments."

I drew my head back. "I what?"

"I swear it's true." Her eyes were bright and shiny. Any second now the lying bitch was going to cry. "You sent me home to call everyone and cancel."

"She's telling the truth," said the girl with the stop-sign red hair. "I was there and so was my dad."

I stared at the girl. The one who had stolen something from the lighthouse. Hidden it here in my home with Grace.

"Mom?"

I spun around. Pulled back my hand. Slapped that lying bitch right across the mouth. Watched her face crumple. The tears fall. If Mary Anne hadn't grabbed her away, I'd have smacked her again. "I don't know what you've cooked up here," I said to Grace. "But it is about to stop." I snatched the scissors from her hands. "Get out. I can't look at you right now."

"Ruby, it's okay," the woman in the chair said. "She does my hair every week. She knows what she's doing. And she's doing a great job."

"A great job?" I had to laugh. "Look at this place. There's water all over the floor. Hair everywhere. And what kind of music is that? This is Chez Ruby. We play Big Band here. Benny Goodman, Artie Shaw. Not this, this, drivel."

"Ruby, really," one of the couch potatoes said.

"It's okay," Grace said. "I understand. She's been sick. She had cancer."

The couch potatoes said, "Oh my." Mary Anne's eyebrows shot up and the woman in the chair said, "You poor thing."

I looked over at Grace. "What are you talking about?"

"Mom, I know," she said. "I know."

I shook my head, punched a button on the CD player. Blessed silence. Except for that bird. I pointed the scissors at the window. "Will someone kill that thing?"

"Mom, please," Grace whined, and I turned on her.

"Just answer me this. If I did tell you to cancel the appointments, then what are they doing here?"

"I didn't think it would be good to cancel. I thought that if they just came I could—"

"What? You could what? Handle my shop alone? Make it Chez Grace for a day? Who were you kidding? You're not capable of it, Gracie. Not for an instant. Do you hear me?"

"Ruby, put the scissors down."

I turned, saw Mark in the doorway. "I can't," I told him. "I have work to do."

"No, you don't. We're going canoeing, remember?"

"I can't go anywhere now. I have clients. Grace can't handle this alone." I looked around. "Where's my notebook? I need my notebook."

"I don't know about the notebook," Mark said. "But I do know that Grace is doing okay on her own."

I stared at him. "Mark, look around. She's made a mockery of everything. And she's taking too long, she always takes too long. Judy needs to be out by noon. She'll never make it." I turned to the woman in the chair. "What's your name?"

"Ruby, it's me," she said. "Joannie from Algonquin Island."

"Do you need to be out by noon?" She shook her head. "Then get out of the chair. Call Judy. Tell her to get in here." I swung around to the women on the couch. "The rest of you . . . I don't know. I'll figure something out. But right now I need my god-damn notebook."

Mark put his hands on my shoulders. "Ruby, give me the scissors."

Maybe it was the way the silence suddenly pressed in on me or the looks on the faces all around me. I don't think I'll ever know what stopped me, what made me come back to the moment. But for some reason, I was acutely aware of what I had just done.

My daughter was outside, crying. My best friend was on the verge herself, and my clients—women I'd known for years, women I considered friends—were staring at me as though they'd never seen me before. They were right. They hadn't. This was the new Ruby. Big Al's girl. And she was down by more than a few points.

"I'm sorry," I said softly and handed him the scissors. "I'm so sorry."

Sweet, wonderful Mary Anne put her arms around me. Turned me away from all those accusing eyes and rounded mouths. "It's okay," she said. "You had a really rough night. It's no wonder you're a little tense."

Avoid stress. Meds, exercise, sleep. Please God. I needed to sleep.

Another woman from Algonquin Island appeared at the door. This one I knew.

"Don't get upset," Mary Anne said. "I called her. She's here to help."

It was Lori, who worked at a salon in the city. Lori, who wanted to open her own place here on the Island. Lori, who was my worst nightmare and had somehow become the cavalry.

I had to laugh. It was that or cry and Grace was doing enough of that for both of us. "I'm sorry," I said again.

Mary Anne waved a hand. "No more of that," she said, guiding me past Lori to the door. "You take yourself canoeing. We'll talk later." She lowered her voice. "And Ruby, we will definitely talk later."

I nodded and let her pass me off to Mark. "I have to kill that bird," I told him as we stepped outside.

"Later," he said, and for the first time in my life, I let myself be led away.

# LIZ

The last time I woke to the sound of cartoons, I was nineteen years old and married to Antony Andreou. We'd only known each other six weeks when we decided it was meant to be—and the announcement of our engagement was equally appalling to both families. While his mother wept for days over the tragedy of a son brought low by the siren song of a barbarian, Ruby assumed the whole thing was about her—one more way for me to thumb my nose at her lifestyle, her choices, her many, many sacrifices.

She couldn't understand that my decision to marry Tony had nothing to do with spite and everything to do with a match made in heaven, love at first sight, two hearts colliding—all of those wonderfully romantic notions that can still make me sigh if I'm ever dumb enough to turn on *Sleepless in Seattle*, or *Ever After*, or any of those made-for-women movies that offend me deeply on one level and are irresistible on another.

I can't explain this weakness other than to say that I was young and impressionable when Mark moved in with us. Maybe it was the way he looked at my mother, or the way he defended her even when she was wrong, or the fact that he wasn't afraid to say "I love you" out loud and often that made my little girl's heart believe in charming princes and happily ever after.

Poor Grace was equally afflicted, and even though my mother's fairy tale ended with Mark's bags at the ferry dock and every lock on our house changed, it was too late for either of us. The damage had been done. We were full-blown romantics, and when I said "I do" at City Hall, promising to love, honor, and spend my life with Tony, I meant it. How could I have known that Scooby-Doo would turn our love into to a lie?

The problem was that while Tony was prepared to fight for the right to marry the woman he loved, he saw no reason to fight the offer of a free room in his parent's basement. *We have to buy a house, right? Houses cost money, right? So we move into my old room, you finish law school while I go to work, and in five years, bam, we got a down payment. Makes sense, right?*

It might have if not for the big TV in Tony's room.

In all the weeks leading up to the wedding, no one had ever mentioned the fact that his five-year-old brother, George, had been eating breakfast and watching early morning cartoons on Tony's television every day since he was born. I know for a fact that this omission had nothing to do with subterfuge and everything to do with being Greek, because if his mother had foreseen any difficulty in our future, she would have told me about it the moment her baby boy presented the barbarian slut as his intended.

The reason no one mentioned George's little ritual was because no one saw it as a problem. Not even Tony. *You have to get up for school, right? I have to go work, right? So where's the problem? Unlock the door. Let the boy watch the TV.*

Even if I refused, Georgie had his own controller and at 5:30 A.M. on the dot, the fat little bastard would flick on the TV, crank up the volume, and wait while the Flintstones or the Freakazoids or Scooby Doo came blasting into our room. *Rets ret roing, reryrone.*

The little shit knew he had me because not only was that television huge, it also had a five-speaker sound system and a subwoofer that could make your chest hum. The moment Scooby opened his mouth, I'd sit bolt upright, Tony would leap out of bed, and his mother would start stomping on the kitchen floor above us. *What, are you crazy down there? Let him in before we all go deaf.*

The few times I unplugged the goddamn television, the kid stood outside the door and howled like I'd cut off his arm or something. Which of course brought everybody down those stairs in seconds, all of them hollering and pointing fingers at the selfish bitch. I didn't stand a chance in that ten-by-twelve-foot hellhole.

By the end of the first month I'd thrown the clock, the phone, and our remote control at the television. By the end of the third I'd smacked Tony with all of them, and by the end of the sixth, our marriage was over. Tony couldn't tell the little shit no, I couldn't live with the kid barging in every morning with a smirk on his face and toast in his hand, and his mother couldn't get me packed up fast enough. *Rets ret roing, rararian.*

Ruby laughed when I turned up with my bags. "Nothing lasts forever," she said. "But six months is embarrassing, even for you."

She didn't understand that I wasn't embarrassed, I was heartbroken. My lifelong love, my vow eternal, shattered by Scooby fucking Doo. And I can honestly say that cartoons have never been heard in my home since—until this morning.

I was lying there with my eyes closed—because I knew from experience that it was going to hurt to open them—listening to what could only be cartoons and thinking about Tony for the first time in years. While it wasn't Scooby I was hearing—or the Flintstones or anything else I recognized—the music, the voices, the overdone sound effects left no room for doubt. Cartoons were definitely playing close by, and my poor hungover brain could only wonder where I was and who had turned on the television. And how come my left shoulder hurt?

Raising my right hand to block out the light, I finally opened one eye. Saw a black bedside table, a glass of water, a bottle of Extra Strength Tylenol, and a framed picture of Grace and me as kids—tongues out, eyes crossed, index fingers up our noses. Definitely my room. But who was in here with me?

I lowered my hand and closed my eye again. "Whoever opened those curtains is dead."

"Finally, you're awake," a woman said. "Do you have any idea what time it is?"

Her voice was close, familiar, and slightly pissed off—which was funny considering it was my place, my television, and my curtains that were open. "Happily no," I said, lifting my head this time and squinting into the light.

"Well, it's noon," Brenda the Former Bartender said and rose from the sofa in front of the television. On the screen, a new show began—Bugs and Daffy stepping out in top hat and tails. *Overture, curtains, lights.* I half-expected George to come bounding into the room and smear jam on my pillow.

I shuddered and sat up a little more, scowled as Brenda threw back yet another curtain. "What are you doing here?" I asked. "More important, how did you get through the front door? And why the hell are you watching cartoons?"

"I'm here because I need to talk to you. Your roommate let me in, and it was either this or some fuzzy French channel." She looked over at me. "Is there a reason you only have rabbit ears?"

"I don't watch a lot of TV." Not since they cut off the cable at any rate. But I couldn't come up with a reason why that should be any of her business. Or why my crazy Russian roommate had decided we were holding open house today.

"Probably better for you," Brenda said, and yanked back the last curtain, filling the room with sunlight and making me wince.

Why I had ever believed that a room with east-facing windows was a good idea was beyond me.

She came over to the bed and picked up the glass of water on my night table. "You should drink this."

It was all too much, too soon. "I'll drink it later. Right now I need to sleep." I lowered my head, pulled the covers up to my neck. "Come back later."

"I've already been here for three hours." She put the glass down with a thud, yanked back the covers, and dropped them on the floor at the foot of the bed. "Liz, this is important. Hal was at the house this morning. I'm scared and I'm not going away until you talk to me. So you might as well get up."

She stood firm, looking down at me with her tiny little hands on her tiny little hips while on the other side of the room, Wile E. Coyote banged a hammer against an Acme anvil again and again and again. I groaned and pressed the heels of my hands against my eyes. Welcome to Liz Donaldson's private hell.

"What do you need to talk about so badly?" I muttered.

"The suggestion you made to Gary yesterday."

Gary—her very sweet brother. I could picture him clearly, loping across the baseball field, rolling his shoulders, offering to meet me at the Duck. I felt myself smile in the silly, dangerous way of all romantics. Had he done that? Had he met me in secret?

I remembered sitting at the back table with the boys, drinking shots of something while the service got slower and slower. So much so that I finally went to the bar and asked the new bartender, Stevie, what the hell her problem was. I couldn't remember the answer, but I was pretty sure Gary's face had not been at the table to that point—which might be something to celebrate, depending on how the rest of the evening had gone.

"You should know that silence does not discourage me," Brenda said.

I lifted my hands from my eyes and squinted up at her, thinking of terriers and muzzles—perhaps a nice choke chain. I sighed and lowered my arms. "I'm not trying to discourage you. I just can't remember details right now. What was my suggestion?"

"Petition into bankruptcy. Surely you remember that."

Not immediately, but as I struggled to sit up, things started to come back bit by bit. A guy with a baseball bat. A husband with money problems. And finally, yes. Petition into bankruptcy. Not a wildly popular or even completely legal solution in a case like Brenda's, but doable—if a lawyer had balls.

I propped a pillow behind my back and stretched my legs out in front of me. "Did you talk to your lawyer about this?"

"I called him last night. First he wanted to know if I'd been reading legal advice blogs on the Internet again. Then he said that a petition into bankruptcy was complicated and started using terms like 'quantum of unsecured debt' and '*pari passu*,' and I pretty much stopped listening until he said, 'Brenda, you can't do this. So stop thinking about it and stop worrying. I have everything well in hand.' When I suggested he might like to meet Hal and his baseball bat, he told me I was overreacting and to be patient."

"Sounds about right." Clearly, there were no balls on Mitch's legal team. While that was obviously a problem, what was less obvious was why it should be *my* problem. Or why I was wearing yesterday's jeans and T-shirt. Or why there were now holes in the knees of those jeans.

I assumed the holes were related to the pain in my shoulder somehow, yet I had no memory of falling down or anything else remotely uncomfortable happening. Of course it was still early on the morning after to be piecing together the night before, and why bother anyway? No doubt someone at the Duck would be more than happy to fill in the blanks for me tonight.

"So I hung up and decided I was finished being patient," Brenda went on. "I wanted to know more about this thing I shouldn't be thinking about before I stopped thinking about it. That's why I'm here." She opened the bottle of Tylenol, shook two tablets into her palm, and held them out with the glass of water. "You really should take these."

Admitting defeat, I took the pills and popped them into my mouth. Swallowed them and then sipped the rest of the water slowly but with purpose, resisting the urge to gulp. When I was finished, she took back the empty. "Can you handle another?"

I nodded carefully. "Kitchen's at the end of the hall."

"And the bathroom is the second door on the left, and the boys who live downstairs aren't allowed to use it." She went out the door with the glass. "I've been here a while, remember?"

"Three hours," I said, cautiously putting my feet over the side of the bed. "Do you know how creepy that is? Especially since you wanted nothing to do with me yesterday."

I heard her stop and come back along the hall. And was pleased with the suitably guilty look on her face when she poked her head into my room again. "I'm sorry about that, okay? I was worried about Mitch and the kids. And there you were, getting in my face, trying to be the helpful drunk—"

"I was sober by then," I said, pushing myself up to standing position.

"Fine, you were sober. But there was still no reason to believe you were qualified to talk to me about anything but the weather."

"Thanks a lot," I said, steadying myself with a hand on the wall just in case.

She came over to stand beside me. "Come on, Liz. It's not like you ever advertised your skills or talked about what you did. Even now, when I look at you, I see Car Bombs and Highland flings, not briefcases and closing arguments. How was I supposed to know you were a brilliant lawyer?"

"Who told you that?" I asked, and started walking, making my way slowly, carefully toward the sofa. It wasn't far, no more than fifteen feet, but with a hangover it might as well have been a football field.

"Gary said it first. And your mom backed him up."

Gary. What a nice name. Strong. Sexy. Still out of bounds.

I stopped and gently turned my head. "Ruby said I was brilliant?"

"She said and I quote, 'Liz is both a brilliant lawyer and a crushing disappointment.'"

"That sounds more like her," I said, and turned back around, waited patiently for my brain to catch up before taking another step.

"You can say what you want, but I like your mom. And after talking to her, Mitch and I both agree that the airport should be shut down."

"I'm sure you do." I started walking again, putting one foot in front of the other. "How long did you spend with her anyway?"

"About fifteen minutes."

When I reached the sofa, I stood perfectly still, watching the Coyote plummet off a cliff and feeling my stomach follow him down. I looked away before he hit bottom. "And in those fifteen minutes, she managed to tell you about the bird sanctuary, noise pollution, and the fact that Babe Ruth hit his first professional home run right there on Hanlan's Point, where the airport is today. Am I right?"

"We were surprised about Babe Ruth."

"Most people are." Unable to resist, I looked back at the television, witnessing the emergence of the Coyote yet again from the dust. He lay among the rocks, battered and broken while the Road Runner stuck out his tongue and raced off again, just like that fat little shit George did every morning.

I bent at the knees and picked up the remote. Pointed it at the television and put the Coyote out of his misery once and for all. Blessed silence descended and hell seemed a little more tolerable.

"So did you sign her petition to close the airport?" I asked.

"Yes, and I'm glad I did."

I tossed the remote and took a much-needed break on the sofa. "You only feel that way because Ruby gave you her usual spiel, and she's very good at it. But I wouldn't worry about your sudden conversion. You should be fine in a day or two."

Brenda shook her head and went off with the glass again. "I hope not, because I kind of like being one of the rebels."

"That'll wear off too," I called, and touched a hand to my shoulder, feeling for the tender spot. Discovering it was large and extended all the way around my upper arm. I lifted the sleeve, revealing a huge purple bruise. Heat, unpleasant and stinging, moved through me. What the hell had happened last night?

Brenda reappeared with a full glass. "You should know that even though you don't support their cause, everyone at the protest had only nice things to say about you."

"That's because they're nice people. Just horribly misguided." I lowered the sleeve, afraid there were more surprises waiting for me beneath the holes in my jeans.

She pressed the glass into my hand. "This one guy, Mark, was a big fan. He said you were not only brilliant, but you also used to be the shining star at his firm."

"I was." I sipped the water slowly again, feeling myself waking up, my brain clicking faster. I'd forgotten Mark was at the protest, and I smiled, remembering how odd it had been to see him standing on the curb after all these years. Waving signs, chanting. Getting hit by a taxi.

Shit. The taxi.

I sputtered and lowered the glass. "Was he okay?" I coughed. "After the taxi hit him, I mean. Was he okay?"

"He seemed fine." She took the glass and patted me on the back. "Said the car just bumped him and refused to go to the hospital no matter how much your mom nagged."

"Good for him." I spotted my cell phone on the coffee table and thought about turning it on, calling to make sure he was okay. But after thirty seconds of niceties, he'd find a way to turn the discussion to Ruby, and I was in no shape to have that conversation now or in the foreseeable future. Better to send a text. *Sry abt taxi. Glad UR feeling better. Luv, Liz.* He'd expect nothing less from his former shining star.

But that could wait. Right now, I needed to focus on my shoulder. And my knees. And what had happened at the Duck.

"Can you explain petition into bankruptcy now?" Brenda asked. "Mitch is waiting to hear from me."

And Brenda's situation, of course. Mustn't forget Brenda's situation.

"Sure," I said, and crossed to the door.

"Then where are you going?"

"I need to pee."

She followed me out to the hall and past my crazy roommate's locked door. "I need you to tell me what it is in plain language."

"Guaranteed." I paused at the bathroom door. "But what about Mitch? Doesn't he want to know what it's all about too?"

"I told you, he's waiting for my call. He said he'd trust my judgment."

"That's my kind of man." I closed the bathroom door, leaving her in the hall while I gingerly pulled down the jeans and inspected my knees. The scrapes and bruises weren't as bad as I'd imagined, but they would make short skirts awkward for a few days. And I still had no recollection of falling.

I pulled a handful of tissues out of a box and dabbed at the scrapes. I was sure I had a phone number for one of my buddies around somewhere. I'd call and find out what happened last night. They'd all had their share of bruises and black eyes over the years, and the stories were usually good for a laugh a day or two later.

I dabbed again at the scrapes, figured they'd be fine until I took a shower, and pulled the jeans back up. Risked a quick glance in the mirror and wished I hadn't. Puffy eyes, pale skin, hair everywhere. Hangover face was never pretty. I washed that face, brushed my teeth, and pushed at my hair. Even dug around in the medicine cabinet for an elastic. A ponytail didn't make the picture prettier, but at least the hair was out of my face. And the good news was that I was hungry, which meant a trip to Willy G's—my favorite dive on College Street—because there is nothing like strong coffee and a high-fat breakfast to ease a hangover. And with luck, Brenda's guilt would encourage her to say, *My treat*. She had come to my house, after all. Woken me out of a sound sleep. Made me think too soon. It was worth a shot.

"Your lawyer was right," I said, stepping out of the bathroom to find the hall empty and the aroma of coffee all around me.

"I thought you might be ready for a coffee," she called, and smiled at me from the kitchen door.

Oh shit, I should have warned her. "Stop!" I called, and hurried along the hall. "You can't make anything in there. Not coffee, not tea. Definitely nothing that requires food."

She took two mugs from the hooks under the cupboard and looked over at me. "Why in the world not?"

I stood in the doorway, watching in horror as she picked up the coffeepot and filled those two ill-fated cups. "Because none of the food in this kitchen is mine."

"None of it?"

"Just the overripe banana in the garbage pail." She raised a brow and I shrugged. "What can I say? I hate to shop. The point is that everything here is the legal property of my roommate. And she will kill me if she finds out we so much as looked at her stuff."

"Don't be silly." Brenda went to the fridge and swung back the door, blocking my view. "Nadia's not like that."

I could only stare as she rummaged through the cartons and plastic containers. "You know her name?"

"It happens when you spend an hour talking to someone."

"You spent that long talking to Nadia?" Brenda nodded and set something on the counter. Sweet Jesus, not the cream. "I hope she paid you," I said, putting the cream back where it belonged and hoping I got the positioning right.

"There was no need. I found her charming." Brenda snatched the container out again before I could close the fridge. "But rest assured she doesn't have anything good to say about you either."

"And here I thought we had nothing in common." I closed the door, figuring I'd water the Russian's cream later. Seemed to work fine the last time. And the bitch could use less fat.

Nadia had moved into the room next to mine three months ago, the only other adult in a house full of students. She was older than me, which was comforting, and much taller with broad shoulders and a permanent scowl. I figured she used to be a judge at the Olympics. Figure skating, no doubt.

Since we were the only tenants on the second floor, I'd tried to be friendly, even asked her to come to the Duck for a drink. But in all the time she'd been here, she'd spoken exactly four words to me in heavily accented English: "Nevair touch my stuff."

I had no idea what kind of work she did or if she ever had any fun. All I knew was that she thumped around in her room a lot, locked up before she went down the hall to the bathroom, and kept a chart on the fridge, accounting for every scrap of food in the kitchen including a tea bag count, the weight of the rice, and the ounces of milk, cream, and juice. If the landlord had allowed padlocks on the cupboards, I'm sure she would have installed them immediately.

I'd used a lot of words to describe her to my buddies at the Duck over the last few months, but *charming* was never one of them.

"Have some coffee," Brenda said. "And tell me how the petition works."

"It pushes the company that owes you money into bankruptcy," I said, my eyes moving from the cups on the table to the chart on the fridge. Nadia would have weighed the coffee tin that morning. Now it would be fourteen ounces less two scoops. Perhaps I could add a little sand.

"Is that what we'll be doing?" Brenda asked. "Bankrupting the other company?"

I turned away from the chart. "That's not the goal. All you want to do is get them to write you a check. But they won't know that." I motioned to the door. "We should go get breakfast somewhere."

"You mean lunch?" Brenda pulled out two chairs. "We'll go later, okay? My treat. But I want to hear the rest of this in private."

She sat down, letting me know the matter was settled as she dragged a cup toward her. That was when I noticed the slight shaking of her hand, the dark circles under her eyes, the way her freckles stood out against the ghostly white of her skin. I sat down across from her. "Jesus, Brenda, you look like shit. Are you all right?"

"Are you kidding? Of course I'm not all right. Did you hear what I said about Hal?"

"Of course I heard. But not all of it stuck."

"Nadia was right. Talking to you *is* like talking to a wall."

"How would she know? She's never tried."

*Fuck you very much*, *Nadia*, I thought, and picked up the cream, tipped it over my cup. Kept pouring until the coffee reached the brim and slopped over onto the table. I shook the container and smiled. Should be down enough to be noticeable. I set the carton in the center of the table. Screw watering anything down anymore. I was done hiding. Let the bitch do her worst.

"Okay, let's talk about Hal," I said and went to the pantry. Reached my hand deep into forbidden territory and came out with a sugar bowl. "Tell me what happened."

"He was sitting outside the house when I got up this morning. I don't know how long he'd been there, but he had the nerve to wave to me when I went out to get the paper. Like he expected me to bring him coffee or something."

I sat down and passed her the cream. "Did you call the police?"

"He was gone by the time they arrived, of course. But he's not smart enough to be scared off by the police forever. Hal is a man on a mission." She picked up a spoon. Stirred her coffee without adding anything to it. "The guy's an idiot, but he's got Mitch spooked. He wants to sell the house to pay him off. He even called a real estate agent to come and give us a price."

"He doesn't need to do that."

"He doesn't know that, does he?" She kept her eyes on the spoon, watching it go round and round. "I told him to hold off. At least wait until I talked to you."

"Good. And as weird as it was, I'm glad Nadia let you in."

Brenda glanced up at me. "I didn't think she was going to when she answered the door. I'd never seen anything like her. A giant in bicycle shorts and a wifebeater T-shirt. She scared the crap out of me, if you want the truth." She went back to stirring her coffee. "But she was polite enough while I explained that I needed to talk to you. Then she said you were passed out and wouldn't come to for hours. 'You come back later,' she said, and went to close the door."

"And yet you're here."

"Only because I started to cry."

"Oh, Brenda—"

"Save the sympathy. It was my own fault. I've seen you on enough Friday nights to know that Saturday mornings probably don't exist for you." She laughed and dropped the spoon. "I don't know why, but I had this foolish idea you might have given the Duck a miss last night. Stupid really, when you think about it."

I winced, feeling like a traitor. "I probably should have done that, but if it's any consolation, I missed you."

"Too bad, because I didn't miss you at all." She picked up her cup but didn't drink the coffee. Just held the mug between her hands, as though needing the warmth. "In fact, it was nice to be home for a change, to put the kids to bed myself and watch a movie with Mitch. Would have been a perfect evening all around if goddamn Hal hadn't kept calling the house every half hour. Two o'clock in the morning, he finally stopped. But come six A.M. there he was outside, smiling and waving, letting me know he is never going to stop until he gets his money. It's enough to make you crazy."

"I can imagine."

"Then you can also imagine how grateful I was when Nadia opened the door and invited me in. Brought me upstairs and showed me which room was yours. Proved to me that your door is never locked and then put a huge hand on my arm and asked why I thought you could help me with anything. 'She is alcoholic,' she told me. 'Very unreliable.'"

"She doesn't even know me."

"Are you kidding? She lives in the next room. Apparently you rarely close your door, and everybody knows you drink too much."

I rolled my eyes. "Define 'too much.' No, don't. Just tell me why you sat there so long. Why you didn't just wake me up?"

"You think we didn't try? We rolled you over, we shook you, we even shouted in your ear, but you wouldn't wake up. Nadia suggested a hose, but I said no, out of courtesy to the boys downstairs. So we went back to the kitchen and again she put one of those huge hands on my arm and asked what was so bad that I needed advice from a drunk."

"She had no right."

"No right to what? Be concerned? Understanding? Compassionate?" Brenda rose again, went to the pantry, and took out a tin. "We sat here for over an hour, talking while we waited for you to wake up. We went through two pots of coffee and she served me these." She banged the tin down in front of me and opened the lid. "Her own homemade chocolate chip cookies, which are probably delicious, but I don't know for sure because once I opened my mouth, I couldn't stop talking long enough to eat one."

She stood with her chin thrust out and her shoulders tense, every part of her holding fast, staying strong. Refusing to give in to the tears that were making her eyes shine. "I told her everything, Liz. All about Mitch, the business, the guy who won't pay, and stupid Hal with his baseball bat."

She sucked in a long breath and sank into the chair as though all the energy had suddenly left her body. "I can't believe I told my life story to a stranger in bicycle shorts and a wifebeater." She picked up her cup again. "I feel like such an idiot."

"I know that feeling. I spilled my guts to a bartender at the park yesterday. I'm still not over that one." I opened the tin and took out a cookie. "I thought I might never have to see her again, but no such luck." She glanced over and I risked a smile. "I thought maybe I could thank her for listening by explaining what a petition to bankruptcy is."

Brenda smiled a little. "Sounds a bit dry, but she might be interested."

I laughed and got up. "Then she might also want to take notes."

I went down the hall to my room. Took my time searching for a pen and a piece of paper under the newspapers, final notices, and clean underwear that covered my desk because I had no clear idea of what I was going to say to Brenda. I'd spent the last two years purposely avoiding anything to do with courts and legal issues. Using Car Bombs to destroy the files in my head and tequila shooters to pick off the stragglers, only to be standing here hoping for a few survivors.

"Petition to bankruptcy," I whispered as I searched. "Petition to bankruptcy," over and over, as though it was an incantation capable of bringing my training back from the dead. I guess being a lawyer is a little like riding a bicycle because it wasn't long before a few of those files started to open. Words and bits of information floating slowly, haphazardly to the surface. Trustee, court, Application for Assignment . . . and then nothing.

No matter. That was enough to get her started. My fingers closed on a pen first, a pad of paper next. I hauled both out from under the rubble, ripped off the first three sheets of drunken doodling, and headed back to the kitchen to deliver a little free legal advice—the only kind I was capable of giving anymore.

Still, as I handed her the pen and paper, my heart started to beat a little faster and my body grew restless, just as it always had whenever I was making a presentation to a client.

"First things first," I said, leaning back against the counter, not yet ready to sit down. "What's the name of the company that owes you money?"

"Champlain Aerospace. They make parts for jet engines."

"Has your lawyer already made a formal demand for the money?"

"A couple of times." She scribbled *petition* at the top of the page. "Last time he signed off with 'govern yourselves accordingly,' and they stopped taking Mitch's calls."

"Trust me. Once the petition is served, they will be on the phone to Mitch within a matter of hours, guaranteed. And since they've already had a formal demand, all we need now is two things: a lawyer to draw up the application and a name to deliver it to."

She put the pen down. "That's all?"

"That's all. Then we pray that the delivery of the petition results in a check, because your guy was right. Unless Champlain really is in financial trouble, you can't see this through."

Brenda looked at me blankly. "I don't understand."

"Okay, let me ask you this. Do you think Champlain Aerospace is in danger of going bankrupt? Could that be why they're not paying you?"

"I don't know. They're pretty big, but everybody's feeling the pinch right now, so Mitch figures they're using our money to pay the suppliers they still need."

"If they're doing that, then it means they're tight for cash and this will work. If they're not tight for cash, however, then they could fight the petition, the court would throw it out, and they'd probably sue you."

Her eyes opened very wide. "But you want me to do it anyway?"

"No, I want you to *act* as though you're going to do it. Like when you're playing poker and all you have is a pair of threes, but you keep a straight face and keep on bidding, hoping the other guy blinks first."

She tapped the pen on the page. "You're saying this is a bluff?"

"A bluff that will work." I hadn't done a presentation in so long I had to remind myself to slow down. Speak clearly. Take a breath now and then. "The moment your lawyer puts the papers into their hands, the directors of Champlain will shit themselves. The petition will be accompanied by a letter from your lawyer stating that a copy of the petition will also be delivered to their bank, and that they have one week to pay you out in full, or you will see them in court. Of course, their lawyers will call your lawyer and tell them you're nuts, you can't do this, and they'll threaten to sue, blah, blah, blah. But your lawyer will say, Who cares? If Champlain doesn't pay you, Mitch's company will be gone soon anyway. That is the case isn't it?

She nodded. "We probably have another month left."

"So they'll be suing a shell."

I started to pace. Eight steps from the sink to the door and back again. "You have nothing to lose," I continued, "while they, on the other hand, will have nothing to gain from continuing to hold on to your money. The moment that thing is delivered to their bank, all hell will break loose. Even if Champlain isn't in any danger of going under, the letter will start a chain reaction.

"Their bank will immediately remove the amount of your claim from their line of credit, in case the petition is successful. If we're lucky and they are indeed using the money they owe you to pay other suppliers, then their checks will start bouncing, suppliers will slap them on COD, and customers will run the other way. Even if they're not strapped for cash, the petition will make their bank nervous, and no one likes a nervous bank.

"The directors will have to start tap-dancing to explain why they haven't paid your bill, and nothing they say will make their bank smile. My guess is that whatever their financial situation, Champlain will cut you a check to keep any of this from happening."

I smiled and straddled the chair next to her. "Trust me, Brenda. This is not business as usual, but it will work."

"A bluff," she said, and sat up straighter. Smiled and threw down the pen. "What a great idea! When do we start?"

"Should be soon as possible," a voice with a thick Russian accent said.

We both turned to see Nadia in the doorway, huge and sweating in her bicycle shorts and beater shirt. As usual, her black brows were pinched, her mouth was a tight white line, but for the first time in months, her pale blue eyes were looking straight at me.

"So, brilliant lawyer," she said. "who gave you such good idea?"

My spine stiffened. "Nobody gave it to me. It's mine."

"If you say so." She looked past me to Brenda. "You are happy with bluff?"

Brenda smiled. "I'm delighted with it. In fact, we're down to the details now and should be out of here in a few minutes."

"Take your time," Nadia said. "Is important discussion." She came into the kitchen and plunked herself down at the table. "Is coffee still fresh?"

Brenda rose. "I'm sure it is. I'll get you a cup."

While she poured, Nadia reached across me for the cookie tin, as though I weren't there.

"We don't want to keep you from anything," I said. "I know Saturdays are always busy."

"Not for me." She spooned sugar into her cup. "I have all day free now."

"That's great." Brenda topped up her own cup and sat down. "How was the yoga class?"

Nadia frowned. "Good, but is hard work."

"Those downward dogs can be a bitch," I said. "But it explains all the thumping and banging in your room." She finally looked at me. I smiled and held out a hand. "Nadia, isn't it? I'm Liz. Nice to meet you."

She ignored my hand. "I know who you are. And yoga is not just downward dogs." She reached into the tin, took out a handful of cookies, and lined them up beside her cup. One, two, three, four, five. "I am on journey of self-discovery and spiritual clarity. Every day discovering potential for limitless joy."

"Of course you are."

She scowled at me. "You find that funny?"

"On the contrary, I find it fascinating." I leaned over and nicked cookie number three, leaving a gaping hole in the middle of her lineup. "Should I assume that counting slices of bread and tea bags is one of the pit stops on this journey to limitless joy?"

"No, that is petty revenge." She watched the cookie travel to my mouth. "But first night here, I find you on floor eating barbequed chicken I bought that afternoon."

I shrugged and took another bite. "I don't remember that."

"No big surprise, but does not make it okay. I was furious landlord had not warned me about alcoholic next door." She slid her remaining cookies into a line of four then pushed the tin toward me. "Take another."

"Thanks," I said, helping myself to one from the tin and one from her lineup. Number three again—always a lucky number. "They really are good. And I'm not an alcoholic."

"No?" She eased her bulk forward and leaned on her arms. "Then what are you?"

"Nadia," Brenda said. "This is not the best time—"

"No, is fine," I said. "I will tell you I am drinker. I like to party. Have good time."

Her smile was enough to make the cookie stall halfway to my mouth. "Did you have good time last night?"

I should have backed off right there, gone out to fetch some sand for her coffee. But I was still feeling good, even a little cocky after my talk with Brenda, and it made a strange kind of sense to take a real stand. To put the cookie down and lean forward on my arms with my nose only inches from her. "As a matter of fact, I did."

"You should tell us about it," she said. "About your good time. And where you got this." Her hand shot out and lifted my sleeve, revealing the bruise.

Brenda drew back. "My God, Liz. Did you know that was there?"

I slapped at Nadia's hand. "Of course I knew it was there."

"But you do not know how it got there, do you?"

Heat moved through my body again, up into my face. "Not off the top of my head, no."

"Or why there are holes in your jeans." I watched her sit back in the chair, fold her hands on her stomach. "If you like, I can tell you, because I was there."

"You're lying."

"No, is true." She picked up cookie number one, held it daintily between her thumb and forefinger. "You were on College Street, sitting on streetcar tracks, holding up streetcar and swearing at driver."

"Bullshit," I said, ignoring the sudden dryness in my mouth, the roller-coaster drop in my stomach. "She could say I was dancing on top of the CN Tower or running naked through Nathan Phillips Square. Wouldn't make any of it true."

"But she did know about the bruise," Brenda said softly.

Nadia took a bite of her cookie. "Bruise came from man trying to pull you off tracks. Long hair. Beard." She screwed up her nose. "Not attractive."

"I don't believe you," I said, trying to picture the table at the Duck. Trying to remember a man with long hair and a beard, a man who might have been buying me drinks. A man I might have been going home with. Nothing came. Nothing at all.

Nadia shook her head slowly, heavily as though it was her lot in life to deal with dolts. "Does not matter what you believe. Is what happened."

"Go on," I said, and managed a smile. "I always like a good bar story."

"Is natural you are curious. Lost nights are always problem." She brushed crumbs from her T-shirt and went for the next cookie in line. "Time was two fifteen A.M. I was in taxi, coming home from friend's house. I saw woman on tracks. I told taxi to stop and bearded man to leave you alone. He said you passed out in bar and got kicked out. Then you got belligerent in streetcar and driver kicked you both out. Bearded man called you pain in his ass and grabbed you again. I knocked him down and picked you up. Taxi would not let you in, so I carried you home."

"You carried me? Why?"

"Because you passed out again. I could have left you on curb for police, but is not like me." She wagged a finger at me. "Do not think this makes you special. I would have done same for any woman in trouble." She went back to the cookie. "Still think you had good time last night?"

"Up to that point, I'm sure I did," I said, trying not to think about what would have happened if the police had come. If I'd gone to jail. If Nadia hadn't shown up in a taxi. "The rest is Brenda's fault anyway. If she'd been there to put me into a cab, none of it would have happened." I watched Brenda's mouth fall open and gave myself a mental slap. "Sorry," I said quickly. "I don't know where that came from. I know it wasn't your fault."

"Sadly no," Nadia said. "She does not."

I shoved my chair back and stood up. "Why are you such a bitch?"

"I am not bitch. I am only worried your friend will trust you with important matter. And you will let her down." She lifted a shoulder, let it fall. "Is way of all drunks."

"How have I let her down? I've already told her what she has to do."

"It's true," Brenda said, and smiled at me. "And I'm ready to do whatever is necessary. Just tell me when we start."

"You start by finding a lawyer who'll take you on."

She looked confused. "Aren't you my lawyer?"

"Me?" I laughed and shook my head. "Trust me, you do not want me as your lawyer."

"You see?" Nadia said. "Already she lets you down. I should have left her on tracks."

I stuck a finger in her face. "You can shut up any time."

For a big woman, she was extremely quick, towering over me before I could make a break for the stairs. "And you can help friend any time. But you will not because you are useless drunk."

"I'm not useless. I'm just not the best person for the job. I'm not even a lawyer anymore."

"Why?" Nadia asked. "What happened to you?"

"Nothing. I'm just taking a break. Can't a person take a fucking break?"

She glanced over at Brenda. "Drunks always lie too."

"I hate you," I said.

"Is mutual."

I wasn't surprised when Brenda squeezed herself in between us, exactly as she had when Mitch and Hal were squaring off in the park. "This is ridiculous," she grunted as she tried to nudge Nadia backward. "Both of you need to cool off."

Nadia stepped back on her own. "You are right. Is not productive." She scowled at me over Brenda's head. "What is productive is to stop taking break and help your friend."

Brenda looked as though she was about to argue, to point out that Nadia was butting into a situation that didn't concern her. But then her expression changed, softened toward my overbearing roommate. "Why are you doing this? Why do you even care?"

"Because you need help," Nadia said as though it should have been obvious. "If I was brilliant lawyer, I would do it for you, but I am substitute school teacher. What do I know about courts and laws in this country?"

"You're a teacher?" Brenda asked.

"Elementary only. I love little children."

"On toast," I muttered, and Brenda turned on me.

"Shut up, Liz, she's got a point. You said it yourself—you wouldn't have ended up on the streetcar tracks last night if I'd been there to help you the way I have been for the last two years. Literally saving your ass by pouring you into a cab because I liked you. You were a drunk, yes, but there was something about you that was different, that I thought deserved saving. But now, when I need your help, you won't do it, and I want to know why."

"Because she is coward," Nadia said. "Is obvious something bad has happened to her. That is why she has beautiful, expensive furniture but lives here. That is why she is on break from good job. And that is why she drinks too much and has become pathetic coward."

"I am not a coward."

Brenda advanced on me. "Then prove it. Help me out. Do the petition."

Nadia shook her head. "Be careful. She may say yes now but will not follow through."

"What the fuck do you know?" I took a step back, giving myself room to breathe, but not to think. Because thinking required logic, and logic required rational conclusions. And the only rational conclusion a logical person could come to would be to keep Liz Donaldson the hell away from Brenda's petition. I was the last person she needed on her side—the last person anyone needed on their side.

But Brenda didn't understand that, *wouldn't* understand that, which made a strange kind of sense. She was desperate, and desperation led to illogical thinking, irrational conclusions, and trusting my pushy roommate—and everybody knows you can't trust the Russian judge.

Yet, how could I say no when Brenda was looking at me like I was the answer to all of her problems? And Nadia was looking at me like I was a bug under a magnifying glass and she'd found the perfect angle for the sun. The situation seemed impossible, like there was no way out. But I have always been resourceful. "Even if I wanted to do this," I said. "I don't have the money, the staff—"

"I will be staff," Nadia said. "You tell me what you need and I will get it."

Brenda nodded. "I can help too. And Mitch will pay your expenses. I have a checkbook in my purse. I'll give you a down payment or a deposit or whatever it is you call it, today."

"A retainer," I said, my resourcefulness slipping away, trumped by their enthusiasm. "It's called a retainer."

"Would a hundred dollars be enough to start things off?" Brenda asked.

I smiled. "Sure, why not."

"Okay," Nadia said. "You have money and staff. What else do you need?"

The idea of the three of us pulling this off was ludicrous in the extreme. But some part of me must not have been paying attention because without me even trying, the files began to open up again, the words floating up slowly into the light. "Information about the company," I said. "Names of the directors, address of the operation, and all pertinent phone numbers. Copies of the invoice, the purchase order, the letters you've sent to them. Notes on any communication that went on between them and Mitch's company. I need pictures of the building and where the big guy sits so I can hand him the notice." I laughed, a high-pitched, slightly hysterical sound. "I know there's more, but I have no idea what it is."

"You will," Nadia said more gently than I would have thought possible.

"You'll really do this for me?" Brenda asked.

"Yes," I said, my skin already clammy, my legs rubbery. "I'll do it."

Brenda screamed and leapt up, wrapping her skinny arms around my neck and hugging me hard. "Thank you, thank you." She kissed my cheek and dropped to her feet again. "Oh my God, I feel so light, so happy." She leapt up again, hugging me even harder. "I am so happy!"

Nadia clapped me on the back. "You see, every day possibility for limitless joy."

Limitless joy. Sounded like the name of a cocktail—something I could use right now.

"We will be like three amigos," Nadia said, her round face shining, beaming. "Fighting for truth, justice, and really big check. And as sign of good faith, of new beginning, there is no more chart." She went to the fridge and took down the list of food and measures. Tore it into eight pieces and dropped them into the can under the sink.

"Thanks," I said.

She gave me her one-shoulder shrug. "You are skinny anyway. How much can you eat?" She motioned us to follow her out of the kitchen. "Now we go for first official business lunch. My treat. I will keep receipt, of course. To claim on taxes."

"I'm so excited," Brenda said to me as we filed out into the hall. "You're doing a very good thing," she said, and went down the stairs.

"She is right," Nadia said, putting out a hand to keep me from following. "This is very good thing." She lowered her voice and came closer. "Like it or not, you are on journey now too. Yoga would be good for you. I will take you some time."

It sounded more like a threat than an invitation, but I was too numb to argue.

"I know you are scared," she continued. "Of petition, of street-car tracks, of everything. But just for today, you do not drink. To-morrow, maybe. But for today, no. Okay?"

What could I say? I can't? I won't? Either way I was screwed. So I gave her a one-shoulder shrug. Said, "Okay," and watched her go down the stairs to join Brenda.

The two of them stood in front of the door, smiling, laughing, united in their belief that we could make this work on one hundred dollars and blind faith. Romantics just like me, I realized, believing in fairy tales and happily ever after.

They turned and held up their hands in a "What are you waiting for?" gesture.

Scared? Nadia didn't know the half of it. Still, I felt myself smile as my legs took me down the stairs. And we went through the door together, the three of us laughing and talking as we burst into the sunshine and the clean, fresh air. The midget, the giant, and me.

Sideshow Legal Services, Limitless Joy Our Specialty.

And just for today, I wouldn't drink.

God help us all.

# GRACE

Of all the rides on Centre Island, the swans have always been my favorite. Liz thought they were kind of lame because they weren't fast like the scrambler or scary like the haunted barrel works. But to me, they were the most beautiful things on the whole Island. Like graceful giants swimming in their own lagoon, just waiting for me to come take a ride.

Each swan is eight feet tall at the top of its beautiful neck and five feet across the middle with a big wide seat between the wings. The motors are electric and really quiet, and those birds are so easy to steer that even a little kid can take a turn with the tiller.

My mom didn't like to take us to Centre because she knew the people who used to live there and where the old streets were and everything. But Mark grew up on the other side of the bay, so he didn't think about any of that while we were standing in line for tickets. He just sat on a bench and waited while Liz and I went on all the rides, and he always made sure we ended with the swans.

Liz would start grumbling after less than a minute, but he

never made us quit early. Sometimes he'd even hand the operator another ticket so we could stay a little longer, because there
was something about gliding across the water, safe between those
wings, that always made me smile.

Still does in fact, but I wasn't heading for the swans when I
left the house this afternoon. I wasn't heading anywhere. I was
just getting away from all the sympathetic faces and the soothing
voices telling me that everything was going to be okay, because I
knew that wasn't true. How could everything be okay when the
last time my mom had been this mad was the day I went to live
with Liz—and everybody knew how long she stayed mad that
time.

She didn't believe me when I said that Liz and I were going
backpacking in Europe. Even after I showed her the travel book
Liz gave me, she just laughed and said that Europe was dirty and
overrated, just like the men. And I should stop being silly and get
ready for supper.

If she'd been home later that night when Liz came over, everything might have turned out differently. But she was out playing
bingo at the clubhouse and Liz said it was a sign. She said that if
I didn't pack a bag and get on the ferry right away, I'd never see
anything but the Island for the rest of my miserable life.

I left a note. *Dear Mom, I went with Liz. Love, Grace.*

The next day, she came looking for me. It was summer then
too, and I was sitting outside the café that was at the bottom of
Liz's building, talking to a man. I didn't know his name, but he
had a condo on the tenth floor and he bought me a cup of tea
because I didn't drink coffee then. He had two Persian cats and he
showed me a picture and said I could see them one day if I liked.

I knew better than to say yes because my mom had taught me
well, but she must have thought I'd forgotten because she came
up to the table and she said to the man in a really loud voice,
"Who are you and what are you doing with my daughter?"

"It's okay, Mom," I said. "We're just having coffee."

"That's what you think," she said, but I was pretty sure it was what the man thought too because I remember the way his eyes got real wide and his mouth opened and closed, but no words came out.

"What exactly are you up to?" she demanded, and people started to stare and the man got up and hurried away without his coffee, which was too bad because the cup was still almost full and he'd said it was good. Then my mom picked up my purse and told me it was time to stop all this nonsense and come home.

She started walking away with my purse, so I got up and followed. "I don't blame you," she said when I was beside her, "but if I get my hands on your sister, I may kill her."

"We were just having coffee," I said, watching the sidewalk pass under my feet as we walked.

She stopped and put her hands on my shoulders. "Grace, how many times do I have to tell you. Where men are concerned, there is no such thing as *just having coffee* for you. They only want one thing. Do you understand?"

I understood that she was talking about sex. And I also understood that I wasn't ever supposed to have any, even though Liz had some a lot, and she liked it too. Or so she said.

My mother put an arm through mine and started walking again. "Sweetheart, I understand that you miss Liz, but all this talk of Europe is just pipe-dreaming. You don't belong there and neither do I. We're Island girls, you and me. Team Donaldson. Together forever."

I kept watching my feet. You and me. Me and you. Together forever.

That's when the words finally came together and I stopped walking.

She almost tripped from stopping so fast, but she didn't yell. Just cupped a hand on my cheek and said real soft, "I'm sorry this is making you unhappy, Grace, but please don't worry. We'll be home soon and everything will be fine again."

That was the problem. If I went home, nothing would be fine. If I went home, we'd watch a movie and go to bed and get up in the morning and go to work and nothing would change. I'd never see Europe or have coffee with a man, or have sex or even get a chance to figure out if I wanted to, even though I was sure I did. But I didn't know how to say any of those things without causing a fight. So I did the only thing I could think of—I went limp. Just crumpled on the sidewalk the way she'd showed us so many times at the protests.

*Passive resistance, girls. Works every time.*

"What are you doing?" She took hold of my arm. "Get up right now."

I shook my head and tried to go even limper, become part of the sidewalk so she couldn't budge me. *Like a tree standing by the water*. That's the song she used to sing when we were little and helping her do the dishes. She'd start singing and waving her soapy hands in the air, and Liz and I would sing the chorus and dance, and those dishes were always done before I knew it.

I couldn't remember the last time we sang that song, but lying there on the ground with my eyes squeezed shut, the chorus came right back, and I started saying it real soft, over and over again. "Like a tree standing by the water, I will not be moved."

"Stop embarrassing yourself," she yelled and that's when she hit me, hard—the same way she hit me today. "Don't I have enough trouble without you acting like your sister?"

She pulled my hair to get me to stand up, but I wouldn't, and finally a lady came over and told her to stop, and my mom shoved her and said it was none of her business.

"You don't understand," she said when a policeman came and told my mother to back away. "This is my daughter," she explained. "She suffers from mild intellectual delay, and she's run away. I'm trying to take her home where she'll be safe."

"Ma'am, I need to you step back now," the officer said, and his partner took her by the shoulders.

"How dare you!" she yelled, and tried to break free.

She should have known that would only make him hold on tighter. But it wasn't until he said, "Ma'am, if you do not step back immediately, I *will* use the handcuffs," that she finally stopped struggling and let him move her back where I couldn't see her anymore.

Then the first policeman got down on his knees beside me. He was kind of cute with blue eyes and brown hair and when he leaned close I could smell peppermint and cigarettes, and I said, "You shouldn't smoke, you know." And he said, "You're absolutely right. Do you smoke?" I shook my head, and he said that was good. Then he started asking me more questions. My name, my address, how old I was. And finally, why was I lying on the sidewalk?

"Passive resistance," I told him, and he smiled. "Works every time," he said, and held out a hand. "So tell me, Grace, why don't you want to go home?"

I let him pull me to my feet. "I want to go with Liz," I said, and once the words started, they just kept on coming. I told him about Europe and backpacking and all the other things Liz said we were going to do. Then I pointed to her building down the street. "That's where she lives. On the twelfth floor, in a perfect little jewel box."

The officer nodded and said I should wait with his partner. And then he told my mother he didn't see any problem with me at all. I knew what I wanted and where I was going, and I was old enough to decide for myself. And it broke my heart when she started to cry. "Gracie, please," she whispered. "You can't do this to me."

Watching those tears fall on my mother's face might have been enough to make me change my mind, but suddenly Liz was there, talking to the police, telling them I didn't have to go home. I could live with her. And when the officer said I could go and Liz tugged on my arm, I didn't fight, so I guess they weren't enough after all, which made me cry too, because I'd left my mother there on the street with tears on her face, begging me to come home.

Liz took me shopping for clothes and that night we went out to a bar. I had a Cosmopolitan and we clinked our glasses and toasted the dirty men of Europe. For the first time in my life, I danced with a man I hadn't known all of my life. A man who held me close and made my head swim and told me I was the most beautiful woman he had ever seen, and I couldn't understand how any of that could be bad.

When we got home, I phoned my mom, but she wouldn't answer. I left a message, but she didn't call back. Not only was she *being consistent* and *sticking to her guns*, she was mad and she wasn't going to forgive me for a long, long time. Which is why I was drifting around in a swan by myself in the middle of the afternoon, because who knew how long it would be before my mom forgave me for not canceling those appointments—and I was in no hurry to find out.

Lucky for me, Ryan James was the operator that day because I'd known him since he was born and my mom did his mom's hair, which counted for more than most people imagined. I handed him a dozen tickets when I got there, and he said they weren't that busy and I could stay on the swan as long as I wanted. But after two hours, he was starting to look at me funny every time I went by the dock. So I kept as far away as I could, hoping he'd concentrate on the other swans and forget all about the one floating in the shade at the far end of the lagoon.

In fact, I was so busy trying not to look at the dock, I might have missed Jocelyn altogether if she hadn't hollered, "What is up with you? A person could die trying to find you in this heat."

She was standing beside Ryan, all bright red hair and sweaty white makeup with black eyeliner slowly running down her cheeks. She held up both of her hands and hollered, "Well?"

So much for not being noticed.

I smiled at the people who had turned their swans around to see who the strange-looking girl was yelling at, and then I aimed my swan for the dock.

"What are you doing here anyway?" Jocelyn asked. "People are looking for you."

"I'm riding a swan." Ryan reached out with his hook and dragged me the rest of the way in. "And I really hope I'm not finished yet."

He shrugged. "Get in," he said to Jocelyn, then held the swan steady while she climbed into the seat beside me. "But you gotta get out soon."

"We will," I promised, and headed the swan over to the shade again.

"This is what you've been doing all afternoon?" Jocelyn raised a brow at me. "Why?"

"Because it's fun."

"Are you kidding? This totally sucks." She smacked my hand away from the tiller. "Let me drive."

I took a tissue out of my pocket and held it out to her. "Who's looking for me?"

She waved it away. "No one's looking for you. I only said it to make you feel bad. Did it work?"

"Not even a little." I sat back and let her steer. "What happened at the house after I left?"

"All your clients went over to Lori's and said they were never coming back." I stared at her and she shook her head. "Jesus, Grace, I'm joking. Don't take everything so seriously. Where's the gas pedal on this thing?"

"There isn't one." I passed her the tissue again. "You really should take this because you've got eyeliner down to your chin."

"That's how I like it." But she took the tissue anyway and dabbed at her cheeks, her chin, and the delicate area under her eyes. "So how do you make this thing go faster?"

"You don't, which is why I like it." I reached a hand over the side, trailing my fingers through the water. "They won't do donuts either, so don't even try."

She sighed heavily, then aimed our swan for the tail of another that was carrying a couple of girls about her age.

"And it's not bumper swans. If you hit someone, Ryan will throw us out." I put a hand on the tiller and turned us just in time. "If no one went to Lori's, what did happen?"

"They all dried their hair and went home. Said they'd come back next week."

"Everybody?"

"Except that Judi person. She went over to Lori's, but everyone else was willing to wait. People seem to like you, although I can't figure out why."

I felt myself relax a little more and this time it had nothing to do with the swan. "What about the mockingbirds? How are they?"

"They're fine. The male is still busy chasing all the other birds out of the yard, and Mary Anne is making sure the cats don't get lady mockingbird." She frowned. "I still feel like an idiot saying that."

"I don't know why. It's what she is. Did she eat anything?"

"She drank a little water. Some lady came by and said we should take her to the wildlife refuge in the city, but I told her the bird would probably die if we moved her around again and she should mind her own business. And I think the male agreed because he dive-bombed her on the way out."

I smiled, picturing it. I still felt bad about leaving them, but knew that Mary Anne would take good care of the lady. "Did you hear from your dad?"

"He called twice. Said they went back to the house on Algonquin after canoeing and your mom was feeling a lot better." She kept her eyes on the swan in front of us. "What happened today wasn't your fault, you know that, don't you?"

"Of course it was my fault. My mom told me to do something and I didn't. I messed everything up."

"You didn't mess up. Nobody cared that there was water on the counter or hair on the floor. And what was that shit about the music being wrong? Who doesn't like Motown?"

"Nobody, but it's not what she plays. She likes to create a certain mood and I didn't do that."

"So what? You created a new mood, and people liked it." She punched me in the arm. "You did good. Your mother overreacted because she's crazy."

"You sound like Liz." I put my hand over hers, turning the swan before she could ram those girls. "You drive the swan like her too."

"Is that a bad thing?" she asked, heading us straight into the sun this time.

I laughed and shielded my eyes with a hand. "It was fun because she'd get bored real fast and start making up games, like Pirate Swans and Spy Swans."

"Pirates could be good," Jocelyn said, weaving us around and through the other swans, the way Liz did when we played Slalom Swans.

"Pirates were okay, but my favorite was Getaway Swans. We'd pretend we'd stolen something big, like diamonds from some lady at the yacht club, and we had to make our getaway in a swan. We'd pretend that all the other swans were cops, and we had to keep from being cornered by any of them. If we got surrounded and couldn't get out without touching one of them, the game was over and we had to start again."

"Could be fun," Jocelyn said, turning us back to the shade.

"It was." I smiled, remembering. "She used to promise that one day, we'd do it for real. Steal a swan and make a run for it. If anyone tried to stop us, we wouldn't pay any attention. We'd just wave like the queen and keep right on going, straight out of the lagoon and into the lake. We wouldn't stop until we reached St. Catharine's or Niagara Falls or even Rochester."

Jocelyn shook her head. "The battery wouldn't last that long. You'd probably make it to Grimsby. Maybe even St. Catharine's. But Rochester? I doubt it."

I laughed. "Grimsby would have been fine. Anywhere would have been fine."

"Did you ever do it? Did you ever break out?"

"No because it can't be done."

"My dad would say there's no such word as can't." Jocelyn took us over to the black plastic strip that marked the end of the swan lagoon. "Looks like it's just a matter of getting over this line."

"Won't work. The propeller would get stuck, and then the operator would have to come and pull you off and your ride would be over. But it doesn't matter anyway because even if you could get over the line, you couldn't get past that bridge." I pointed to the footbridge by the café. "It's built low so nothing fits underneath. No canoes, no motorboats. Definitely no swans." I lowered my arm and closed my eyes. "The only place the swans can go is around this lagoon."

"Then I was right. They totally suck." Her phone beeped, and I knew that meant she had a text message and not a phone call. She let go of the tiller and flipped open her phone. "Let's go do the flume ride," she said while she read her message. "That looked kind of fun."

"Definitely Liz." I took control of the swan and pulled Mark's phone out of my pocket, checking to make sure it was still on for the four-hundredth time that day. I must have called Liz a dozen times since I got in the swan, but she wouldn't have recognized the number, couldn't have known it was me on the other end, so she never answered. Just kept letting it go to voice mail. I left a bunch of messages but who knew how long it would be before she checked them?

"Shit," Jocelyn muttered. "They're on the ferry already."

"Who?"

"My friends. They said they were coming tonight to see the mockingbirds. But they're coming now." She dropped her head back and stared at the sky. "Shit, shit, shit."

"I'll bet your dad doesn't like it when you swear."

She sat up and typed real fast with her thumbs, sending a message back. "He's never said anything."

"He's probably hoping you'll grow out of it. Like he's hoping you'll grow out of your hair."

She smoothed her bangs down over her forehead. "I like my hair. It makes a statement."

"Like stop?"

"More like, I don't care what anyone thinks." She stuffed the phone back into her pocket. "I gotta go. I can't be seen in this thing. How come that guy hasn't called our number yet?"

"Because he's waiting for me to wave and let him know we're done."

"Then wave because I have to get off."

When I didn't, she reached for the tiller, but I kept a firm grip on it and held my phone out to her. "Show me how to do that first."

"Do what?"

"Send a text."

She waved to Ryan on the dock. "You don't know how to send a text?"

"I never had a phone." I shook my head at Ryan and he put his microphone back on the hook. "You can wave all day if you like, but he won't pay attention. He'll keep waiting for me."

"You really are the evil re . . . girl." She turned back to me. "If I show you how to text, can we go in?" I nodded and she took the phone. "Hey, this is my dad's."

"He gave it to me last night."

"Thank God. I felt like such a tool knowing he carried around a second phone just for me.  The Jocelyn Hotline he called it, which is so lame it hurts. But as cell phone's go, this one's pretty good, plus it's got a QWERTY keyboard." She turned the phone on its side and opened it in a way I didn't know you could. "See? It's like a regular keyboard. All you have to do is hit Favorites, and then Text Message." She showed me how to use Contacts, and where the symbols were and how to make capitals and numbers, and I knew I wouldn't remember any of it.

When she finished I said, "Show me again."

She gritted her teeth and growled at me. Then she checked the shore on both sides and held out the phone. "You take this and I'll walk you through it. Pay attention this time. First you have to pull up Favorites. Push that button there. Not that one, the one under Favorites. Oh my God, Grace, can you even say favorites?"

She growled and rolled her eyes a lot, but she did go slower this time and she didn't call me names, which was nice because I could tell how hard that was for her. We went over it again and again while we cruised the lagoon until bit by bit, I learned where the buttons were and how to type the message and even how to put capitals on the words. I didn't think I'd ever learn how to put in symbols, but who cared? I was ready to send my first text ever to Liz!

With Jocelyn watching closely, I punched in her number, I hit Next, and I typed my message: *Hi Liz this is me Grace I have this phone now Send a message back Your sister Grace*

"She knows you're her sister," Jocelyn said. "The point of a text is to be brief, to keep it short and snappy. So take that line out."

I took it out and pressed Send. "How long before she writes back?"

"Who knows? It's up to her now." She pulled out her phone again and wrote a message of her own. *Whr R U?* I repeated that in my head a few times and finally figured it out. She meant *Where are you?* If that was short and snappy, it would be a while before I mastered it.

My phone made a funny jingling noise. "Is that a text or a call?"

"It's a text. Press this to read it."

She didn't have to show me that one twice. I pressed the button and up popped a message from Liz: *Holy shit, UR texting!!! Whr RU?* Short and snappy struck again. Rats.

"Hit Reply," Jocelyn said. "Then answer her."

*I am in a swan with Jocelyn.*

"Too long," she said. "Just say 'In swan with Jocelyn.'"

Within seconds, Liz came back. *Send a pic!*

I held out the phone to Jocelyn and she did the usual eye roll. "You don't know how to take pictures either?"

I shook my head, she sighed, and we went around the lagoon a few more times before I could say "Got it" with confidence. Then I held the phone in front of us and she leaned in until our heads were touching and I pressed OK. "Now what?"

"Now you send it."

It didn't take me as long to get the sending part, so the picture went off to Liz and then I typed a message. *Jocelyn is Marks daughter.*

In under a minute a picture and a message came back. *Hi Mark's daughter. This is me.*

Liz was sticking her tongue out. Jocelyn laughed and we took a picture of us sticking our tongues out and the two girls in the swan giggled as they went past.

The picture went to Liz and a text came back saying, *Very attractive. How is Mark?*

*Mark is fine Whr R U*

*Cemetery.* She included a picture of herself among the headstones.

Jocelyn drew her head back. "Your sister goes to cemeteries?"

"Just this one."

Jocelyn tipped the phone so she could see the screen better. "Why?"

"Because I can't." I sent back a message. *Did U put flowers*

Jocelyn sat back. "I hate cemeteries. People always think it must bother me that my mom wanted to be buried in Quebec with her parents instead of here where we could visit more often, but it doesn't. In fact, I'm kind of glad because cemeteries are sad places. Why would you even want to go to that one anyway?"

I felt my face warm and kept my eyes on the screen. "Because that's where my son is buried."

*Flwrs alwys*, came back followed by, *Want a pic?*

Jocelyn stared at me. "You had a son?"

I nodded.

"What was his name?"

"William," I whispered, because that's what I always do. Because my mom doesn't like me to talk about him. Because that's dredging up the past and I'll only get sad all over again.

The phone jingled. Liz asked one more time. *Want a pic?*

"She wants to send you a picture of the grave?" Jocelyn pointed at the screen. "Now that's creepy."

"It's not creepy. She knows I've never seen it."

A mother with two little boys stared at Jocelyn as they went past. Jocelyn smiled and gave them the finger. "You haven't seen your own son's grave? What the hell is wrong with you people?"

I pushed her hand down and mouthed *Sorry* to the mom. "Nothing's wrong. I just wasn't allowed."

"Not allowed? You're an adult. He was your kid. Who could possibly stop you?"

"You'd be surprised."

I realized my palms were sweaty. Did I want to see a picture? Did I want to *dredge up the past*? I automatically turned and checked the dock. Half-expecting to see my mom shaking her head, telling me no, making my mind up for me. Only she wasn't there. I had to decide for myself.

I wiped my hands on my shorts, swallowed the first trace of a lump in my throat, and typed, *I think so* before I could change my mind.

The picture was in front of me so fast it felt like magic. A small bronze plaque on a board with a bunch of other small bronze plaques. There wasn't much information. No room to say that he'd had a beautiful smile and a real belly laugh that made everyone who heard it laugh too. But his name was written out in full. William James Donaldson. Named for his great-great grandfather.

Liz sent another picture. The flowers she brought for him. White daisies. "The happiest flowers in the world," she always said, and even in winter she took white daisies and scattered the petals on our boy.

"That's not a grave," Jocelyn said, tipping her head to the side. "What is that?"

"A plaque. He was cremated, like all the other Donaldsons."

Only his ashes weren't buried in the garden with Great-Grandma Lucy and Granny Rose. William's ashes had been left there in St. James Cemetery. Tossed in the Scattering Garden because it was better for me that way. No daily reminders of what I'd lost.

I'd never seen the garden, so Liz's third picture was a surprise. The thing looked more like a concrete bathtub than a garden to me. But the roses inside it were pretty, and the petals from Liz's happy flowers looked like snow on the ground around them.

That lump in my throat got bigger and the end of my nose started to sting and if I didn't put the phone down I was going to cry. And you don't cry in a swan. That's a rule. You can cry on the Ferris wheel or on the sky ride but not in a swan. That would ruin everything.

I typed as fast as I could. *Got to go Call U later*
*Say hi to Mark 4 me.*

I closed the phone and slipped it into my pocket and wished I had a water bottle with me. "We should go in now," I said to Jocelyn, pointing the swan at the dock.

"Thank God." She leaned back with her hands behind her head. "You can send that picture to your e-mail you know. Save it on your computer and print it if you want."

"I can't do that. My mom would say it's morbid and make me take it down."

"Then leave it on the desktop as wallpaper."

"I can't do that either. She checks my computer to see what I've been doing. She doesn't know I know, but I do, so I have to be really careful."

"Or you could use a password."

"I've tried that. She always finds a way in."

"She won't if you use one of my passwords, guaranteed." We were almost at the dock when suddenly she sat up straight and said, "Oh shit," and then ducked down into the bottom of the swan. "Turn us around! Turn us around!"

I made a hard left, taking us back out into the lagoon. "Why? What's wrong?"

"My friends are there by the ticket booth."

Sure enough, a group of four kids around Jocelyn's age were standing in line. Two boys and two girls, wearing jeans and T-shirts. No stop-sign red hair, no black eyeliner. Only Jocelyn had both of those. Funny how she'd gone to so much trouble to stand out, and now all she wanted to do was disappear.

"What are they doing?" she asked.

"I think they're buying tickets."

She groaned. "Why can't they ever just do what they say they're going to do?"

"What did they say they'd do?"

"Send me a message as soon as they got here."

"Maybe they're giving you a little more time."

"Maybe." But she didn't sound convinced. "Give me that tissue again." She started rubbing the rest of the black off her cheeks. "What are they doing now?"

"Getting tickets." I glanced down at her. "What difference does it make if they see you anyway? I thought you didn't care what other people think."

"They're not people, they're my friends." She kept rubbing. "Are they gone?"

"Nope, in fact they're coming this way. Maybe they're going to ride the swans too."

"That would not be good." She huddled deeper into the bottom. "I can't believe this. They're supposed to be here to see the mockingbird, not ride a stupid swan. And they weren't even supposed to come in the day. They were supposed to come tonight to hear him singing."

"Maybe it's better they're here now. Maybe he won't sing at night now that the lady mockingbird has found him," I grinned at her. "It'll be fun to find out."

"Or maybe it'll be so boring they'll never come back. And if my dad doesn't let me start taking the ferry on my own soon, I'll be stuck riding this swan all summer." She glanced up at me. "No offense. It's just not doing for me what it does for you. How's my face?"

"You've got a bit right there. And I'm sure your friends will have a good time with you no matter what."

"That's because you don't know my friends. Are they in line for a swan?"

"No, they're walking away." I smiled at her. "It's safe to come up now."

She poked her head up and took one last look around before getting back into the seat. As soon as she was settled, she whipped her head around and pointed a finger at the man in the swan beside us. "What the fuck are you looking at?"

The family who had been watching us turned their swan away as quickly as they could and headed for the dock.

"He's probably going to report you for using bad words. Happened to Liz all the time."

"So what? We're done here anyway." She knocked my hand off the tiller. "We're going in now. How's my face?"

"Fine," I said, dabbing at one last spot of black on her cheek.

When we reached the dock, Ryan said the man had definitely reported her, but he didn't care. We could keep going if we wanted. I shook my head, told him thanks but we had to go, so he reached out with his hook and hauled us into the dock. The moment her feet were on the ground, Jocelyn took out her phone and started hitting the buttons. "I need to find out where they are," she said, her head bent over the phone as we walked up the ramp. "Get them to meet me at the fountain."

"That won't work," I said, "because they're right there."

She snapped her head up. "What? Where?"

"By the tree." I started to raise a hand to show her, but she slapped it down.

"I see them. Shit. And they see me too. Shit again."

The taller of the two boys called, "Hey, Goth girl. How's it going?"

"Good," she called back, and I watched her face soften and her smile turn shy as the four of them came toward us. "Do not follow me," she muttered, and walked away.

I understood her need for privacy, but I was curious, I couldn't help it. So I took out my phone and practiced my texting skills while I listened. I found out that the taller boy's name was Sean and the girls' names were Alex and Courtney. The two of them giggled the way some girls do, and Jocelyn smiled and nodded with them, but her eyes kept returning to the shorter of the two boys. His name was Josh—the one who'd had the party.

"You're so lucky," the one named Courtney said. "It would be so cool to spend the summer on the Island."

"You wouldn't say that if you had to be here." Jocelyn turned that shy little smile to Josh. "How was the party?"

He was thin but good-looking. Clean-cut, my mother would have said. The kind you should instinctively mistrust. Then again, you were supposed to be watchful around long-hairs, business types, tradesmen, men who were unemployed, and anyone who worked at the park, so what difference did it make? But Josh seemed okay. He had a nice smile and when he said, "It would have been more fun if you'd been there," and put an arm around her shoulder, Jocelyn looked surprised but she didn't pull away, so I figured he must be a nice boy.

"Let's go see that bird," he said, but as they turned to go, the girl named Alex glanced over at me. Her eyes flicked down from my face to my shoes and back up again, pausing a moment to read my WHAT WOULD BUDDHA DO? T-shirt before returning to my face. "Is that the retard?"

Jocelyn's face went as red as her hair. "Her name's Grace. Let's get out of here."

She glanced back once as they walked away. And I was the only one who saw the little wave of her fingers.

# RUBY

Within a few hours of my meltdown, I was fine again. Medicated, exercised, and more than lucid enough to grasp the full impact of the disaster I'd created. Mark kept me away from the house for the rest of the day, canoeing in the lagoons, hiding out in the café, even napping at his place. Anywhere was fine by me as long as I didn't have to face Grace's tears or tell Mary Anne the truth or think about clients who might or might not come back again. If Mark was hurting from his run-in with the taxi, he kept it to himself while we paddled and ate and talked—about the Boy Scout jamboree on Snake Island, the flashy new sailboats at the yacht clubs, the fabulous food at the Rectory Café. Anything but what had happened or what it meant, while Big Al sat smugly between us, smiling and waiting for my next performance.

It was almost dark when Mark finally took me home. Jocelyn and her friends were there, the five of them huddled around the bird-in-a-box while the other one, the healthy one, sat up high in the lilac bush singing for them. Someone needed to shoot that thing.

Grace was there too, of course, sitting alone by the birdbath, still tiptoeing around me, giving me a wide berth, as though I might bite if she got too close. Mary Anne must have been at her window all day because the moment Mark opened my gate, she came trotting over with a box of my favorite cookies—white chocolate and macadamia nut—to have our little chat.

I sighed and let her follow us into the house, let her make tea and set out her cookies. When the first cookie was halfway to her lips, I finally said the three little words that would change everything forever. "I have Alzheimer's."

Her face froze for a heartbeat and then it began. The falling cookie, the watery eyes, the gentle, fluttering touch—that god-awful sympathy I'd been dreading since the diagnosis.

"Why didn't you tell me?" she asked, sliding her chair closer.

"I didn't tell anyone." I stared at her hand on mine. Wanted to pick it up, put it back where it belonged, and tell her to stuff her sympathy. But it seemed a lot of bother for nothing.

"You obviously told Mark," she said, her tone only a little accusing, only slightly hurt.

"Just a few days ago," he said. "And only because she needed a lawyer."

"Liz knows too," I said. "For all the good it did." I met those watery eyes again. "But Grace still hasn't been told and I want to keep it that way. You can't say a word to her or anyone else, do you understand?"

"But—"

"Mary Anne, I'll make it public when I'm ready."

Which might be tomorrow. The story of my meltdown was probably all over the Island by now anyway, so what difference did it make.

I got to my feet. "I'm going to bed. Tell Grace I said good night. And tell her I don't bite."

"She's just afraid you're still angry with her," Mary Anne said. "You really scared her."

"That makes two of us." I went up the stairs, leaving her and Mark to discuss me, my condition, my prognosis, anything that made them feel better while I popped an extra sleeping pill and hoped it kept me from hearing that goddamn mockingbird.

The next morning I slept in, waking up at nine to the sun streaming through my window and the mockingbird still in good voice. Ignoring my own notes and signs, I didn't pull on my shorts and T-shirt. Didn't tie up my hair. Didn't do anything but close the bedroom door and go down the stairs. Mark was there already, or perhaps he'd never left, standing at the stove flipping French toast with cinnamon, another favorite. Mary Anne was there too, sitting at the table, sworn to secrecy and twitching with questions. She rose and hugged me, kissed my cheek, asked how my night had been.

"Uneventful," I told her, leaving out the dreams, the sweats, and the fact that the pills hadn't stopped me from hearing that damn bird.

"Breakfast is almost ready," Mark said.

"Where's Grace?" I asked.

"Outside with Jocelyn." Mary Anne nodded at the window. "Keeping the cats away from the mockingbird."

The bird-in-a-box. Yes, I remembered.

I glanced over at the answering machine. Saw the flashing light and wondered how long it had been doing that. Pressed the button and wished I hadn't as soon as the first message started. "Oh, Ruby, I do hope everything is okay," from Audrey, who had been here yesterday. "We were so worried about you, Ruby," from Joannie on Algonquin, who was probably spreading the story even as I listened to the message. And the one that truly bothered me: "What the hell was that?" from Grace's client, Marla.

I drummed my fingers on the counter and stared at the phone, knowing damage control should start immediately with a call to each and every woman who had been caught in the storm. Followed by a visit to the neighbors, anyone who might have heard my outburst and be wondering, talking about what was wrong with Ruby. And there was Grace to consider as well. Poor Grace who was still outside with the crippled bird. On the lookout for cats so she wouldn't have to come near me.

I could see her through the window, sitting by the birdbath with Jocelyn, the two of them watching the healthy mockingbird dance high above them on a wire. Flicking his tail and flapping his wings, putting on a show for his biggest fans.

The thing might be cute if he'd shut up once in a while. I'd never heard anything like it. He went on and on, sounding like a robin one minute, a cardinal the next, and God only knew what kind of bird after that. He even sounded like a cell phone a couple of times, which was entertaining at first, but was truly annoying at three in the morning.

I turned back to the answering machine. Thought about making those calls. Was reaching for the receiver in fact, when Big Al asked if I had a story ready. Something believable to explain my behavior.

I drew my hand back, closed my fingers up tight, and was still staring at the machine, waiting for inspiration, when Mark announced that breakfast was ready. I walked over to the stove, looked into the pan.

French toast with cinnamon. My favorite.

"Sit here," Mary Anne said, pulling out a chair in front of a place mat laid with cutlery and a napkin. A glass of orange juice on the left, a cup of tea on the right. When had she done that? I wondered and glanced over at the answering machine. There was no rush, Big Al said. I had all day to make those calls.

I spotted my notebook on the counter as I sat down. I should pick it up. Start today's list, keep it current so I didn't forget anything. But again, I had all day and Mark had set a plate in front of me. French toast with cinnamon. My favorite. So I left the notebook where it was and picked up the fork instead. Ate the toast, drank the tea. Heard Mark ask, "Do you want to go canoeing after breakfast?" I shook my head, took both meds and vitamins with the orange juice, and Big Al and I went back to bed.

By Monday morning, both Mary Anne and Mark had stopped being nice. They made me call the doctor. Stood beside me while I explained what had happened, adding enough of their own observations to the conversation that the doctor finally asked who was with me. "Former friends," I told her.

"Were either of them with you when the outburst happened?"

"Both."

"Put one of them on."

And by eleven o'clock, the three of us were sitting in her waiting room, waiting.

Instead of having the receptionist call my name, Dr. Mistry came out herself and scanned the room. For the first time since I'd started coming to her, my impossibly young and pretty doctor had come looking for me. She spotted me in the corner. Smiled like she was genuinely glad to see me. "Come on in, Ruby," she said. "And bring your friends."

Friends? I looked from Mark to Mary Anne, and then back at the doctor. "Why would I do that?"

"Because I need to talk to all of you."

"They have nothing to do with this."

Her smiled hardened, became frighteningly professional. "Ruby, things have changed. It's time to talk about your options whether you like it or not. Your friends clearly care about you, and it's best if they're there when we do."

Then she walked away, discussion closed. Making it clear my opinion mattered for nothing, and Big Al laughed.

Mary Anne rose. "You heard the doctor. Let's go."

Mark offered me a hand. "She did sound like her mind was made up."

I let him help me up, let them lead the way. I'd probably get lost anyway.

My doctor's consulting room was large, bright, and filled with plants. Spider plants, Boston fern, ficus trees, and potted palms. Together with the bamboo furniture and soft chintz cushions, they give the room the feel of a conservatory instead of a medical office. The only giveaway being the massive oak desk in the middle, with her on one side and the patient on the other.

I took my usual chair, the one closest to the door. Mary Anne sat on my left. Mark dragged over a third chair and sat on my right, blocking my exit. Dr. Mistry smiled again and folded her hands on the desk. "Ruby, I'm not the bully you think I am right now, I'm simply worried about you. But I do need to confirm that you're okay with having me discuss your situation with your friends present before we go any further."

I shrugged. "Sure, why not?" There were no secrets anymore anyway. What was the worst that could happen?

"All right, then." The doctor sat back, clearly relieved. "Why don't you tell me again what happened on the weekend."

I went over it for her, leaving nothing out because honesty with your medical practitioner is the key to good treatment. When I was finished, she turned to Mark. "Tell me what happened."

He told the same story I did, and when he was finished she asked if Mary Anne wanted to add anything. She shook her head and Dr. Mistry turned back to me, the monkey in the middle.

"Ruby, I know how difficult that episode must have been for you, but I believe it was the wake-up call you've needed, and having your friends here today is a real step forward. It means you're finally moving past the anger and denial into acceptance, which means you're ready to deal with the future in a realistic manner." She leaned forward, her earnest-doctor expression sitting awkwardly on her lovely young face. "I can't tell you how relieved I am to finally look across this desk and see people with you. But before we proceed, I need to be sure that they're fully aware of what it means to be a caregiver."

And there it was, the worst that could happen.

"Caregivers?" I shook my head. "Absolutely not. No. Never."

"I can be whatever she needs," Mark said.

"The same goes for me," Mary Anne added.

"She needs someone to look after her," Dr. Mistry chimed in, the three of them completely ignoring me. Paying no attention at all when I repeated, "Absolutely not. I forbid it."

"Do you both know what that will entail as time goes on?" the good doctor asked.

Mary Anne smiled at me. "Ruby and I have been friends since we were children. She's more like a sister than my real sister ever was. I know what this illness does, the toll it takes on relationships, and I will be with her whether she likes it or not."

"And I plan to be with her for years to come," Mark said.

"You would," I muttered, and he smiled. Bastard.

"Very well," Dr. Mistry said, and launched into one of her tedious, inspirational speeches. "It's important to know that we're all on the same track."

I wanted to stop her, to point out that both Mark and Mary Anne worked full time, and Mark didn't even live on the Island. He was merely a summer visitor with a daughter and a law practice. Neither of my dear, stupid friends had time to worry about me on a daily basis.

But Dr. Mistry was on a roll and I couldn't find an appropriate break in her monologue, a spot to interject and object. So I sat back and listened to her talk about *the need for a positive attitude* and the *trouble with depression* and *getting myself a buddy, someone else with Alzheimer's whom I could e-mail or visit with*. Nothing that was new or even vaguely interesting, until she said, "I'm going to adjust your medication again." At last she had my full attention.

She dragged her prescription pad toward her and started to

write. "We've been seeing success with smaller doses given more frequently throughout the day. Fewer side effects like nightmares and restlessness. I'm also going to give you something to relax you, something to help keep your stress in check."

Something to relax you. And thus it began. The slow march toward medicated numbness.

Contrary to what the good doctor assumed, I had been taking a realistic approach to my future from the moment she gave me the bad news. Not only had I read every book and pamphlet, visited every blog, and watched every movie or documentary ever made, I also volunteered at a long-term care center for a while, just to be sure I was making the right decision.

As a result, I was well aware of the rush to quell all negative emotion and outbursts, all depression and sadness in Alzheimer's patients, and the success of antidepressants in the treatment of this problem. So successful in fact that a sort of apathy took over, leading to that "oh well, what will be will be" attitude that I'd found so frightening in the people I'd met.

Some of them felt nothing anymore. No tears or anger, certainly, but also no laughter and no joy. No extremes of any kind. Just a constant, frustrating calm, which must have caused even more stress in its own way and kept the cycle of medication going. And now it was my turn.

Dr. Mistry put down her pen and handed me two separate pages from her little pad. "You're going to be taking medications several times a day, and Mark, Mary Anne, that's where you come in. I need to know she's getting what she needs when she needs it." Then, as if she'd been reading my mind, she said, "You're both probably still working and undoubtedly have busy lives. No one can reasonably expect you to be with her all the time, so she'll need to start thinking about hiring someone to come in on a daily basis." She opened a drawer, took out three pamphlets, and slid one across the desk to each of us. But it was only me she looked at.

"I'm talking about a companion, Ruby, not a nurse. Someone to oversee the medications and help you get through the day. Do a little light housework and cooking as well." She stood up and came around the desk. Knelt down in front of me. "I know it's not something you've wanted to think about, let alone investigate, but the time has come to call a few of these agencies, get their prices, and discuss services. You'd be surprised how many of my patients develop a real attachment to their companions. It's a win-win situation for everyone."

Win-win. That was one way of putting it, I suppose. Although woe-woe felt more apt.

Mary Anne was reading the pamphlet in her slow and careful way, but Mark folded his up and put it into his pocket without looking at it. There would be time later, I supposed. While I was sitting neatly in a chair bothering no one. My difficult nature safely stored in a bottle and put away on a shelf so those around me could get on with their day. A little light housekeeping. A little cooking.

My mouth went dry and I drew in a deep breath. I opened my purse, put the pamphlet and the prescriptions inside. Snapped it shut.

"Make sure you fill those prescriptions today." The doctor rose, and repeated it to Mark and Mary Anne. "Make sure she fills them today."

They both nodded, but said nothing. They were probably as overwhelmed as I was. And no wonder. You took someone to a simple appointment and wound up tethered to a nut bar for God only knew how long.

Dr. Mistry went to the door, opened it, and waited for us to approach. "One of the agencies I've been talking about holds a meeting downstairs every couple of months as a service to Alzheimer's patients and their caregivers. There's one starting in a few minutes and I think you'd all benefit from it." She followed us out into the hall and down to the receptionist's desk, where she picked up a card and handed it to Mark. "Take the elevator down to the basement and look for room B114." She checked her watch. "They'll just be assembling now, so hurry."

The three of us hurried as instructed, arriving at the same time as most of the other participants. Men and women from fifty to ninety, all shapes, sizes, and colors. Husbands and wives, parents and children, friends and friends—patients and caregivers two by two. We were the only group of three and I suppose I should have felt special, but to be honest I just felt empty.

We joined the line, smiling and nodding to the people around us. Sometimes it was easy to tell who was patient and who was caregiver, but in most cases it was more difficult. Like the three of us I hoped, standing straighter, smiling brighter, wondering if anyone could tell just by looking that I was the one who danced with Big Al.

We shuffled forward, finally reaching a table just inside the door where a perky young woman greeted us with a cheery, "Hello and welcome. Have you been with us before?"

We shook our heads and she smiled more. "Well, you couldn't have picked a better day. Dr. Gregory Bonnett is here to talk about the Stepping-Stones to Happiness."

I was thinking that red wine should be one of the steps when she pointed to a clipboard. "Sign in there please and I'll give you these stick-on name tags. First names are all we need." She laughed and pushed a handful of Sharpie markers toward us. "Can't expect everyone to remember everyone else right away, can we?"

We nodded, smiled back, and wrote our names on the tags. Stuck them to our shirts and moved on to the clipboard. Six columns: *Date, Name, Caregiver or Patient, Phone Number, E-mail, Address.* "You don't have to leave your personal information," Perky said. "But if you'd like to be contacted about upcoming events, we'll put you on our mailing list."

While Mary Anne and I had never been fans of group encounters—except those that happened naturally in my shop on

a regular basis—Mark had always been a true believer in organized support groups, regularly referring his legal aid clients to
everything from anger management workshops to sex addiction
networks. I always suspected the sex one was more social than
self-help, but I knew that AA had been a big help to Mark when he
was younger, and his faith in group hugs was real, so I had always
kept my opinion to myself.

Given his views, it was only natural that he started to relax
as Perky went on to name a few of the workshops they were excited to have on their Upcoming Events list. And he was the first
Musketeer to put his name on the clipboard, complete with a
phone number and an e-mail address. Mary Anne followed suit,
and I went them both one better, providing not only my phone
and e-mail but my home address as well. *In for a nickel, in for a
dime*, as Grandma Lucy used to say. Who could tell? Perhaps the
good doctor was right. Perhaps this would be good for me. And
perhaps with a few antidepressants under my belt, I'd even come
to believe it.

Another woman, far less cheerful than Perky, herded us forward. The room was typical of basement meeting spots. White
walls, brown stacking chairs lined up in rows in front of a podium,
a screen for the presentation, and two doors leading into smaller
areas. Along one wall was a table with coffee and cookies, and
along another a few tables with flyers, cards, and a display board
highlighting those Upcoming Events and a man signing copies of
a book—Dr. Gregory Bonnett and the Stepping-Stones to Happiness. Fifteen dollars, tax included.

We wandered past the board and the tables, Mary Anne and
Mark picking up a few more flyers, politely sidestepping the line
for Dr. Bonnett's book. I paused beside a stand-up display for
something called a Caregivers Expo. A two-day event to be held
in some convention center that promised to be "filled to bursting with businesses and nonprofit agencies catering to the needs
of caregivers, each offering ideas, products, and services to make

the care-giving journey more enjoyable and assist in problem solving."

A trade show for Alzheimer's. Who knew?

"Ladies and gentlemen," Less-Than-Perky called. "Today's meeting will start with a special presentation of Stepping-Stones to Happiness, "Finding Your Way Forward through Alzheimer's," courtesy of our guest, Dr. Gregory Bonnett. After that, we'll break for coffee and then we'll move on to the separate caregiver and patient meetings." Here she indicated the two doors. Caregivers on the left, patients on the right. I could hardly wait.

Seats were filling up quickly, leaving us to choose between the front row and the three seats left in the back. We went with the back row, nodding and murmuring hellos to the people around us as we settled in and Dr. Bonnet took his place behind the podium.

"Good afternoon, ladies and gentlemen, and let me say how pleased I am to be part of this very special lunchtime presentation."

He was short and blond with the overeager look of a salesman. Glad that I hadn't thought to bring cash, I shoved my purse under the seat and leaned back while he continued. "Ladies and gentlemen, I'm going to take you on a journey along the Stepping-Stones to Happiness." He picked up a clicker and got things rolling with a PowerPoint presentation, complete with music.

The Stepping-Stones were merely a repackaging of the things Grandma Lucy used to say, including *Be Positive*, *Have Respect*, and *Trust in God*. He added a few that were Alzheimer's specific like *Do Puzzles*, *Keep Active*, *Find a Buddy*, and I knew what Dr. Mistry had been reading lately.

"The challenges of Alzheimer's affect us all," he said, and after about fifteen minutes, I started thinking that the coffee smelled good and cookies would be nice and that the man in front of me must be a hundred years old, when finally, the doctor stopped talking and started a movie.

"This is something very personal that I want to share. A video I made about a year ago when my wife was in the late stages of the illness. I think it illustrates the importance of what I've been saying. The need to look for joy, a silver lining in every day, even when there seems to be none."

The lights dimmed and the movie began with a musical introduction and the title, *Debbie Is My Darling*.

Debbie was tragically young. Early fifties at most. Tall, slim, and blond, she wore black pants and a white shirt that were both fashionable and expensive—befitting a doctor's wife. The film was set in a large and beautifully appointed living room where Debbie paced back and forth in front of a fireplace.

Her expression was blank, almost childlike. She kept her head down and constantly rubbed the back of one hand with the other as she walked back and forth, back and forth in an area bounded by two wing chairs, a coffee table, and a wide-screen television. It took a moment, but I finally realized she was pacing back and forth because she couldn't find her way out. Couldn't figure out how to get around the chairs or bypass the coffee table. So she went back and forth, back and forth. At least she was getting some exercise. Silver linings. Silver linings.

"Debbie, darling," the voice behind the camera—Dr. Bonnett's voice—called.

She paid no attention. Just kept on walking despite the fact that he called her name over and over again. "Debbie. Debbie sweetheart. Debbie darling."

He snapped his fingers, but she still didn't respond and I expected him to whistle for her at any moment. *Come on, Debbie, come here, girl.* Instead he moved on, addressing the audience and taking his camera with him to a gallery of portraits hung on the wall above a white leather chesterfield. "We mounted these pictures to help Debbie remember us," he said, pointing out their daughter and her children. Their son and his partner and finally their own wedding portrait.

Debbie had been truly beautiful. The kind of woman who took your breath away, and there was an audible silence in the room when the camera returned to the present-day Debbie.

Dr. Bonnett went on to explain that even though Alzheimer's had stolen so much from them, there were still moments of joy, still silver linings to be found each and every day. We just had to look to find them.

To illustrate where he himself liked to look for such moments, he led Debbie and the audience out to the garden where apparently she liked to walk. He showed us the roses she had loved and how he had removed all the thorns so she could touch them and smell them and find joy in these small and simple things. Only Debbie didn't smell or touch them. She simply stood still, rubbing her hand and staring at the ground, trapped between the camera and a pair of gardening gloves someone had left on the ground. At least she wasn't likely to wander off. Another silver lining.

Done with the flowers, the doctor took us all back to the living room, sat Debbie darling on a chair and called, "Here, Skipper, here, boy." A fluffy little dog bounded onto the scene and leapt into Debbie's lap, making her jump and then almost smile before he leapt away again.

As the dog ran in circles and a day in the life of Debbie trudged on, faces all around me were softening and people were nodding. Mark reached out to take my hand and I was almost ready to be seduced, lulled into looking for silver linings and shining moments, when the doctor said, "This is my favorite part," and I turned my attention back to the screen.

Debbie was on her feet again, pacing and rubbing, oblivious to his voice telling her to look his way. So he went to the stereo, pushed a button, and that silly song *Build Me up Buttercup* burst from the speakers. Debbie stopped walking. Looked at the stereo and for one split second her face changed. In that brief moment, you could see the woman she used to be. Confident, strong, and heartbreakingly beautiful. And she started to dance. Moving her head, her arms, her hips. It didn't last for more than fifteen seconds, and then she was pacing again, the connection lost.

The doctor was obviously pleased with the result. Called it *Debbie's moment of joy*, and hit the button one more time. Again, she stopped, faced the music, and danced. It was her party trick, I realized. The one he probably had her do for company. Dance Debbie Dance, and I knew from the portrait on the wall and that fleeting look on her face, that the woman she had been would not have been amused. If that woman knew what he was doing to her, what he was showing the world, she would have smacked the shit out of him. And he'd deserve it.

"What are you doing?" I called out, not because I was out of control, but because for the first time since the outburst, I felt I was *in* control, fully aware of what was going on and who I was. I was Ruby Donaldson. Alzheimer's patient. And I would never be anyone's one-trick pony.

"Do you honestly expect us to believe that Debbie is finding joy in any of this?" I demanded.

"I assure you, madam, my wife loved to dance—"

"I'm sure she did when it was her choice. But this—" I flicked a hand at the screen. "This isn't choice, this is response to a stimulus. Like Pavlov's dogs or a rat in a maze. Flick the switch and get a treat. Watch Debbie dance."

"I beg your pardon," the doctor said.

"Dr. Bonnett, your film is despicable," I continued, knowing Less-Than-Perky and a few men of the committee were already on their way. "You're treating your wife like a dog. Getting her to do tricks for you. Tell me, Doctor, what will you have her do when she can't do this one anymore? Will she still be your darling, or will she no longer have anything film-worthy to offer? No moment of joy for you to peddle to the world?"

"Madam," Less-Than-Perky said, and Mark and Mary Anne rose at the same time. Both were probably finding me offensive as hell, but they were ready to defend me against security if necessary. All for one and one for me and all of that.

"If Debbie knew what you were doing," I continued, "she would hate you, sir, I guarantee it."

The ladies two rows in front of me nodded, and a man behind me whispered, "She's right, you know," and I knew I'd hit a chord.

"Alzheimer's steals our dignity," I said to my comrades instead of the doctor. "The least we should expect from our caregivers is a little respect."

"Absolutely," a woman to my right said. "I'm as appalled as you are."

"We demand respect," the hundred-year-old man yelled. "Do you hear me, son? Respect!"

"Ma'am, please," a man from the committee said.

"Don't you ma'am me and don't you touch me either." I thrust out my arm, pointing straight at the doctor. "Do you want to know what the real Stepping-stone to Happiness is for an Alzheimer's patient? There's only one and it's real simple. Take yourself out while you still have some happiness. While you still know who you are and what you want. Before they start toileting you and setting you in the sun like a potted plant." I lowered my arm, turned to the group. "If we were smart we'd be lobbying for the right to die with dignity. To thumb our noses at the Alzheimer's industry and say no to mind-numbing drugs and meaningful activities and warehouses that pose as nursing homes, prolonging our lives for their own monetary gain."

The hundred-year-old man burst into tears. "I've been saying the same thing, but no one ever listens. 'Don't be silly, Dad.' 'Life is precious, Dad.'" He whacked his son with his hat. "It's bullshit, I tell you. Bullshit!"

"Ma'am, we're going to have to ask you to leave."

"You don't have to ask me anything. I'm already on my way."

I slid back my chair and headed for the door. Stopped at the table long enough to tear the page with my name off the clipboard. "If any of you want to sign their form again, go ahead. As for me, I am out of here."

I turned and started walking. Stopped again and spun around. "Mark! Mary Anne! Get my purse. I forgot it."

# LIZ

Mark Bernier is a prick.

Sure, he comes off all concerned and caring, nodding and mur-muring "I see, I see" while you talk his ear off. Never interrupting even when you're little and ranting about silly schoolyard shit. Or when you're older and need someone to let you talk without always offering advice. Leading you to believe that you can count on him to understand, to help you out when it matters most. But watch out, because just when you were feeling confident, just when you least expected it, wham! The real Mark came out and bit you on the ass.

I should have known something was up when he didn't tell me he was spending the summer on the Island. I found out from Grace, for chrissake. But fine, he was busy or whatever. I got over it. Assumed everything was back to normal until this morning, when I asked him to meet me at Hanlan's Point—a quick and invigorating bike ride from his new home on Algonquin—and the bastard said no.

Pointed out that it was a workday for most people, and if I wanted to see him badly enough, I could come to Ward's, meet him at the Rectory Café. He'd give me an hour and he'd pay for lunch, but that was as far as he was willing to go. The choice was mine.

"I don't believe this," I'd said. "You want me to abandon my principles just to save you from riding out to Hanlan's?" He'd laughed at that. Said it wouldn't be the first time.

I knew what he was getting at and I wanted to tell him to go fuck himself. Point out that I hadn't had a drink in ten days. Not because I didn't want one—which I did—but because I was going to need a fully functioning brain if I wanted to pull off this petition.

Brenda, Nadia, and I had spent the first weekend drinking nothing stronger than coffee while we set up the official head office of Sideshow Legal Services in Nadia's room. And I was still dead sober when I sat down the following Monday to make up a list of things I'd need and figure out exactly what I had gotten myself into. It hadn't taken more than a few hours to realize I was not only rusty in the practice of law, I was also in way over my head. Still, I'd pressed on, drawing up the papers, searching for a trustee, and waiting two full days to hear him say yes. Now, ten days later, we were ready. All the hurdles crossed except one—serving the petition. Walking in and plunking that paper into the hands of Mr. Klaus Vandergroot, CEO of Champlain Aerospace—the man who had stopped taking Mitch's calls.

And last night when I was sitting in my room alone, staring at the blank space at the bottom of the petition, the space where Brenda's representative would be named, the space where it would read "Elizabeth Donaldson, Attorney at Law," I had wanted a drink so badly I would have parked my butt at any bar in the city and stayed for a week. But I didn't because that was when it hit me. If we wanted this to work, we needed a different name in that spot. A name with clout, with weight, with credibility. And I'd best have a clear head if I was going to have a hope in hell of convincing Mark that the name should be his.

"I'll be at the Rectory at noon," he'd repeated. "If you want to talk to me, you'll be on the eleven thirty ferry."

So I was at the Ward's Island ferry dock at eleven twenty-five, wearing dark glasses and a floppy hat, trying to blend in with the tourists while I followed the bikes and the grocery carts up the ramp to the *Ongiara*. Recognizing old Benny Barnes, of course, as well as a kid's photographer from Algonquin and a feral cat crusader from Ward's. Hoping none of them noticed me huddled there against the railing. Barely breathing until the ferry bumped the dock on the other side of the bay.

When the deckhands finally lowered the ramp, I risked a glance at Benny, watched him wheel his bike off the ferry and along the dock. I waited until everyone else was gone before walking across that ramp myself. The Rectory was only minutes from the dock and I moved quickly, head down, figuring I was home free until someone called my name.

"Liz Donaldson." I jerked around. Sly old Benny Barnes waved at me. Fuck. I waved back and he came toward me. Double fuck.

"How are you then?" he asked. "Better than your mom, I hope. She's been some odd lately, eh? Lots of stress, though, running that business and all."

The Island drums had obviously been beating, carrying tales of the Donaldsons once more. "I guess. Listen it's been nice talking to you—"

"Yeah, lots of stress." He sniffed the air and cleared his throat loudly but thankfully didn't spit. "Good thing she doesn't know about Grace gallivanting off to the airport every morning. Or those picnics the two you have on the nude beaches. Probably kill the old girl, eh?"

Double double fuck.

*The old bugger's smarter than he looks*, Great-Grandma Lucy used to say. Then she'd wink at me and smile, and I'd always wondered if they'd had an affair back in the day.

"Really hope your mother's all right," he continued. "She's a right corker, Ruby is. Just like her grandma." He smiled at me. "You're a lot like them, Lizzie Donaldson. A lot like them."

"God forbid," I muttered.

"And don't you worry. I won't mention I saw you to a soul." He started back toward his bike. "Wouldn't want people talking about the Donaldsons again, would we?"

"Thanks, Benny," I called, and hurried on to the Rectory, grateful the Island drums had been silenced—for a while anyway.

Mark was waiting for me by the bike rack outside the café. He looked good—slimmer with some color in his face. But he was clearly in work mode—dress pants, white shirt, a tie loosened at his throat. It occurred to me that I should have dressed more appropriately too. Pants instead of jeans. Shirt instead of tank top. Definitely no floppy hat. Promising myself I'd be more dignified next time, I waved and ran toward him, looking forward to having lunch at the Rectory again.

The café had been just another home slated for demolition back in the fifties and sixties, but the concrete construction of the grand two-story building had proved too much for the city's bulldozers and they'd left it intact. Since then, it had filled a number of roles—including home to the priest of St. Andrew–by–the–Lake—but now it housed the Island Trust offices, the art gallery, the café, and a summer patio that was one of the most beautiful spots on the Island.

"Nice disguise," Mark said, giving me a hug and a kiss on the cheek. "I almost didn't recognize you."

"Liar," I said, checking the perimeter for old classmates, even older neighbors, before pulling off the hat and shucking the sunglasses. "Thanks for meeting me. Did you get a table?"

He nodded and I followed him through the gate to an oasis of wrought-iron tables shaded by trees and banked by flower boxes. Only a few tables were occupied—no one I knew—but the place would be jammed soon enough.

"We're sitting over there, by the boardwalk." He pointed to the far end of the patio and a table where Jocelyn and Grace sat drinking Cokes and passing their cell phones back and forth. One all in black, the very soul of adolescent angst, the other a picture of innocence in a kitten and puppy T-shirt. No wonder people were staring.

Grace spotted us and waved, a big dopey grin on her lovely face. Jocelyn's expression didn't change. Was she ticked at something or just staying in character? I didn't know the kid well enough to tell. I'd only met her twice, at our weekly beach picnics. I was surprised the first time Grace brought her along, but they seemed to like each other. And Grace could definitely use a friend, even if she was a twelve–year-old Goth.

"I hope you don't mind," Mark said. "But Jocelyn's never had a meal here, and Grace could use one."

"A little privacy would have been nice—"

"Let's cut to the chase, Liz. Do you need money? Because if that's what this is about, then I can give you some work at the office. Filing mostly. They're overloaded right now—"

"It's not about money. I have a friend who needs help."

"Are you already married to him?"

I felt my face warm. "My friend is a woman. Someone I've known for a while who now finds herself in a financial bind through no fault of her own."

He looked over my shoulder, checking on the girls. "I'm not writing anyone a check, Liz. We both know how that turned out the last time."

God, I sounded like a screwup when he talked that way. No wonder he wasn't taking me, or my request for a meeting, seriously. I composed my face and adopted a lawyerly stance. "Mark, I don't want a check, I want you to listen."

A waitress delivered salads to our table. "The girls were hungry," Mark said. "I ordered them something to start." He folded his arms. "So tell me about this friend. Just keep it brief."

Mark in work mode was rarely patient. I'd do well to remember that.

I took a breath and started in, laying out Brenda's story and the problem they were having collecting the money. But I was rusty after two years away from the practice and I went off on tangents again and again. He wasn't tactful about bringing me back, forcing me to stay on track. By the time I finished, I was sweating but excited, certain he'd see the value in performing this one small task.

"Petition to bankruptcy? Forget it. You don't have a case."

He started to walk away. I put a hand on his arm, holding him back. "I'm not trying to make a case. I'm only trying to shake these people up. Make them see that Brenda and Mitch mean business so they'll pay their fucking bill."

"Watch your language. My daughter has a foul enough mouth as it is without you adding to it."

I held up both my hands. "I'll be good, I promise. In fact, I'll be a paragon of virtue if you just let me put the application in your firm's name. Mark, I'm rusty and I don't want to make a mistake. Plus, I'll be going up against Hodgeson and Levi. If they see 'Elizabeth Donaldson, Attorney at Law' on the petition, they'll eat me alive." I paused and took a breath. Went for the heart. "Mark, these are good people. They deserve a little justice."

He sighed and rubbed a hand over his face. "What you're trying to do is foolhardy at best. You can't use the court to collect a bill." He held up a hand when I started to object. "Let me finish. I understand you don't think it will go that far, but the company you're going to do this to might feel differently. They may continue to do nothing about the bill and agree to see you in court on the appointed date. After your case is thrown out, they might very well turn around and sue your friends. Are they prepared for that possibility?"

"It's a nonissue. If they don't pay, there will be nothing left to sue."

He shook his head, frowned at a planter box. "I still don't like it."

I took a breath. Prepared to close. Reminded myself not to swear. "Mark, I know it's unorthodox, but it's their last shot. They'll be bankrupt inside of a month without this."

He thought for a moment, jaw working, eyebrows scrunching. I kept my mouth shut, let the silence play out as he'd taught me—once the deal was on the table, never be the first to blink. At last he folded his arms again and lowered his chin—the judge returning from chambers.

"Okay, I'll sign your application, I'll deliver it, *and* I'll field the calls from Hodgeson and Levi, on one condition."

My breath left in a rush, leaving me weak and a little giddy. "Anything." I threw my arms around his neck. "Anything at all. As long as it doesn't involve Ruby."

"Then you can forget it." He removed my arms and started walking. Brushed my hand away when I tried to stop him a second time.

"Mark, be reasonable," I said, chasing him through the tables.

He stopped and turned on me. "Don't speak to me about reasonable. You asked me earlier to listen to you, and I did. Now I'm asking you to listen to me. Your mother needs you to come back to the Island, and I need you to agree."

I stared at him. "I can't."

He was on the move again. "Then you're on your own with the petition."

I hurried after him. "But I can't do it on my own. I need the backing of your firm in order to pull this off."

"Then take the deal." He pulled out a chair when he reached the table. "Hey, girls, sorry we took so long. What looks good today?"

Grace smiled and said, "Everything," but Jocelyn ignored him.

Snatched her phone back from Grace and slouched lower in the seat. Obviously pissed off. And the target was Mark. Interesting.

He waved me into the chair across from him. "Have a seat, Liz. We need to order."

I stayed where I was. "Why are you being such a prick about this?"

The girls went quiet. Mark raised his head and looked at me with the steady practiced gaze I had always admired—the one that always reduced his opponents to ash. "I warned you about that kind of language. Now sit down."

"I can show you the new pictures of the mockingbird," Grace said, trying to ease the transition.

"I'd like that," I said, setting my hat on the table, my backpack on the ground as I took my seat. When the waitress arrived I handed her the menu and pointed to Grace. "I'll have whatever she's having. And bring me a double vodka with soda and a twist."

"Bring her the soda with a twist," Mark said. "No vodka." He raised his water glass. "You can drink on your own nickel. Not mine."

My face burned. "No lemon," I told the waitress. "Just ice."

She slunk away and Grace held out her phone. "See? That's the new cage. It's bigger with branches for her to climb on. And we made a nest from a hanging planter."

I looked at the screen. Saw a cage. "That's great," I said while Mark opened his menu, took a pair of glasses from his pocket, and perused the page. I'd been dismissed. Turned into another child at the table. Any minute now he'd ask the waitress for crayons.

"And here's the male dancing on the lawn." Grace frowned. "It's hard to tell, I guess, but he really is dancing."

"I told her to video it," Jocelyn said. "But she doesn't know how."

"Then you should show her," Mark said, flicking his napkin open and setting it in his lap.

"Here's the lady mockingbird," Grace said, pushing the camera at me again. "We've been feeding her dog food mixed with berries and it seems to be working. She seems a lot better. See?"

I don't know much about birds, but she might have been right. It was alive at any rate. "She looks great. Maybe she'll be flying soon."

"If the cats don't get her first," Jocelyn said.

"We're all working hard to make sure that doesn't happen," Mark said. "Jocelyn even came up with a warning system. Why don't you tell Liz about it?"

"It's bells," she said, pushing lettuce around her plate. "And why can't I go to the sleepover?"

"We'll talk about this later," Mark said.

"You're the one who dropped it on me the moment we sat down." Jocelyn raised her chin. "I still don't know why you're being so mean."

Definitely pissed. And too good to pass up.

I leaned my arms on the table. "Whose sleepover is it?"

She looked straight at her father. "One of my friends in the city. It's her birthday and everybody's going except me."

"You can go to the party. You just can't stay overnight. I don't like the idea of you being over there after the ferries stop running."

"Like it's my fault they stop so early." She slumped back in the chair. "I hate you."

I leaned closer and lowered my voice. "Your dad can be a pain in the ass sometimes."

Jocelyn nodded. "Yeah, he can."

"Liz, that's enough," Mark said.

I smiled at her. "Laying down the most ridiculous rules for no reason at all."

She smiled back for the first time. "You got that right."

"Liz," Mark repeated, the warning clear. Stop now. Back away from the kid.

But he was the one who'd drawn the lines, treated me like a child. And everyone knows that two twelve-year-olds at a table are always more fun than just one. I sat back. "It's like he wants to fuck up your life, just for the hell of it sometimes, don't you think?"

Grace sprayed Coke out of her nose, Jocelyn laughed, and I tried to remember if Mark's face had ever gone that red when I was a kid. The waitress delivered my soda. "Definitely a pain in the ass," I said, and took a few small ladylike sips.

"You're using the wrong tack, Liz," he said. "I'd change course now if I were you."

A waiter chose that moment to arrive with salads for Mark and me. I shook out my napkin, ceding the round to him. The game, however, was not over yet.

Grace plunged into the awkward silence, filling it with tales of the mockingbirds. Explaining how the male brought bits of food to the lady, and sang all night long so she'd know he was still there, waiting for her to come out of the cage and join him.

"How romantic," I said. "And where exactly does he do this singing?"

"In the tree outside Mom's window."

"She must love that."

"She hates it," Jocelyn said. "Said it's too bad *To Kill a Mockingbird* isn't an instruction manual."

"I'm sure she'll find a way." I sat back as our lunches were delivered. "Seems there's always someone around to do her dirty work. Someone to make sure she gets exactly what she wants, no matter how hard it is on anyone else."

Mark rose and dropped his napkin on the table. "Girls, will you excuse Liz and me for a moment? We need to talk."

I picked up my fork. "After lunch. Don't want the pasta to get cold."

"Now," he said, leaving the table, heading for the gate.

Round two had begun.

"Be right back," I said to the girls and hurried after him.

He was waiting for me at the edge of the lawn, out of earshot of people at the bike rack and the hostess at the gate. "You think this crap is going to help your case or your friend?" he asked, his voice low, his tone that of a lawyer who knows he has the upper hand at the bargaining table. "You've lost all perspective, Liz. You've become so accustomed to playing the victim that you've lost the ability to be rational. To figure out what's legitimate rebellion and what's nothing more than sheer pigheadedness."

"I have *never* played the victim."

"Come on Liz, every drunk plays that role. To be honest, I blame myself. I should have dragged you to AA long ago. Or shoved you into rehab and kept sending you back till you snapped out of it. But I told myself you were a smart girl. You were hurt, but you'd find your way through, only you haven't. Two years later and you're still wrapped up so tightly in your own grievances, your own troubles, you can't think about anyone else anymore. Not your sister, not me, not even the friend you say you want to help so badly."

I kept my voice down, my tone level, matching his. "You're so full of shit it's a wonder your eyes aren't brown. I'm only standing here because of my friend. Otherwise I would have told you to shove your ultimatum where the cat won't get it. And I have always cared about Grace. All I've ever wanted to do is help her."

"Well, it won't be much help to her if Ruby sells the shop, will it?"

"What are you talking about?"

"Your mother's plan. She's going to sell the business because she wants to tie up all the ends before she dies. I've tried to talk her out of it because it's not necessary and it's going to devastate Grace, but there's no changing her mind. You know nothing of this, of course, because you haven't once called to see how your mother is doing."

I threw up my hands. "That's ridiculous. I've never called about Ruby before."

"She's never had Alzheimer's before."

I let my arms drop. "Fine, how is she?"

"Not good. She refuses to take some of the medications because somehow she's got her hands on some pot instead. And she's started a blog. 'Show Me the Ice Floe.' That's how she is."

I wrapped my arms around myself and turned away. "Sounds like she's doing just fine. And a little pot is probably good for her. Takes away the anxiety."

"Don't be smart with me, little girl."

I sighed and looked back at him. "Mark, what do you want from me?"

"I want you to move back home."

"But what if that isn't what's best for her?"

"Don't try and turn this around. Ruby wants you here. You know that."

"Alzheimer's patients are supposed to avoid agitation and stress, right? Well, talking to me, even seeing me from afar, only causes more of both. I can only imagine how horrible it would be for both of us if I lived there. Like it or not, Mark, the best thing, the most loving thing I can do for Ruby, is to stay the hell away from her."

"You tell yourself that if it makes you feel better."

"What would make me feel better is knowing why you're pushing me this way. Why you won't just leave it alone?"

"I can't leave it alone because your mother is going to kill herself. She has pages of notes, Liz. And a spreadsheet with more ways to kill yourself than I ever imagined possible. She even has a column of risks associated with each one. Risks that aren't death."

"She always was thorough," I said, and had no trouble picturing a spreadsheet with precise rows and neatly labeled columns: Method, Equipment, Pain Factors, Risks. While the last column probably wouldn't have occurred to me any more than it had to Mark, I suppose she had to take the risk factors into consideration, be prepared for outcomes that weren't part of the plan. Dismemberment, for instance. Or paralysis. Any number of fates that would definitely be worse than death, if that was the goal.

"Not just thorough," Mark said. "Meticulous, which leaves no doubt in my mind that she'll try."

"And you intend to stop her?"

"What else can I do?"

"Leave her alone. Let her handle this in her own way."

"Even if her way is wrong?"

"How dare you decide that for her. How dare you think you know what she needs, what's good for her. My mother may have been a bitch, but she always knew her own mind and precisely what she wanted. Now that mind is telling her to get out while she still can, and I can't fault her for that."

"Can't fault her? You just said that her mind is telling her to do this, and her mind has Alzheimer's for God's sake. Her decision isn't rational."

"Come off it, Mark. She's always felt this way and you know it. 'Take me out and shoot me,' she used to say every time Great-Grandma Lucy took off all her clothes at the ferry dock or threw tea bags at the tourists. I was just a little kid, but I remember it clearly. 'If I ever get like that, take me out and shoot me.'"

"But no one ever took Lucy out and shot her, did they? Because life is precious."

"No one shot her because we didn't have a gun. And the winter they found her body in the woods on Hanlan's Point, we were sad, but we all breathed a sigh of relief, didn't we? We were all glad the crazy old coot was gone and Ruby could finally fix up the house. Add the second floor we'd needed for years but couldn't do until the queen bee agreed, which she wouldn't do because she was fucking crazy. So don't give me clichés about the preciousness of life, Mark. Give me one good reason why Ruby shouldn't kill herself instead."

His shoulders slumped, his eyes closed, and he looked tired all of a sudden. Old and tired and vulnerable in a way that I hadn't seen since the day Ruby packed his bags. "Because suicide is the end of hope," he said, and opened his eyes. "It's giving up and giving in. Turning your back on the possibility of miracles."

"You mean a cure."

"Yes, a cure. And if not a cure, at least something that will slow the progress better. Something to hold the illness where it is and prevent further loss." He paused and drew in a breath. Shook off whatever had been weighing him down and pushed his shoulders back. Mark returning. "There's research being done all over the world, scientists searching for answers every day, and that gives me hope. It should give Ruby hope too, but it doesn't, and that's not like her. Your mother has never been the kind to give up hope, no matter how pointless the cause. If anything, she's been the patron saint of lost causes all of her life, fighting to save her home or stop the expressway or—"

"Ban the ban on altar girls."

"Exactly. She knew she wouldn't win all of her fights, but she never gave up trying, she never gave up hope. She still's fighting the airport, for God's sake. What kind of crazy optimism is that? Yet she won't fight to save herself, and that's not your mom, that's not Ruby." He put his hands on my shoulders, looked into my eyes. "She needs you, sweetie. She needs you because you're right about avoiding agitation and stress. Both of those things will only cause the disease to advance faster, steal her from us that much sooner. And the biggest stress in Ruby's life right now is the house. She needs to know the house will stay in the family."

I pushed him away. "Then let her leave the goddamn house to Grace. I don't want it, I never wanted it."

"Grace can't handle that house on her own. She'll always need help."

"And that's my problem, is it? The fact that Ruby needs to hold on to her piece of the Island is my responsibility."

"Yes," he said, so simply and with such conviction that I realized he believed his own shit. He honestly expected me to come home and take over that goddamn house. How in God's name was I supposed to answer that?

"Liz," he went on. "You don't have to come forever. Just for a year, six months even. Just long enough for your mother to know that she can relax. Once she does that, then together we can show her she's wrong about the suicide. Prove to her that this illness is worth fighting, and we'll be with her every step of the way."

I didn't say anything. Couldn't make sense of it. But he mistook my hesitation for a way in, and he put those hands on my shoulders again. Weighed me down and held me in place while he made his closing argument. "I know it won't be easy. I know you and your mother can fight at the drop of a dime, but that's not how it has to be. You're the healthy one, Liz, the one with the ability to think and reason. That's why you need to be the one to change things. Your mother is who she is. She'll always find fault, but only because she loves you and wants the best for you. *Her* idea of what's best, yes, but that's all she has. That's all she's ever had.

"So I'm asking you to stop fighting with your mother. I'm asking you to come home, bite your tongue, and be the daughter she needs you to be. Not forever, just until she settles down. Comes to see that the future isn't as grim as she imagines." He paused there and smiled. "Can you do that, Liz? For Grace. For me. Can you do that for all of us?"

I looked away, watched the line for the patio growing longer. Thought of the pasta congealing on my plate, of Grace waiting to show me more pictures of the mockingbird, and Ruby plotting ways to kill it.

I smiled, imagining her walking back and forth under the lilac tree, shaking her fist and muttering threats. Determined to get that bird off her property one way or another because, by God, this was Donaldson land and no bird was going to get the better of her.

If nothing else, my mother was interesting. And I tried to

imagine myself on the lawn with her, yelling at the bird, shooing it away. Trying to be the daughter she'd always wanted. The one who would bite her tongue until it bled while Ruby pointed out that she was shooing the bird the wrong way. Or wearing the wrong clothes, or thinking the wrong thoughts.

The daughter who would play lady-in-waiting to the queen bee. The girl who would march at the airport and live in the house and keep her mother alive and take away the tea bags and follow in her footsteps long after she'd buried her mother's ashes in the garden. And that was where my stomach started to heave and that image, that horrible twisted image, faded to black. Because I wasn't that daughter. I never had been. And Ruby and I both knew it.

I turned back to Mark. "As much as you'd like to believe otherwise, the last thing my mother needs is to have me in that house. Because if she didn't kill herself, I probably *would* take her out and shoot her. I can't move back to the Island, Mark. I simply can't."

Disbelief moved across his face, followed by disappointment. I'd expected both, was ready for both. It was the disgust that brought tears to my eyes.

"I'm sorry you feel that way." He checked his watch, glanced back at the café. "I need to get back to work. I've arranged payment for lunch. Go ahead and order something else. Your pasta will be ice by now." He hugged me briefly, as you might a cousin with an odd smell at Christmas. Then he released me, stepped back, putting distance between us. "You're so alike, you and your mother. But as much as I love you both, the fact is that Ruby needs me more, and I won't be the go-between any longer. You're on your own, Liz. Take care of yourself."

He turned and started walking away, and I knew a moment of real panic there on the lawn in front of the Rectory. Mark had never in my life turned his back on me. He had always been my champion, my white knight. The one man I could always count on, until now.

*You're on your own, Liz.*

I ran after him. "Is that it then? You choose one of us and then just walk away?"

He didn't stop. Didn't turn around. Just kept on going. I slowed down as a chill moved around me, through me. I picked up a rock and threw it, missed him by a good ten feet. "Fine," I hollered. "Keep walking. I don't need you or her. I fucking hate both of you. Do you hear me? I fucking hate you."

"Liz?" I spun around, saw the feral cat crusader staring at me, open-mouthed. Benny on his bike across the road. Was it always Old Home Week on the Island?

"Are you okay?" he asked.

"I'm fucking perfect," I said, and went back to the gate. Walked past the stuttering hostess. Between the tables of staring faces. Sat down with Jocelyn. "Where's Grace?" I asked.

"Bathroom," Jocelyn said. "They took your lunch."

"Figures." I reached under the table for my backpack. "We might as well go."

"Or we could get you a new lunch." She held up a credit card. "My dad left me this. We can order everything on the menu." She smiled slowly. "Twice if you want."

"You are my kind of girl, Jocelyn." I smiled back and let my backpack slip to the ground as the waitress approached. "Bring us one of every dessert you have," I said to her. "One at a time, and keep them coming. And while you're in there, might as well bring me that double vodka. Don't worry about the soda. I already have plenty."

# GRACE

My mom's day off is Wednesday, but she doesn't usually go anywhere. She usually stays here and does paperwork. Ordering stock, paying bills. "Mundane tasks that are part of running a business," she always says, and then she smiles. "And you don't have to worry about any of that. How lucky does that make you?"

Pretty lucky, I guess. Especially since it seems like all those tasks are getting harder and harder. She used to sit at the table with her laptop while I worked, talking to me and my customers while she wrote checks and studied bank statements and counted stock and she always finished before lunch. But just after Christmas, she started taking her laptop upstairs where it was quiet, and lately she was still counting stock at dinnertime.

"Banks and governments exist to make our lives more difficult," she says when she finishes. "And I swear they're getting worse every day."

So I guess I was pretty lucky I didn't have to worry about any of those things. But that didn't stop me from wishing I knew something about it when she came back from canoeing with Mark this morning, and said she wasn't doing paperwork today.

"Don't make me any eggs," she said when she came through the door. "Mark and I are going into the city, so we'll grab breakfast over there." She picked up the teapot and carried it with her to the window. "That stupid bird is barking like a dog. What kind of bird does that?"

"A smart one. But what about the stock order? We're almost out of peroxide." I went to the stock cupboard. Took out the bottle and shook it. "We'll be in trouble come Saturday." I set the bottle back on the shelf and picked up two bills from the table. The hydro bill and the telephone bill. "And you left these in the bathroom yesterday."

She looked at me as though I was making it up, then laughed and gave her head a shake. "Well that is the quietest room in the house." She opened the appointment book and stuck the bills inside. "I'll take care of them when I get back."

"What about the peroxide?" I asked.

"Grace, we're fine. We don't need as much now that summer is in full swing. You know that."

Sure, I knew that. Business always slowed down when the days got hot. But still, it wasn't like her to let the stock get this low. Wasn't like her to leave bills lying around either. Something was wrong and my stomach did a flip-flop when I thought about it some more. Was she sick again?

"Now that silly bird's got the real dogs barking." She carried the teapot to the fridge. "Honestly, Grace you have to do something."

I didn't know what she thought I could do, or what she was looking for in the fridge. All I could think about was the color of her skin and the state of her hair. Both looked fine to me. Like she'd been using the sunscreen and wearing her hat, but what did I know? I'm not a doctor. Just a worried daughter.

"We need milk," she said, and closed the fridge. "Can you put that on the list for me?" She carried the teapot back to the stove. "Do you want a cup?"

"Sure." I unclipped the list from its spot on the fridge and wrote *milk* underneath *salt*. "But I still don't understand. We've never had so little stock any other summer."

She turned me around and laid her hands gently on each side of my face. Smiled and drew me closer so our noses were touching. "Grace, honey, trust me. We'll be fine."

I couldn't understand how that could be, but Mark and Jocelyn were coming through the gate and there was no more time to talk. So I quickly added *peroxide* to the bottom of the shopping list and stuffed the page into her ant bag.

Maybe if she saw it written down, she'd change her mind. And I could ask her later if she was sick. Hope she told me the truth.

"The lady mockingbird looks great," Mark said as he came inside. "She was even poking her head out when I came up the stairs. Jocelyn's waiting to see if she does it again. Who knows, this might be the day she flies."

"We can only hope." My mom opened the ant bag to throw in her Tilley, saw the shopping list, and pulled it out. "Grace, what's gotten into you?" She scratched the line off the bottom and stuffed the list back in her bag. "Sometimes I swear you do things just to annoy me."

My face got warm and I wanted to ask why she was being so stubborn, so stupid about a bottle of peroxide. But Mark shook his head behind her back and made "calm down" motions with his hands. So I said, "Fine, no peroxide." But it still didn't make any sense.

"Who's that going by the gate?" my mom asked, pointing out the kitchen window.

I took a quick look. "Kylie and Brianne. They're getting really good on those stilts."

I was surprised when they stopped and Kylie called, "How's the mockingbird?" to Jocelyn.

I was even more surprised when Jocelyn said, "Good," and walked a little closer to the gate. "She's even poking her head out of the cage. Do you want to see her?"

"We can't right now," Brianne said. "Our summer camp is having a garage sale at the clubhouse this weekend and we said we'd help put price stickers on stuff."

"But we can come later if that's okay," Kylie added.

Jocelyn smiled. "Sure. I'll be here."

I shook my head. Was everything going to be weird today?

The girls waved and stilt-walked down the street. Jocelyn was still smiling when she sat down at the table. "The lady mockingbird is almost all the way out. She's going to fly soon, I know it."

My mom poured a glass of orange juice for her. "I hear that garage sale is an important fund-raiser for the theater camp. Without it, they can't afford new costumes or sets, and I'll bet someone with something great to donate would be a big hit with everyone over there."

Jocelyn looked up at her. "What are you saying?"

My mom smiled and sat down. "I'm saying I have a shed full of brand-new power tools that you can take over there. And I guarantee you'll be the hero of the summer."

"Are you sure?" Mark asked. "Those tools are worth a lot of money."

"Which is exactly the point."

"And I can just take them?" Jocelyn asked. My mom nodded and Jocelyn narrowed her eyes. "What's the catch?"

"No catch. I'll just be happy to see them gone." She rose and picked up the ant bag. "You don't have a lot going on today, Grace, so have some fun." She kissed my cheek on her way to the door. "And don't worry about the peroxide. We'll be fine."

Jocelyn waited until they were gone, then turned to me. "That was weird. Nice but weird." She skipped over to the toaster and popped in two slices of bread. "Will you help me take the tools over?"

"As soon as I'm finished working." I took a sip of the tea and put the cup right down again. It was stone cold. She hadn't waited for the kettle to boil.

"I'll need a wagon or something." She opened the fridge door and stuck her head inside. "Do you have any of that good jam?"

"Not till they get back. It's on the shopping list."

"Shoot." She closed the door and went to the cupboard for peanut butter. "And what was that about peroxide?"

"We're almost out, but she won't order any more." I carried my cup to the sink and plugged in the kettle. "And I don't know why because we can't do any kind of color without it."

"Then order it yourself." The toast popped. She grabbed the slices and juggled them over to a plate. "Do you want one of these?"

"No, thanks. And I can't order anything. That's my mom's job. She handles the business side of things. I just do the hair."

"Well, if your mom's being stupid, it's your duty as a responsible partner to order the peroxide."

"I'm not a partner. I only work here." It didn't matter that I was right, that we were going to be in trouble by Saturday. What she said was what we did. Always and forever, amen.

So I focused on setting up the shop for the day instead—something I could definitely do on my own. Pulling the kitchen chairs out of the way and shoving the table back against the wall, making room for Chez Ruby while Jocelyn hummed and spread peanut butter on her toast.

"Are your friends coming today?" I asked.

She shrugged. "Who knows. They never make plans till the last minute. It used to be okay when I was in the city, but now it makes me crazy. Speaking of crazy . . ." She grinned at me over her shoulder. "I believe this is the day I get my iPod back."

I'd been hoping she'd forget and I'd have another day or two of music on my morning bike ride. I was getting really good at loading songs, and I had a whole section just for myself now. But she was right, today was the day.

"How much are these things anyway?" I asked as I handed it back.

"About sixty bucks."

Sixty bucks. Did I have that much in tips? Maybe by the end of today.

Her phone jingled with another text message. She flipped it open, grunted at the screen, and closed it up again.

"Are they coming?"

"They're still deciding."

"You're allowed to ride the ferry alone now. Why not go across and surprise them?"

She stood at the counter, eating her toast. "Not a good idea. I could get there and be really surprised to find out they've planned something great and didn't invite me."

"Why would they do that?"

"Because they can be mean."

"Then why are you friends with them?"

She shrugged and picked up the juice my mother had poured for her. "Because I've known them all my life. We've been friends forever, and it's hard to make new ones."

I smiled. "Not when you've got power tools."

She rolled her eyes. "You're such a goof."

I laughed and went into my room for my workstation. Jocelyn came in behind me and sat down at the computer. Touched the spacebar and a picture of daisies came up. "Are you ever going to let me load a desktop that isn't so lame?"

I rolled the workstation to the door. "Go ahead, just don't pick something that will give my mother a heart attack."

"Is she still snooping in your computer?"

"She was in there this morning." I knew because I had this detection system. It was just a bit of plastic thread on the side of the keyboard drawer, but if it wasn't there when I came back, I knew she'd pulled it out. I knew she'd been looking. It was almost funny. Almost like a game she didn't know we were playing.

I positioned the workstation beside the table, locked the wheels, and went back into the bedroom for my styling chair. Jocelyn was still at the computer, moving the mouse around, and tapping the keyboard, searching for a desktop that wasn't so lame, whatever that might be.

"It would make me crazy if my dad was looking around in my computer," she said as I went past with my chair. "I can put a really good password on here if you want. One she'll never figure out. All you have to do is say the word."

I shook my head. "It'll just make her mad and I think she's sick again."

"It doesn't matter if she's sick. She shouldn't be nosing around in your stuff." She went back to tapping the keys. "Besides, if you're not supposed to know she's doing it, what's she going to say if she suddenly can't get in? I was dusting your computer and I notice you have a new password?"

"She doesn't dust my computer. And I already said no. Just do the desktop."

I rolled the chair in front of my station, locked down the wheels, and was on my way to the laundry room for the roller cart when Jocelyn appeared again. "You now have a great desktop. Your mom will love it." She spun my chair once, sat down in it, and turned in a slow circle to the right. "So how long will it be before you can help me with the power tools?"

"You don't have to wait for me. Just borrow Mary Anne's cart and take them over."

"It's okay, I'll wait." She spun the chair again. "So how long will you be?"

I smiled and lifted the cover on the full-length mirror. "I have three regulars on Wednesdays. Mrs. Charlton, who likes nice soft waves, at nine. Mrs. Walker, who likes tight, tight curls, at eleven. And Mrs. Rose, who likes her hair cut so short it's almost buzzed, at one."

Jocelyn grunted as she spun. "I don't know how you stand it. Every day the same thing."

I flipped up the wings on my workstation and spread a hand towel on the top. "It's not the same all the time. Even if it was, I wouldn't mind. I like my clients and my job."

"You like tight, tight curls?"

I laughed and headed to the laundry room for towels. "I like Mrs. Walker. And she feels pretty when she leaves, and that makes me happy."

I came back with an armload of folded towels to find her rinsing her toast plate and putting it back in the cupboard. She'd finally learned that this wasn't a house during business hours. It was a salon, and dirty dishes could not sit in the sink. "Okay, so what's the best part of the job?" she asked. "What would you do more of if you could?"

"I like mixing colors. Getting the right shade for each customer." I laid the towels on the counter beside the sink, large ones on the left, smaller ones on the right, nice and handy when I'd need them. "And foil streaks. I really like those too." Pulling open the drawer on my station, I took out my kit and laid it on the towel. Undid the string and unrolled it slowly, revealing my scissors, my brushes, my combs. "I think I'd like to do manicures and pedicures one day too. And facials and waxing. I think we'd get more customers that way."

She sat in my mother's barber chair this time. "Couldn't hurt."

"That's what I told my mom." I opened the cupboard on my station. Reached way into the back, past the blow-dryer and the curling iron and the box of customer files. Put my fingers on the manila envelope my mom told me to throw out a long time ago, and pulled it out carefully.

"I even looked up the equipment and training," I told Jocelyn. "It's expensive, but I think we can make more money if we offer more services." I handed her the envelope. "It's all in there. Everything I found. My mom could have signed up for the courses and then she could have taught me how to do it and—"

"Hold on. Why would she take the courses? Why wouldn't you take them?"

I took out the dryer, the curling iron, the box of files. "Because she learns faster and she can teach me better. My mom's always been my teacher, for high school, hair dressing, everything. But she won't take the courses because she doesn't think we need to add services to our list. 'You can't be all things to all people,' she always says. Just like a pizza place doesn't serve barbequed chicken. They specialize, and so do we."

"Except most pizza places also serve wings and pasta now because people want more choices."

I shrugged and finished setting up my station, getting ready for Mrs. Charlton at nine. "I told her that too, but she said I don't understand business. And we don't talk about it anymore."

"You and your mom don't talk a lot, do you?"

"We talk all the time."

"Just not about anything important."

I ran my fingers across the neat line of combs and brushes. "We talk about what she thinks is important."

"Well, this is important." Jocelyn held up one of the pages. "You're smart enough to learn how to paint nails and yank out hair. And you'd be good at it too, because you like it."

"I don't know," I said, and opened the box of files. Flipped through the *A*s and the *B*s, until I came to the *C*s. *C* for Mrs. Charlton.

"Grace, listen to me. All you have to do is sign up for an online course, order a nail kit, and hang out a new shingle. Grace's Aesthetics at Chez Ruby."

I liked the sound of that. Grace's Aesthetics at Chez Ruby. But as my mom would say, *That's not an idea whose time has come, Grace.* I laid Mrs. Charlton's card on the towel, next to the dryer. "It's a nice thought, but I can't do it."

She walked with me to the sink. "If it's about money, I'm sure my dad will help."

I took out the shampoo and conditioner. Set them on the shelf and bent down to get the hose and the special attachment that lets the customer lean back without hurting her neck. "You don't understand. I can't just order equipment and supplies. Not without my mom's permission."

Jocelyn raised her arms. "Why the hell not?"

"Because it's her house. I can't just say, 'I hate the kitchen,' and order a new one because it's *her* house. The only place I can change things is in my room. And even there, she still has control of everything that matters."

Jocelyn lowered the pages and took a step back. "That sucks."

"It doesn't suck." I picked up the hose again. Attached it to the tap. "It's called respect."

"It's called nuts." She went back to the chair and slipped the pages into the envelope. "I don't even know why you stay."

"I don't have a lot of choice. And I have work to do."

She dropped the envelope on my station and herself in front of the television. She didn't turn it on, just sat there with her arms crossed, glaring at the blank screen, reminding me so much of Liz it made me smile. No wonder she couldn't understand why I stayed. Some days, I didn't either.

Leaving her to decide just how crazy I really was, I secured the neck rest to the sink and checked the clock. Nine fifteen. I went to the window, certain I'd see Mrs. Charlton at the gate, but there was no sign of her there, or on the street.

I checked the clock again. Nine sixteen. She should definitely be here by now, unless she changed the time. I pulled the appointment book across the table and flipped it open. Her name had been crossed off. As had Mrs. Rose's. The only one coming was Mrs. Walker at eleven. The rest of the day was blank and my mom had written, *Surprise! Extra time off. Enjoy it!*

Extra time off? Why would I want extra time off? Tomorrow was Thursday, and that meant Liz would come and we'd take Jocelyn to the nude beach, and we'd lie on the blanket and have KFC and try not to let Jocelyn get sunburned eyeballs again. But not today. Today was a workday. Only now it wasn't. Now it was extra time off.

Jocelyn came over to the table. "What's wrong?"

I showed her the page. "Mrs. Walker is the only one coming."

"You have the afternoon free?" She bumped me with her shoulder. "Bonus. Can we take those tools over now?"

"But this isn't my day off." My body felt numb, but I saw my hand reach out, saw my fingers lift the corner of the page. Turn it over to Thursday, my official day off.

All of my mom's appointments were canceled there too. Every name crossed off the list. The page turned again. Friday. Only two left. One for her. One for me. I slammed the book shut, afraid to look at Saturday. I backed away from the table. What was going on? What was happening?

"Grace, are you okay?"

I looked over at her. "They're all canceled. Everything. Canceled."

"Maybe it's a coincidence. Maybe they all decided to take holidays at the same time."

I shook my head, pointed at the book. "This is why I don't like surprises. This is why."

Jocelyn came toward me. "I don't understand. Why can't you just enjoy a day off?"

"Because if it doesn't stop, there will only be days off, don't you see?" I went to my station, picked up Mrs. Charlton's card, tried to read her phone number, but everything was a jumble, nothing made sense. I closed my eyes, and tried again. This time the numbers made sense and I took the card with me to the phone, punched all of those numbers, and waited while the line rang once. Twice. On the third one, Mrs. Charlton answered. I recognized her voice.

"This is Grace," I said. "From Chez Ruby."

"Grace, how are you?"

Shaky, confused. "You canceled today," I said.

"You didn't know?" I didn't answer and she said, "Oh my goodness, Grace. Your mother called yesterday. Said she wasn't feeling well and she's starting to wind down the business."

Wind down the business. Wind down. Wind down.

"I just assumed you knew."

No. Of course not. Who ever tells me anything?

"I didn't," I said, my voice no more than a stupid whisper. "I didn't know. I have to go."

I put the phone down. Turned to Jocelyn. "She's sick again. I knew she had to be sick. Otherwise she would have ordered the peroxide."

Jocelyn stood beside me. "She didn't tell you?"

"Like you said, we never talk about anything important."

I walked to the door. Pushed it open and went outside. Saw the lady mockingbird, half in, half out of the cage. Mr. Mockingbird flying down from the tree, flying back to the tree. Down and back. Down and back. Trying to make her follow, make her fly.

"Grace, talk to me," Jocelyn said, joining me on the step, her hand on my arm.

"What's the point?" I asked, and went down the stairs and across the lawn. Stopped at the rose garden and sat down in the grass. Tried to feel it tickle my legs, my fingers. Tried to feel anything all. But the numbness was still there and it was all I could do to breathe.

"It's always been this way," I said when she sat down beside me. "My mother never tells me anything important, and we never talk about anything unpleasant like men who leave or babies who die. The whole time we were growing up, Liz and I were never allowed to talk about our dads, never allowed to ask where they came from or what they looked like. The bits we know came from Liz eavesdropping or tempting Great-Grandma Lucy with scotch. But there are no pictures of them anywhere, no letters, no special things. 'What's done is done,' as my mother likes to say. 'No point in dredging up the past, poking old wounds. Better to move forward, always forward.' Of course, the same went for William. 'There can be no pictures, no booties, no locks of hair preserved in paper. There is to be a clean slate, Grace. A fresh start.' Even if that start came with house arrest and an ankle bracelet that kept me within a hundred yards of this front lawn for a solid year."

Jocelyn shook her head. "Wait a second. Go back. Why were you under house arrest?"

"Because I killed my son." Funny how I could say that now without choking. Say it matter-of-factly, I killed my son, as if it was true. As if I could ever have done anything to hurt my baby.

"Did you really?" she asked me straight out, the way kids always did.

"No," I said just as simply, and turned back to the roses. The red and white climbers. The pink and yellow hybrids. The pair of little stone angels at their feet, and the shower of petals on the ground around them. The same kind of shower that I now knew would be covering William's ashes on the other side of the bay.

"Then why did you say that?" she asked, and just like on the swan, I found myself looking over my shoulder, searching for my mother. Half-expecting her to come flying out the door, shaking her head and telling me no. Making me keep the story to myself long enough that the faces all faded and the details got fuzzy, and even I didn't care anymore.

But she wasn't there, and even after two years, I hadn't forgotten any of it. Not a night in that prison, or a moment with my son, or a word of the speech the prosecution made when he sat me down and offered me a plea. All of it was right there, waiting for me to start dredging.

I turned away from the roses, turned back to Jocelyn, hoped she'd be able to pull me out if I dug too deep. "They think I did it because I confessed. Because I said his death was my fault."

Her mouth drooped. "Why would you do that?"

"The prosecutor said I'd do less time if I took responsibility."

"But if you didn't kill him, you shouldn't have done *any* time."

"That's what Liz said too. She said she would convince the jury that my baby was dead when I picked him up. That the most I was guilty of was sitting in a chair and rocking him because it was too late to save him. But the police didn't see it that way. They said the least I was guilty of was criminal negligence because I didn't call 911. I wasn't a doctor or a nurse or anyone else in a position to say whether he was dead or not when I picked him up. I was just a mother who sat in a chair and did nothing to save her son."

"Is that true?"

"Yes," I said again, gathering a handful of rose petals and letting them fall through my fingers. "I sat with him and I rocked him because I knew he was dead. And if I called, they'd have come and taken him away and I wouldn't have been able to hold him ever again. So I left a message for Liz to call home. And then I sat down and I rocked him and I sang to him until she called, and I'd do the same thing all over again. But that wasn't a good thing to say, and the prosecution told my mother that if the jury didn't like what I said, if they didn't believe the baby really was dead when I picked him up, then I could go to jail for a very long time."

"So the rat bastards offered you a plea and you took it."

"I got two years, less time served, which equaled one more year in jail."

"Shit," Jocelyn said and shook her head. "I wish my dad had been there."

"He was there. He was the one who convinced the judge to let me serve my sentence here, under house arrest."

"I can't believe he didn't get you off."

"He didn't have a chance. Liz was my lawyer, and she was furious when I took that plea. But my mom said it was for the best. She said it wasn't worth the risk, and Liz still doesn't talk to her because of that, which is too bad because maybe my mom was right. Maybe I'd still be in jail right now if I hadn't done it."

"Or maybe you'd have cleared your name."

"We'll never know, will we? We'll never know if that ankle bracelet was the best or the worst thing that could have happened. All I know is that I spent that year right here, on this street. I couldn't go more than a hundred feet from my front door. From that house to that house. That's why my mom closed the shop on Queen Street and moved the whole thing here. For me, so I could stop crying and go to work and maybe not go completely crazy.

"Most of my customers came with her, but we weren't allowed to talk about the thing on my ankle or the ache in my chest or the constant tightness in my throat. And the whole time that I was swallowing antidepressants and talking about the weather or the price of gas or how beautiful the garden was that year, all I wanted to do was to stand at the gate and tell my story to everyone. Tell them all about his beautiful blue eyes, and his favorite toy. And the way he was starting to push himself up because he couldn't wait to crawl, to walk, to discover the world just like his father. Just like Bobby Daniels who I still hadn't stopped loving even though he turned out to be the worst kind of man a girl could imagine. And most of all I wanted to tell them that I needed to have my boy here with me. I needed him here in the garden, with the rest of the family."

"You have bodies in your garden?" Jocelyn whispered.

I smiled and tried to swallow. "No, there are ashes. Remember?" I pointed to the little stone angels. "That's Great-Grandma Lucy on the right, and that's Grandma Rose on the left. I never met her. Someone pushed her in front of a subway train."

"You sure she didn't jump?"

My God, how I loved this girl. "I'm not sure of anything, because we don't talk about it. We don't talk about why Grandma Rose fell in front of that train or why I wasn't allowed to put William's ashes right there." I reached out and put my hands on the earth beneath the white climber. "Right here between his grannies, where I could visit him every day and tell him I loved him and hope that one day he'd forgive me for not getting to him soon enough. For not knowing a baby could just die like that. And for not standing up for him when my mother said it would be better if his ashes stayed in the city because having that kind of reminder around day in and day out would only make me sadder."

Jocelyn crawled over to where I was kneeling and pulled me back out of the garden. She held my hands and she looked into my eyes. "But not having him here only made it worse."

I nodded and lowered my eyes. It was funny because for the first time in two years, I was saying it all out loud right here in the garden where I used to whisper his name because that was the only way I could do it. Because we were making a new start, with a clean slate. But he didn't go away just because my mother said he had to. He was still right there every time I saw a little boy and I'd think, *William would be one year old now*. Or *William would be two years old now*. As much as my mother wanted to believe that ignoring him would work, I couldn't let go. I couldn't pretend he never happened. And I didn't want to.

"I don't care if your mom is sick," Jocelyn said and pulled me into her arms. "She was wrong about William. And she was wrong not to tell you she canceled the appointments too. She was wrong about all of it."

I hadn't realized how small her frame was, how delicate her bones, until I held tight to her and cried, burying my face in a shoulder that smelled of cotton-candy body spray and trying not to wipe my nose on her bright red hair. And she cried with me as openly as she did everything, the same way Liz had cried with me on the night that William died.

I had no idea how long we stayed that way, but when we finally broke apart, sniffing and dabbing and wishing for tissues, we walked back across the grass together, stopping long enough to watch the mockingbirds.

The lady mockingbird was still where she was when I went out biking that morning, standing half inside and half outside the cage while the male flew back and forth, never stopping. Never shutting up.

"He's trying to get her to fly," Jocelyn said.

I watched her peck at the sides of the cage, rattle it as though she wanted to break the whole thing down. "She doesn't like it in there, but she's scared to leave. She's afraid she'll get hurt again."

Jocelyn shook her head. "That won't happen. She'll be more careful this time."

I nodded. "Maybe."

The lady mockingbird took a step outside, darted back in. Poked her head outside, pulled it back in, making me wonder if she'd ever learn to fly again. If she'd ever get out of that box.

"Grace?"

Mrs. Walker was at the gate, smiling and lifting the latch. And I couldn't remember when I'd last seen anything so beautiful.

"I caught an early ferry," she said as she hurried along the path. "I hope that's okay." She stopped and tipped her head to the side. "Is everything all right?"

"Everything's fine, just fine." I led her to the door and held it open for her. "Go on in and make yourself comfortable."

"Shall I put the kettle on?" she asked.

"Sure," I said, and smiled as Jocelyn came up the stairs. "Can you change that password for me now?"

"I'll come up with one that no one can break." She grinned and punched me on the shoulder. "And you can order the peroxide."

I followed her inside. "Right after we take those power tools to the sale."

# RUBY

**SHOW ME THE ICE FLOE**
**The blog for people who know what they want**

By Ruby Donaldson

*Number 24 in a series*
*Shhhh. Big Al is sleeping.*

*It's early morning, and so far so good. I know I have to go canoeing, I know I have a meeting with Lori this afternoon to work out the terms of the sale of my business, and I know I'm hungry. All good signs, proving yet again that more frequent meds are working, the marijuana isn't hurting, and I do not need round-the-clock supervision despite everything the well-meaning people in my life want me to believe.*

*If you follow this blog regularly, you know that I have Alzheimer's and that I will not be hanging around for the long good-bye. This is not a popular stance. Psychiatry tells us it's depression. Religion tells us it's a sin. Pharmaceutical companies tell us to keep a stiff upper lip—they're working on a miracle and all they need is more money. But to all of them I say, Up yours. I do not have a history of depression or mental illness. I do not hear voices telling me to jump off a cliff. And if there is a God, I'm certain she does not want to see us warehoused and kept alive to feed a growing industry.*

*While I would like to believe in miracles, the truth is that Big Al is tunneling into my brain on a daily basis, leaving gaping holes where facts and names and even time disappear. Sadly, their re-appearance is becoming more and more rare. So as much as the cheerleaders of hope would like me to keep the faith, the odds of this miracle happening before Al wipes me out completely are not in my favor, and I am not willing to roll the dice on my life. I plan to leave while the going is still good, and I will work toward both public and legal acceptance of this idea until the time comes for me to lay down arms and sleep.*

*If you believe as I do that the choice to step onto the Ice Floe is ours alone to make, then join me today at Queen's Park. We rally there at 1:00 P.M. to demand an end to the criminalization of those who would help us. An end to the tyranny of laws that allow family members to interfere, the state to find us a danger to ourselves, and judges to enforce treatments to keep us docile and controllable until we see the error of our ways and decide that life is precious and yes, by God, we want to live.*

*This is the endless paradox for those of us bunking with Big Al. It is not illegal to take your own life in this country. And we are con-sidered competent to make the choice to live or die as long as we don't want to take it. As soon as we decide that, yes, we really would like to get on the Ice Floe, then we are no longer considered competent and the choice is removed. Go figure.*

*But ladies and gentlemen, I promise that we can fight this lu-nacy and we can win because the Ice Floe is a viable alternative. And screw those who tell us otherwise.*

*See you at one o'clock this afternoon. Providing we both remember.*

I sat back from the laptop. Reread the entry, checking for sloppy grammar, spelling mistakes, errors in logic. Certain there were none, I clicked Exit. A box appeared. *Post?* As always, every cell in my body, every natural instinct, screamed, *Yes! Yes! Yes!* But again, as always, practicality won out. In order for Grace to live in this house with enough money and no guilt, my death had to look like an accident. Which meant there could be no record anywhere of my opinions. No references, veiled or otherwise, to my decision. It was just one more part of myself, my nature, that Big Al was stealing away.

I hit No. Do not post. And watched entry number twenty-four disappear, just like all the others. Then I got out of bed, carried the laptop to the dresser, and checked the clock: 6:10 A.M.

Over on Algonquin, Mark would be smacking his alarm clock, rubbing his eyes, and getting himself out of bed to go canoeing with me. He'd been doing it every morning since we visited the doctor, and I had to admit it was helping. He'd lost weight, his face had color, and his posture was starting to improve. He was looking good, and if I thought for a moment that I could get him to stop I would, because I missed my solitary mornings on the water. I missed solitary anything.

I'd taken to setting the alarm fifteen minutes earlier in order to write the blog entries in my room, in secret, instead of sitting in front of the television with Mark at the end of the day, pecking them out on my laptop where he could see and roll his eyes. Start the argument all over again.

Trying to convince him that my plan was not wrong was proving as impossible as trying to convince him that I didn't need a caregiver. He simply wouldn't listen, and now he and Mary Anne had worked out a schedule, taking shifts to ensure that someone was always around, always in the way. It was getting bloody annoying, let me tell you.

To prove I could still do just fine on my own—and to make sure I had my notebook with me at all times—I'd added a sticker to the bathroom mirror, reminding me to leave the notebook beside my bed at night, and another on the bedside lamp just in case. On the notepad itself was a bright yellow strip reading *Open me, you stupid cow*, in keeping with the tone of the other notes in my life.

Did these sound like the actions of a woman who needed constant supervision? Certainly not. These were the actions of a woman who not only recognized her shortcomings but was pro-active in dealing with them. Meeting her challenges head on and fighting back one day at a time. Knowing with absolute certainty that she was having a good day and that it was time for her morn-ing smoke.

I kept the little bag of pot in the medicine cabinet, because con-trary to what Mark believed, that's exactly what it was. Medicine—clinically proven to help the older brain with memory retention while significantly reducing agitation. Little things that ticked off Big Al and were more than enough to keep me puffing for the foreseeable future. Thank God Mary Anne still kept a little on hand, to take the edge off after a rough day in the classroom.

I lit the joint and inhaled slowly, the way she and I used to before Liz became wise and the pot started disappearing. I closed my eyes, letting the smoke work its way into my head, still cough-ing a bit on the exhale, but positive that would pass in time. Rais-ing the joint to my lips a second time, I opened my eyes and was surprised to see Mark standing in the bathroom door. For a big man, he could be awfully quiet.

And he didn't merely look good, he looked great. His jaw had always been strong, his cheekbones pronounced, and he was start-ing to get those wonderful angles back. Starting to look more like the outdoorsman he was born to be, the one I'd welcomed into my home all those years ago. "You're early," I said.

"And you're still at it."

I nodded while I inhaled and said, "I think it's helping," on the exhale. Then I pulled the ashtray across the counter, snuffed out the joint, and held up my hands. "See? Two puffs and no more. It's purely a therapeutic exercise. Although I don't understand why they make the stuff so strong nowadays. I honestly believe there's a market for pot lite." I walked past him, grabbed my notebook from the bedside table, and started down the stairs. "You should look into that one day."

"I'll try and remember," he said, and his steps were much heavier going down than they had been coming up, I was sure of it.

I reached the kitchen in time to see Grace on her way out the door, and Jocelyn waiting for her outside by the birdbath. "See you for breakfast," Grace called over her shoulder.

"You bet," I said, wondering if she ever missed solitary mornings the way I did. She hadn't complained so perhaps not. Then again, she rarely complained about anything so who knew? It was just one of her many virtues.

"I have a conference call at eight," Mark said. "I can't fit in canoeing now. We can go this evening when it's cooling off, or Mary Anne will grab a paddle if you'd rather go now."

Yes, she'd grab a paddle and we'd cruise the lagoons, which would be nice. But the good thing about paddling with Mark was his willingness to go beyond the safety of the inland system. To head out into choppy open water where I could use my arms and work my body, confident we'd find our way back without incident. As much as I hated to admit it, I'd miss that more than the ritual of the morning paddle.

"I'll wait," I said, and went to the door, watching the girls laughing and talking on their way to the gate while the mockingbird flew back and forth above their heads, trying to get the bird-in-a-box to come out. Mark handed me a mug of tea and stood behind me with his coffee, just as he had so many mornings when Liz and Grace were little. Not giving it a second thought as they headed off to school or the beach or a day of exploring on Snake Island. Knowing they were safe here, on the Island, where we watched out for each other's children and the deckhands on the ferry knew them all by name.

Grace and Jocelyn pedaled off, but we stayed where we were,

standing close enough that I could feel the reassuring warmth of his chest, the steady rise and fall of his breath against my back. Without thinking I leaned into that warmth, that reassurance. Felt him adjust his stance, welcoming me, supporting me. Outside, the mockingbird quacked like a duck, singing his song for the bird-in-a-box who hadn't done more than poke her head out the door for days.

"I don't know why he stays," I said softly. "Even if she comes out, she's never going to be the same."

"He probably doesn't care," Mark whispered, his lips grazing my ear, making my breath catch and my skin warm. "He just wants to be with her."

He set his mug down, took mine from my hands, and turned me to face him. Said nothing at all, simply leaned down and kissed me, letting his lips linger, his hands move over my back. Both of us discovering the fit was still right, still worked, exactly as it had for so many years.

I wrapped my arms around him and kissed him back, trying to remember why I'd sent him away, why I'd spent so many years alone, and why he'd only once tried to come back.

He was hard now, his hips pressing against my stomach, making my head swirl and my body ache with a longing as familiar as it was unnerving. I pulled away and he let me go, the two of us awkward now, searching for a way back, a way out, some time to think, at least—finding it in a voice calling, "Good morning, birdies," as Mary Anne came through the hedge to look in on the bird while the four of us were supposed to be out. Looking after me would come later, when Mark had gone to work.

He went out the door to say hello—to discuss my care—and she turned and smiled at him. She was all in white, a floating, gauzy shirt knotted over loose fitting linen pants. She looked old and lovely, like she'd stepped out of an ad for Viagra or extra fiber. When she laughed at something Mark said, then reached out to touch his arm, I couldn't help hating her, knowing she would be around to hear that voice, maybe kiss those lips, long after I was gone.

I turned away from the window, needing a distraction, needing order. Definitely needing meds. Pleased that my mind had gone in that direction, I focused on finding the container with the days of the week written clearly on top of each compartment. I didn't keep it upstairs anymore because it was more convenient for Mark and Mary Anne here in the kitchen. As long as Grace didn't find out what was under those plastic lids, it was all the same to me.

Pills swallowed and ready to make my morning notes, I searched the counter by the answering machine for a pen, the one that always sat there. But Grace must have moved the pen again, so I took the hunt to her room and sure enough there it was, sitting on her desk beside the monitor. She must have been making notes of her own.

Curious, I poked around on her desk a little, lifting bird books, sifting through styling magazines. Sifting, sifting. Opening drawers. Sifting, sifting. Still finding nothing of interest.

I straightened and gave my head a shake. Rolled the chair out from the desk and sat down. Pulled out the keyboard and tapped the spacebar. A small box asked for a password. I had to smile. Another game of hide and seek.

I typed in *bike*, *ned*, *baberuth*. When those didn't work, I tried *lordm*, *ladym*, and *feralcat*. Still no luck so I typed *william* and breathed a sigh of relief when that didn't work either. I wasn't sure I'd be able to cope if we started down that road again now.

Mark came to the bedroom door. "What are you doing?"

"Just a quick check on the Life of Grace, but I think Jocelyn might have given her a password and now I can't get in." I glanced over at him. "Give me a few passwords Jocelyn might use."

"Not a chance. What's on that computer is none of your business."

"Of course it's my business. How else can I know what she's up to?"

I went back to the keyboard. Tried to think like Jocelyn. *Goth*, *hated*, *fuck*. Still no good.

"Ruby, stop." Mark rolled me back from the desk. "Grace has a right to privacy."

He was right. I could corner Jocelyn later. Get the brat to confess.

He helped me to my feet and we walked out into the kitchen together. I sat down at the table while he plugged in the kettle and got out the eggs because Grace and Jocelyn were already back, already coming through the gate. How odd. They must have cut their ride short for some reason.

"Beautiful day, isn't it?" Mark asked as they came through the door, and then somehow they were all working together to get breakfast on the table. Mark measuring coffee, Grace breaking eggs, Jocelyn slipping bread into the toaster. And me? I was sitting at the table. Thinking how quickly this had become a routine and wishing they'd all stop talking at once.

"Then we're going birding," Grace was saying, sliding the eggs onto plates while Jocelyn added toast, and the three of them sat down to join me.

"When we were out this morning, I heard a black-billed cuckoo near the statue of Ned," she continued. "So we're going back to find him."

"A cuckoo?" Mark asked. "Aren't they fairly rare?"

She said, "Not anymore," and went off about changes in migration patterns and sightings while I considered my toast. It needed something. Red stuff. The stuff in the jar in the middle of the table. The stuff that's sweet and bad for you and full of . . . "Strawberries," I said out loud. "Can you pass me the strawberries. The jam. The strawberry jam." Big Al was stirring.

Jocelyn raised a brow and picked up the jar. Handed it to me much more slowly than I thought was necessary. "Anything else?" she asked.

"No, thank you." I smiled and dipped my spoon into the jar. Shook the red stuff onto my toast. Spread it around. Cut the toast in half and dipped it in my eggs. Nope. That was wrong.

"I like to blend the flavors," I said, biting into the dripping yellow and red mass. It didn't taste bad, but I was going to have to be more careful. Think before I made a move.

"You should come with us," Grace said, and smiled at me over her teacup. "See the cuckoo for yourself. Might be nice since you don't have any appointments today."

Mark coughed into his hand, Jocelyn bent her head over her plate, and my sweet daughter kept smiling at me. She'd turned the page in the appointment book. Of course she'd turned the page. Why hadn't I thought of that?

"A surprise day off," she said. "Just like I had yesterday."

"Yes," I said, and laughed. "Isn't it like customers to cancel all at once like that? But it's summer and the weather is lovely, so aren't we the lucky ones?"

"Lucky," she repeated, and I knew she had more to say. Could see it in the way her jaw was moving back and forth, back and forth. My fingers fumbled with the other half of the toast. How many pages had she turned? Did she know that Saturday also held nothing at all? Not even Marla Cohen, who had argued and argued with me before finally hanging up. Banging the phone down and leaving me with a headache. No matter how many times I said it, she couldn't understand that closing the shop was best for Grace, best for both of us. And honestly, how bad could it be for a young girl to have the whole summer off?

Mercifully, Grace didn't make me answer that question or anything else. She simply pushed back her chair and said, "I need to feed Lady M," for which I was grateful. I still needed to plan what I was going to say to her about Chez Ruby, figure out a way to ease into the discussion. Make sure she fully understood what a great idea this was.

She went to the fridge for the container of dog food and berries.

"Perhaps if you stop feeding her," I suggested, "she'll look for food on her own."

"Or perhaps she'll starve." Grace put a dab of the bird food on a plate and shoved the rest back in the fridge. "I'll see you outside, Jocelyn."

The ferry horn sounded. "I'm off to get a paper," Mark said, pressing a quick kiss to Jocelyn's cheek on his way to the door. No kiss for me, though. Not this time. Not in front of the kid. Just as well. No need to give her something more to scowl about.

He poured more coffee into his travel mug and headed out. This was also one of the new routines. On the days he was working from home—which had been every day as far as I could tell—he'd take his coffee and the ferry across to the city, buy a paper at the convenience store, and come back again. The trip took him forty-five minutes from the moment he left the house, and rather than seeing it as a pain in the neck—rather than ordering home delivery—he'd come to enjoy it. To remember what it was to relax, to breathe, to be an Islander again. And his return always gave me the opportunity to be frustrated by yet another crossword puzzle.

"Are you looking forward to birding?" I asked Jocelyn.

She turned to me, her eyes narrowing, warning. Danger ahead. Danger of what? Impending mood swing? Eruption of pimples? Who ever knew what teenagers were thinking?

"Grace makes it interesting," she said. "She knows a lot about birds."

"Yes. She surprises me daily with her bird trivia."

I went back to my toast. Did not dip the second half. Ate it like any other person at the table. Except I wasn't hunched over my plate and scowling. Had my own girls been this wretched as teens? Certainly not Grace, but Liz yes, now that I thought about it. She used to sit just that way, slumping and snarling through every meal. It got so that I preferred dinner in front of the television to one at the table with my daughter. Pity really, now that I thought about it.

I watched Mark through the window, waving to Mary Anne as he sauntered down the path. Breaking into a run when the horn went off again. Another part of being an Islander he'd rediscovered—the stitch in your side from running for the ferry.

"So did you get the power tools over to the clubhouse?" I asked Jocelyn.

"Yes, thank you." She raised her head, those narrowed eyes on me again. "And just for the record, Grace knows you're winding down the business."

I kept my eyes on my cup, breathed normally. "What are you talking about?"

"Don't play with me. Mrs. Charlton told her everything yesterday. 'Winding things down,' is the way she put it."

My stomach tightened around the toast and the eggs and the strawberry jam. Winding down the business, yes. For Grace. So she wouldn't have to worry about anything. So she wouldn't be overwhelmed by paperwork and taxes and stupid government forms. So she could relax and enjoy the rest of her life here on the Island in our house, in our garden. Looking at all the birds she wanted and bringing home as many as she liked with nothing else to worry about.

Yes, I was winding it down. But I needed to have everything done before I told her. A package to present to her. Nice and neat. All the ends tied up. Nothing to trip over down the line. Nothing forgotten. Nothing forgotten.

I rose and carried my cup to the sink. "Why did she call Mrs. Charlton?"

"Because she didn't know the appointment had been canceled. You didn't tell her. You let it be a surprise, which it was, believe me."

I gathered up my plate, my knife and fork. "I thought she might enjoy it."

"You thought it would be easier than telling her the truth. Even this morning, you lied to her. You need to know that you're an asshole for doing this."

"I am not discussing this with you." I dropped my dishes in the sink and carried on to the door. Stepped outside. Looked around for Grace. She wasn't there. I glanced over at Mary Anne's. Probably in there, asking her to keep an eye on the mockingbird while she went out with Jocelyn again. Asking her to babysit because she didn't trust me to keep an eye out for the cat. With good reason.

Jocelyn came out behind me, clutching a brown envelope in her hand. "If you think I'm letting this go, you're wrong."

"Little girl, you're in no position to judge. You know nothing about me, my family, or my business." I tried to go around her, go back into the house. Maybe take another couple of puffs. Relax for a moment. But the bitch wouldn't move. Just stood there with that envelope, like it was some kind of shield. "You know nothing," I repeated, and went down the stairs instead.

"I know Grace," she said, walking beside me across the lawn and around the side of the house. "And closing the shop without even talking to her is wrong. She's good at her work and she loves it. She *needs* it. She wants to do more. She wants to expand into manicures and pedicures—"

"And facials and waxing. I am well aware of my daughter's pipe dreams and happy to say that she's over them." I stopped at the hose reel. Stared at the nozzle. Knew I should do something with it. But whatever it was wouldn't come right now, and no wonder. I needed away from the girl with the bright red hair. Away from everything. It had been a mistake to postpone the paddle.

"They're not pipe dreams, and she's not over them." She held out the envelope. "It's all in here. Costs, courses, equipment, everything she'll need to offer aesthetics here on the Island."

"Pipe dreams." I hurried back across the lawn and into the house. Stood in the kitchen. Looked around slowly. What had I come back for?

The brat was there again. Pop. Right in front of me. Appearing out of thin air, I swear.

"Grace can do this," she said. "Sure, she'll take a while to get it, but once she does she'll be gentle and thorough. What more could anyone ask?"

I spotted my paddle hanging by the door with the life jackets. New inflatable life jackets. A gift from Mark. Latest technology. Light and easy to wear. That was it. I was going for my morning paddle. "I'm not discussing this." I grabbed the paddle and a jacket off the hook and headed back out, walking quickly down the path to the gate. Go canoeing, go canoeing.

"Just like you don't discuss William?" she yelled from the stairs. "Or the trial or the fucking house arrest that you pushed her into?"

I froze with my hand on the latch.

"She told me everything," she yelled. "Everything."

Thank God the street was empty. I leaned my paddle against the gate, dropped the jacket on the ground, and walked back. Stayed calm and in control. But I knew Big Al was watching, waiting, grinning. "You're twelve years old. I don't expect you to understand, but I do expect respect. I will not be spoken to like this in my own home."

"Whatever." She held up the envelope. "The point is that Grace needs to work, she needs to grow. These courses can do that for her."

"What is wrong with you people? I told you on the phone, she can't even get on the ferry. How can she take courses?"

For the first time, Jocelyn looked confused, unsure of herself and the righteousness of her argument. "We didn't talk on the phone. And what's wrong with the ferry?"

"It's not what's wrong with the ferry, it's what's wrong with Grace, and you people with your easy solutions and your quick fixes. Filling her head with nonsense about expansion and added services. Letting her imagine a whole different life for herself, when everything she needs is right here. Not in some stupid envelope."

I snatched it out of her hands and walked around the side of the house again. Lifted the lid on the garbage can. Dropped in the envelope.

Jocelyn snapped it up again before I could get the lid on and held it against her chest. "Why can't she get on the ferry?"

"I don't know and I don't care. It means she stays here where she's safe, and that's good enough for me." I looked around again, not sure what to do next. Took a few steps toward the front of the house, spotted my blessed paddle by the gate, and all the gaps filled themselves in. Snap, snap, snap. I was going for my morning paddle.

But the kid was in front of me again, like a mosquito that won't give up. "You're a horrible mother."

"I'm a good mother." And unlike Debbie Darling, I could still figure my way out of a situation. I went around the brat. "I only want what's best for Grace."

Right now that meant going for a paddle so I could think for two minutes because there was something I needed to do today. Something important. I stopped halfway to the gate. Pulled the notebook out of my pocket. *Open me, you stupid cow.*

I opened it, stared at the blank page. I hadn't written anything down. I flipped to the next page, and the next and the next. I hadn't written anything down.

I looked over at the paddle, looked back at the house. List or paddle? List or paddle?

"What is wrong with you anyway?" she demanded.

"I have—" I slapped a hand over my mouth, couldn't believe I'd almost said it, almost told the one person who would carry it straight back to Grace. I lowered my hand, pointed myself at the paddle. "I have to go."

I left her standing there, staring after me. I kept walking, carrying my paddle down the street and around the corner. Didn't care that my feet were bare and I'd forgotten the jacket, forgotten my hat. Didn't care about anything except getting in the canoe.

Go canoeing. Go canoeing. I walked on. Past the houses, past the dock. Saw the ferry coming in. Heard the horn. Walked on. Past the bridge, past the firehouse, past the Rectory Café where they have very nice tea. I hadn't been there for tea in a long time. But no, that didn't sound right. I'd been there recently. With Mark. Yes. The day I was mad at Grace.

Mad because . . . ? I didn't know. Couldn't remember. So what? Right now I knew that Jocelyn was wrong. I had to sell the business. Protect the house. Protect Grace.

Go canoeing, go canoeing. I walked on. Go canoeing, go canoeing.

When I stopped walking I was looking at the statue of Ned Hanlan and I had no idea how I got there. Or how long ago. Or why my feet were so sore.

I looked down. No shoes. I looked around. I was on Hanlan's Point with no shoes.

I started to laugh, it was that funny. On Hanlan's Point with sore feet and no shoes. I sat down in front of Ned, still laughing. Too funny, too funny. And suddenly I was crying. Sitting there blubbering like a fool, unable to stop.

A young man bent down and handed me a tissue. "Ma'am are you all right?"

He was nice-looking, clean-cut, the kind Great-Grandma Lucy would have liked. Not an outdoorsman with big hands, broad shoulders, and more patience than I had ever deserved.

I took the tissue and wiped my nose. "I have no shoes." But I still had my paddle. I saw it in my hand. My bent-shaft paddle. Where had that come from?

The young man took out his wallet. Tucked a bill into my hand. "God bless you," he said, and walked away.

I stared at the bill. Twenty dollars. He'd given me twenty dollars. He thought I was homeless. Sitting on the ground with no shoes on Hanlan's Point. Too funny, too funny.

I tried to get up. My feet were too sore. I sat back down. What time was it? Time for meds probably. But not here. Not on Hanlan's Point with no shoes.

A plane flew over my head. I got up. Shook my paddle at it. "Assholes," I yelled, and sat down again. "Don't you know there's a black-billed cuckoo here somewhere?"

That's when I saw him. Mark Bernier pedaling toward me. Going really fast. He was getting good on a bike again too.

"Ruby." He dropped the bike, ran to me. Looked at my feet. "Jesus Christ, Ruby."

He pulled me into his arms. Held me tight. I closed my eyes and my head fit perfectly into that spot on his shoulder. "I don't know how I got here," I whispered, and felt those damn tears burning my eyes, wetting his shirt. "I think I wanted to go canoeing, but I'm not sure."

"It's okay," he whispered. "I'm here. It's okay."

I shook my head. More tears on his shirt. "How can you say that? How can it ever be okay? I have to sell the business. I have to protect the house and Grace. How can I do any of those things if I don't even know how I got here?"

"I'll help you," he said, but I shook my head again.

"Help me with the paperwork, yes, and I appreciate that, but what about the house? What about Grace? She can't stay there alone, just as she can't run a business on her own. And if she can't stay there then we'll lose the house. The Island Trust will sell it and my great-grandmother's house will be gone. I can't let that happen, Mark. That house is everything to me, to Grace, but not to Liz, the one person who should be there to take care of it."

"She just needs time."

"I don't have time." I sat up, stared at the paddle. "She needs to come home now because I'm not doing better. It's not slowing down. She needs to take responsibility now, but she won't because she hates me, Mark. She hates me." I started to cry again as the truth began to seep through my bravado, my years of denial. The holes made by Big Al finally allowing it to get through, to penetrate, to show me what I'd done.

"It's all my fault, but she's so stubborn, she'll take forever to change her mind."

"She's a lot like her mother."

"She's a lot like Grandma Lucy." Exhaustion swept through me, making my limbs heavy and my head light, and bringing a fresh wave of tears. "Like it or not, Mark, I don't have years to wait for her to change her mind, and I don't know what to do."

"Marry me," he said.

I wiped my eyes with the young man's tissue. "I don't understand."

"The land trust lets you pass the house to a husband or a spouse. So marry me. I'll take over the house so Grace can stay, and when Liz is ready, I'll sign it over to her."

I stared at him. "Why would you do that?"

"Because I love you. And I'll still do my damnedest to stop you from doing something stupid, from throwing away the possibility that there are plenty of good years still to be had."

"Mark, can you honestly look at me and say that this is a good year? And wish me plenty more like it?"

"Ruby, it's not perfect, but it's better than the alternative because you're here, I'm touching you, I'm talking to you, hell, I'm fighting with you, and that's enough. That's all I need. That's all I've ever needed." He held up a hand. "I know it's not enough for you. I understand that the illness will progress and that provisions will have to be made for Grace. That's why I want you to marry me, so you can pass the house to a spouse and relax. Enjoy the years we have together, knowing it's protected. For you, for Grace. For Liz when she finally realizes what's important."

I looked down at my blistered feet. What he was saying made sense if I didn't dwell on the part about us having years together. Or think about what could happen if he decided to tell the doctor about my plans. To have me declared incompetent in order to protect me from myself.

But when I looked into his eyes, I saw love there. The same love I'd seen on the day he showed up at my front door with a bike and a baby seat. I could only hope that love would let him do the right thing when the time came.

I put my arms around his neck. "I've never believed in marriage."

He pulled me closer. "Then just believe in me."

He kissed me then, tenderly, slowly, making my heart squeeze and the tears start all over again because I probably didn't deserve this. But for now, for the moment, I wasn't going to question, I wasn't going to wonder. I was going to marry him. To hold on and hope for the best.

# LIZ

I have fallen off the wagon. At the turn of the twentieth century, *wagon* referred to a horse-drawn water cart that was used to wet down dusty country roads. Back then, being *on the wagon* meant you'd rather drink questionable water from the water cart than be sullied by drinking the finest demon rum from a bottle. When you finally admitted how boring your newfound respectability really was—and how pointless the fight to hold on to it anyway—you fell *off the wagon* and had to run to catch up with it again.

In my case, I have not only fallen off, I have made camp by the side of the road and the wagon has long since turned the corner. I'm not sure I want to catch up, even if I could. Which made my journey of self-discovery mercifully short, ending here on the floor by the window, the only place in this godforsaken room where you can catch a breeze on a hot summer night.

My tumble began on Tuesday on Ward's Island but oddly enough did not continue with Car Bombs at the Duck. Not out of loyalty to Brenda, but because I'd been banned from the place indefinitely. Found out that little tidbit when I showed up and was told I was no longer welcome. That's what happens when the new bartender tells you to shut up and return to your seat, and instead you dance the Highland fling on the bar and accidentally kick the bitch in the chin.

One of my buddies told me I was lucky they didn't press charges, and I believed him. He also told me the man with the long hair and beard—whose bruises had faded at last—had been a stranger to the place. They'd been keeping an eye out for the bastard, but he hadn't been seen since. I could only assume that when Nadia knocked someone down, they stayed down—and went into hiding later. I should tell her that if the substitute teacher thing didn't work out, she would make a fine bouncer, because one should always have a career alternative in mind.

Lying there on the floor, staring at the ceiling, not even sure what day it was, I wished I had a career alternative, because law was no longer an option. How sad that Ruby had been right after all. Hairdressing would definitely have given me something to fall back on. But that was water under the bridge. *Clean slate, move on. Never look back.*

Looking forward, however, knowing I'd have to tell Brenda that she and Mitch were on their own, had caused me to fall off that damn wagon in the first place. I would not be thinking about it even now if I hadn't run out of booze, proving what I have been saying for some time now—they're just not making twenty-sixers of vodka the way they used to.

The proof was there beside me, empty and cold, yet I didn't feel all that hungover. Didn't feel half bad in fact, except for the crushing weight of Brenda's petition sitting front and center in my mind, making it hard to think about anything else.

I could go to the liquor store, grab another bottle, and start all over again. But even if I could muster enough energy and money for the trip, I wouldn't make it past the top of the stairs because I knew for a fact that both Brenda and Nadia were in the house. I'd

heard them troop up the stairs and into my room earlier. But I'd
kept my eyes closed, pretending to be asleep, even when Nadia
came around the sofa and nudged me with her toe.

"Is not awake yet," she said, and went back out, closing the
door and cutting off all hope of a breeze. Punishing me for falling
off that stupid goddamn wagon. As if it was my fault her stupid
*Don't drink for today* shit hadn't worked.

But it had for a while, hadn't it? Like dieting for a day, or
not calling the man who broke your heart for just one more
hour, it was all about breaking down a long and painful war into
manageable battles. And I had been a real warrior for ten whole
battles. Sitting proudly on that wagon, right up front with the
driver, the two of us laughing and urging his old horse to pick
up the pace. *Git up, boy! Git up!* He'd understood I wasn't like
the rest of the passengers. I didn't have a problem. I was just
joy-riding, showing them all that Liz Donaldson was in control. Reins firmly in hand and facing forward. Who needed the
demon rum anyway?

Then Mark came along and shoved me on my ass, and that
driver didn't even look back once. Fuck him and his wagon. I'd
always liked camping out anyway.

Now, however, with the vodka gone, I needed to break camp.
Mostly, I needed to pee, which meant the time to talk to Brenda
had come.

Familiar thumping and banging began on the other side of the
wall, and I tried not to wonder what they were doing as I stood up
slowly, pleased that my head and my stomach stayed with me the
whole way. As hangovers went, it looked like this one was going
to be a snap. Perhaps there was something to be said, after all, for
sticking to one demon at a time.

I was still wearing the tank top from the meeting with Mark,
but my jeans lay in a heap by the bed and my floppy hat was on the
desk, next to a beautiful arrangement of flowers—a dozen pink,
orange, and yellow Gerbera daisies I hadn't known were there. A

peace offering from Mark, I assumed, which meant there was still hope!

I plucked the card from the plastic holder, tore open the envelope, and read:

*Thanks for helping my sister. I'd love to take you to dinner. Call me. Gary*

Hope gave way to a rush of warmth and pleasure that had twice spelled the beginning of something wonderful, something I'd hoped would last, but not this time. I sighed and slid the card into the flowers. How much better for everyone if they had been from Mark.

The door opened and Nadia stuck her head into my room. "You are up," she said, and seconds later both she and Brenda walked in wearing black bicycle shorts and white T-shirts with I ❤ Iyengar on the front—something Grace would appreciate—both sweating and smiling.

"How do you feel?" Nadia asked, taking a couple of Werther's out of her pocket and offering one to Brenda but not me. "Hungover or sort of okay?"

"Sort of okay." I pulled on my jeans and looked from one to the other. "Why are you both dressed that way?"

"I brought T-shirts from yoga school." She unwrapped a candy and popped it into her mouth. "One for you also. Was now showing Brenda benefits of headstand."

"I wasn't very good," Brenda said, and the two of them laughed. "I kept falling and she kept propping me up."

That explained the thumping but not the lingering grins.

"You sure you're feeling okay?" Brenda asked.

"Yes, I'm sure. But we need to talk."

Brenda looked over at Nadia. "Definitely sharper than usual."

Nadia grinned. "I told you. Works like charm every time."

"What works?" I asked.

"Watering vodka." She walked over and picked up my dead soldier. "Drunk person can taste nothing. Nevair knows difference."

"It's the same at the bar," Brenda said. "We don't water, but after a couple of rounds, we're definitely subbing in regular brands for premium. No one ever knows."

"I don't believe you." I followed them along the hall to the kitchen. "I would know if you'd done that. How much water did you add anyway?"

"A lot," Brenda said, and stopped me at the door to the kitchen, smiling up at me, obviously pleased. "We were late getting here the day after your meeting with Mark, and I was really ticked to find you drunk and passed out when we still had so much work to do. I was ready to smack you around right there on the floor, but Nadia took a more reasoned approach."

"I don't understand."

"It's simple," Brenda said. "Rather than bully you out of your binge the way I wanted to, Nadia said it would be best to let you continue, on a modified basis. Let you come out of it on your own. It seemed weird to me, but what the heck. We were screwed anyway. Might as well give it a shot."

Residual anger was creeping into her voice, bringing color to her face, and I was grateful Nadia hadn't set her loose on me. Made a mental note to thank her later.

"We could see you'd only had a couple of drinks from the bottle," Brenda continued. "So Nadia dumped out all but the last quarter. I was afraid it was too much, but she seemed to know what she was doing."

Nadia shook her head in that slow annoying way. "Would have been problem if she knew vodka, but she is peasant. Buys cheap shit, does not keep in freezer, mixes with soda." She flicked a hand at me. "Was too easy."

Brenda laughed. "Seemed so because we filled that bottle with water, put it back on the floor, and you didn't know the difference. Drank the whole thing, and here you are at the end of the bender, rested, mostly sober, and able to work. Brilliant, eh?"

The two of them had the nerve to high-five each other right in front of me.

"Trick is filtered water," Nadia said, turning to rinse my empty at the sink. "Tap water has chlorine smell and taste. Filtered? Nothing. Is perfect. For peasant."

She walked past us with the bottle and down to her room. I followed again, speechless, sputtering, madder than hell but not sure why.

Because I'd been duped? Because I wasn't hungover? Because I wasn't a goddamn peasant? Then it hit me. "That bottle cost me thirty goddamn dollars!"

"And still is cheap shit." Nadia stuffed my bottle into her canvas shopping bag, then walked over to her desk and sorted through the folders. "I have things to show you."

From the moment she first unlocked her door and invited us in, Nadia's room had never failed to intrigue me. Lipstick-red bed coverings, embroidered pillows, and yards and yards of gauzy red and gold fabric drooping from the ceiling. Walls adorned with paintings of lush women and lusty men framed in heavy gold leaf, and everywhere, bowls of candy and baskets of fruit. Werther's Originals by the bed, apples on the desk, gum balls on the dresser.

It hadn't taken us long to figure out that not only was Nadia efficient and organized, she was also a closet sensualist with a passion for color, texture, and anything sweet—which was why she was always popping something into her mouth. No wonder she'd been so worried about her groceries.

"Now we work," she said, popping another candy and handing me a bulging folder. "We have completed surveillance at Champlain. Here are pictures of building, men in suits, everything you ask for." She paused. "Do you want to use bathroom first? Maybe have coffee?"

"I don't believe this." I dropped the file. "I don't fucking believe this."

"I know, it's amazing," Brenda said, the two of them smiling, looking every inch the circus act in their matching outfits. "You should have seen her in action at Champlain. She knew you needed a floor plan, so she bought helium balloons and a top hat. Told the receptionist she had a singing telegram to deliver to Klaus Vandergroot and the girl led her straight to him."

Klaus Vandergroot. The man who would be receiving the petition to bankruptcy. But not from me.

"Now we know exactly which office he's in," Brenda continued. "And how you'll get there. We even drew you a map." She tapped a finger on the file. "Everything's right here."

"That's great," I said and turned to Nadia. "But the important thing is, did you sing?"

"Of course. Would have blown cover otherwise."

I smiled. This was too much. "What did you sing?"

"Bayu-bayushki-bayu." Nadia gave me her one-shoulder shrug. "Is Russian lullaby warning that little grey wolf is coming to eat you. Seemed appropriate, under circumstances. Horrible man liked it. Even gave me twenty-dollar tip, which I will claim on taxes."

"You make me nuts," I said. "But it doesn't matter because I am out. Can't finish the petition. Can't save your ass." I pushed the folder back at Nadia. "You'll need to take your pictures to someone else."

Brenda stopped smiling and crossed her arms. "Okay, what do you need this time? To hear again how brilliant you are? To have us say that this is the best idea anyone has ever had? Because if your ego needs stroking, maybe we could arrange for a couple of cheerleaders to follow you around. Gimme an *L*. Gimme an *I*—"

"My ego has nothing to do with it. I told you from the beginning I'm not the one for the job. I gave it a shot, but you need to hire someone else."

I started along the hall to the bathroom, but like the little dog that she was, Brenda darted ahead of me, blocking the way. "You self-centered bitch. If anyone's ass was saved here, it was yours. If we'd left you alone with that bottle, you'd be in the hospital right now having your stomach pumped and trying to get over alcohol poisoning."

"Now don't you wish you'd left me the hell alone?" I moved her out of the way. Stepped into the bathroom and closed the door.

She banged it back before I could turn the lock. "Why are you doing this? After all the work we've done, when we're this close. Why are you backing out now?"

"More important question," Nadia said as she lumbered down the hall toward us. "What has changed your mind? What has made you so afraid?"

"I'm not afraid, I'm practical. I've told you over and over again that Champlain is represented by a big firm that never plays nice. I finally took a long hard look at the petition and realized it was not in your best interest to have my name at the bottom. You need a name that has equal strength, equal clout. So I set up a meeting with Mark. I was sure he'd help, but apparently being back on the Island has turned him into a prick, so he refused." I started to close the door again. "Now, if you'll excuse me."

Brenda held it open. "He seemed like a nice guy. Maybe if I talked to him."

"Won't make any difference. He won't help unless I move back to the Island."

"Why would he say this?" Nadia asked.

I sighed, already tired of justifying myself to them, to Mark, to the whole fucking world. "Because my mother has Alzheimer's and she wants me back home." I tried closing the door again. "You really need to excuse me."

"Then you should go," Nadia said. "Look after mama."

"That's not what she wants."

"What does she want?"

"She wants me to take over the house and live there with my sister after she's gone."

"She wants to give you house? But you don't want house?" She turned to Brenda. "Brain impairment also is common in alcoholics."

"I don't have brain impairment, but I am desperate to pee."

Nadia shrugged and moved aside. Brenda finally let me close the door, but Nadia kept talking at me. "So he will not put name on petition and you are afraid your name is not enough."

"What difference does a name make?" I heard Brenda say. "It's the paper that matters."

"You think that way because you don't know lawyers." I rose and washed my hands. Purposely avoided the mirror and opened the door again. "The way the petition works, I have to deliver the papers to Champlain first, the bank second, and then I have to file them with the bankruptcy court. Our plan has always been to avoid that last step. We only want Champlain to *believe* that we're going to register that petition so the bastards write you a check. But once their legal team sees that it's just me out there on a limb, they may tell their clients to hold off. See if I really do get the sucker registered."

"Do you think they'd do that?" Brenda asked.

"If Champlain were my client, and I saw my name on those papers, I would call my bluff." I wandered into the kitchen and slumped into a chair. "I would eat me alive."

Nadia sat down beside me. "Why? What is wrong with your name?"

"It's not worth much anymore."

"Because you are drunk?" Nadia asked.

"Nope, that came later."

Brenda went to the sink. "Anyone want tea? Coffee?"

"Car Bomb?" I suggested. She gave her head a disgusted shake. "Coffee's fine, thanks." I leaned back and closed my eyes. Why anyone thought sober was better was beyond me. I would have given anything to have a Car Bomb going off inside my head right now.

Nadia tapped me on the arm, waited until I opened one eye. "What did you do? Sleep with client? Rob bank? Kill someone? If you killed someone, we are finished for sure."

"I didn't kill anyone." I grabbed the saltshaker. Slid it back and forth between my hands. "But I did ruin my sister's life."

Nadia smacked me on the head. "Stop playing with salt." She grabbed the shaker and put it out of reach. "How did you ruin sister's life? Maybe steal boyfriend? Marry lover?"

"Post ugly pictures on the Internet?" Brenda offered, still busy measuring and scooping—making fucking coffee instead of something a person could really use. Useless twit.

I pulled the sugar bowl toward me. Slid it from my right hand to my left. "Believe me, there are no ugly pictures of my sister. She's the most beautiful woman you have ever seen. And I did not understand how much trouble that could be for her."

Nadia nabbed the sugar bowl on its return trip to the right. "How can being beautiful be problem?"

"Because she's slow," Brenda said, setting out cups, going back for spoons.

"'Mind of a ten year-old,' my mother always said." I put my elbows on the table and propped my head in my hands. "But I never believed her. I was convinced that all Grace needed was a chance to grow, to learn, to experience a few things, and she'd surprise us all by becoming an independent woman."

"You were wrong?" Nadia asked.

"I was wrong," I admitted. Then I told them about Bobby Daniels and William, and how much he'd looked like her, and what a great mother she'd been. And finally I told them something I hadn't talked about in a long time. About the day I came back from lunch with a client and found a message waiting for me. A message that had already been there for two hours.

"'Call Grace,' it said."

I sat back, hands clasped on the table in front of me so I wouldn't be tempted to play with the cream or the cups, or the pepper shaker I'd just noticed. "Nothing else. Just 'Call Grace.' Being the rising star of the firm, of course, I had other calls to make first. Important calls to clients and other lawyers, one of them from the firm that now represents Champlain. Naturally, I made those calls first because the message only said, 'Call Grace.' When I finally did call her another two hours later, she said, 'William's dead.' Not 'William's sick' or 'I'm worried,' just 'William's dead.'"

Even now, years later, just thinking about that call made my skin grow cold.

"She must have been frantic, poor thing," Brenda said, leaving the stupid coffee at last and sitting down on the other side of me.

I shook my head. "Not at all. She was quite calm, which the prosecution used to their advantage later. She just wanted me to come home, because she didn't know what to do next."

"Of course you blame self," Nadia said. "For not making call earlier."

"But you couldn't have known," Brenda said. "She should have said it was an emergency." Echoing the very words my friends and colleagues had said over and over again. *It's not your fault, Liz. You couldn't have known, Liz.* But always, always, there was Ruby's voice in the background whispering, *You should have known, Liz. You should have known.*

"How did baby die?" Nadia asked.

"Quietly, in his bed."

"SIDS?" Brenda asked, whispering the word, not wanting to say it out loud, to give it weight, power.

I pushed myself back from the table, frustrated, restless, desperate for a drink or at least something to play with. I rose and picked up an orange from the basket on the counter. Tossed it back and forth between my hands. Back and forth, back and forth. This time Nadia didn't try to stop me.

"The original medical reports listed the cause as uncertain," I said, "which ultimately led to the broad catch-all of sudden infant death syndrome. But I can tell you with certainty that he was not outwardly sick, he did not fall, and he certainly was not shaken, despite their initial attempts to prove otherwise."

"He just died?" Brenda asked.

"He just died."

She shook her head. "How could that happen?"

"Sometimes there is no definitive reason." I tossed the orange, caught it. Tossed it again. Caught it. "Grace and I learned that little truth the hard way, but the problem is that the public can't accept it. They need someone to blame, something to point to. Something definitive like vaccinations, mattress bugs, infections, even the time of year will do, because it lets them believe in a root cause, a concrete reason for the death. A root cause that could have been avoided by a discerning parent.

"And every time, every single time this happens, there are those who believe the mother is the root cause. She must have done something. Was he in her bed? She must have smothered him. Was he crying a lot? She must have shaken him. She must be guilty because babies don't just die. But the thing is, sometimes they do."

I smacked the orange down. "My sister did not kill her son. Her only crime was in not calling 911. In knowing he was dead, not by measuring brain waves or lines on an EKG, but by being his mother. By touching his skin, feeling for a heartbeat, listening for a breath, anything that would have given her a sign that he could be saved. But she saw none of that. She only saw her baby, her son, lying in his bed, lifeless, cold, dead. She knew from experience what would happen if she called 911. And all she wanted was to hold him a while longer, without medical staff and social workers and all the other things that would have kicked in if she had made that call. So she called me instead. Then she wrapped her baby in a blanket and she rocked him, she sang to him, and she waited for me to call."

"And that was start of problem," Nadia said.

I leaned back against the counter. "They charged her with criminal negligence causing death. I acted as her lawyer."

"This was not best decision."

"I know that now," I said, keeping my eyes on the floor. "But at the time, no one could talk me out of it. I was convinced a jury would see that my sister was innocent and she would be acquitted. And for the first time in her illustrious career, the shining star lost a case."

"How could that happen?" Brenda asked. "Your sister was obviously traumatized, even if she didn't show it. Her reaction was completely understandable. How could the jury have convicted her of anything?"

I smiled at her indignant tone, her unqualified support. Even if she didn't have a clue what she was talking about, it was nice to have Brenda on my side. "The trial was a difficult one with expert testimony on both sides, conflicting autopsies, and psychological evaluations that didn't always put Grace in a good light. It was hard enough for the legal teams to wade through everything, harder still to gauge which way the jury was leaning. My sister was facing at least ten years in prison if I lost. So my mother went behind my back and convinced her to take a plea. To admit to the lesser charge of failing to provide the necessities of life, leading to death. Grace went home with a security bracelet around her ankle and I went to my favorite bar to start working on her appeal."

I left the kitchen. Walked back to my room. I didn't expect them to follow. Didn't *want* them to follow. All I wanted right now was to get dressed up and go out. Find someplace that was loud and fun. A place with music and dancing, where they didn't water the vodka and limitless joy was an all-you-can-drink happy hour.

I opened my closet and hauled out fresh jeans and a sparkly tank top—jade green, my best color—and threw them on the bed. Was rooting through the underwear on my desk when the two of them came to my door. Brenda crossing her arms and planting her feet, Nadia scowling and tossing jelly beans into her mouth—Sideshow Legal at your service.

"I do not see how this affects your name," Nadia said. "Everyone loses cases. Is nature of business."

"True," I said, tugging a jade green thong out of the tangle of bras, panties, and still more thongs. "And everyone has to learn to put those losses aside and move on. But I couldn't do that. All I could think about was the appeal. Grace hadn't even agreed to one, but I was already on the job. Couldn't eat, couldn't sleep, couldn't think about anything but getting her acquitted."

"This was when you started to drink," she said. Not a question, just the truth.

"Only one before going to bed. To get some sleep, smooth things out a little."

"But one became two," Nadia said softly.

I gave her a tight smile. "And two became three, and three become four and so on and so on, and still I never slept past three A.M."

I tossed the rest of my clothes onto the bed and went to the window, looked out at the street. Aware of a woman walking a dog, and little kids running, but seeing only Grace leaving the courthouse. The police escort. The throng of brash and pushy reporters. And Ruby screaming at me to leave my sister alone, just leave her alone.

"But I kept working on that appeal," I told them. "And I started hanging around the Island more too. Blowing off appointments and hopping on the ferry. Hoping for a glimpse of Grace, a moment when I could get her alone, make her understand how important it was that we strike back hard and fast. Ruby wouldn't let her speak to me, of course, and the local police escorted me onto the ferry, three, four, times a week." I stepped back from the window, looked over at them. "It's no wonder my mother took out a restraining order."

Neither one had moved from the door, and neither one said a

word. Then again, what was there to say? I was setting out the evidence clearly and concisely, making my case step by step. When I finished, they could only come to one conclusion, the right conclusion—Liz Donaldson was not the one they wanted.

"Slowly but surely, my name became a joke. Clients refused to have me on their team, other associates refused to work with me. It got so bad that Mark told me to take a leave of absence. 'Go have some fun,' he said. 'Think about something else,' he said. So I took the leave, found a lot of fun at the Duck, and never went back."

I picked up my clothes, grabbed a towel from the floor. I needed a shower. The time had come to close. "So Brenda, that is why I cannot help you. That is why you need a lawyer whose name will be respected. A name that is anything but mine."

Again, they didn't move, didn't speak, for another full second. Then it was as though someone had fired a gun and they were off.

"That's nonsense," Brenda said, "This is the perfect opportunity to win their respect. Come back with a bang. Show them you're still a shining star."

"She is right," Nadia said, popping the last of her jelly beans into her mouth. "Problem with sister's case was that jury never decided. No one knows if you would have won or lost." She dusted her hands and walked toward me. "This time you will find out. This time you will see if you win or you lose."

I dropped the clothes on the bed, sat down beside them. "But there's so much at stake."

"Which is why I'm betting on you," Brenda said. "I'm betting I'll have a check in my hands three days after you walk out of Vandergroot's office." She thrust out a hand. "What do you say? Three days, twenty bucks."

"I am thinking four," Nadia said and held out a hand to her. "Four days, twenty bucks."

"You're on." Brenda pumped her hand and grinned at me. "Come on, Donaldson. What do you bet? Three days? Four?"

In my head, I could see her with pom-poms and a little short skirt. *Gimme an* L. *Gimme an* I. The self-appointed captain of the Liz Donaldson cheerleading squad, laying a lot more than twenty bucks on the line. Willing to risk it all on me in spite of the mountain of evidence laid out before her.

I rose, humbled, terrified. Resigned. "I'm betting two," I said softly.

"Two days!" she shouted, and high-fived with Nadia. "I am going to win me forty bucks." She looked me up and down. "You do have something other than jeans?"

"In the closet," I said. "Far right."

We shook on the bet and Nadia went back to her room for a pen and paper to duly record the details of our bet while Brenda opened my closet door. Pushed everything to the left, revealing what was on the right. Hanger after hanger of crisp white shirts, cashmere sweaters, silk dresses, none of which had seen daylight in more than two years.

She stood on a chair to go through each item one by one. "Holy crap. You've got designer suits in here. Real leather jackets, suede skirts." She glanced back at me. "You must have looked amazing in a courtroom."

"I did." I wandered over. Pulled out my favorite black suit. Short jacket, fitted skirt. Crumpled and a few years out of style but exquisitely tailored, superbly finished—the signature look of a star attorney.

"Put it on," Brenda said. "Let me see how a brilliant lawyer dresses."

I shook my head, handed her the hanger. "Probably doesn't fit anymore."

"Just try it on," she insisted. "That way we'll know if we need to go to the dry cleaners or if we need to go suit shopping."

"I love suit shopping," Nadia said. "But if jacket fits . . ." She slid the jacket off the hanger and held it up, waiting for me to slide my arms into the sleeves. "What is worst that can happen? You find out you are too skinny and suit needs altering."

"I'm not too skinny." I shoved my arms into the sleeves, feeling the cool glide of the lining against my skin. The nip at the waist as I did up the buttons one by one. Nadia was right. I was too skinny now. I started to take it off.

"Wait," Brenda said. "It needs shoes." She got down on her knees and reached into my closet, under my suits. Came out with an electric-blue shoe box. Gave it a shake. "What's in here?"

"Not shoes," I said, taking the box from her. Pushing it up on the shelf above the clothes, out of her reach. "Shoes are to the left."

Nadia glanced up at the box then turned to me. "Is vodka?"

"I don't hide my vodka. Although maybe I should so no one will put water in it."

She shrugged. "Okay. Not vodka." She jerked her chin at Brenda. "Find shoes."

Brenda shifted to the left, reached in, and came back with a pair of black heels that had once made a judge forget to breathe while I was walking into his chambers. She set them on the floor in front of me. I slid my feet into them one by one, not certain if I'd be Cinderella or one of the stepsisters after two years in running shoes and flip-flops. The fit was still remarkably good—I guess feet don't lose weight—but it was going to take me a while to remember how to walk.

"One more thing," Brenda said, dragging the chair around behind me. She climbed up again, gathered my hair into a ponytail and piled it up on top of my head.

"Now look in mirror." Nadia pushed back my closet door, revealing the full-length mirror on the other side. "What do you see?"

I saw a woman in a crumpled black jacket, fabulous high heels, and blue jeans, with a midget in bicycle shorts holding her hair up.

"I tell you what I see." Nadia stood beside me. In my heels I was almost as tall, but not quite. "I see brilliant lawyer back on track again."

"I see *my* brilliant lawyer back on track again," Brenda said.

"Now look again." Nadia raised my chin. "What do you see?"

I looked again. Saw the crumpled jacket, the jeans, the fabulous shoes, and the beaming faces of my friends. Two odd women who saw more in me than I had in a very long time. Who believed in me more than I deserved.

I heard the wagon coming around the corner. Heard the driver tell the horse to slow up, to wait.

"Well?" Brenda said. "What do you see?"

"I see a lawyer who is going to be forty dollars richer two days after that petition is delivered."

Brenda whooped and let my hair fall down around my face. Nadia grinned and clapped me on the back. "Is good decision. Good decision."

"I've been meaning to ask you," Brenda said, taking the skirt from the hanger and looping it over her arm. "Who sent you the gorgeous flowers?"

I slipped off the jacket, looked over at the happy faces of the Gerbera daisies. "Just a man I met."

Brenda smiled. "Is he cute?"

"Very. Just not my type."

"Too bad." She took the jacket and headed for the door. "We should get these to the cleaners. I'll grab my purse."

"Get mine too," Nadia said, and then leaned close, whispering, "And just for today . . ."

"I don't drink," I told her. "Tomorrow maybe. But not today."

I kicked off the heels and climbed up into the wagon. Nodded to the driver and took my place in the back, knowing I'd have to earn a seat in the front this time.

# GRACE

Jocelyn and I were sitting in her kitchen on Algonquin, ready to go to the nude beach for the usual Thursday picnic—and to look for the cuckoo along the way—but waiting to hear from Liz first.

It was already ten and I'd started sending *RU coming?* text messages at eight, but she still hadn't answered back. I finally called her phone and left the same message three times. But when it got to be ten thirty and she *still* hadn't called, I said to Jocelyn, "Maybe we should pack a lunch, just in case."

Jocelyn shrugged and said, "Whatever," and we went back to my house. Her phone started going off the second we were through the gate, and she sat outside tapping keys while I went inside and took a look through the fridge, making note of what we had and what kind of sandwiches I could make, just in case. All the while knowing Liz wasn't coming, but not saying it out loud. Just waiting and checking the clock and sending the same text message over and over again *Whr RU? Whr RU?* Until it got to be eleven thirty and I finally went outside with two boxes of cookies and said to Jocelyn, "Do you want chocolate chip or vanilla cream with your lunch?"

She stopped tapping her keys. "I don't care. But do you still want to go?"

"Well, it's Thursday, and I always go to the nude beach on Thursday."

"But do you want to?"

I hadn't thought about it, but now that Jocelyn had asked, I realized the answer was no. Even though it was Thursday, I didn't want to go to Hanlan's Point. I wanted to be home when the peroxide arrived and when my mom got back from wherever she went because I wanted to talk to her. Wanted to ask her what was going on and hope she'd explain what *winding things down* meant. Most of all, I wanted to be there in case the lady mockingbird flew.

I put the cookies on the railing. "No. I don't want to go anywhere."

"Good, because I don't want to go anywhere either." Her phone went off again. She growled and started hitting keys and I went back inside and put away the cold meats and the cookies. I was about to pick up the phone to find out if the beauty supplier had shipped my order, when the door opened and Jocelyn stuck her head into the kitchen. "Get out here right away! I think the lady mockingbird is going to fly."

We ran down the stairs but slowed down as we rounded the corner so we wouldn't startle the bird. Sure enough, she was sitting on top of the cage, bobbing up and down, up and down, looking for all the world like she was going to fly.

The male must have thought this was the day too because he had stopped working on the nest and was sitting on top of the lilac, singing like a cricket.

Mary Anne appeared at the break in the hedge, a wide-brimmed straw hat on her head and a pair of gardening shears in her hand. "How's she doing?"

"I think this is it," Jocelyn said, waving her over.

"Is she going to fly?" a voice called from the sidewalk.

We turned to see Kylie and Brianne and four other girls standing with their bikes at the gate, all craning their necks to see what was going on. Jocelyn smiled and waved them in too. "Hurry up. Or you'll miss it. But you have to be quiet so we don't scare her."

The bikes dropped and they all tiptoed through the gate and over to the cage. They ranged in age from ten to thirteen and I knew each of them by name. They all whispered, "Hi Grace, Hi Mary Anne," and then Kylie said, "Everybody, this is Jocelyn." She grinned at Jocelyn. "And Jocelyn, this is everybody."

The other kids introduced themselves and Jocelyn nodded to each one. "You all live on the Island?" she asked.

They all nodded and the youngest one whispered. "How long you here for?"

"The summer," Jocelyn said.

"How are you liking it?" another girl asked.

"It's good," Jocelyn said, her smile bright, genuine. "Really good."

"Jocelyn's the one who brought all the power tools for the sale," Brianne said.

"We are going to make soooooo much money with those," Kylie added.

"You should totally come to Wonderland with us on Sunday," another girl said.

"If you'd like to," Kylie said, and Jocelyn grinned and whispered, "I'd love to," and Kylie grinned back and said, "Great!" And while Kylie gave her all the details, Mary Anne and I arranged the girls in a group about ten feet back from the cage—putting the shortest ones in the front and the taller ones in the back while the bird bobbed up and down, and danced to the left and then to the right, her eyes on the honeysuckle bush across from her.

It wasn't far. Maybe six feet. I crossed my fingers. Tried not to hold my breath.

"Look!" Kylie said. "She's going to go!"

The lady mockingbird bobbed once, bobbed again, and flew! Fluttered was more like it, landing on the ground in front of the table. But it was enough to get all of us up on our toes and leaning forward, whispering, "Come on, come on. You can do it."

Suddenly she took off again, reaching a branch about a foot off the ground. From there, she flew back to the top of the cage and tried again. This time, she made it to the honeysuckle bush. From there, she made it to the birdbath where she paused to freshen up for her mate, and we all looked at each other and said, "What the heck?" and then she took off again, flying all the way to the top of the lilac!

"She did it!" Jocelyn shouted and the whole group of girls squealed and jumped up and down while Mary Anne and I laughed and hugged and dabbed tears from our eyes and said we'd known all along she could do it.

Above us, the male performed his dance of love, swooping and diving while he barked like a dog, rang like my mother's alarm clock, and finally sang his own sweet song, all for the lady mockingbird who had made it to the top of the lilac. She seemed to like his show and they flew up and around and down together, calling hew, hew, hew to each other until finally he led her to the nest he had built and the two disappeared into the leaves.

"Proving once again that love conquers all," Mary Anne said and leaned in close. "I'm so glad your mom wasn't here to spoil it."

"Me too," I said, wiping away another silly tear.

"Where is your mom anyway?" Mary Anne asked.

"I guess she went canoeing with Mark."

Her smile faded. "Did you see him with her?"

"No, but Jocelyn saw her leave with her paddle and when we came back his bike was gone, so he must have been meeting her somewhere."

"I hope so." She looked back along the street. "I only slipped out for a moment . . ."

"Mary Anne, is something wrong?"

She smiled again and patted my arm. "Not at all."

"You'd tell me if my mother was sick again, wouldn't you?"

Jocelyn punched a fist in the air. "This calls for a celebration!"

"With cake!" one of the girls said.

"What a marvelous idea," Mary Anne said, avoiding my question and heading back to the hedge. "I have a white cake mix and a tub of chocolate frosting in the pantry. I'll bring it over for you."

I shrugged at Jocelyn and pointed to the kitchen. "You know where the pans are."

"Great!" She smiled at the girls. "You guys want to help me bake a cake?"

And they all trooped up the stairs and into the house.

I didn't know Jocelyn had left her phone on the arm of the chair until it started to buzz. She came back, watched the phone until it stopped, then switched it off and left it behind again when she headed back into the house.

"You have to love a girl with priorities," Mary Anne said, handing me the cake mix and frosting over the hedge. "I'll go make some of my world-famous lemonade."

"Mary Anne, wait. You would tell me this time, wouldn't you?"

"Grace, your mom is just fine," she said, and hurried on before I could ask anything else.

I handed everything to Jocelyn at the door then wandered over to the empty cage. Ran a finger along the bells of Jocelyn's cat-stopping contraption, hoping my mom was indeed *just fine* and listening to the clatter of pans, the whirr of the mixer, and the music of seven voices all talking and laughing in my kitchen. Thinking that maybe it was a good thing we had no clients today after all.

When the cake was frosted and ready, I brought the folding table out to the yard, spread a cloth on it, and set chairs all around. Jocelyn served, Mary Anne poured, and we toasted the happy couple who were too busy finishing their nest to pay us any attention.

I was helping myself to a second piece of cake when my cell phone buzzed. Liz had sent me a text.

*Sry sry. Wrkng on case. Cmpltly frgot. Hp UR not md. Wll cll ltr.*

I sent a message back. *Not md. Gd lck. Mkngbird flew!*

I didn't know she was working on anything, but if she had a case then she couldn't be drinking, so how could I be mad? Especially when I'd purposely missed the picnic myself.

We were gathering up the last of the dishes when my mom and Mark came up the street on his bike, my mom riding on his handlebars. I smiled and handed my stack of plates to Kylie, who took them into the house where Jocelyn was washing, Mary Anne was drying, and the girls were sorting out what went where.

"Don't you know that's dangerous?" I said as they rolled up to the gate. But when my mom got off the bike, I could see she wasn't riding the handlebars because she wanted to, she was riding them because she was having trouble walking. "What happened to your feet?" I asked, holding the gate open for her.

"Blisters," she said, tiptoeing off the walkway and onto the grass. A burst of Mary Anne's laughter drew her attention to the house. But it was the ripple of giggles after that held it. She looked from the house to the table and back to me. "What's going on here?"

"The lady mockingbird flew," I said. "How did you get blisters?"

"Walking. And that bird flying does not explain why my house is full of kids. What are they doing in there?"

"Dishes by the sound of it." Mark drew up beside her. He had her paddle in his hand. "Are those Jocelyn's friends I hear?"

"Not the ones you're thinking about. Some of the local girls came by to watch the takeoff with us."

"That's great," Mark said. "When did she fly?"

"A couple of hours ago." I pointed to the lilac. "They've been working on the nest since." I turned back to my mom. "Where were you walking?"

"Hanlan's Point." She tiptoed over to the table and sat down. "Can you get everyone who is in the house out of there? I have something to discuss with you."

"Did you ride on the handlebars all the way from Hanlan's?"

"No," Mark said, pulling out the chair beside her. "We took the ferry across to the city and then hopped on the *Ongiara* back to Ward's."

"Can you get me a glass of water?" my mom asked.

"Daddy, did you hear?" Jocelyn called as she came down the stairs, the rest of the girls streaming through the door behind her. "The lady mockingbird flew."

"I need a glass of water," my mom repeated.

"I'll get you one," I said, but then the girls were all around us, the seven of them talking at once. "The male sang just like a cricket!" "*And* an alarm clock!" "I've never heard a bird like that, have you ever heard a bird like that?" "I swear it was the bravest thing I ever saw." "She flew right up to the top of the lilac, no stops at all." "No, she made one stop." "I'm sure she made two."

Then Brianne said, "I almost forgot. Did you know a bunch of people started a pool over at the tennis courts? It's called Fly or Die, and they bet on what day the bird would either fly or die." She put a hand on her chest. "I bet five dollars she would fly, of course."

"We should go over and spread the good news," Kylie said, leading the troops to the gate.

"And give the finger to anyone who bet against her," Jocelyn added.

"You're not going anywhere," my mom said. All the girls froze and looked back. "Not everyone, just Jocelyn." She turned to me. "Can you get me that water now?"

Jocelyn's eyes narrowed at her dad. My mom's narrowed at her. This was not going to end well. "Would you rather come inside for that water?" I asked. "Put your feet up. Relax—"

"Will you stop arguing and just get me a goddamn glass of water!"

"Right away." I was halfway to the house when I heard Jocelyn say, "She can't tell me I can't go to the tennis courts."

"Then I'm telling you," Mark said. "Because we need to go home. I have something I want to talk to you about."

Mary Anne was still at the sink, rinsing the last traces of cake batter from the cloth.

I snatched a glass from the shelf and held it out to her. "I need a glass of water, quick."

She held it under the cold-water tap. "What's wrong?"

"My mom," I said, heading back out with the glass, and Mary Anne right behind me.

"I don't understand why it can't wait an hour," Jocelyn was saying as I handed the glass to my mom.

"We won't even be that long, Mr. Bernier," Kylie said.

Brianne nodded. "We just want to post a notice at the tennis court."

"Somebody's going to make a lot of money," the youngest girl said.

"Not my dad," another added. "He bet against the mockingbird."

"Then you know what he's getting," Brianne said. They all laughed and started to slowly raise their middle fingers.

My mom banged her empty glass down. "Oh, for God's sake, we're getting married. There, it's done. Go post your notice."

I stared at her, Mary Anne stared at her, even the girls stared at her, their fingers still poised in midair. Only Mark spoke. "Ruby, what are you doing?"

"Making it easier for her to go and have some fun." She turned to Jocelyn. "Any questions?"

"Just one. Are you fucking kidding me?"

Mark squeezed his eyes shut. "Jocelyn, that's enough."

She turned on him, face red, fists clenched. "Enough? You spring this shit on me and then expect me to be polite?"

Faces appeared in windows and doorways across the street. My mom waved. "Hi, Renata. Benny, you visiting her again? And, Carol, how have you been?"

The faces disappeared, but the houses are close and we all knew they weren't the only ones listening to another installment of *Oh, Those Donaldsons*—an Island exclusive since 1943.

"We should take this inside," Mary Anne said.

"You go inside. I'm staying right here." My mom folded her arms and sat up straighter. "By the way, I want you to be my maid of honor."

"I'm thrilled." Mary Anne slumped into the seat beside her. "Does anyone besides me need a cup of tea?"

I started for the door. "I'll make you one."

My mom pointed a finger. "Grace, you stay right there. Jocelyn isn't the only one affected by this."

"We should go," Kylie said, herding the rest of the girls toward the gate.

Jocelyn walked with them. "I'm coming with you."

"No she's not," Mark said, standing in front of Jocelyn while the girls filed through the gate and picked up their bikes.

"We'll wait for you over there," Kylie called.

Mark sighed as they pedaled away. "Jocelyn, I swear this was not the way I wanted to tell you."

"What difference would it have made? The news would still have been the same."

"Why don't we go home and continue this conversation in private?"

"Because there's nothing more to talk about. You're getting married. Congratulations." She grabbed her bike and kicked back the stand. "But it would have been nice if you'd mentioned your plan *before* you asked someone to marry you."

"Jocelyn, believe me," my mom said. "We didn't plan this. It just happened."

She laughed. "It just happened? While you were out canoeing the thought just came to you? 'Hey, let's get married and screw up Jocelyn's life forever.'"

"We won't be screwing up your life," Mark offered.

"Really? Okay, then answer me this. Where are we going to live?"

My mom laid her head on the table. "We haven't worked out all the details."

"They're not details," Jocelyn said. "They're my fucking life." She started walking her bike to the gate. "I just wish I could understand the rush. We've only been here a few weeks. There's food in the fridge we've known longer, for God's sake."

"It hasn't been just a few weeks for Ruby and me," Mark said.

"Yeah, yeah, you used to be lovers." She stopped and glanced back. "As gross as that is, why can't you just do the same thing? Why do you have to get married?"

"Because we're not getting any younger." My mother raised her head and looked across the street. Twiddled her fingers at the crack between the curtains at Renata's house. A crack that slowly, discreetly disappeared as my mom turned back to Jocelyn. "It was now or never."

"*Never* would work just fine for me." She glanced over at me. "And you, standing there like a lump, not saying a word. What do you think about all this?"

"I think it's great," I said softly. "It's something I wanted for years."

She shook her head. "Why would you want this?"

My mom sat back. "Because when Liz and Grace were little, your father lived with us here in this house. He was their dad too."

Her eyes widened at Mark. "You're their father?"

"Not biologically, no. But in every other way, yes."

"So you used to live here in this house. With her. With them."

"For thirteen years, yes."

Jocelyn dropped her bike and walked back to the table. "Why didn't you tell me this before we came?" She turned on me. "And why didn't *you* tell me after we got here?"

"You never asked." I felt kind of stupid saying it, but I wasn't going to lie. There was enough of that going on around here already. "You knew your dad lived on the Island years ago, but you never even asked me what house. I figured you didn't want to know anything about it."

She screwed up her nose. "I didn't ask because I didn't care. It was ancient history, like asking who his third-grade teacher was. Honestly, who gives a crap?" She focused on her father again. "But living with them, being part of a *family*, is totally different from just being a guy who lived on the Island for a while. Why didn't you tell me before we left the city?"

He ran a hand over his face and sank into a chair. "Because it would have meant a long, complicated discussion and I didn't think it was going to matter. I didn't think we'd be getting married."

"You can still change your mind," my mom said, as though expecting nothing less.

He covered her hand with his. "I'm not going to change my mind. You don't get out of it that easily."

Jocelyn said, "I think I'm going to puke."

Mark turned back to her. "Will it help if I admit that you're right? I should have told you before we came here, but everything happened so fast I didn't get the chance."

"Exactly my point," Jocelyn said. "Everything's been done so fast. The decision to come here, changing everything at your office, and now this. I've never understood the rush. It's like you're in a race or something."

"We are," my mom said.

"Because we're not getting any younger," Mark added. "And yes, this marriage probably seems like a sudden decision, but believe me, it's been years in the making."

Jocelyn closed her eyes. "Just tell me you weren't screwing around with her when my mother was alive."

More faces at the windows, more shadows by the doors.

"Absolutely not," Mark said at the same time my mom said, "Never." She looked out at the street and raised her voice. "Did everybody get that? I was not sleeping with Mark while he was married. Benny, you might want to write it down in case you forget later."

"I have a perfect memory," he called. "And congratulations to you both."

I had to laugh as the shadows disappeared and faces ducked out of sight. Too bad Liz wasn't here. She would have loved this.

Jocelyn went back to her bike. Stood with it half inside the yard and half out, her eyes moving back and forth between Ruby and Mark. Like she couldn't decide what to do and didn't know what to think anymore. I understood how she felt. I've always been the last to know what was going on in my own life, but it still hurts every time I find out someone has kept something from me for my own good or because it's too complicated for poor Grace to understand. Like why my clients had been canceled, and how much Mary Anne wasn't telling me, and why my mother thought it was okay to look through my computer whenever she felt like it.

If it was hard for someone like me to be left out, I could only imagine how much harder it was for someone like Jocelyn, someone who had never been last. But she was better at making decisions than I was ever going to be because a second later she said, "I'm going out," then she pushed her bike all the way through the gate and let it close behind her.

"Jocelyn, for what it's worth," my mom called to her. "I'd like you and Grace to be my bridesmaids. You can pick your own dress. Whatever color, whatever style. I won't say no."

Jocelyn looked back and smiled a little. "Wanna bet?" she said, and started walking her bike toward the tennis courts.

My mom turned to Mark. "Aren't you going to say something to her?"

"Dinner's at six," he called.

"I meant aren't you going to stop her?"

"Why would I? She was given the news of the wedding a little more abruptly than I'd planned. She needs time to absorb it, think it through."

"But you don't even know where she's going."

"I don't have to know every move she makes. I trust her."

My mom shook her head. "You always were naïve where kids are concerned."

"Ruby, this one is *my* daughter. Don't forget that."

"I'm sure I won't." She gave me a tight smile. "Can you put the kettle on, please?"

"I have to talk to Jocelyn," I said and ran to the gate.

She was two doors down, still walking her bike. "Jocelyn wait," I called. "I'll come with you."

She shot a quick glance over her shoulder, but kept on going. Not riding, just walking. Fast enough to let me know she wasn't going to wait. Slow enough that I could catch up easily.

"Grace, what are you doing?" my mom asked.

"I'm going out too." I dashed up the stairs and into the house, grabbed a copy of the movie *Family Man* from the shelf in my room, and went back outside. Tossed the movie into the basket on my bike, and ran with it to the gate. Jocelyn was almost out of sight.

"Grace, sit down right now," my mom said.

"She can't," Mary Anne said. "She's going out. Now leave the girl alone and come inside. We have a lot of planning to do." She rose and pointed at Mark. "You too. Inside."

My mom grimaced as she got to her feet and tiptoed behind Mary Anne to the door.

"I have always loved weddings," Mary Anne was saying. "The flowers, the dresses." She frowned as my mother hobbled up the stairs beside her. "Oh, for heaven's sake, what on earth have you done to yourself now?"

Jocelyn was still walking her bike when I finally caught up to her. "What do you want?" she asked.

I got off and walked mine too. "Just to tell you I'm sorry you had to find out everything this way."

"Me too."

"But the good news is that when they get married, we'll be sisters."

"Have I mentioned how much I like being an only child?"

I laughed, but she didn't laugh with me, and we walked on in silence. Past the cutoff to the tennis courts to the path that leads to the ferry dock. People were already starting to gather and more were coming along the road and across the field. Jocelyn shoved her bike into the rack and went to stand by the railing, away from the crowd, her face turned toward the city. On the other side of the bay, the *Ongiara* was leaving the dock, making its way back to the Island.

"Are you very mad?" I asked. She nodded and I said, "I can understand that. But I hope you don't do anything to make Mark change his mind, because that would be the meanest thing you could do to him."

"Stopping him from marrying someone he hasn't seen in years would be mean?" She gave a short laugh. "I don't know, Grace, sounds to me like it might be the kindest thing anyone could do for him right now."

"You think that way because you only know Mark as your dad *now*. You didn't know him back then. You didn't know how happy we were." I walked back to my bike and took the movie out of the basket. Popped the case and lifted up the cassette. Underneath was an envelope with three photographs inside. "Take a look at these."

The one on top was a man holding a chubby blond baby up over his head. Both laughing, looking into each other's eyes. Behind them to the right, a woman watching, her eyes soft, her mouth relaxed, smiling. Beside her, another little girl with her skirt raised up over her head. On the back: *Our family, 1981.*

The second, a strip of three shots. Same man, same woman, same little girls, older now—six and eleven. The four of them squeezed into a photo booth, flashing peace signs, sticking out their tongues, each trying to outdo the other to make the strangest face—all of them laughing so hard it hurt when they left the booth. On the back: *Our family, Disney World, 1986.*

The third, same couple, a rare shot of them dancing. Her head on his shoulder, his head resting on hers. Arms around each other. Eyes closed, no idea a picture was being taken. On the back: *Mom and Dad, 1987.* That was me, pipe dreaming.

These were the only pictures I'd managed to save once he was gone and my mother was crying and wiping the slate clean. Liz had hidden six inside a book, Richard Scarry's *Best Mother Goose Ever*, and stuck another three to the bottom of a drawer. I always hoped my mom had a couple of her own hidden somewhere. Secrets she didn't admit to anyone, not even herself.

Jocelyn went through the shots one by one, taking her time, seeing her father as a much younger man, living a life she hadn't been part of, a life where he had obviously been happy, in a world that had never been the same without him. After the third time through, she stacked the photographs together, leaving the one of my mom and Mark dancing on top. "How old were you when he left?"

"Twelve. Just like you."

"He was like your dad, and he just up and left?"

"He didn't leave. My mom kicked him out."

"Why?"

I sighed and waited for the captain of the *Ongiara* to stop blowing the horn. "She said it was *irreconcilable differences* and *incompat-*

*ible parenting styles.* Liz said she was just jealous. Afraid we were starting to love him more than her."

"Were you?"

"Liz, probably yes. Me, no. I loved them both the same. I still do."

She handed them back to me. Stood with her hands on the railing as the *Ongiara* slowed and prepared to dock. It was hard to say what she was seeing. The city, the water, maybe something else completely.

"I wish we'd never come here," she said at last. "I wish we'd stayed home, and I'd never met any of you."

"I'm glad I met you."

She gave me a small half smile. "You would be."

The ferry bumped the dock. The deckhands prepared to lower the ramp. The crowd on the dock moved to the sides, making space for the passengers waiting to leave the *Ongiara.*

"Jocelyn, I didn't know your mom, but I'm sure your family was happy, and I'm sure you have pictures you love as much as I love these. And I guarantee that if you make up your mind to stop them from getting married, you'll win because you're his daughter and he loves you. But he's been alone for a long time now, hasn't he?"

"Six years. Almost seven."

"My mom's been on her own for a lot more than that. She's seen other men during that time of course, a lot of them if you want the truth, but there was never anything serious after Mark left. Certainly no one she would have married. And even though I live with her, I know she gets lonely."

Jocelyn bent her head, kicked at a stone on at the ground. "My dad's never seen anyone seriously since my mom died. He goes out with his friends all the time, but not with women much. The last time I can think of was almost a year ago. That wasn't even a date really. She was just some woman he met at AA. They had lunch a couple of times but then she started drinking again, so he didn't see her anymore. Since then, nothing." She sighed and stared out over the water again. "That's kind of sad, isn't it?"

"I worry about that for myself sometimes. That I'll end up here, alone. Just another crazy old Donaldson woman ranting at the tourists."

She turned suddenly and took my arm. "We need to get off this Island and go into the city. Do something totally nuts, something you can't do here, like go to a movie."

The ramp came down. Passengers started to flow out onto the dock.

"Come on." She tugged on my arm. "Let's get on the ferry. Let's go have some fun."

I held back. "Your dad said we should be home at six."

"You've got a phone. We'll call them from the other side." She tugged again. "Come on, Grace. We'll be fine."

People still flowed off the ferry. "I don't have any money."

"I do." She pulled a flat leather wallet from her back pocket. "Twenty bucks and a debit card. What more do we need?"

"Jocelyn?" We turned. Kylie smiled as she and Brianne rode toward us. "You okay?" she asked when they stopped.

Jocelyn let go of my arm. "Yeah, I'm good. I'm sorry I didn't come to the tennis court."

"Don't worry about it," Brianne said. "We told everyone about the bird. Some guy who's dating your neighbor Carol won two hundred dollars."

"But we didn't say anything about your mom and dad," Kylie added "We figured they could tell whoever they want."

"Jocelyn?" another voice called. "Oh my God! It's Jocelyn!"

Her friend Courtney stood on the ramp of the *Ongiara*, smiling and waving while Alex, Josh, and Sean urged her to keep moving forward. "I've been calling you all day!" she shouted as they walked. When they hit the dock, she edged through the crowd, sidestepping strollers and bicycles, then broke free and ran toward us.

"Where were you?" she asked as she hugged Jocelyn. "I was starting to get worried."

"I forgot to recharge my phone." That was a lie. She'd turned it off, but who was I to tell?

"Airhead," Courtney said, and smiled at me. "Hi, Grace." She turned to Kiley and Brianne. "Hi, I'm Courtney."

The girls introduced themselves while the rest of Jocelyn's friends joined us.

"Hey, Goth girl," Josh said, but I didn't know why because Jocelyn didn't look Goth at all anymore. She just looked like herself.

"We're heading over to the beach," he said. "Gonna light a little fire, smoke a little—"

"You go ahead," Jocelyn said. "I don't feel like it."

"Why not?" Courtney asked. "What's wrong?"

"Nothing's wrong," Jocelyn said. "I just want to go into the city tonight."

"Then we'll go with you." Courtney gestured to her friends. "Back on the ferry, everybody. Jocelyn needs to go into the city."

"Hold on," Josh said. "We've got plans here." He looped an arm around Jocelyn's shoulder. "What's the problem, Goth girl?"

"Stop calling me that." She pushed his arm off. "There's no problem, okay? I just don't want to stay here."

He held up his hands and backed away. "Whoa, settle down. You do whatever you want, but we're not getting on any ferry for a while. Courtney, you coming?"

"I'm going with Jocelyn." She leaned closer and lowered her voice. "And you're going to tell me what's going on."

Jocelyn gave her a small, uncertain smile. "Sure. Why not."

Alex strolled away with the boys. "Have fun you two," she said, and smiled at Jocelyn over her shoulder.

"What was that about?" I asked.

"Nothing. She's just a bitch." Jocelyn turned to Kylie and Brianne. "You want to come with us? I need to go to a movie. It feels like I haven't been to one in a year."

"We'd have to call home first," Kylie said.

"There's no time," Courtney said. "The ferry's loading now."

"We can call from the *Ongiara*," Kiley said to her sister. "Have you got any money?"

"Five bucks," Brianne said.

"My treat," Jocelyn said. "You can get me next time. Let's go."

Kylie laughed. "Okay."

The twins parked their bikes in the rack and ran ahead with Courtney to the ramp, the three of them already talking at once. "Does anyone know what's playing?" "No idea." "I am *sooo* getting nachos."

I smiled. They were going to have a great time.

Jocelyn turned to me. "You coming?"

I shook my head. The captain blew the horn. A few stragglers were running full out across the field. A woman picked up a wailing toddler and started to jog. She probably didn't stand a chance.

Jocelyn took my arm again. "Grace, please. I want you to come. You know I didn't mean what I said earlier, right? About wishing I'd never met you?"

"Of course I know that. You love me."

She laughed and pulled me along. "I wouldn't go that far, but I do want you to come to the movie."

The other girls were already on the ferry, waving, calling, "Hurry up, hurry up."

The captain blew the horn. The woman with the toddler was still jogging, still closing the distance. Maybe she'd make it after all. And Jocelyn held on to my arm, leading me along the dock, all the way to the end of the ramp.

I stopped there, my heart pounding, the blood swooshing in my ears. Jocelyn tightened her grip. "Grace, listen to me. There's no reason you can't do this."

I moistened my lips. Told myself she was right. There was no bracelet on my ankle, no poster on the bulletin board, and none of the deckhands were on the lookout for me anymore. I was free to get on that ferry any time I wanted. Like right now.

I took a step forward. My skin suddenly got all hot and tingly as the woman with the toddler ran past me and thundered across the ramp, red-faced, sweating, victorious.

A deckhand came out to meet us. Held out a hand. "Come on, Grace," he said softly. "You can do this."

I looked up into his eyes. He knew me. After all this time, he still knew me.

He was tall with eyes so brown they were almost black, and I wasn't supposed to talk to him. *Pay them no attention, Grace. None at all.* But he smiled and I smiled, and I couldn't think why I should be rude. "Hi, Joe," I said and reached for his hand.

His fingers closed around mine. "Hi, Grace."

He waited while I took a deep breath.

"Come on, Grace," Jocelyn whispered. "You can do this."

At the other end of the ramp, Courtney looked confused, but Kylie and Brianne were nodding and smiling. "She's right," they said. "You can do this."

I tried to take a step but my legs were numb, my feet like concrete. I could feel Joe's fingers against my skin. Rough, strong. I looked up at him again.

His smile was kind, his touch gentle. "Grace, it's okay. Just don't look down."

Don't look down. Like the lady mockingbird, look up, look up. I could picture her there on the top of her cage, bobbing and dancing, bobbing and dancing, getting ready to fly, to go. Maybe I should bob and dance too. Maybe that would help. If I could have moved my feet, I might have tried.

The horn blew again. The toddler started to cry. "What's her issue?" the mother said. Jocelyn shot her a nasty look. "What's *your* issue?"

I let go of Joe's hand. "Next time."

"Next time for sure," he whispered, and stepped back onto the ferry.

Jocelyn came back to the dock with me. "It doesn't matter. We can go home."

"Don't be silly. One of us has to get on that stupid ferry and go to a movie."

Kylie, Brianne, and Courtney started across the ramp too. "No," I called. "Get back on." I pushed Jocelyn forward. "Go with your friends. Have fun."

They hesitated and the captain blew the horn one more time.

"You coming or not, girls?" another deckhand asked.

"They're coming." I motioned to Kylie. "Take Jocelyn with you. Take her now."

The twins each took an arm and led her across the ramp. Joe pushed the lever and the ramp slowly rose and locked into position. The engine kicked up a notch, the water churned, and the *Ongiara* slowly backed away from the dock.

"Have fun," I called, and waved my arm in a big arc. *I'm fine, see? Everything is just fine.*

The four girls lined up along the railing. Three waved back with equally big arcs. *Okay, you're fine.* Jocelyn crossed her arms. *Liar.*

The woman with the toddler stood slightly back from them, looking at me like I was indeed the crazy woman of the Island. The way things were going, she was probably right.

I sniffed back tears, made my smile bigger. "Be sure to come back," I called to Jocelyn.

She smiled at last and blew me a kiss. "Count on it."

# RUBY

Never having been married, I had no idea a wedding, even a simple one, required so much organization, documentation, and tulle. Tulle for decorating, favors, headpieces—as far as I could tell, no wedding was complete without miles and miles of white, frothy tulle. Apparently brides sold it on eBay after the big day. People who made a living planning such events knew these things. Lucky for me, Mary Anne had been planning hers since the day she turned ten.

Within twelve hours of our engagement, she had a wedding checklist in front of us with stars beside the first three items: *Fix a date. Book the church. Rent the clubhouse.*

By Sunday night, Mark and I had completed items one and three. However, because he is stubbornly Catholic and I am third-generation agnostic, we skipped item two and hired a justice of the peace to do the honors instead. It was either that or risk having me burst into flames at the altar, which might have made Jocelyn smile, but would have meant a messy cleanup for the church ladies, and that hardly seemed fair.

Along with the checklist, she had also gave me a file marked VENUE with pictures cut from magazines, showing me how fabulous the clubhouse would look with white tablecloths, satiny chair covers, and all of that tulle draped and pouffed on every conceivable surface.

Mary Anne hadn't mentioned tiny white lights, but judging by the pictures, I would doubtless be looking for miles of those on eBay as well because as unlikely as it was, I admit I had been sucked into this wedding madness. Entranced by fairy-tale settings, swept up in the search for a theme, and amazed that cakes could be art. She had not yet tried to convince me that I needed someone to walk me down the aisle, which meant that so far, the only point of contention had been our choice of date.

"You cannot pull a wedding together in three weeks," she'd said. "It takes longer than that to print the invitations."

"Why don't we just put the invitation on the phone chain?" I suggested.

"Or why not run off a few flyers and staple them to lampposts." She lowered her chin and looked at me over her reading glasses. "This is not a rave, Ruby. This is a wedding. And the invitations are always engraved."

I was beginning to understand the terror her students must know on a daily basis.

Now, on Monday morning with a rush order about to be placed for invitations, and two and a half weeks to go, the biggest decision facing us now was the menu. A file with our choices was sitting in the middle of the table when we came back from canoeing this morning. Right next to the large manila envelope Lori from Algonquin had dropped off as well—the envelope containing her offer to buy the assets and client list of Chez Ruby.

"Mary Anne left that for you," Grace said, taking a sip of tea and disappearing around the corner into the storage room to join Jocelyn in a search for sponges.

The two of them were getting ready to take down the mockingbird cage and eating breakfast on the run—morning glory muffins from the clubhouse instead of eggs, which had left me staring at the stove for a moment. Grace didn't seem bothered by the change, however. In fact, she looked happy as she rooted around in the cupboard under the sink.

Reminding myself to be grateful for small things, I put it down to wedding madness and poured tea for myself, coffee for Mark.

"These are really good," Grace said, retuning to the table to pop the last bit of muffin into her mouth. "You should try one."

Jocelyn said nothing, of course. Just kissed her dad on the cheek, curled her lip at me like a mongrel, and followed Grace out the door. But as mad as she still was at me about the wedding, she had not resorted to covering her face with white makeup and black eyeliner. And she stopped wearing her Hated skirt after only a few hours on Friday. Seems it was not conducive to birding in the bush. I learn something new every day. And usually forget it the next. But not today. Not so far.

"They do look good," Mark said, peering into the muffin bag. "You want one?"

"Why not?" I shook this morning's pills into my palm and swallowed them down with pomegranate juice, pleased that Big Al had not yet joined us for breakfast.

In fact he'd been rather lax about coming down at all these past few days, leaving me with most of my marbles, most of the time. Perhaps he was taking a vacation. Resting up after our last dance. While it would be nice to believe Dr. Mistry's latest shift in meds was finally paying off, I knew better than to count on anything where Al was concerned. Told myself not to get excited. Take things day by day and keep that notebook handy at all times.

Speaking of which, I took the notebook out of the back pocket of my shorts and set it down in front of me. *Open me, you stupid cow.* That sticker still made me smile, but Mark had been horrified the first time he saw it. "Why would you write that?"

Because it was the first thing that came to mind. No longer

confident that there would be a second thing, I'd scribbled it down right away, only later realizing I'd come up with a theme without my even trying.

I flipped open the book, printed *Today's List* at the top followed by: *Sign papers. Meet Lori. Find out about cuckoo.* I laid the pen down. What kind of cuckoo? Not the clock kind. Something else. A black something. Close enough. I crossed out *cuckoo* and printed the more precise, if not entirely complete, *black something cuckoo*.

Mark set a muffin in front of me. Kissed the side of my neck and sat down. "What's Mary Anne have in mind for the menu?"

It was more curiosity than a genuine need to be part of the wedding madness that had prompted the question. His involvement in the process had ended on the night of his proposal when he handed me his credit card and said, "Whatever you want is fine by me."

He hadn't shown any sign of regret either when he climbed into bed with me the following morning—his first foray up my stairs since he arrived on the Island, possible only because the girls left for their bike ride before I was even up—still searching for the elusive black something cuckoo as I understood it.

Seemed that bird was proving harder to find than any of the others, and I was beginning to wonder if there was more going on during those morning bike rides than Grace was telling. But the worry drifted away when Mark started kissing my lips, my throat, the ticklish spot behind my ear. And when his hands moved down the length of my body, only to come right back up, sliding my nightgown up and off, my mind filled with memories of other mornings, other nights when he'd kissed me just this way before starting the slow, tender trek down between my breasts to my stomach and beyond.

I was grateful that Big Al slept on, mercifully oblivious to the sighs, gasps, and occasional hoots of laughter going on all around him. And that he stayed that way while Mark and I lay in each other's arms afterward, sweaty and smiling, waiting for skin to cool and breath to calm. It was with a clear head that I decided then and there that I really did want to get married. Not just to save the house or to protect Grace but for myself. For Ruby Donaldson who could finally admit she'd been an idiot to throw him out and wanted a chance to make up for all the lost years. To have him there in her bed every night and every morning for as long as possible. To go out remembering the touch of this man, this love, on her skin.

Sitting at the kitchen table now, watching him read the menus, I knew I'd made the right choice. Invitations be damned. Three weeks was long enough to wait.

"I'm leaning toward number three," he said, laying the pages in front of me. "What do you think?"

All three menus were from Mary Anne's most trusted caterer and included assorted hot and cold appetizers, chef's wedding soup, green salad, and a lemon cheesecake rich enough to satisfy the most expensive taste. The only difference was the main course. Chicken, veal, or roast beef. I didn't need to look to know that menu number three must be the roast beef.

I picked up the envelope instead and held it out to him. "I think we should look at this first. Lori said she'd come by this morning for a decision, and I'd like your opinion."

"You know my opinion." He went to top up his coffee. "Why the rush? What difference will it make if you sign your company away today or wait until after the wedding?"

"I'm not signing my company away, I'm selling it and making a nice profit in the process." I dropped the envelope back on the table and reached for the milk jug. "Besides, I can't wait any longer even if wanted to. Grace knows something is up because dear Mrs. Charlton told her I was winding things down. She hasn't said much, but that bottle of peroxide is proof enough that she's feeling her oats, pushing my buttons to goad me into a discussion about this, and I do not want to open that door."

"Why not? What would be wrong with a discussion?"

"It would upset her, that's what. Grace functions best with structure, and I'm sorry she found out anything at all. I wanted to present her with a done deal so she could adjust to her new situation without any advance fretting and worrying. Like the wedding. We didn't ask her if she minded if we got married, we simply told her what was going to happen, and she adjusted. It's different with a girl like Jocelyn, but it works well for Grace."

"What are you plotting for me now?" We both jerked around as Jocelyn came through the door. "An all-girls school in Switzerland?"

"Something much more important." Mark slid the envelope to one side and held up the menus. "The wedding dinner. What do you think we should serve? Chicken, veal, or roast beef?"

Jocelyn did the eye roll that was always so attractive. "Who gives a shit?"

It was the first time we'd agreed on anything. I would have been happy with potluck. Let everybody bring something and see what happened. Three tables of desserts, a tray of deviled eggs, and one chickpea salad, if my guess was right. But that menu wouldn't fit with the white tablecloths and satiny chairs of my shocking new fantasy, leaving me no choice but to set the notion adrift and say, "Roast beef could work," setting myself up for an in-depth analysis of au jus versus gravy when Mary Anne came over later.

"I can't believe you two," Jocelyn said. "Doesn't anybody want to talk about the stuff that really matters? Like where we're going to live?"

Mark carried his plate to the sink. "We can discuss that tonight. Right now, Mary Anne needs a decision for the caterer."

"Will you stop the bullshit?" Jocelyn said. "The wedding will last one day. Our living arrangement will last the other three hundred and sixty-four. That should be item number one on your fucking checklist."

"Jocelyn, if you don't watch your language—"

"She has a point," Grace said.

None of us had heard her come in and we all turned at the same time.

"I've been wondering where we'll live too," she said, crossing to the sink and opening the cupboard again. She reached in and pulled out a bottle of bleach. "I mean, it's okay if she shares my room. It's pretty big, and we could move in another bed. Or we could have bunk beds." She closed the door with a smile. "That might be fun."

"I am not sleeping in a bunk bed. I need my own room." She turned to Mark. "So here's the deal. I'll agree to live here as long as I have my own room."

Mark raised a brow. "You're agreeing to live here, just like that? No discussion, no fighting, no more Hated skirt at breakfast?" He folded his arms and leaned back against the counter. "Why?"

She threw up her hands. "Because what choice do we have? Our beautiful four-bedroom house in Rosedale perhaps? The one with a flat-screen TV, heated pool, and your house-swap buddy, Seth, in the hot tub? We all know that isn't going to work for Grace."

Color burned its way up into Grace's face and she turned away. "Don't worry about me. I'll be fine."

"You won't be fine anywhere but here," Jocelyn said. "While I'm sure that will change in the future, I know it's the case now and I'm okay with living here. I just need a room of my own." She pointed at me. "And for her to stay out of my face." She turned back to her dad. "Are these things going to be possible?"

"I suppose we can tie Ruby up for a few years. As for your own room . . ." He shrugged and took a look around. "We'd have to have an architect look at the place. See if another floor is feasible—"

"Not necessary," I said, because this was still my house and I would not be tied up or left out of any discussion concerning what would or would not be added or subtracted. "The solution is right in front of us." I rose and walked to the sink, gestured to the storage/laundry room off the kitchen. "That used to be Liz's room.

We renovated so we could bring Chez Ruby here. But there's no reason we can't put it all back the way it was for Jocelyn."

"Except that's where we keep all the salon stuff," Grace said, and walked over to the storage room. "We can probably fit the roller carts and your workstation in my room, but that would still leave the towels and the washing machine and . . ." She stopped and faced me. "Unless you've got something else in mind. Unless you're *winding things down*." She came a step closer. "What does that mean? And why did you cancel my appointments without telling me?"

Definitely feeling her oats. I sighed, remembering only too well where that had led the last time, and wishing Lori had already been and gone with those papers. But since Grace was determined to open the door, there was nothing left but to walk through and hope for the best.

"I canceled the appointments because I wanted us both to have more time off. And 'winding things down' simply means slowing things down, enjoying life more. That's what I'm doing with Chez Ruby. Slowing it down so we can enjoy life more." I got up from the table and cupped her face in my hands. "Sweetheart, I'm fifty-five. I want to relax, retire. I thought we'd try it out by taking the summer off. Find out what it's like to have a little time to ourselves."

Grace's eyes widened. "You want me to try out your retirement? Mom, I'll be thirty next week. I don't want to retire. I want to work. I like to work."

"I understand that, but as you know I haven't been well—"

"The cancer, yes," she said, her beautiful face filling with compassion and empathy, making my own flush with guilt. "You didn't tell me about that either."

"That's because I only found out recently myself," I said, refusing to acknowledge Mark's cough or his sudden need for more coffee, because it was true—I had no idea where the cancer notion had come from. Something was going on with Grace. Something more than birds, I was sure of it.

I sat down and picked up my cup. "Of course, I'm perfect now. Right as rain, but I want more time to myself. And running a business takes a lot of time and energy—"

"I have time," Grace said. "And energy. Lots and lots of energy."

"If only that was enough. But there's also bookkeeping and paperwork—"

"We can hire a bookkeeper," Mark offered, and had the audacity to look all wide-eyed and innocent when I scowled at him. "It's just a suggestion."

"A really good one," Grace said, beaming, dreaming—both equally dangerous. "If we hire a bookkeeper, then I promise to keep everything else the same." She all but danced over to the table. "I'll make sure the floor is swept after every client and the water cleaned up after every shampoo. I'll book the appointments every forty-five minutes, just like you do, and I'll always play Big Band music." She pulled out the chair and sat down beside me. "I've done almost all of your clients' hair at least once or twice, and most of them like what I do." She grinned at Jocelyn. "Mary Anne really likes what I do."

"So do Marla and Audrey," Jocelyn said.

I waved a hand to cut her off, to cut all of them off. "No one has ever disputed Grace's ability to cut and color hair."

"You'd think that was the most important thing in a salon, wouldn't you?" Jocelyn said. "Otherwise people would go to their bookkeepers or their bank managers or someone else who was really good with paperwork when they wanted their hair done. But they don't. They go to someone with the ability to cut and color hair."

I closed my eyes. "My God, it's like having Liz in the house."

"Jocelyn, that's enough," Mark said.

"But she's right," Grace said. "If people are happy with their hair, why won't they keep coming back just because someone else is doing the paperwork? And I won't change the name or the color of the towels or anything. All you need to do is give me a chance."

"Sounds good to me," Jocelyn said.

Even Mark was carried away. "She certainly has the drive."

I turned to her again. "Grace, sweetheart. You know I love you, but running a business is more than bookkeeping. There's inventory, ordering—I can't begin to name all the things that are second nature to me now. I can't possibly teach you everything else you'd need to know."

"How can you say that?" Jocelyn demanded. "You haven't even tried."

I rounded on her at last. "Little girl, you have no idea what you're talking about. For seventeen years, I've been showing my daughter what it is to run a business. Hoping she'd start to get it, to understand even the basics, but she hasn't. And the proof is right here in front of us." I went to the supply cupboard, picked up the brand-new bottle of peroxide, and plunked it down in front of Grace. "Do you know where this came from?"

She had the sense to lower her eyes, to look sheepish. "We were almost out and you wouldn't get any. I was afraid we'd run out completely, so I called and they shipped it out right away. It arrived on Saturday."

"Did you put it in the cupboard so I wouldn't see it?"

"I put it there because I wanted you to see it. I wanted you to ask me about it." She breathed deeply and lifted her chin, faced me again. "I wanted you to ask me because I thought if we started talking about it, then maybe you'd tell me the truth for a change."

I threw up my hands. "Fine, let's speak the truth. Let's start with that bottle of peroxide. When it arrived on Saturday morning, did you wonder why? Did it strike you as odd since none of our regular orders ever arrive on a Saturday?"

She shook her head. "I just thought it was special."

"You're absolutely right. It was special." I walked over to the desk, snatched up an envelope, and handed it to Grace. "You didn't open this when the order arrived, did you?"

"No, because you always open the envelopes."

"Yes, I do. So I opened this one and discovered that our peroxide had arrived by special delivery from a supplier in Buffalo. Do you know where that is, Grace?"

She didn't shake her head this time, just stared at the envelope.

"It's across the border, in the United States."

She looked confused. "I don't know what happened. I just called the number in your book."

"You obviously picked the wrong one. You couldn't tell that the area code you were dialing was wrong, and you placed an order with a supplier in Buffalo who had my credit card on file from an order I placed a year ago. The bastard on the other end didn't ask why you were ordering a stock item like peroxide. Didn't suggest you call someone local. Just took the order and slapped me with a bill for fifty-five dollars in delivery, duty, and taxes. Plus the cost of the product." I picked up the bottle. "This is officially the most expensive bottle of peroxide in the world."

"It could have happened to anyone," Mark said.

"I was with her," Jocelyn said. "I didn't notice any of that stuff either."

"You're twelve years old. Grace has been been working in a salon for longer than you've been alive. You'd think she'd have picked up something as simple as the name of our regular supplier, but she hasn't." I shifted back to Grace. "She hasn't."

"It won't happen again," she said softly.

"But something else will."

"Then we'll hire an office manager," Mark said. "Someone to take care of the details so Grace can focus on the hair."

"My God, Mark, we're talking about a cottage industry here. Not a huge downtown salon. Besides, this isn't simply about Grace's ability or inability to run the business."

She closed her eyes. "I don't understand."

I sank into the chair beside her. "Grace, the truth is that even if you were up to running the business, I would say no because I want my house to be a house again. The place is small. Even if we add a bedroom for Jocelyn, we still couldn't separate the business from the living area, and I don't want to come down and have clients in my kitchen anymore."

"That's it then," Jocelyn said. "You don't want the business, so screw Grace."

"I'm not screwing Grace, I'm relieving her of the burden." I held up the manila envelope. "I'm selling everything to Lori. The papers are here. That's all there is to it."

Grace was on her feet so fast she made us all jump. "When were you going to tell me this? When Lori was rolling my workstation out of my room?"

I rose to stand with her. "Grace, you need to calm down. Take a deep breath—"

"I need to go and finish the cage." She banged back the door and went down the stairs.

"You bitch," Jocelyn muttered on her way by, and I noticed Mark did not correct her before she crashed out the door as well.

"That went well," he said.

"Shut up." I went to the sink, turned on the tap, and let the cold water run. "You might have been more helpful."

"I didn't once say that I agree with them. I think that was being very helpful." He tore open the envelope. "Might as well look this over. Your mind is made up anyway."

I splashed water on my face while he laid Lori's offer on the table and picked up a pen. I didn't care what was in it anymore.

Whatever the offer, I'd take it, just to have this whole thing over with. To be rid of the workstations, the roller carts, the daily reminders of what had been my life. I glanced over at the barber's chair. Even that could go. I'd always wanted a wicker couch anyway.

I walked to the door. Grace had taken the cage apart and laid the pieces on the grass. I watched her snap on rubber gloves, pick up a brush, and go at the bottom section of the cage, scrubbing harder and harder. Her face was red, her hair coming out of the ponytail. Her arms were slick with sweat and her T-shirt starting to cling, Kiss Me I'm Irish straining across her chest with each brutal stroke.

"You're Scots," I whispered, fearing an outburst, knowing I'd earned one. Wishing there had been another way, certain there was none.

Jocelyn sat down beside her, picked up a section of cage, and went at it with equal fury. Glancing over at Grace now and then, saying nothing, just being twelve and trying to help, to show loyalty. She looked different from the girl who had first arrived at my door all those weeks ago. Tanned, healthy—still an awkward adolescent, but I could see signs of the woman she was going to be in the curve of her cheek, the cut of her jaw. *Striking* was the word that came to mind.

Grace's movements began to slow, her shoulders to slump. She closed her eyes and finally took a long, deep breath. I took one myself, hoping the storm was over.

The gate opened. Kylie and Brianne came into the garden, no longer needing to be invited. "Hey, you guys," Kylie said. "What's up?"

"Cleaning the cage," Jocelyn said. "What's up with you?"

"We're going to Centre. You want to come?"

"I don't know." Jocelyn turned to Grace. "What do you think?"

Grace sat back. Dropped her brush. Stared at the section of

cage that had never been so clean, then rose and smiled at the girls. "Sounds like fun. You should go."

"You don't mind?" Jocelyn said, dropping the brush and stripping off her gloves.

"Why would I?" Grace picked up the hose, aimed it at the cage bottom, and squeezed the trigger. All four of them leapt back, screeching as the water splashed back. I could have told her that was going to happen, but Grace hadn't known, couldn't see it, which would always be the problem. She could never see trouble coming. Now she was soaked but laughing. At least she was laughing.

"This isn't a bad offer," Mark said. "Straightforward, nothing hidden or tricky."

I was about to go back to the table when the gate opened again. Two men this time. One a deckhand from the *Ongiara*. Thirtyish, nothing special to look at, with too much dark curly hair. Italian probably. Or Portuguese. I couldn't think of his name. The other was a neighbor from down the street. Stewart? Yes, Stewart. Doris's husband. Tall and round-shouldered, like his wife.

The deckhand had a fried chicken box in his hand and he was in a hurry. "Grace," he called.

She stopped laughing and turned. Dropped the hose. Straightened her shoulders. Pushed at her hair with the back of her hand and smiled. A gesture so feminine, so adult, it took my breath away. "Hi, Joe," she said.

*Hi, Joe*? She knew him? What the hell was going on here?

He held out the box. "Some kid was trying to get on the ferry with this."

"I heard it when they came on board," Stewart said. "I asked the kid what he had and he said it fell out of a tree."

She opened the lid and peeked inside. "A baby robin."

Another bird-in-a-box. More proof that there was no God.

"Let me see!" the girls said, the three of them clamoring around her, trying to get a look in the box.

Grace knelt down and lifted the lid. "He's very scared. So you have to be quiet."

The girls were instantly six years old, peering into the box, eyes soft, mouths round. Their fingers twitching, eager to touch but holding back, being quiet.

Grace covered the box again and stood up. "Why did you bring him here?" she asked this deckhand, this Joe who should be working, not talking to my daughter.

"I couldn't let the kid take it to God only knew where," he said. "And once I had the box in my hand, I thought of you."

His smile was awkward, shy. He wasn't sure of himself around her. The deckhand liked her. My spine stiffened. Not this, not now.

Behind me, Mark said, "Ruby, don't." I turned my head. How long had he been standing there? "He's just a nice guy with a baby bird. She's fine."

"Everybody knows what you did with that mockingbird," Joe was saying. "I thought maybe you could help this little guy too."

A nice guy. That's what people said all the time after they found out a serial killer was living next door. 'He seemed like such a nice guy.' Not that Joe looked like a serial killer. Just large. And hairy. And what did he want with Grace anyway? Why hadn't he stayed at his post on the *Ongiara*? Let Stewart come with the bird on his own. Irresponsible, that's what he was. And standing far too close to my daughter.

"Fly or Die," Brianne said, and held out a hand to her sister. "Five bucks to fly in three days."

Kylie shook on it. "Five bucks to fly in four."

Stewart shrugged. "Put me down for five to die in two." He headed out the gate. "Sorry, Grace, but he looks pretty shaken up. I don't think he's going to make it."

"You're on," Jocelyn shouted after him. "I'll take five to fly in five."

"We should set up a board at the tennis court," Kylie added. "A lot of them there will take 'die.'" She gave Grace a small, embar-rassed grin. "Sorry, it's just the truth."

"That's all I ever want," she said. It just wasn't always what she needed.

Kylie motioned Jocelyn to follow her to the gate.

"I should call Courtney," Jocelyn said as they walked.

"Tell her to get over here right away," Brianne said, letting the gate close behind them.

Grace peeked into the box again. "Poor little thing."

"Can you help him?" Joe asked.

"I don't know." She held the box close, as though keeping it warm. "He's got lots of feathers so he might have been on the ground on purpose. He might have been learning to fly. Did the kid say where he found him?"

"Near the fire station I think."

"Then you should take him there and put him back on the grass." She held the box out to Joe Deckhand. "His parents may be looking for him. That will be the best chance he has."

He looked disappointed. "Are you sure?"

"At this age, he'd need to be fed every few hours, and I don't have anywhere to keep him. That cage is too big, and besides he shouldn't get used to one. He needs to be outside where he can see other birds, learn what he needs to do." She glanced up at the lilac. "Once the lady mockingbird lays her eggs, the male will probably try to run him off or worse." She held the box out again. "You should try the fire station first."

He still didn't take it. What was wrong with that man? Irre-sponsible and pigheaded.

"What if it doesn't work?" he asked. "What if his parents don't come for him?"

She peeked into the box again. "Someone should stay with him to make sure they do or at least make sure no one picks him up again until they have a chance."

The ferry horn sounded, still at a distance but on the way, and none too soon.

"I have to get back to work." Joe moved in a little closer, peeked into the box with her. "I'll take him back, but could you stay with him?"

"I don't know." She turned her head. They were the same height, standing eye to eye and much too close. "I have to think a minute."

"That's okay," he said, and gave her that same awkward smile. "I can wait."

"Oh no you don't." I hit the door and was on my way down the stairs before Mark could stop me. "What's going on here? What are you up to?"

"Nothing." He backed up one step, then another. "I just brought her a bird—"

"Mom, stop."

"I saw that. And I need to know why you felt it necessary to bring it yourself. Why didn't you let Stewart bring it down?"

"I didn't mean any harm," Joe said. "I was just worried about the bird—"

"And I'm just worried about what you want." I glanced over at Grace. "Is this the black something cuckoo you've been looking for so hard? Is this the reason you go out early every morning?"

"No. Mom, I swear."

"I don't know anything about cuckoos," Joe Deckhand said. "But I give you my word I don't want anything—"

"Liar." I put a hand on his chest, pushed hard enough to get him moving. "She's asked you to take the bird and leave. I suggest you do that. We're not running a wildlife rescue here." I gestured to Grace. "Give him the box."

"No." She backed up, clutching the box to her chest.

"Grace, give him the box now."

She lifted her chin. Looked me straight in the eye in a way she hadn't since she came home from the city. "I'm taking the bird to the fire station."

Joe smiled. "You'll do that?"

"And I'll sit with him till his parents come. And if they don't, I'll bring him back here."

"Grace, don't be ridiculous," I said. "You said yourself he needs to eat every few hours. How will you manage that?"

"I'll figure it out." She turned to Joe. "Let's go," she said, and went through the gate with the deckhand and his damned fried chicken box.

It was happening all over again. Grace turning her back, walking away.

I gripped the post. "Grace, don't do this. You know what happened the last time."

She drew up short but didn't turn around.

"Grace, you said yourself you need to think."

The ferry horn blew again. Closer now. Joe Deckhand reached for the box. "It's okay. I'll take him."

Grace shook her lovely head, straightened her back, and turned. There was no anger in her face. No confusion, no hesitation. Just a steely determination that froze me to the spot. "I have thought about it, and I'm going to the fire station. I'll see you later."

She started walking again. Joe Deckhand said to me, "I'll take care of her," and ran to catch up.

I stood with my fingers wrapped around the post and my feet stuck in one spot, watching my daughter, my baby, walk away with a man whose hands were big and probably far too strong, but I couldn't move, couldn't say a word. My head was filled with bits of thoughts. Go get her. Stay here. Where's Lori?

But I was clear on where I was and what was happening. I could see the tourists approaching, snapping pictures of our houses, pointing at our gardens. I could hear the ferry horn and wondered if Joe would be on it when it left. And how he possibly thought he could look after my girl who would sit by the fire station watching a baby robin for who knew how long.

I started to sweat. Blood roared in my ears. Any second I expected the fog to descend, to wake up somewhere else in an hour or six, with Big Al laughing and saying, *Gotcha last*, just for the hell of it. But it was Mark's voice I heard saying, "Still winning hearts and minds, I see." And his hands I felt on my shoulders. Big hands. Strong. Slowly kneading away the tension, making me relax.

"You should go after her," I said. "Bring her back."

"I don't think so," he said, his fingers moving, working out the knots, the worry, the stress. "If she said she was going to the fire station, then I believe her, and so should you."

"You are so naïve," I said, the roar slowly quieting, calming.

"Yes I am," he said. "And we should stay right here."

# LIZ

Tuesday morning dawned overcast and muggy. By eight o'clock I was showered and by eight fifteen, I was feeling like I could use another. At nine forty-five, Brenda pulled up to the curb in front of my house. By nine fifty-five, the entire staff of Sideshow Legal was belted in and ready to go—taking our show on the road to Champlain Aerospace in Oakville, a town about forty minutes west along the Queen Elizabeth Way.

As clown cars went, Brenda's wasn't half bad. Sunshine yellow with air-conditioning—thank God—a decent stereo, and enough leg room in the back for Nadia, if she sat behind Brenda. As the star of the show, I had been granted the front seat and control of the buttons on the stereo, Brenda's gift to me for still having a seat on the wagon after four days. Hitting Seek for the tenth time in as many minutes, however, it occurred to me that one simple drink before we left could have saved us all from the agony of my musical indecision.

Rock? *Seek*. Jazz? *Seek*. Talk radio? Please Lord, *seek*.

"I like easy listening," Nadia said, shoving a fist between the seats and opening it to reveal a handful of Werther's. "Take candy and find easy listening."

I shook my head. "It's too early for candy. How about country?"

"Whose country?" she asked.

"Never mind." I hit Seek again and promised myself it would be the last time. How could I have known it would come up punk/heavy metal/angry?

"Get rid of that crap," Brenda said, smacking Seek herself and shooting me a look that said, *Touch that button and die*, when Sting growled *Rrrrroxanne*. "Oldies work," she said, tapping the steering wheel and nodding her head. "You look great by the way. The suit came out real nice. And I love your hair."

"I took her to Olga." Nadia unwrapped a candy and held it out to her. "She did cut, manicure, pedicure, even waxing of eyebrows and hairy upper lip. All for one hundred bucks. Such good friend."

"Such good job," Brenda said, which was true. But I still felt guilty about the hair.

I'd only let Olga wash and trim it a half inch, but I shouldn't have let her do even that. I should have asked Grace to grab her kit and meet me on Hanlan's. Dunked my head in the lake and then let her work her magic on my unruly mop. Not only would that have given me a great cut, it would also have given me a chance to make up for missing our picnic, and to catch up on all the wedding news.

I still couldn't believe that one. What had Ruby been feeding Mark anyway? Poor guy was going to wake up one morning and wonder what the hell happened to his balls. Then he'd remember. He'd given them to Ruby as a wedding gift.

"You are quiet," Nadia said to me. "Are you going to throw up again?"

Brenda immediately started to pull over.

"No, I'm fine. Just drive."

I wasn't fine. I was nervous and shaky and I wanted off the fucking wagon so badly I would have sold more than my soul for just one drink. That would be enough, I swear. But Nadia had been like a bodyguard since Thursday. Always there, hovering, chatting, and offering food. Turned out she was a great cook, and since I wasn't drinking I'd developed an appetite again. Four days of cabbage rolls, pierogies, and lasagne, and the suit had gone from sagging to merely slack. Another week and I'd have been out shopping for this meeting.

Brenda had spent the weekend with Mitch and the kids of course, which had left the two of us to finish up the last-minute details. We'd had cards printed with my address and cell phone number. We'd picked up legal seals, heavy vellum paper, and envelopes. Nadia had typed the petition, then proofread and printed it. All I'd done was sign the thing and let Olga make me presentable. The only step left was the delivery, and my legs were already rubbery just thinking about the long walk to Klaus Vandergroot's office.

The drive was fast and uneventful, getting us to Champlain's front door in thirty-five minutes flat. The company occupied five units in a nondescript grey brick industrial complex—roughly 250,000 square feet, the average for a medium-sized business such as this. The plant was on the left, the executive offices on the right, and Klaus Vandergroot sat in a back corner office. According to Nadia, I would take the main hall leading from the reception area, turn left, and there he'd be—the shit who had caused all of this trouble.

We'd chosen Tuesday because our surveillance indicated that he was always in the office on Tuesdays. To be sure, Brenda drove around to the side of the building.

"There's his car." She hopped out of the driver's seat and Nadia hopped in. "I'll text you if he's in his office," Brenda said, and jogged off across the grass toward the building.

She was light and quick and our hope was that no one would

notice her prowling around, peering in windows. Watching her go, I realized this was probably one of those plans that sound better than they work. But there was no calling her back. Nadia already had the car in gear and was heading around to the front door.

"Do you need picture again?" she asked, putting the car in park and opening the door.

She had blown up a photograph of Klaus Vandergroot and posted it on the fridge on Saturday. Now, three days later, it was unlikely I would ever forget the pale and pudgy face with the neatly combed blond hair and perfectly trimmed mustache.

I shook my head, gathered up my jacket, and stepped out into sunshine and a breeze, proving there were indeed advantages to life in the suburbs. Slipping on the jacket, I reached back into the car for my new briefcase. Butter-soft black leather with brass locks—a gift from Nadia. "To make good impression," she'd said, after discovering I had used my old briefcase to start a marijuana crop one long, drunken weekend last winter.

Her phone chirped with a text message. "Is Brenda. He is not in his office. You wait."

I set the briefcase on the hood of the car, unsnapped the locks, and lifted out the first of two envelopes. This one was addressed to Klaus. The other was destined for the manager of Champlain's bank. I tucked one into the side pocket of the case, dropped the other back inside, and grabbed a couple of cards while I was there. Shoved them into my jacket pocket, closed the case, and told myself I would not throw up here in the parking lot.

"Squeeze this." Nadia held out a small blue ball. "Will help."

I took the ball. It was soft and squishy, yet gave just the right resistance and returned to its original shape quickly. I squeezed again. And again. "You're right, it does help."

"Bounce like this, one hand, other hand. That's it. Good. Should have brought two. Let you try juggling."

I laughed and bounced the ball, one hand, other hand. "Thanks. I needed this."

"All drunks need something." She held up a butterscotch. "That is why I have this." She frowned as she unwrapped it. "Ball has fewer calories. I wish I needed ball."

I watched her pop the candy into her mouth, suck it slowly. We stood like that for a few minutes, staring at the front door of Champlain, waiting for Brenda's text. The giant and the freak, bouncing and sucking. It wasn't much of an act, but it was all we had.

"You were a drunk?" I finally asked.

"Smoker too. Double whammy."

I watched her with that candy. Brow furrowed, chin working. Never had I seen anyone suck a butterscotch with such determination. "How long have you been sober?"

"Three years, not one drink. Olga helped me. Taught me what I told you. Today, don't drink. Tomorrow, maybe. She is good friend."

I tossed the ball high in the air. Caught it. Tossed it again. "Will it disappoint you if I said I would kill for a drink right now?"

"It would disappoint me more if you said you would not, because I would know you were lying." Her hand shot out and caught the ball. "I am three years sober. But still are days I would kill too. Today is one."

"What would you want?" I asked, a stupid question to ask a recovering alcoholic, but I was curious. "Vodka?"

"Straight up, out of freezer." She kissed her fingertips. "Heaven."

"I'll have to try it sometime." I held up my hands. "Kidding. Just kidding."

"No. You are not." She handed me the ball. "So today we help each other. I do not let you drink, you do not let me. Deal?"

I bounced, she sucked, and we both wanted a drink. Lucky Brenda. What a team to have on your side.

"Deal," I said, and tossed the ball high in the air. I wasn't sure how to stop a 250-pound woman from doing anything, but I could give it a try. I caught the ball, tossed it again. Maybe a bat would help.

Her phone chirped. I jumped, startled, and missed the ball. It hit the ground with a surprising thud but didn't roll. The perfect toy for drunks.

"Is Brenda. He is in office." She snapped the phone shut and held out a hand. "Give me ball." She dropped it into her pocket. "I go now. You follow ten seconds after I am inside."

She lumbered across the parking lot, up the walkway, and through the front door. I started to count. Smoothed my hair. Tugged on the front of my jacket. When I reached ten, I picked up the briefcase. Checked for the envelope in the side pocket and raised my chin.

"Good luck to us," I whispered, and followed her path across the parking lot on legs growing shakier and shakier by the second. By the time I reached the front door, my stomach was reeling, my knees were rubber, and I could feel sweat trickling down between my breasts.

I walked into a wall of air-conditioning. Shivered and took a look around. Marble floor, dark wood reception desk with a pretty young redhead in a heavy sweater answering the phone—a novelty these days. Their customers must get a kick out of it.

Nadia was at the desk talking to her. "I was here few weeks ago. Singing telegram, remember?"

The girl smiled. "Yes, of course. How are you?"

"Not good. I have lost earring. I think when I leaned over desk, it fell off." She went around behind the girl's desk. "I will look quickly. Not bother you at all."

"No, no," the girl said. "You'll have to go back around . . ." She spotted me on the move, making my way across the reception area to the main hall. She held up a hand as she came out from behind the desk. "Excuse me, you can't go in there."

"I'm just visiting," I said, and kept going. "Won't be a moment."

The girl started to follow me. Nadia opened a drawer. "Maybe in here," she said, and started taking stuff out. Files, pens.

"What are you doing?" The girl went back to the desk. "You can't be back there." She turned to me a moment before my foot was in the hall. "Miss. You can't go in there!"

"Found it!" Nadia cried. "Oh no. My mistake. Is someone else's."

"Will you get out of there?"

And I was on my way, walking along that hall, smiling and nodding at the faces that popped up above cubicles and appeared in doorways. "Hello. How are you. Lovely day."

Passing the boardroom. Paneled walls, leather chairs. Reaching the corner, turning left. Seeing the door ahead of me. Open. Bingo.

A voice behind me. Male. "Miss, you can't go down there. Miss."

Hurrying now. Trotting in high heels, afraid one would snap, hoping I didn't fall if it did. Arriving at the door, breathless. Pausing, wiping sweat from hairless upper lip. Seeing that pudgy face bent over papers at a fabulous rosewood desk. Leather chair, matching credenza. Art on the walls. Champlain was doing well. Now, so would Mitch.

"Do I have the pleasure of addressing Mr. Vandergroot?"

He looked up. Smiled and put down the pen. "You do indeed. How can I help you?"

Behind him, I could see Brenda through the window, pointing at him and making stabbing motions.

*Gimme an* L. *Gimme an* I . . .

I walked toward him, my hand already sliding the envelope out of the pouch. "Mr. Vandergroot, my name is Liz Donaldson."

"Miss, you can't—" A man came to the door—young, eager, a toad in the making. Brenda dove, hitting the ground hard, I was sure of it. "Mr. Vandergroot," the man said. "I'm sorry. I don't know how she got in here."

"I walked," I said, and turned my most charming smile on the shit in the fancy chair. "I'll just take a moment of your time. Do you recognize the name Mitch Bradley? How about the firm, Bradley Mechanical?"

His face started to fall. "Get her out of here."

"I thought you might." I gripped the envelope, drew it all the way out of the pocket, and prayed I didn't drop it between there and the desk. I saw my hand extending, his mouth rounding, the envelope falling, landing faceup on the blotter in front of him.

"Mr. Vandergroot, that is a petition into bankruptcy. Consider yourself served."

Vandergroot jumped up, as though I'd dropped a dog turd in front of him. "You can't do this."

"I can and I have. My next stop is your bank."

"Get her out of here, God damn it!"

"Miss, I need you to leave." The young man grabbed my arm.

I shook him off. "I am an officer of the court, here in the performance of the court's duty. If you touch me again, I will charge you with assault. Do you understand?"

The toad nodded.

"Do you understand?" I asked louder.

"Yes, I understand. Yes."

I turned back to Vandergroot. He was already on the phone. "I'm calling my lawyer. You can't do this."

"Mr. Vandergroot, you have three days in which to pay Bradley Mechanical the sum of one hundred and fifty thousand dollars in full, or we will be filing that petition with the bankruptcy court."

"Jim?" he said into the phone. "I have some woman in here trying to serve me with a petition to bankruptcy. I don't know her name. Just some bitch in high heels and an expensive suit."

"Tell Jim it's Liz Donaldson." I took a card from my pocket, tossed it on the desk. "I'll be expecting his call."

I shook back my hair, saw Brenda's head peeking over the edge of the window, and turned sharply. Shot the toad in the corner a warning glance, and looked back at Klaus. "And Mr. Vandergroot. Make sure the check is certified."

I marched back out the door and down the hall. Past those same faces, now gaping, gossiping, tossing curious looks at me, at the office of the CEO and back to me.

"Have a nice day, people," I said when I reached the door to the reception. "You too," I called to the redhead on my way through. "And tell them to turn down the air-conditioning. Then maybe they can pay their bills on time."

I went out the door into the heat. My legs were shaky but still on the job, carrying me along the walkway, to the parking lot. Across the parking lot to the clown car.

The midget leapt up and hugged me. The giant whooped and hugged us both. I thought I'd die for lack of breath, and then she let us go and we high-fived and high-fived again. Laughing, congratulating ourselves, finally climbing into the car as my cell phone went off.

We froze. I looked back at the front door, saw Vandergroot standing there, phone to his ear and a big smile on his face. Shit.

My stomach clenched as I flipped open the phone. "Liz Donaldson," I said, hoping my voice conveyed more confidence than I felt.

"Is this the Liz Donaldson that used to work with Mark Bernier?" the caller asked.

I could tell I was on speaker phone. "Who is this?"

"It's Jim Hodgeson, Liz. Of Hodgeson and Levi. You must remember me."

I wished I didn't. "Of course, Jim. How are you?"

Nadia and Brenda huddled closer, watching, listening. I gave them a thumbs-up and smiled, hoped I was convincing.

"Well, I'm a little troubled, Liz," Jim said. "And I'll tell you why."

I could picture the smug bastard, leaning back in his chair, sure of himself, more sure of me. Vandergroot wasn't the only one at the door now. Most of the company was there too, standing behind their leader, waiting to see what happened.

"I hear you're making some trouble for my good friend Klaus over at Champlain. He's on the line with us now. Say hi to Liz, will you, Klaus?"

Klaus waved to me. Had everybody there with him yell, "Hi, Liz."

"What's going on?" Brenda whispered.

"Vandergroot is being shit," Nadia whispered. "Liz is in trouble." She smiled and gave me a thumbs-up. Obviously, I hadn't convinced anyone.

"Something about petition into bankruptcy," Jim was saying. "Is that right, Liz?"

I took a breath, spoke slowly, in my low and controlled lawyer voice, not the high, squeaky, scared shitless one that was threatening to break through at any moment. "I suggest you speak to your client, Jim. He's got the paperwork and I hope he's opened it. Ignoring the petition will only get him deeper into trouble."

"Well, Liz, that's what I wanted to talk to you about. Frankly, I'm surprised by all of this. It's been a while since you've practiced law, and I know you've had some trouble with the drink these past few years. Don't try and deny it, Liz, because this is a small world we work in, you and me. Things get around. Bad things sometimes, but usually true. So I was surprised when Klaus told me you had the balls to walk in there and drop a petition on his desk."

"That's exactly what happened. And—"

"He said the card read 'Elizabeth Donaldson, Attorney at Law,' so I'm assuming you're not back with Mark again. Is that true, Liz? Is it really just you and your girlfriends out there by a little yellow car, trying to bully my client into paying a bill that should be handled through normal channels? Is that what's happening here, sweetheart?"

I looked into Brenda's frightened face, then back across the road at Vandergroot's cowardly one. Felt my shoulders relax, my spine straighten. "I'm not bullying anyone, Jim. I believe your client must be in financial difficulty. Otherwise they would have paid Bradley Mechanical when the bill came due. I am on my way to the bank now—"

"You don't want to do that."

"Why is that, Jim? Why don't I want to go to their bank?"

"Because you'll only cause trouble where none is due. Plus, if you do file that petition with the court, the judge will throw it out in less than five minutes. Then we'll come after you and your client, personally and through the business. We will end you, Liz. Do you understand me? We will end you before you even get started."

I moistened my lips, swallowed hard, and gave Brenda another thumbs-up because this was not the time to show weakness. Then I fixed my eyes on Vandergroot. Took a few, measured steps in his direction. Spoke in that nice clear way that Mark had taught me. Remaining calm, focused on the facts, confident that what I was doing was right. "You can threaten all you like, Jim, but you should advise your client that I am on my way to the bank now. He has three days to decide. Pay the bill in full or take his chance with the court."

I snapped my phone shut. Kept my eyes on Vandergroot while the message was relayed.

"Open the briefcase," I said to Brenda. "Get out the other envelope now."

I watched the bastard shake his head and wave his entourage back inside. Smiled when they scurried like mice from a cat. We had his attention at last.

Brenda handed me the envelope. I tapped it against my leg while he kept talking to Jim. When he finally closed his phone, I held up the envelope. "This is the one that's going to the bank now," I called. "You have three days."

I turned and walked back to the car, Nadia and Brenda hurrying along on either side.

"What now?" Brenda whispered.

"Get in the car," I said. "Don't talk, just get in the car."

We climbed into the clown car. "Drive," I said once the doors were closed. "And don't look back until we are out of here."

The three of us rode out of that parking lot like visiting dignitaries. When we were safely around the corner I hollered, "Pull over, pull over," leapt out, and threw up on the curb.

Brenda handed me a bottle of water and a tissue. "What now?" she asked again.

"Now we go to the bank." I rinsed my mouth and wiped my face and the two of us climbed back into the car. I slumped back against the seat. *Christ, I need a drink*, I thought, as she pulled away.

# GRACE

It was a good thing my mom didn't follow me to the fire station and try to haul me right back home again because I was right about the baby robin. He'd been on the ground because he was learning to fly, and that boy had picked him up too quick. And if she'd tried to make me dump that baby on the grass and leave, we'd have started fighting all over again, because somebody had to make sure no one else picked him up again.

Joe and I knew right away where the little guy belonged because his poor parents were still calling for him and flying all over the place, looking and looking. I was a little afraid they would dive at us when they saw us opening the box with their baby inside, but once we laid him on the grass, we backed away real fast so they'd see we weren't going to hurt him.

Joe had to go back to work, but I stayed like I promised even though I didn't have to because those robins were good parents and they came down right away. First one, then the other, giving him bits of food and yelling at him, probably telling him he was grounded for making them worry, and all the time trying to get him to fly.

I pulled out my cell phone and took pictures while he hopped around after them, mouth open, begging for more food. But they wouldn't give him any more and after a while he tried to fly again. Just like the lady mockingbird, he went a little bit farther and a little bit higher each time. Landing on a garbage pail, then a bush, then a branch in one of the trees until he finally made it all the way to the next tree and disappeared.

I should have gone home myself then, finished cleaning up the rest of the cage. But if my mom was signing those papers, giving Chez Ruby to Lori, then I didn't want to see it. And I sure didn't want to be there if they started moving everything out right away.

I couldn't imagine the kitchen without the barber's chair. Couldn't picture our house without women lined up on the couch, their heads wrapped in towels or slathered in hair color. All of them laughing and talking while my mom and I worked and the Andrews Sisters sang in the background. And I didn't want to think about any of that right then either because it made my throat get all achy and the end of my nose start to burn, and it was too nice a day to cry.

I headed over to the ferry dock instead, to tell Joe the good news about the bird. But it was the middle of the day by then and the dock was jammed with people and I could see from the railing that he was really busy. So I went for a walk. Over the Algonquin bridge, and up and down all the streets. Except Lori's. I didn't want to see her street or her house. Didn't want to know if she had a sign outside now or what she was calling the place. Or if some of my clients were there that very day, letting Lori do the back-combing and roller sets that should have been mine, all because they got the call from my mom days ago. *I'm winding down the business. Don't tell Grace.*

*Bitch.*

That was Liz's voice inside my head, and for the first time ever I didn't tell myself that voice was wrong. I just kept walking because once Mark and Jocelyn left Algonquin and moved into my mom's house, there was a good chance I would never walk over the bridge again.

I spent a long time wandering around, looking at what people were doing with their houses and their gardens. Wishing I wasn't so mad at my mom because she'd like to know that the pink house with the white shutters was now a grey house with no shutters. But I wasn't going to tell her anything. Just like she didn't tell me anything.

When I got tired of walking, I went back to wait for the *Ongiara*. But when the ferry docked this time, it wasn't Joe lowering the ramp. I couldn't see him on the deck at all in fact and I figured he must have finished working and gone home. I told myself not to be disappointed. Just because he smiled and talked nice to me didn't mean a thing. He was probably being polite, and I'd be silly to waste any more time thinking about that smile or those brown eyes, or the way his fingers touched mine before he left to get back on the ferry.

My mom always said there were no Prince Charmings in this world. But she'd found one, hadn't she? And she was going to marry him, wasn't she? And they were going to live happily ever after in her little castle where she would be queen forever and ever.

It was just me who couldn't have a Prince Charming. Or a castle. Or a job or even a room where I could lock the door and say, *Stay out of my stuff!*

Jocelyn would probably put a lock on her door. I hoped so, anyway.

Leaving the dock, I hurried over to the tennis courts to see if that Fly or Die list was posted someplace and if anyone had bet on the right day. I didn't know what to think when I saw my mom's name in that spot. *Ruby Donaldson, Five to Fly in One.*

As curious as I was about why she put her name on that list, I didn't ask her about it when I got home. I just took my dinner into my room, put a chair under the door, and stayed there all night. Lying on my bed, sending text messages and pictures of the baby robin to Liz.

She sent me pictures of her new friends, Brenda and Nadia, and they looked like they were having fun playing video games and drinking strawberry milkshakes. I was happy for her, glad she'd found some new friends. I didn't tell her about Lori. Why spoil her night too?

The next morning, my mom left the stack of five-dollar bills on the table where I'd be sure to see it when I came down to go biking. She tried talking to me like it was any normal day. "Have you thought about a dress for the wedding? Would you like to see the invitations?"

I purposely hadn't thought about a dress because there was never going to be anything fancy enough at the Bridge Boutique. And I *did* want to see those invitations more than anything, but I still couldn't talk to her, couldn't hardly look at her without that dumb lump in my throat starting all over again. So I said, "Maybe later," and I didn't tell her about the baby robin. Even though she'd won the Fly or Die bet, I still didn't ask her about it.

"When is Lori coming to take everything away?" That was all I wanted to know.

She sighed. "Around ten today. We could use your help getting things packed up."

"I won't help," I said, and she didn't argue. Just watched me take my binoculars from the hook by the door, and my bird book from the shelf above that.

"Grace, you can't keep this up," she said when I got on my bike.

But she was wrong. I kept it up all the way down the walk and through the gate. As much as I wanted to, I didn't look back once as I rode down the street and around the corner. I wasn't going to wait for Jocelyn this morning, and I only hoped Mark had some groceries at his house for a change because I was not going home for breakfast either.

I thought I might run into Mark and Jocelyn along the way. But I was on their walk and almost to their front door before they stepped out onto the porch with Kylie, Brianne, and Courtney—all of them yawning and blinking in the sunlight.

"My dad let me have a sleepover," Jocelyn said.

"Weak moment," Mark mumbled on the way to his bike. "Is your mom up?"

"She was in the kitchen when I left. Are you helping her pack up everything?"

He looked down as he kicked back the stand. "I don't like it any more than you do, Grace, but I can't let her do it alone."

I nodded because it was true. She would be his wife after all. And I would be what? There, I guess. I would just be there.

"Tell Lori to watch out when she's moving my workstation around," I said. "If you bump it over a cord or anything, one of the wheels will fall off."

I should have warned him about my chair too. Told him that if you turned it round and round too many times to the right, the seat would pop off. But I didn't. Lori could find that out for herself one day.

"If my mom goes looking for my kit," I added, "tell her I took it out of the workstation last night and I'm not telling her where it is. Those are *my* scissors and *my* combs, and no one else is getting their hands on them."

Even if I only threw the kit in the Eastern Gap one day, it was my kit to do it with, not hers. And never, ever Lori's.

"I'll let her know." He gave Jocelyn and the girls a wave and left, pedaling slowly toward the bridge.

"I still think her mom's a bitch," Jocelyn whispered to the girls then came down the stairs. "I told everybody they could come biking with us this morning. And that we'd look for the cuckoo too. Is that okay?"

We wouldn't get to watch the planes, because that was still a secret—one Jocelyn was really good at keeping—but I didn't care. We could see them tomorrow. Or not.

I looked from one girl to the other. "Do any of you have binoculars?"

Lucky for us, Kylie and Brianne's mom and dad had two pairs of binoculars, so there would be enough to share. Mark still didn't have a lot of groceries, but there was toast and peanut butter and orange juice, which was okay. Funny, but I didn't miss the eggs as much as I thought I would.

After breakfast, we rode across the Island to the woods near Gibraltar Point and pulled our bikes off the road where Jocelyn and I had last heard the cuckoo. I showed the girls the picture in the field guide and told them how to use the binoculars, explaining that you had to move them nice and slow over the branches or you wouldn't find anything.

They nodded and said, "Yeah, yeah," pressed the binoculars to their faces and took off into the scrubby brush before I could tell them anything else. They were back in about two minutes, all of them frowning and shaking their heads.

"I think the only cuckoos around here are us," Courtney said.

"He's in there," Jocelyn assured them. "I heard him."

Brianne looked around. "I hear all kinds of birds. How do you find the one you're looking for?"

"You have to listen carefully." I put a finger to my lips to keep them quiet, closed my eyes, and listened. "Hear that? Four notes, really low, all the same. Cu-cu-cu-cu. Cu-cu-cu-cu. Then ten notes, higher but still all the same. Now back to four." When I opened my eyes the three of them were still looking at me like I was making it up. "Close your eyes. It helps."

They closed their eyes and scrunched up their noses and listened.

Kylie shook her head. "I don't know what you're . . ." Then all of a sudden she stopped talking and opened her eyes wide, like she was real surprised. "I heard it. He's not as interesting as the mockingbird, but I heard him."

Brianne scrunched her eyes up tighter. "I still don't hear it."

Her sister punched her on the arm. "He's over there. Listen that way."

Within a few more minutes, all the girls had heard him, and could make out the low cu-cu-cu-cu, without closing their eyes.

"Now all we have to do is find him," Jocelyn muttered.

The girls headed off again, searching the branches, still finding nothing. "They like to hide," I reminded them. "And the leaf cover is thick this time of year so you have to take your time. You have to be patient."

"Come on, you stupid cuckoo," Jocelyn said. "Where are you?"

"You're not looking in the right place, any of you," I said. "He's over to the right."

Courtney glanced back at me. "How can you tell?"

"Because I can hear him, clear as a bell, right through there."

Jocelyn stuck her tongue out at me, then shifted the glasses to the right. The other girls did the same and started checking again, passing the bins back and forth, checking the branches from left to right a little more slowly this time.

After a few more minutes Brianne froze, binoculars pinned on something. Then she flapped a hand frantically. "Everybody, stop," she whispered. "I see it. I see it!"

Kylie adjusted her position. "What's it look like?"

"Brown on top. White chest. Just like the picture." She grinned and held out the binoculars to Courtney. "You want to see?"

Courtney put the binoculars to her eyes. Brianne helped point her in the right direction and after a few seconds, Courtney's mouth fell open. "I see it, I really do." She lowered the binoculars and grinned at me. "Oh my God. I see it!"

"I still don't see anything," Jocelyn grumbled, then stopped moving the binoculars, held perfectly still, and grinned too. "It *is* there." She held out the bins to me. "You want to see?"

I stared at the binoculars. Shook my head. "Cuckoos are pretty cautious. He's probably gone by now."

Jocelyn kept holding the binoculars out to me. "You don't know that for sure."

I took the bins and snapped the covers on the lenses. "Don't worry. I'll see it another day."

"That was kind of cool," Courtney said to her. "How come you never told me you were doing this?"

She turned to her friend. "Are *you* going to tell anyone you did this today?"

The girls all shook their heads. Probably not, they agreed.

"But it *was* fun," Kylie said, obviously as surprised as Courtney.

"You're really good at teaching people how to do it," Brianne added.

"You should take people out birding and charge for it," Courtney said. "Make it like a business, now that you're not working and all."

Jocelyn whacked her on the head. "Shit, Courtney, what is wrong with you?"

"It's okay," I said. "Plus it's true. I'm not working and all." I bent down to pick up my bike. "But I'm not a good enough birder to charge anybody anything. Maybe in another ten years, I can think about it."

Kylie looked down at my bike. "Are we finished here already?"

"I think so." I took a slow look around, hearing waxwings and warblers, finches and phoebes. Even a Lincoln sparrow, and all I could think was, so what? He'd be there tomorrow too. Or not. What difference did it make? There would always be another bird somewhere. If anyone wanted to find it.

I rolled my bike forward. "The birds are getting quiet now. Makes them harder to find."

Jocelyn narrowed her eyes. She could hear that Lincoln as well as I could.

"Where to now?" Brianne asked.

"Feels like a swan day to me," Jocelyn said, and wiggled her eyebrows when I glanced over at her. "What do you say?"

I smiled. "You hate the swans."

"But we love them," Brianne said, then shrugged, embarrassed. "We just don't tell anyone that either."

Jocelyn started to roll her bike forward. "Let's go do some swan. Last one there sucks."

The three other girls hopped on their bikes and shot out ahead. "How do we swan?" I heard Courtney asking just before they were out of range.

"You should hurry," I said to Jocelyn. "Or you're going to suck."

She looked over at me. "You're not coming, are you?"

I threw my leg over the bike. "Not this time."

"What's wrong with you?" she asked in her wonderful, blunt way.

"I'm just tired. I didn't sleep much last night. And I promised Mary Anne I'd help her with wedding stuff today, so I should get back."

She seemed to accept that and we started riding, neither of us hurrying to catch up. "I wanted to thank you for yesterday," I said as we rolled along. "For telling your dad you don't mind living on the Island. I know it's not what you want and I wish things could be different—"

"One day it will be." She smiled at me. "I really believe that."

It was funny. In seven weeks, Jocelyn would start junior high school. In ten, she would be a teenager. But right now she looked like a little girl. Nose freckled, eyes shining—trusting that everything was going to work out fine. And I felt nothing but old.

# RUBY

I knew there were eggs in the nest the moment the mocking-bird launched a surprise attack on a group of tourists. It happened around ten this morning. I was outside deadheading roses when they stopped by the gate, but they barely had time to raise their cameras before the male went to work. Diving, reeling, diving again—moving those interlopers along as efficiently as any of Grandma Lucy's belly dancing routines, and without a single visit from the authorities. They were birds after all, protecting their nest. Not a dotty old woman with cymbals on her fingers.

To be honest, after everything the female had been through, I was surprised there were eggs at all. With the nest only five feet off the ground, I assumed it would be easy to take a quick look, find out how many she'd been able to lay. But those two birds drove me back before I had the first leaves parted. Flying at my head, beating their wings in my face, making it clear that I was tolerated as a neighbor but would never be a member of the family.

I went inside and asked Grace to take a look, certain she could find a way to take a peek, find out how many babies we could expect. But she shook her head and said, "We'll know when they hatch," which made sense but wasn't at all what I expected of a committed birder.

Then she gathered up the box of Styrofoam balls and dowels that Mary Anne had assigned to her and went outside to work on centerpieces for the wedding—just as she had done for the last three days, ever since Chez Ruby changed hands. She was out there now, sitting on a blanket with a few of the neighbors, all of whom Mary Anne had recruited to help with her endless projects. Centerpieces, table favors—there was no end of silly things that needed doing. While Grace had never been the type to take up crafts, I could see she was enjoying herself. Laughing with Mary Anne, fishing for sequins with Carol, helping Renata with a glue gun—finally discovering that life without a blow-dryer could be fun.

I'd been busy with my own wedding jobs, of course. Trying to shop for a gown and flowers while helping Mark find new homes for the washing machine, the winter boots, the Christmas decorations—all so Jocelyn could have her own room. With my closet bursting and Grace's room jammed, I'd come to the conclusion that a third-floor addition would be a good idea after all. But the most important discovery I'd made was that without customers coming and going, and without equipment everywhere I turned, this house was starting to feel like a home again. And the wicker couch didn't take up half the room that old barber's chair had.

Being free of the business, I was learning how to really relax for the first time in my life. Sleeping in if I felt like it, going for a walk when the mood struck, these were small luxuries I hadn't known in years. And having Mark around to enjoy them with me wasn't hurting at all.

I still chafed at the term *caregiver* and refused to put the label on either him or Mary Anne, but if I was honest, I'd admit that knowing one or the other was always around—that they'd make sure I took those stupid meds—had made my life easier. And so far, Big Al hadn't objected.

He woke up briefly on moving day, shuffled a few things around inside my head, and went back to bed, leaving me searching frantically for a file marked WEDDING VOWS, which I found in the microwave before anyone else was the wiser. But for the most part, he'd been pretty quiet. And sitting at the kitchen table now, with Grace outside and Mark washing down the last wall in the storage room, a tiny thought pushed at the corner of my mind.

It had been there before, popping in when we were canoeing, refusing to be ignored when we were making love. I recognized it immediately as hope. That nasty four-letter word that could make a fool of anyone, put the idea in my head that maybe Mark had been right all along. Maybe I was being hasty with my poisons and my Ice Floe. Maybe with a more relaxed lifestyle and the right meds, I could be Ruby awhile longer after all. And Mark and I could spend a few years making up for all the ones we'd lost.

Still afraid to face that thought, to give it room to grow, I ignored Hope's smiling face and set to work writing my vows. And tried not to think about what Mark might be planning for his.

"All finished," he said, coming into the kitchen with the bucket and mop. "Jocelyn can start painting any time." He poured himself a soda and sat down beside me. Put an arm around my shoulder, kissed me. Made me glad all over that he hadn't listened to me that first day. That he hadn't gone back to the city where he belonged. "I'm starving," he said. "You want one of those hot dogs from the clubhouse?"

"You go ahead." I held up the file. "I've got vows to write."

"Don't remind me." We both turned at the sound of high-pitched squeals, watching Jocelyn and her friends at the gate, trying to fend off the mockingbird with paint rollers and brushes. He seemed to know Jocelyn and left her alone, but the rest were fair game. And he would not stop just because the girl with the stop-sign red hair said so.

But as soon as Grace ran over, the bird flew up to the top of the tree. As though the silly thing trusted her to let only the best kind of people into his yard. "Hurry," she said to the girls. "You have to get away from the lilac."

The girls dashed through the gate and straight into the house. All of them talking at once while they dropped tins of paint, bags of rollers, and armloads of drop cloths in the middle of the kitchen. "She picked a great color." "Show them the chip." "Do we have to stir the paint after they shook it?"

Mark held up his hands. "Hold everything. I'm going for hot dogs. Who wants to come before we start?" And as quickly as that, they all trooped out the door and down the stairs again. Blessed, blessed silence restored.

Grace did her trick with the mockingbird again, standing by the gate so he wouldn't attack Mark and the girls on their way out. But she didn't go straight back to the blanket. Instead she stood a moment longer, looking down the street the other way, toward the dock.

Thinking of what? I wondered. The baby robin we had yet to discuss? The deckhand I had yet to forgive? For all that she was laughing again and working on projects, Grace was still stiff with me, still cryptic when she came home from biking, or helping Mary Anne. I didn't even know if she'd ever found that black something cuckoo. Everything would straighten itself out eventually, I was sure of it, but if I could help things along . . .

I strolled over to her bedroom door. Pushed it back a little and was about to step inside when I heard footsteps on the stairs, the back door flying open.

"Forgot the paint chip," Jocelyn said, squatting down to root through the bags on the floor. "Got it," she said, and glanced over. Saw me standing by Grace's door. "You'll never figure out that password."

I leaned a shoulder against the frame. "I don't suppose you'd give it to me."

She laughed. "Dream on."

"You really do think the worst of me all the time, don't you?"

"It's hard not to." She looked me up and down, stuffed the paint chip into her pocket, and started for the door. "But my dad likes you, so maybe there's something I've missed."

"I love your father. You know that, don't you?"

"I hope so, because I know he loves you."

She turned around, came back toward me. "He got all sappy when we were playing Frisbee the other day. Said he's loved you from the first moment he saw you at some protest rally."

"That's nice to know," I said, and walked away from Grace's door.

"I guess." She studied me a moment, then folded her arms and leaned back against the counter, a move so like her father I almost smiled. "He also said you're difficult to know, but if I give you a chance, I might come to like you. If not, at least I'd respect you, but I'm not sure about that."

"Because I snoop on Grace's computer?" I sat down at the table. "You have to believe me when I say that everything is done with Grace's best interest in mind."

"And you have to believe me when I say that sometimes you screw up. Like selling the business. That was a screwup for Grace."

"Jocelyn, you're wrong. It was hard on her, I know, but I had no choice. And she's adjusting beautifully." I pointed out the window to where she was juggling Styrofoam balls for Mary Anne and Carol. "Look at her. She's having fun, she's moving on." I turned back to Jocelyn. "I know my daughter. And I know this was for the best."

"If you say so." She walked back to the door.

"Aren't you interested in knowing how I feel about you?"

"Sure," she said in the offhand way of adolescents, then turned and smiled at me. "And don't hold back."

This time, I did smile. "I think you're foul-mouthed, precocious, and extremely bright, just like Liz was. I also think you have your father wrapped around your finger. If you weren't devoted to him, I'd be afraid that you would be a terrible influence on Grace, exactly the way Liz was. But you love your dad, and you haven't gone out of your way to make his life miserable, so I'm hoping you'll show more sense than Liz as you grow. I'm curious to see what kind of woman you'll become, and I hope it's one your father will be proud of." I rose and crossed to where she stood. "I don't know you well enough to like you yet either, but for Mark's sake, I'm also willing to look for a reason."

She considered a moment, then said, "Okay, here's the deal. You won't pretend to be my mother, I won't pretend to be your daughter, and we'll be polite to each other, for my dad's sake."

"I can do that."

"You won't go in my room or look through my backpack. And you will never, ever look on my computer for any reason whatsoever."

"Just as you won't go through my dresser or look at my files. And you will never, ever open my purse for any reason whatsoever."

She smiled again. "I can do that."

"One other thing. You won't encourage Grace to engage in dangerous behaviors."

And the smile was gone. "Define dangerous."

"Anything that will result in her getting hurt emotionally or physically."

"This may surprise you, but I love Grace too. I'm glad she's going to be my sister and I won't let anything hurt her. Not even you."

I was a little taken aback but pleased. "Then we should get along just fine."

She held out a hand, her face solemn as we shook on our deal. "You want to see the paint color I chose?" she asked, and as she held out the paint chip I could feel myself starting to like the kid already— even if her room was going to be Festive Coral Rose.

"Your dad will love it."

"I think so." She shoved the chip back in her pocket. "Gotta go. Hot dogs await."

She stopped halfway out the door and looked back at me over her shoulder. "Did you mean it when you said I could wear anything I want to the wedding?" I nodded. "And can I be Grace's personal shopper too?" That one took a moment, but again I nodded and she gave me her first unguarded smile. "I am soooo looking forward to this."

I watched her trot down the stairs and pause at the blanket, taking time to admire the topiary centerpieces, the plantable-daisy table favors, even the god-awful feathered guest book. She laughed at something Mary Anne said and I realized I had a lot to learn about Jocelyn. Oddly enough, I was looking forward to it.

"Ruby, come out here and give us your opinion," Mary Anne called.

Fortunately, she wasn't looking for input on the guest book. The topiary centerpieces were the issue—ribbon or ivy around the dowels. Apparently brides lose sleep over things like that.

"I vote for ribbon," I said before Mary Anne had time to list the benefits of ivy. "All in favor." Jocelyn raised a hand. Grace smiled and did the same. A small victory, but I'd take it.

Grace rose and walked toward me. Then someone screeched at the gate and she was gone again, keeping the mockingbird at bay so the girls and Mark could get back into the yard. They came to the blanket bearing hot dogs and cans of pop for all.

"We need mustard, relish, and ketchup," Jocelyn called, and was on her way up the stairs when another screech drew everyone around.

I expected to see a tourist with a camera, but it was Lori from Algonquin, red-faced and frantic, as though she'd ridden all the way over at top speed. But this time Grace didn't work her magic with the mockingbird. She stood watching Lori bat the bird as she struggled through the gate. "Go and help her," I whispered.

"No," she said, and turned her back, heading for the house.

Mark went to the gate instead. The bird didn't stop his attack for him, of course, but Mark was big enough to block the way so Lori could make it up the walk relatively unscathed.

She looked close to tears now that I saw her up close. "Thank God, you're here," she said, shoving hair out of her face and trying to catch her breath. "I've been calling and calling, but there was no answer. So I took a chance and came over."

"I'm sorry," I said. "The phone must have come unplugged when we were cleaning up the storage room."

Grace and Jocelyn carried the condiments past us to the patio table. Lori looked from me to Grace and back again. "I wanted to ask her something."

I gestured to Grace. "She's right there."

Lori walked over to the table. Grace ignored her. Took the lid off the mustard, put a spoon in the relish. Lori touched her arm. "Grace, I need to ask you a favor."

Grace jerked away and called to the group. "Come and get it."

The girls and the craft circle descended on the table. Grace turned and walked back to the house. Lori followed her to the steps. "Grace, please. Marla Cohen is at my place right now, and she's making me crazy. I can't do anything right. She keeps saying, 'Grace did things this way, and Grace did things that way.' I told her I'd see if you'd come over and help. Show me what she likes."

Grace stopped at the top of the stairs. Turned her head slowly, like a queen. "No," she said, and went inside. Lori started to cry, sudden heaving sobs that stopped the voices at the table and drew Mark over to the stairs. She had everyone's attention except Grace.

"Grace, don't be so rude," I called, and went after her, leaving Mark outside to deal with Lori.

Grace was in her room, lying on her bed, staring at the ceiling. "What are you doing?" I demanded. "Lori needs your help. You know how difficult Marla can be."

"Yes, I do."

"Why won't you help her?"

She rolled over, putting her back to me. "Because I'm not a hairdresser anymore, remember?"

Jocelyn came to the bedroom door and squeezed in beside me. "Grace, are you okay?"

"I'm not a hairdresser. I can't help her."

"You're being ridiculous," I said, but Jocelyn took hold of my arm, urging me to follow her out. "What are you doing?" I asked when we reached the kitchen table.

"Making sure Grace doesn't get hurt."

The bedroom door closed. Something slid across the floor. I tried the handle. She'd barricaded herself in with a chair. "Grace, you open the door this instant!"

"Leave me alone."

"You should probably do as she asked." Jocelyn turned to leave. "And while you're at it, keep telling yourself that she's doing just fine."

# LIZ

Day three. Nine A.M. and still no call from Champlain or their fucking lawyer.

If I didn't hear from one of them by five o'clock that afternoon, Sideshow Legal would have two choices: register the goddamn petition and have a judge throw it out a week later. Or forget the registration, admit defeat, and try to get Mitch out of town before Hal found out there wasn't going to be any money after all. Either way, Klaus Vandergroot came out the winner courtesy of Jim Hodgeson—the real lawyer.

"Fucking bastards," I muttered, and threw the little blue ball at the wall. It dropped with a thud on the floor. "Why won't they call?"

Nadia shrugged. "You said yourself, is like game. Seeing who closes eyes first."

"Blinks," I said evenly. "Seeing who blinks first."

"That too." She picked up the ball and sat down beside me. "I know is hard and you are reaching end of rope, but just for today—"

"Say it and die," I snarled, staring her down through narrowed and painfully sober eyes.

Wisely, she closed her mouth. Put the ball in my hand. And when the phone in her room started to ring, she went to answer it. Leaving me alone for fifteen glorious minutes, during which I squeezed that ball, willed my own phone to ring, and tried not to think about Car Bombs.

"That was Brenda," Nadia said, smiling and holding up a sheet of paper. "And we have come up with plan to keep you busy."

We both knew she meant—*We have come up with plan to keep you from drinking*—but I appreciated her subtlety. So when she slid my phone to the side and set her paper in its place, I didn't go for her throat the way I otherwise might have. Instead, I tossed that poor little ball from one hand to the other while she laid out their plan to keep Liz busy.

"There is new place close by. Has all kinds of games. We start with laser tag and glow-in-dark bowling this morning. We break for pizza, then we play mini-golf this afternoon." She punched me on the arm. "Some fun, eh?"

I dropped the ball on the page. "Did Brenda's boys make this list?"

"I added laser tag. You will like it. They give you big gun. And do not worry about mini-golf. I am certain call will come before then."

Such was her faith in good versus evil, even though lawyers were involved.

I slid the page back to her. "I can't go anywhere. I have to be here if they call, so I can put on a goddamn suit and go pick up the goddamn check."

"I told you, place is not far. Ten minutes, tops. When call comes, we bring you back, you change, and we go pick up check." She got to her feet. "Do not argue. Brenda is on the way."

"Fine," I said, and flipped open my phone. Sent Grace a text confirming our picnic on Saturday. Regardless of what happened today, I wouldn't disappoint Grace again.

She wrote back within minutes. *OK.*

Nothing else. Not *Love Grace* or *Whoopee*. Just *OK.*

I sent another message. *RU ok?*

Again, she sent back one word. *Yes.*

I started to send another, but Brenda was already downstairs, double-parked, leaning on the horn. I squeezed into the back of the clown car with the boys, and stared out the window as she drove, looking forward to a really big gun.

Despite Nadia's faith, we worked our way through laser tag, bowling, and the pizza lunch without a call from Champlain. It was now 1:15 P.M., a storm was threatening, and the two of us were standing under the Welcome sign at Pirate Bay Mini-Golf. The attendants were dressed accordingly and said "Argghhh maties" a lot, and the course was decked out with a sinking pirate ship, several rope bridges, and a number of water obstacles that smelled slightly off and were rumored to contain buried treasure.

Brenda and the boys were already at the first hole. Distant thunder rumbled, a parrot squawked, "Walk the plank, walk the plank," and I turned to Nadia.

"Why are we doing this? It's hot, it's crowded, and it's going to pour any minute." I pointed my putter at the restaurant/souvenir shop. "You play if you want, but I'm going to wait over there for the call."

She fell into step beside me. "Liz, do not do this."

I squeezed the ball in time with my steps. "You don't have to worry. The club doesn't serve alcohol, I don't have keys to Brenda's car, and it's too hot to walk anywhere. I'll just sit inside where it's cool and be good."

She took hold of my arm and hauled me around. "Stupid bitch. Do you think any of us wants to play silly game?"

I stared at her. "Then why did they come? Why didn't they just stay home?"

"Because Brenda could not stay home. This is last day. Hal is sitting outside her house, waiting for answer."

My stomach tightened as I squeezed the ball. "He's there already?"

"Arrived this morning early. He is not threatening, just waiting. Gary is with Mitch in case call does not come."

"Why didn't you tell me?"

"I found out when we got here." She flicked a hand at the golf course. "Boys were too quiet, I knew something was wrong. She finally told me when we were buying tickets."

I glanced back at the turnstile. "I had no idea."

She snatched the ball away, dropped it into her bag. "Of course not. Everything is always about you, so you do not see that Brenda is on verge of tears and children are frightened. You think they want to spend time with grumpy lawyer always checking phone and frowning?"

"I'm not always frowning."

She held up three fingers. "Three days, no smiles."

"What do you want from me? This is serious shit, okay? Jim Hodgeson is playing with me. Trying to wear me down and it's working. I can't sleep, I can't think—"

"And you cannot drink. My heart breaks for you." She turned me around and shoved me toward the golf course. "No more selfishness. You will play, and you will let little boys win."

Brenda spotted us coming back and waved us over.

More thunder rumbled.

"Pretty ladies in the house," the parrot squawked. "Walk the plank."

"Remember to smile," Nadia said and handed me back my blue ball. "Who knows? Might even be fun."

"Might be," I said, putting on a bright smile when we reached the first hole, and picturing Jim Hodgeson on that bloody plank.

"You're just in time," Brenda said, edging us into line ahead of her and ignoring the muttered disapproval of the group behind. "Boys, you go first."

Nadia was right. There was no excitement in Aaron's step, no anticipation on Ethan's face. Now that I took the time to notice, I saw the tension around Brenda's smile, the quick, nervous movements of her hands. It was time the Bradleys had their own cheering squad.

I slipped the ball back into Nadia's bag and started clapping, whistling. "Come on, Ethan. Give us a hole in one. A hole in one."

Brenda raised a brow and Ethan looked over, clearly shocked to see me grinning and doing the whoop-whoop circle in the air with my fist. He gave me a small, uncertain smile, then looked down at his ball. Repositioned his feet. Checked the shot one more time—a straightforward putt up a slight incline with the cup on the curve to the right.

"Whoo-hoo," I called, circling my fist in the air again.

Aaron joined in this time, chanting, "Hole in one, hole in one."

Ethan grinned, flexed his fingers on the club, and took the shot. The ball rolled up the incline, curved right, and came to rest a few inches back from the cup.

"Hole in two," I called, and Aaron picked up right away. "Hole in two."

Nadia joined in, Brenda's smile relaxed, and Ethan completed his play, shooting the coveted hole in two. Since three was par for the first hole, we gave him a well-deserved round of applause and did the same for Aaron when he also took no more than two shots.

The boys hooted when Nadia also managed it in two, booed loudly when Brenda took three, and were clapping and calling, "Liz sucks," when it was my turn.

I inclined my head graciously, knowing I'd earned that. "Maximum of five," the attendant reminded me while I lined up my feet with the ball, and the ball with the hole. I drew the club back and swung, whacking that ball right out of bounds and into one of those questionable ponds.

"Ball in the water," the parrot squawked. "Walk the plank."

Nadia laughed. The kids behind us started to titter and the attendant handed me another ball. "Try again, matie."

Thunder rolled, coming closer. I lined up that ball again. Tapped it, and muttered, "Come on, come on," as it rolled up to the cup, circled, and slowly rolled all the way back down. Honestly, who puts a hole at the top of a mountain anyway?

"Clap her in irons," the parrot hollered.

I tried twice more and could have wept with gratitude when my phone finally rang.

"Play through," I said to the kids waiting behind us. "Play through."

Nadia put her hands together prayer style and followed me off the course.

I flipped the phone open on the third ring. "Liz Donaldson," I said, and held my breath.

"Liz? This is Jocelyn."

I gave Nadia a thumbs-down. Said, "Jocelyn, I can't really talk now."

"It's about Grace. She doesn't know I'm talking to you."

I stopped at the end of a rope bridge. "Is she okay?"

"Yeah, it's just—"

The beep went off in my ear. I had another call! I had another fucking call!

"Jocelyn, I have to go. I'll get back to you." I pressed Flash, said, "Liz Donaldson," and my heart all but stopped when the voice on the other end said, "This is Jim Hodgeson. We need to talk."

I flapped my hand at Nadia. Nodded yes, yes, yes when she put her thumb in the air and watched her take off to get Brenda. Children leapt out of her way, adults scattered, and even the pirates gave her plenty of room—there was nothing as daunting as Nadia in full flight.

"Walk the plank," the parrot hollered.

"Where are you?" Jim asked.

"With clients."

Nadia appeared with Brenda and the boys. I motioned for them to follow as I marched away from the parrot toward the shade and relative calm outside the men's rooms.

"So, Jim," I said. "When can I pick up a check?"

Brenda had her own phone to her ear, talking to Mitch. "She's asking about the check," she was saying. "I don't know. We're waiting."

All eyes were on me when I said, "What are you talking about? What kind of deal?"

Nadia shook her head slowly, heavily. Brenda looked worried and Ethan asked, "Is she screwing it up royally, Mommy?"

*Could be*, I thought. But to Jim I said, "They want to pay seventy-five percent? If this is your idea, Jim, you're not doing your clients any favors."

Brenda bounced up and down. "Take it, take it, take it."

I made slashing motions across my neck, then turned my back. "Forget it, Jim. We're not negotiating. My client delivered one hundred percent of that equipment and he expects to be paid according to the contract. Call me when you have a check for the full amount. Certified."

I hung up. Silence hovered around me, heavy and accusing, broken only by the rumble of thunder, closer still. "He'll call back," I said, for my own sake as much as theirs.

"She hung up on him," Brenda said to Mitch, and held the phone away from her ear while he hollered, "What the fuck? What the fuck?"

"Daddy swore," Aaron whispered.

"Today it's allowed," Ethan whispered back, both he and his brother standing close to their mother, eyeing the woman who was screwing up royally.

Lightning flashed. More thunder.

"I'll call you back," Brenda said to Mitch, and we started running, making it across the parking lot to the clown car just as big fat drops of rain started to fall.

"Get in, get in!" Brenda yelled, and the thunder pressed down all around us.

We made it into the car and closed the doors as the sky let loose, dumping rain so hard and fast it was impossible to see the car in the next spot. The windows steamed over, the sky lit up like a giant camera flash, and my phone rang again just as the thunder started to roll.

Every head in that car turned to look.

"Liz Donaldson," I said, my heart still beating fast, making my voice breathless, ineffective.

"Liz, it's Jocelyn."

"Jocelyn, I can't talk now," I muttered, and the heads groaned and turned away. "I'll call you back." I closed the phone. Jumped when it rang again right away. If it was Jocelyn again, I swear the kid's life was over. "Liz Donaldson," I said.

"Jim Hodgeson here."

I gave a giant thumbs-up to the faces around me. No one reacted. Just kept staring at me while Brenda pressed a button on her phone and put it to her ear. "He's calling again," she said, still no expression on her face.

"Do you have a check for us, Jim?" I asked, and prayed for the right answer.

"No, I have a bank draft."

My breath came out in a rush. "A bank draft, you say."

Four pairs of eyes widened. Four mouths dropped open.

"For the full amount," I repeated, and would have gotten out of the car so I could hear the rest of what Jim was saying if the rain hadn't still been coming down hard.

I checked the clock on the dash. Two ten. By the time I got home, changed, got back in the car . . . "I'll be there at four to pick it up."

"No good. Champlain is on summer hours. They close at three."

"Then I'll pick it up at your office."

"Nope, I'll be on my way up north at the same time." I could hear the bastard smiling when he said, "Since Vandergroot and I both take Mondays off, I guess we'll see you Tuesday."

The cheering in the car had stopped. Brenda said, "Hold on, Mitch," and all I could think was, *Three more days of Hal.*

I glanced down at my shorts and tank top. What the hell. Jim had heard about the expensive suit. He didn't need to see it. "I'm leaving now, Jim. I'll be in Oakville by three."

"I'll wait for you at reception. You're not to go past that desk. And if you're later than three ten, you'll have to wait until Tuesday."

"I'll see you at three," I said, and closed the phone.

Brenda said, "Gotta go, Mitch. We have to be in Oakville in less than an hour."

The thunder and lightning stopped as we pulled onto the highway, but the drive was slow, with rain still falling and the water so deep at times we could see the tires making waves as we drove. We pulled into the lot at five past three. Brenda took me as close as she could to the front door, but it would still be a thirty-foot dash through stubborn rain and huge puddles in sandals. If I was lucky, I wouldn't slip halfway there and end up on my butt in one of them.

"Have we got a bag or something I can put the draft in?"

Brenda had a zipper-lock bag with cookies for the kids in her purse. She handed three each to Nadia, Ethan, and Aaron, then sent the bag back to me. I zipped it up and pushed it into my back pocket. "Wish me luck."

Ethan leaned over and hugged me, pressed a kiss to my cheek. "Good luck."

I threw back the door to a chorus of voices calling, "Good luck." "Don't get too wet." "We love you, Liz."

"Limitless joy," Nadia hollered, as I ran full out for that front door.

Fortunately, the rain was warm and I was grateful for shorts as I splashed through the puddles. Jeans would have been heavy and dragging by the time I reached that door, but the shorts were light and clinging nicely to my ass—the perfect complement to the wet T-shirt thing I had going on when I walked into the reception area.

The icy cold blast of the air-conditioning made for an even more interesting visual and I was pleased to see Jim's mouth drop open and the police officer with him swallow hard. Silver linings, as Great-Grandma Lucy used to say. Silver linings.

I smiled sweetly. "Nice to see you again, Jim."

I walked toward them, dripping all over the expensive marble and sliding a little in my sandals—prompting a helping hand from the nice police officer who was there, I supposed, to make sure I didn't violate the inner sanctum again. If nothing else, we had shaken things up at Champlain Aerospace.

A crowd hovered at the doorway to the offices and I flashed them a smile, twiddled my fingers, then turned my full attention to Jim, who had finally composed himself enough to say, "Nice to see you too, Liz. I only wish it could have been under different circumstances."

As I watched him pull an envelope from his jacket, I took the zipper-lock bag from my back pocket nice and slow. "As you can see, I'm a little wet. Can you open the envelope and show me the draft? I wouldn't want to ruin it and have to get you to issue another one."

He opened the envelope and I sidled up beside him, not close enough to get him wet but close enough to feel the heat coming off him. Everything looked to be in order, so I stepped back and held open the bag. "Just drop that puppy in here and I'll be on my way."

With the draft safely tucked inside the bag, I zipped up the top and held out a reasonably dry hand to Jim. "It's been a pleasure."

He shook my hand and walked with me to the door. "It took moxie to pull this off, Liz."

I smiled up at him. "I think the word you're looking for is balls."

He laughed and opened the door. "What would you say to a drink some night?"

"I'd have to say no." I smiled as I stepped outside. "You see, I don't drink anymore."

The door closed between us. I turned around to see that the rain had finally stopped and Mitch's black pickup was parked beside the clown car. He and the kids, along with the staff of Sideshow Legal, were all standing outside, giving me a standing ovation as I came back through the puddles.

Nadia put her fingers in her mouth and whistled, the boys jumped up and down, and Brenda started to cry when Mitch took the zipper-lock bag and started pumping my hand.

"I hope you don't mind if I don't hug you," he said. "But you're a little wet and I have to get to the bank."

"I am, and you do," I said, laughing and bending over at the waist to give Brenda and the boys a safe, long-distance hug.

"We're taking you and Nadia for dinner tonight," Mitch said.

"Decide where you'd like to go," Brenda said, walking with him to the truck. "And make sure it's expensive!"

The boys splashed along beside them and Nadia stepped forward at last, wrapping her arms around me and lifting me up off the ground.

"Limitless joy," I grunted, which was a mistake because I thought she might crack a rib when she hugged me harder.

# GRACE

"Grace."

The voice was familiar. Calling softly. Bringing me up from a sound sleep.

"Grace, wake up."

I opened my eyes. Blinked at the dark. "Liz?"

Warm breath on my forehead. "No, idiot. It's Jocelyn."

I smiled at the shadow above me. "Hi, Jocelyn."

"Hi, Grace." I could hear her smiling back. "It's time to get up."

Get up? I turned my head to the window. Saw moonlight on the black trees outside. "It's still dark. We can't go biking in the dark." I rolled onto my side and closed my eyes again. "I don't want to go today anyway. Maybe tomorrow."

She climbed on the bed and bounced up and down by my feet. "This is the fourth morning in a row you've said that."

"It is not."

She bounced harder. "Doesn't matter because we're not going biking. Now get up."

"No."

"You are such a pain." She climbed off the bed, grabbed my arm, and tried to drag me over the side. But even if I wasn't completely awake, she was still smaller than me and I did not want to end up on the floor. So she did instead, plop, right on her butt.

"Asshole," she muttered, and scrambled to her feet. "If that woke your mom up, then we are totally screwed."

"My mom takes sleeping pills, so I don't think that would be enough. And why would we be screwed?" I propped the pillow under my head and opened my eyes really wide as though that would help me see in the dark. All I could make out were the shapes of my furniture against the walls, black holes where I knew there were posters, and Jocelyn's shadow crossing the room, opening the door and checking the kitchen anyway. "What's going on?"

"It's a surprise."

"I've had enough surprises." I turned my head. Stared at the grey square that was my window. "I don't think I can take any more."

"You'll like this one, I promise." She plunked a canvas bag beside me. Started digging around inside. "But it's not going to be dark for long, which means you'll miss it if you don't come with me this minute."

"Are you planning ghost stories at the lighthouse? Because if you are—"

"It's better than ghost stories. So stop arguing."

"Why won't you tell me what it is?"

"Because that would ruin everything." She pulled a flashlight out of the bag and clicked it on. "I brought this so you can see to get dressed."

She stuck it under her chin and made scary noises the way Liz used to do.

I smiled, but I guess she couldn't see me because she said, "Well, I thought it was funny," and put the flashlight in my hand instead. "You need to find some shorts, fast."

I didn't use the light to look for shorts. I used it to check the clock instead. "It's four A.M." I turned off the light and laid it down beside my head. "I'm going back to sleep."

"I don't think so." She shone the light in my face.

I put a hand in front of my eyes. "Why are you being so awful?"

"If I'm being awful, then I learned it from you." She knocked my hand away. "Get up, get up, get up, get up—"

"Okay, okay, you win!" I threw my feet over the side and sat on the edge of the bed.

*You're up before the birds, Grace*, my mom used to whisper when I was little and standing beside her bed in the dark. She never minded me being there, and she never took me back to my own bed either. She just lifted the covers and said, *Hop in*, and she and Mark would make room for me in the middle.

I guess that's why I didn't mind when William used to get up early too. Everything was so quiet and dark, it felt like we were the only ones awake in the whole world. Just me and William and a little night-light shaped like a swan. Liz gave it to me when I brought him home from the hospital. She said it would give me enough light to see what I needed to see in order to take care of the baby but not so much that he'd wake up completely and not go back to sleep.

She'd read all the books about babies, and when she said I wasn't to play with him at night, I figured she wasn't being mean, she just knew more than I did. She said I could talk to him and change him and feed him and then I could take him back to bed with me, which was my favorite part because he loved to snuggle. It didn't take long to figure out that Liz was right about the light, because every night, William and I would go right back to sleep. And lots of times, Liz would already be gone to work when we woke up again. Lots of times.

Jocelyn shoved the flashlight in my hand again. "You've got one minute to get dressed." She went out into the hall. "Otherwise, you're going in your jammies."

It was a good thing I knew where my shorts were because I don't wear jammies in the summer. Just underwear and a camisole. And like Jocelyn said, it wasn't going to be dark out there much longer.

I pulled on my shorts and tugged a T-shirt over my camisole—I'd Rather Be Sailing, which was a lie—and walked into the kitchen. Outside, the streetlights were still on, making it easier to see her waiting for me by the back door. "Did you make sandwiches?" I asked.

"No."

"Did you at least pack some cookies?"

"Why would I?"

I shook my head. "You don't do this kind of thing much, do you?"

She swung her bag up over her shoulder and held open the door. "Just get on your bike."

No sandwiches, no cookies. None of it made sense. Then again, we weren't going to tell ghost stories, so what did I know? Not much, as usual.

We passed the ferry dock and I realized she might be right. It might have been four days since I'd gone riding. Four days making centerpieces and watching the mockingbirds. Relaxing. Enjoying my summer like I was supposed to. Going to bed early. Getting up late. And eating.

I don't know why, but ever since Chez Ruby closed, I'd been hungry all the time. An ache in my stomach always there, a giant hole begging for ice cream or leftover cake or another hamburger. Anything at all as long as it filled that spot for a while.

Four days of eating and lying around didn't seem like much until we reached the bridge and suddenly it felt like ten. My legs were already stiff and my whole body felt heavy. "How far are we going?" I asked, that hole in my stomach wide awake now too. Making me wish I'd slapped some cheese sandwiches together. Grabbed a whole box of cookies.

"Gibraltar Point. Be quiet until we're past the fire station."

That was the first thing she'd said that made sense.

But even when we were past the disc golf course and on our way to Centre, we didn't talk. Just kept following the dull yellow glow of the streetlights past the empty pier where the moon sat watching us to the even lonelier road heading out toward the lighthouse. Even though the birds were starting to stir, it was still too early for the artists, so no one was around to see two bikes gliding past the retreat and turning left onto the first path leading down to the lake.

Jocelyn stopped at the end of the path and got off her bike. "You are going to love this!" she said, grabbing her bag and my hand and running with me across the grass onto a small, secluded beach shouting, "We're here! We're here!"

I had no trouble at all seeing Kylie, Brianne, and Courtney racing toward us, the three of them screeching and talking at once, as usual. "Oh my God, Grace!" "Wait till you see, Grace!" "This is the coolest thing ever!"

All of them were pulling me now, dragging me down to the water. That was when I saw it—one of the giant swans, bright white against the dark water. Freed from the lagoon and floating not two feet from the shore.

Jocelyn bounced up and down, her smile wide, her eyes bright. "Isn't it great? And look what else we have." She shoved her hand into the bag and came up with two sparkly tiaras. She danced them back and forth in front of me. "One for you and one for me."

I looked from the girls to the swan and back again. "I don't understand. How did the swan get here?"

"We brought it!" Jocelyn said.

"On a Sea-Doo trailer!" Courtney added.

The swan bobbed gently on the water, her graceful head going up and down as if she were agreeing. *Yes, yes. I came on a trailer!* I felt myself smile. I couldn't help it.

"The park guys move them around with a fork lift," Brianne said. "But we figured there had to be another way."

Courtney squeezed my arm. "Oh my God, Grace, those two know so much about boats and trailers, it's amazing. And you should have seen Kylie driving the golf car!"

The only golf cars I knew about were used by the park people who cleaned the bathrooms. "You stole a golf car?"

"I didn't steal it," Kylie said. "She left the key in her basket of cleaning stuff when she went into a stall, so I borrowed it."

Courtney put her hands on her hips. "It's not like we had a choice or anything. I mean, how were we supposed to move the trailer without it?"

"I have no idea." I looked back at the nodding swan. "How did you even get her here? Aren't the swans locked up at night?"

"Not locked, just kind of corralled together with a big wire," Brianne said. "The worst part was walking through the water to get to them."

Courtney shuddered. "That was gross. But we did it and she's here."

A light breeze came up and the swan started turning in a slow circle, bobbing as she went, like she was dancing. Happy to be the lucky one.

"The hardest part was getting the swan on the trailer," Jocelyn said.

"And the trailer up the slope," Brianne groaned.

"But it was smooth sailing after that," Courtney added. "You should have seen her riding along behind the golf car looking sooo majestic."

Kylie nodded. "And sooo big."

The swan went round again, turning in happy circles, taking my head with her.

"How long has the poor thing been out there?"

The girls looked at each other. "About two hours, wouldn't you say?" They looked back at me. "Yeah, about two."

The swan swung around again, nodding on her way past. "Yes, yes. Two at least."

Kylie smiled. "And the golf car and the trailer are back where they belong. All that's going to be missing now is a swan. No one will know how it got out or who did it."

Brianne lowered her voice. "Which is why we are sworn to secrecy."

"Absolutely sworn," Courtney agreed.

They formed a circle. Each girl put one hand over her heart and the other in the middle of the circle so they were all touching. "Come on, Grace. You have to swear."

The swan nodded and I didn't know what else to do anyway, so I put one hand over my heart and the other on top of theirs.

"What happened this night remains a secret until death," Jocelyn said solemnly.

"Until death," they all repeated, and looked at me.

"Until death," I said, still confused but certain I'd never tell anyone. Mostly because I didn't think anyone would believe me. I hardly believed it myself as I wandered down to the water and watched the swan dancing on the water, happy to be out here. Happy to be free.

"You should get in now," Brianne said.

I shook my head. "Get in?"

Jocelyn took my arm. "This is our Getaway Swan. So we can get away from all the shit that's been going on. Just float away and wave at the world like the queen." She put one of the tiaras on her head. "Come on, do the queenly wave with me." She cupped a hand, held it at shoulder height, barely moving it side to side while she looked down her nose at her friends and said, "Lovely to be here. Lovely to be here." She laughed and pulled me toward the swan. "Let's go. It'll be fun."

A wave brought the swan around to face me, her nod firmer, more definite this time. *Yes, yes! Time to go.*

I hesitated all the same. Not sure I should get into a stolen Getaway Swan.

*You have to be careful all of your life now, Grace,* my mom had said when the baby was born. *You can't take silly chances anymore.*

As if I ever had.

Brianne took my other arm. "It's now or never. The sun is coming up and you don't want to be here when the people start moving around."

I dug my heels into the sand. "Where do I want to be?"

"Grimsby!" the girls said at once, pulling me forward.

My eyes lifted to the shore in the distance. "Because Rochester's too far."

"Where's Rochester?" Courtney asked.

The water lapped gently on my toes. It was horribly cold, as always. "Somewhere over there. I don't know exactly. But then, I don't know exactly where Grimsby is either."

"We have a map." Kylie pulled a folded page from her pocket and held it out to me. "If you follow the shore, you can't get lost."

A map to Grimsby. The swan danced and Jocelyn bounced.

"I can't do this," I said, shaking myself free, marching back across the sand. "I don't know what you were thinking about. Stealing a swan, dragging me out here in the middle of the night—"

"We were thinking about you," Jocelyn said, taking my arm again, making me stop. "Because you've been so unhappy and we thought this might help. We thought that if you and I went out there on a swan and just gave the finger to everyone and everything on the Island, that it might make you feel better. Might even make you smile again."

Jocelyn wasn't smiling now. None of them were. Only the swan was still happy, still dancing, as if she really liked their plan, could hardly wait to get going. I had to admit I was starting to like it too.

"We just go out there and give the finger to everyone?" I asked.

"Anyone you want," Jocelyn said. "Lori. Your mom—"

"Especially your mom," Kylie muttered. Adding, "Well, she deserves it," when Jocelyn elbowed her.

"She does deserve it," I said quietly, looking back along the beach. Back toward Ward's Island where the sun was rising, turning the sky pink and purple and painting the horizon with a thin line of pure gold while that hole in my stomach grew larger and larger.

"She deserves it," I told the sun. "For making me retire and not telling me until it was too late."

"For not letting you do manicures and pedicures," Jocelyn muttered.

"And for wanting to kill the mockingbird," Kylie said, adding, "My mom told me that a while ago. I'm sure she doesn't want to kill it now."

"She will if it starts singing again," I said, and turned back to the sun. "And I hate her for that." I looked back at Jocelyn. "I hate her."

"That's okay," she said.

I shook my head. "It's not okay. None of it's okay." The ache in my stomach was getting worse and I started to walk toward the sun, my voice rising, getting louder and louder with every step. "It's not okay that I hate my mother or that Joe didn't come back to see about the baby robin. And it's not okay that Marla Cohen and Mrs. Charlton and everyone else went to Lori's so easily. They didn't even come to the house to say good-bye. Just got off the ferry and went to Lori's, like it was no big deal." I stopped suddenly and bent down. Picked up a handful of stones and threw them at the sun. "Well, it was a big deal to me!" I yelled. "It was a big fucking deal to me!"

I didn't even know I was crying until Jocelyn put an arm through mine and the ache spread out across my chest. "So let's do it. Let's get in the swan and tell them all to fuck off."

I turned slowly. Saw the girls watching me while the swan danced on the water all by herself, not caring one way or the other what I did. I could hop in and make my getaway, or I could get on my bike and go home. Shove dowels into Styrofoam and never again say that I wanted to escape on a swan because I'd been given the chance and I'd said no.

The swan stopped dancing and faced me again. *What will it be? Get in or go home?*

Didn't matter to her which way I chose. She'd be fine either way. Someone would find her and take her back. I was the only one who would still be lost.

Jocelyn held out the second tiara. "What do you say?"

I took the crown, pushed the combs into my hair, and kicked off my sandals. "Let's do it."

Brianne cheered, Courtney did a cartwheel, and Kylie kicked off her shoes and splashed into the water with us, holding the swan steady while we climbed in. We all crossed our fingers when Jocelyn flicked the switch, and breathed a sigh of relief when the motor began to hum softly behind us.

Brianne unhooked the anchor, gave us a push, and went back to the sand. "Just beach it and run when you're finished," she called. "And if anyone asks where you got it—"

"It was floating on the water when we got here," Jocelyn called, taking control of the swan as usual, heading us out into the lake.

The wind was calm, barely ruffling the surface of the water, and we kept going, farther and farther into the lake. Kylie, Brianne, and Courtney were still on the beach, and they cheered when Jocelyn turned the swan around and we gave them our best queenly wave.

"Are you ready?" Jocelyn asked.

I nodded and we pointed our middle fingers at the Island. Raised them up over our heads. "Fuck you, Ruby!" she hollered.

"Fuck you, Lori!" I added.

The girls on the beach held their middle fingers high. "Fuck 'em all!" they bellowed, and the five of us whooped and hollered, while I banged the side of the swan and Jocelyn thumped her feet on the bottom.

"Getaway Swan!" she yelled.

"Goin' to Grimsby!" I answered, and we laughed and high-fived while she turned us around and headed out into the lake again. Aiming the swan at the distant shore. Straight ahead. You can't get lost.

I could hear the girls on the beach chanting, "Grims-*bee*. Grims-*bee*," as we chugged on, the swan skimming across the water, her head bobbing, agreeing. *Yes, yes. Going to Grimsby.*

Their voices faded, but we were still moving. Heading for that distant shore, Jocelyn laughing and waving over her shoulder. "Grims-*bee*. Grims-*bee*."

I looked back at the Island. The girls were growing smaller and smaller as we went farther and farther. I could see them walking back to the grass, making their own getaway. Leaving us behind.

*You have to be careful all of your life now, Grace.*

I wiped my palms on my shorts. We should have brought sandwiches.

*You can't take silly chances anymore.*

Like leaving the Island. Following Liz.

Going to the city. Going to the city.

Jocelyn turned back around, still laughing, pounding her fist on the side of the swan. "I told you this would be great. Didn't I tell you this would be great?"

Her tiara sparkled in the sunlight. "Grims-*bee*. Grims-*bee*."

*You need to be careful all of your life now, Grace. You can't take silly chances anymore. Not with a baby.*

Not with a baby.

"Are you okay?" Jocelyn asked.

I saw the water all around us, the swan's beautiful head still pointed south.

*You need to come home, Grace. You need to bring that baby home.*

"Grace?"

I looked into her eyes. "I should have taken him home."

"Taken who home? What are you talking about?"

I spun around in my seat again. Looked back at the Island.

*That baby would still be alive if she'd brought him home.*

"I knew I should have gone back," I whispered, saying it out loud for the first time. "The day he was born, my mom said, 'Bring that baby home,' and I knew I should have. But I didn't."

"Grace, you can't dwell on that."

"But she was right." I snapped around again, looking east toward Ward's. "I should have gone back right away. I shouldn't have taken silly chances. It's not safe away from the Island. It's never been safe."

The next thing I knew I was in the water. It was colder than I'd expected. And I couldn't see the shore anymore.

# RUBY

Mark arrived early this morning, hurrying over after waking up to find Jocelyn's bike already gone. And he'd taken my stairs two at time when he discovered that Grace's was gone as well. I was as happy that Grace had finally come out of her snit and gone off to look at birds as I was to welcome Mark into my bed. Happier still that Big Al slept on while we made the most of our stolen time together, and I was looking forward to round two when someone knocked on the front door.

"Let it go," I said, kissing a path down his chest.

But whoever was out there knocked again. And again. Louder each time. The next thing I knew, I was on my back and Mark was throwing his legs over the side of the bed. "Someone really wants to talk to us," he said, dragging on jeans but not bothering with a shirt. Letting me know he'd be right back once he'd killed whoever was down there.

But the voice drifting up the stairs sounded agitated, and then

Mark was calling my name. "Ruby, get down here. The girls are in trouble."

And bam. Big Al was awake, snapping and hungry. Keeping that single word running round and round inside my head as I leapt out of bed and ran down the stairs. *Trouble, trouble.*

A man was at the door. I recognized him from the fire station, but I couldn't think of his name. He looked all of fifteen.

"Ruby," Mark said. "This is David Bell. He's with the Emergency Medical Service and he came to tell us that Grace and Jocelyn were pulled from the water near Gibraltar Point. He's going to take us to them now."

"From the water?" I repeated. "Grace and Jocelyn from the water?"

"I'll explain on the way," David said. I must have looked confused because he added, "I assumed you'd want to go straight over, so I have the van waiting outside."

"We'll be right there," Mark said. "We'll only be a minute."

But Big Al had a question he wanted answered right away:

"Where are they?" I asked while Mark closed the door.

"Where are they?" while I pulled on my clothes.

"Where did you say they were?" on our way down the stairs again.

And once more, just for kicks, while we were running to the gate for God's sake, with my head pounding and my hands clutching his shirt, holding us back, wasting precious seconds. "I'm sorry. I know you told me where they are, but I can't remember."

I could see he was as frustrated and scared as I was, but he didn't raise his voice, didn't call Mary Anne for backup, didn't try to leave the useless, weepy sidekick behind as I would have. Simply held my face between his hands, looked into my eyes, and said, "There's no time for questions. Just follow me. I'll take you to them, I promise."

No doubt Big Al would have preferred a scene, another riveting Ruby meltdown. But he must be learning to deal with disappointment because I was able to remain calm. Take a deep breath and trust Mark enough to stop talking and just follow him into the van. Feeling like everything was happening in slow motion. Certain only of one thing: If Grace was in the water, then something must have gone horribly wrong.

"I don't understand," I said as we passed the ferry dock. "She's an Island girl for heaven's sake. She's lived around water all of her life. What could have happened?"

"We're getting more details all the time," David said as he drove. "What I can tell you is that someone at the art center called to report two girls in trouble. One was in the water, the other was in one of those giant swans."

"In a swan? So they were in the lagoon?" Mark asked.

"No, sir, they were out on the lake, near the lighthouse. Apparently the one in the swan jumped into the water to help the other."

"I don't understand any of this," Mark said, giving me a lot of comfort. Assuring me I wasn't the only one having trouble with this conversation. "How did they get a swan out there?"

"We're trying to determine that, sir."

"Are the girls all right?" Mark asked.

"As of the last report, they were fine. Paramedics are with them on the beach now, and they'll be able to tell you more when we get there."

But where was *there*? That fact kept slipping away no matter how many times I asked or how hard I tried to hold on to it. Disappearing into the same hole where Big Al was keeping the names of people I'd known for years, along with a few phone numbers I used to take for granted. I touched my back pocket, felt the edges of my notebook, and smiled. I didn't remember putting it there, but Big Al would not be pleased.

I turned back the cover of my lifeline. Ran my fingers over the clean, blank page. "Mark," I said quietly. "Where is Grace?"

"The beach near the lighthouse," he said just as quietly, then asked the driver for a pen. My coconspirator, helping to keep Ruby's problem a secret. When I had the pen, he repeated the information without being asked. We made a good team, Mark and me, and I couldn't imagine trying to get through this without him.

I scribbled, *Grace in the water off the beach near the lighthouse* at the top of the page. Not that the knowing helped make sense of what was happening. My girls had always been strong swimmers with a healthy respect for the lake. They knew the dangers of currents and hypothermia. The need for proper safety equipment on the water. But according to the next report, none of that made any difference this morning. This morning, Grace had decided it was perfectly acceptable to go out on the lake without so much as a life jacket. In a swan of all things.

David parked on the road past the art center. A few early risers had gathered at the foot of the path down to the lake, but a police officer from the marine unit—female, maybe sixteen—was holding them back. David led us past the curious and across the grass to a small secluded beach, passing us off to an Officer Stokes when we reached the edge of the sand.

"Grace and Jocelyn are still being examined," Stokes said. "You'll need to wait here for now, but you can see them once the paramedics finish."

Farther down the beach, the girls sat about fifty feet apart—presumably so they couldn't talk to each other until after police had questioned them—both pale and coughing, both wrapped in a blanket, and both being tended to by paramedics. The relief when Grace turned and gave me a tiny wave was enough to weaken my knees, bring tears to my eyes. But relief quickly gave way to anger when Stokes drew our attention to the giant swan chugging around in a circle out in the lake, and the marine rescue boat trying to corral it.

"What were they thinking?" I asked, hearing Grace cough again and again. Knowing I should be grateful she was alive, but furious all the same. "Why would she do something like this?" I looked up at Mark. "She knows better."

"We'll find out everything soon enough," he whispered while the paramedic with Jocelyn packed up his kit and signaled to the female officer. The investigation was about to begin.

"Jocelyn is twelve," Mark said to Stokes. "I should be with her when she's being questioned."

"Just give Officer Grant a moment to determine if Jocelyn is up to answering questions."

"She is." The paramedic smiled as he came toward us. "Are you the parents? I tell you, luck was definitely on your daughters' side today. The current is strong here, and that water is cold, but they made it to shore under their own steam. They've both swallowed a bit of water, and they're coughing some, but nothing that warrants a trip to the hospital. Just get them home and keep them warm. Let them get some rest and they should be fine in a day or two." He glanced over his shoulder. "The bigger issue is that swan, and how they ended up inside it."

"We're working on that," Stokes said, then nodded at Mark. "You can go ahead now."

While Stokes stayed back to ensure that the curious came no closer, we hurried across the sand to where Jocelyn sat—a tiny bundle in a blanket, staring down Officer Grant.

"Tell me again how you got the swan out there," she asked.

"Like I said, we didn't *get* it there. We *found* it there."

"And you decided to get in?"

Jocelyn raised a brow, like the officer was missing a few screws. "Wouldn't you?"

She scribbled in her book. "How far from shore were you when Grace fell in?"

"About a hundred feet."

Mark said her name and Jocelyn raised her head. Reached for her dad. "It's okay," he whispered, kneeling down, pulling her into his arms. "It's okay."

"I just have a few more questions," the officer said. "We've learned that a golf car went missing last night, only to reappear this morning. Do you know anything about that, Jocelyn?"

Mark released her. Rearranged the blanket back on her shoulders. "Officer Grant, the paramedic advised that my daughter get some rest. Can we pick this up at the house later?"

"Of course." She closed her book and smiled at Jocelyn. "You take care," she said, and headed back across the beach to join her partner.

When she was out of earshot, Mark turned to Jocelyn. "You need to tell me exactly what happened. And if you give me that crap about finding the swan, I swear I will ground you until school starts."

She started to protest, thought better of it, and slumped against him. "What difference does it make? The swan is safe, we're safe. What's the big deal?"

Mark kept his voice low. "The big deal is stolen property. Police are involved, paramedics are involved, even the bloody marine rescue unit is involved. And not one of them believes that swan magically appeared on the beach. I doubt it's something you could have arranged on your own, so I figure you're protecting someone, which I respect. But if you want me to help you get out from under this, you need to come clean. Do you understand?"

"Fine." She cast a suspicious glance at the officers by the path and kept her own voice to a whisper. "We took the swan because Grace was unhappy after all that stuff with Lori, and I thought it might cheer her up."

"Not this again." I got to my feet. "Jocelyn, you have to let this nonsense go."

She shot up, the blanket falling behind her. "You keep telling yourself whatever you like, but I know Grace was miserable. About Chez Ruby, about you, about everything." She turned back to her father. "I probably should have thought it through better, but I wasn't planning to go far. Just back and forth so she could give the finger to the Island and tell everyone to fuck right off."

I spun her around. "That was your big plan? You put my daughter's life at risk so she could yell *fuck off* at the world from a swan?"

"She yelled it mostly at you, Ruby."

"Jocelyn, enough," Mark said.

"It's just the truth. And I know it sounds like a stupid plan, but I swear it's what Grace wanted. I wish you could have seen her out there, Daddy, sailing away on a swan with a big grin on her face and a fist in the air, shouting, 'Fuck off, we're goin' to Grimsby!'"

I shook my head. "This is ridiculous. Grace has never said a word to me about sailing away on a swan."

Jocelyn rounded on me. "I'll bet she never said anything to you about getting on a plane at the Island airport either, but that's another route she thinks about every single day."

I grabbed her by the arm, jerked her toward me. "How dare you."

Mark put a hand on my shoulder. "Ruby, let her go."

I loosened my grip, but she didn't pull away. Leaned into me instead, teeth gritted, voice low. "You should know that Grace goes to the airport every day to watch the planes. And she has picnics with Liz every Thursday at the nude beach on Hanlan's Point. In fact, there's one planned for today. She'll be here on the ten thirty ferry."

"Jocelyn, back off," Mark warned.

But Big Al had already perked up. *Picnics with Liz?* he said, and roared with laughter, filling my head with noise.

"That's a lie." I put my hands over my ears. "A bloody lie."

"I tried to tell you before," Jocelyn said. "You don't have a clue about Grace. Not a goddamn clue."

"I know my daughter better than any of you—"

"Do you know she has a cell phone? Did she tell you my dad gave her one?"

"Ruby, it's nothing," he said. "She borrowed it one day and I told her to keep it."

I looked up at him. "But you didn't tell me?"

"Because everyone knows you'd just take it away," Jocelyn said. "Or start snooping around in it, the way you snoop around on her computer."

"I'm trying to protect her!"

"And she's trying to protect herself! That's why she sneaks around. That's how she survives." The kid stuck her face in mine again. "Why do you think you never found anything in her computer? Because she's too smart to leave it there!"

Mark pulled her back. "Jocelyn, that is enough!"

"Sir," Officer Stokes said, "is there a problem here?"

I turned, searching for Grace. Spotted her, still huddled in a blanket, still being examined by that paramedic, oblivious to what was happening at our end of the beach.

"No problem at all," Mark said, leading Stokes away. But leaving Jocelyn behind.

She leaned close again, whispering. "You've been lucky up to now because Grace always found a way to make things right for herself. But she couldn't do it this time. Not after what you did to her with Chez Ruby."

It was my turn to curl my lip. "So you made things right by putting her in a swan out on the lake?"

"Grace got in that swan all by herself. And she was having fun. Laughing and cheering, like she'd won something. Until she jumped, and it was all over."

My stomach dropped. "Jumped? Why would she jump?"

"Are you that dense? She jumped for the same reason she can't bring herself to get on a ferry. Because you taught her that it's not safe to leave the fucking Island."

Big Al chuckled. *So she climbed into the swan because of you and jumped back out because of you. Nice work, Mom.*

"It's not my fault," I muttered, and backed up a step. Thought how nice it would be to climb into a swan and give Al the finger.

Tell him to fuck right off and go to Grimsby. I turned, searching for Grace again. Seeing that bloody paramedic still with her.

"It's not my fault." I raised my voice. "It's not my fault."

"What the hell is wrong with you?" Jocelyn demanded, bringing me back, making me focus. She tipped her head to the side. "Are you sick? Grace thinks you might be. That you might have cancer again—"

"I don't have cancer. I never did. Where did she get such an idea?"

"From Liz."

"Why would Liz tell her that?"

"How should I know? But she said it was a basal cell and you had laser treatments."

I stared at her. Liz had lied to Grace? Elaborately? For me? She must have been really drunk.

"If it's not cancer, then what do you have?" Jocelyn jerked a thumb at me when Mark returned. "What does she have?"

"Nothing," he said at the same time I said, "Alzheimer's." I hadn't known I was going to say it, but now that it was out there, I couldn't take it back. And Big Al was quite amused when both of their mouths fell open.

Jocelyn recovered first. Hauled back a fist and plowed her dad in the stomach. Doubled him over, bringing the paramedic tending to Grace running.

"You're going to marry a woman with Alzheimer's?" Jocelyn growled. "Why would anyone do that?"

"Probably because he loves her," the young man said, helping Mark to bend over, catch his breath. "I see that kind of devotion all the time. Especially in couples who've loved each other for years." He smiled when Mark straightened. "So how many has it been for you, sir?"

"Twenty-eight." Mark struggled to draw in a breath. "And I'd like twenty-eight more."

The paramedic gave us one of those horrible *I'm so sorry* looks.

"He knows that's not possible," I told him. "He's just an optimist."

"He's an idiot," Jocelyn said. "I can't believe you're going to saddle us with a . . . a—"

"Lump?" I finished for her. She shot me her trademark scowl and I laughed. "I'm the one it's going to happen to, and I'm even more surprised than you are that he wants this."

"With all the research being done today," the paramedic said, "you have every right to be optimistic."

Mark smiled and there she was behind his eyes—Hope. Waving her little pixie fingers, trying to make me believe he was right. Luck was on our side, just like with Grace and Jocelyn. Miracles for all today!

I sighed and turned back to Grace. With the paramedic busy here, Officer Stokes had wasted no time taking his place. I hurried across the sand and sank down beside her. "Grace, honey? Are you okay?"

She held out her arms to me. "Mom, I'm so sorry."

I drew her close and laid her head on my shoulder, her damp hair brushing soft against my neck, her breath warm on my skin. "There's nothing to be sorry for. Nothing at all." I glanced over at the officer. "Can your questions wait until we get her home?"

"I don't see why not." He tucked the notebook into his pocket. "Maybe a little rest will help trigger her memory. Help us figure out how that swan got all the way over here."

"It's a mystery." Grace sat up straighter, wiped her nose with the back of her hand. "But if I think of anything, I'll let you know."

"You've got my card." He turned to me. "We've arranged for the art center shuttle to take you all back to Ward's. I'll come by the house to speak with the girls later today."

Out in the water, a man with a hook finally caught the swan and guided her back to the marine rescue boat. Once she was alongside, another man climbed in, turned her motor off, and settled back for the ride to the dock. The drama was over. The curious started to leave. Like Jocelyn said, the swan was safe, they were safe. What else mattered?

Mark and Jocelyn were already making their way to the shuttle, Jocelyn marching ahead, talking, talking, talking, and Mark hanging back, silent—giving her the right to be angry, to say her piece. Probably feeling bad because he'd kept the Alzheimer's from her, but confident that eventually she'd shut up and start asking questions instead. Giving him a chance to explain, to mend the rift with an open and honest discussion, because that was his way. Had always been his way, even when the girls were little. Encouraging them to ask tough questions, develop opinions, and learn to voice them effectively—as if Liz had ever needed encouragement. He'd made me crazy if you want the truth, but maybe he'd been right all along. His daughter wasn't the one who had jumped out of the swan after all.

"We should get you home," I said, helping Grace to her feet. "But I have to ask. How *did* that swan get there?"

"It was the strangest thing," she said. "We got to the beach and saw her floating in the water, right over there." She went on to tell me the Tale of the Swan. How the big bird had danced on the water, turning in a circle, nodding her head like she was happy to be there.

"We were nervous at first," Grace said. "But how could we not get in?"

She looked down at the sand, avoiding my eyes while she gave me her version of the story that she and Jocelyn must have cooked up before the police and the ambulance arrived. Not trusting me with the truth the way Jocelyn had trusted Mark. Telling me instead about the beautiful sunrise, the fun of riding on the lake at dawn. Steering clear of the darker truth, brushing the unpleasantness aside, because that's what I'd taught her, because that's what we did. We swept aside the pain and sadness, pushed the tough questions and the guilty answers under the carpet and then we walked on the lump. Told ourselves we were moving forward, giving ourselves a clean slate, a fresh chance. And all the while, we kept walking on that bloody lump, pretending we didn't feel a thing, until one day we tripped over it and fell flat. Found ourselves drunk in a park, or swimming from a swan, or taking the handyman to bed, with that lump lodged in our throats, making it harder and harder to breathe.

"It was fun," Grace said. "Until I fell in the water and ruined everything."

The lie stung, but I'd earned it. She could no more tell me she'd jumped from that swan than she could tell me about her picnics with Liz or her trips to the airport or why she let Jocelyn put a new password on her computer, because they were all criticisms of me. Blatant rejection of my policies, my rules, and guaranteed to start an argument she knew she couldn't win. Unlike Liz, effective communication had never been Grace's strong point. So she was doing exactly what Jocelyn said she would—lying to protect herself. From me.

"I'm not sorry we went out in the swan. I'm just sorry it ended like this." She dug a toe in the sand. "I wish I hadn't been so stupid."

It would have been easy to let her go on lying. Pretend I didn't know the truth and avoid a long, humbling conversation. Let everything go back to the way it had always been. Both of us keeping secrets, telling the other what she wanted to hear—or what we thought she could handle.

Or I could tell her the truth. Give us yet another fresh start, another clean slate, with nothing left behind to trip us up later.

"Grace, you weren't stupid, you were scared, which I understand. But really, you should be proud of yourself." She looked at me curiously and I threw an arm around her shoulder, started walking with her across the beach. "You made Donaldson history out there today. We've always fought against tyranny. Given the finger to authority. Told the despots to fuck off and leave us alone. But you're the first one to do it in a swan. And I'm proud of you, even if you were aiming that finger mostly at me."

She stopped dead and pulled away, her face stricken. "Mommy, I didn't do that. I wouldn't do that."

"Yes you did, and that's okay because I deserved it." I draped my arm over her shoulder again, kept walking. "I kept secrets from you too, and I didn't treat you with the respect you deserve as an adult. But I promise things will be different, I'll be different. And when I'm not, when I yell or try to give you your opinion, you have to promise to stop me, to remind me of this conversation. Can you do that for me, Grace?" She nodded and I smiled. "I'll hold you to it. And while we're making promises, I promise I will never keep secrets from you again. Which means I have something to tell you." I stopped when we reached the path. "And I need you to listen carefully, okay?"

# LIZ

The call came at 10:15 A.M. Nadia and I were already in line at the ferry dock with KFC, potato salad, everything we needed for a fabulous picnic on the nude beach, waiting for the next crossing to Hanlan's Point. When the phone rang, I thought it was Grace—finally answering the texts and messages I'd been leaving her since early that morning—and I answered with, "Well, it's about time," only to have Mark say, "Liz? Thank God I reached you."

I hadn't spoken to Mark since our lunch at the Rectory—neither of us willing to be the first to say *I'm sorry* or *I was wrong* or, better yet, *I miss you*—and my breath caught when I heard his voice. "I'm calling to let you know that Grace won't be meeting you today. There's been an accident."

My whole body went cold and the bucket slid from my fingers. "What happened?"

Nadia caught the chicken while Mark told me about Grace and Jocelyn in a swan, the three of them going to Grimsby. "Getaway Swans," I said, suddenly remembering Jocelyn's phone calls.

"That's what Jocelyn called it," Mark said. "Did you know about this plan?"

"For years," I said softly. But I was always just talk. Jocelyn was the one who had pulled it off, made the dream come true for Grace. And I hoped she didn't blame herself for the accident. "Are they okay?"

"They're both fine and they're home. They just need to rest."

"Can I talk to Grace?"

"She's with a friend right now—"

"Friend? What friend?"

"Liz, I don't have time—"

"Okay, okay. How about Jocelyn? Can I talk to her?" Make sure she understood the gift she had given Grace and how much I would have loved to have been a part of it all.

"Jocelyn is with friends now too, but I'll tell them both you called."

"What is wrong?" Nadia asked when I closed the phone.

"My sister and Jocelyn aren't coming." I looked up at her and sniffed back unexpected tears. "There was an accident on the lake."

While I explained what had happened, she fished a tissue from her purse. "They are all right?" she asked when I finished. I nodded and dabbed my eyes. "And they are home?" I nodded and dabbed again. "Then there is no need to cry. We will take picnic to them."

"I can't do that," I said, but Nadia held the bucket tighter and grabbed my arm, dragging me across the dock to the gate for the Ward's Island ferry. Naturally, the *Ongiara* was there and loading, and Nadia kept going, taking me across the ramp and along the deck while I said, "This isn't going to work," and "What do you think you're doing?" and grabbed at bikes and tried to dig my feet into something, anything to hold my ground, convince her that I was not going to Ward's.

"I do not understand," she said when she finally stopped at the railing, setting the basket and the bucket down and turning to me with a scowl. "You want to be sure sister is okay, yes? Then what is problem?"

"Problem is Ruby. It's her house. She'll be there." I bent to pick up the bucket. "We need to get off."

She put a foot on top of the chicken. "Why? Because your mother made mistakes and you cannot forgive her? Is time you learned universal truth—all mothers make mistakes. You must forgive anyway."

"Why? Because she's sick?"

"Even more because she's sick."

I almost laughed. "So you're one of those people who believe that even if you're a shit all your life, once you get sick, you're automatically entitled to forgiveness? A moral do-over regardless of the mess you've left behind? Sorry, Nadia, I disagree. My mother has not earned a do-over."

I started to walk away. Let her keep the goddamn chicken. But she latched on to my T-shirt and yanked me back. "What your mother has or has not earned should not concern you. Is what you have earned that matters. You forgive your mother so you can stop being little girl, stop being affected by things she did. And then you forgive yourself for what happened to sister so you can get on with your life."

I tried to pry her fingers off my T-shirt. "Is this part of your limitless joy philosophy because, frankly, it lacks punch."

She tightened her grip, yanked me in close. "You want punch? Okay, here is story you will like. I used to have husband and little boy. Uri and Gregory, both very handsome. Uri and I, we liked to have good time, liked to visit friends every Friday and Saturday, have a few drinks. One time Uri would drive, one time I would drive. Always Gregory came with us, played with other children. But one night, both Uri and I are drunk. It is his turn, so I give him keys and tell him, 'You are driver.' Then I put Gregory on my lap because he does not want to sit in the back, and a drunk mother will let you do anything you like. He is only seven, but already he knows this."

Nadia released my shirt and turned away, looked out over the water. "We are in car," she continued. "Uri drives, I fall asleep with Gregory. Next thing I know, car is swerving, horns are honking, and bam! We hit something. Uri dies instantly. Gregory . . . he takes longer. Me, I am fine because my little boy was like air bag, keeping me safe. I walk away from accident. They are both dead."

Her face was blank, her voice flat, dull, as though she had told the story many times, to herself, to Olga, to strangers just so she could say it out loud. Hear the words and hope that with each telling she might come closer to understanding, to making sense of a loss that made no sense at all.

I laid a hand on her back. "Nadia, I'm so sorry."

She did that one-shouldered shrug, kept staring at the water. "Of course I blame Uri and I blame myself. I start drinking to get some sleep, but it doesn't work. So I drink more and more, and soon I am sleeping all the time and hoping I will not wake up, because guilt and anger are too much. But like I said, I have good friend in Olga. She steals my vodka and tells me I have two choices. Forgive Uri and myself and go on to be good teacher, or die. Those were my choices."

She turned back to me, her eyes no longer blank, her voice no longer flat. "So I made choice." And just like that, the Nadia I knew was back, and in my face—and I could not have been happier to see her.

"Olga was good friend," she continued. "She helped me to forgive Uri, to forgive myself. She helped me get my life back. Now I will be good friend to you. And we will start by taking picnic to sister."

The ferry bumped the dock. The deckhands readied the ramp. I backed up a few steps. "Nadia, as much as I appreciate the offer, I'm just not ready."

I walked to the other end of the ferry, getting ready for the trip back to the mainland. She left the bucket where it was and strolled over to stand beside me at the railing. "Okay, this is your lucky day. There is alternative. We will live together. Your room is bigger. Nicer window." She smiled at me. "I like right side of bed."

I stared at her. "What are you talking about?"

"Drinking. Same as always." She leaned her elbows on the rail and lifted her face to the sun while the rest of the passengers filed across the ramp, onto the dock. "If you do not grow up and find way to forgive both your mother and yourself, I guarantee you will drink again very soon. Probably tonight. So will be easier for everyone if I move in to keep eye on you. Can I have right side of closet too?"

"Will you stop? You're not moving in with me."

"Then you should go to bar now, get it over with."

"I'm not going to a bar."

"You are thinking about it."

"I am not." I sighed. "Fine, I was thinking about it, but only for a moment."

"Is where it starts. And before you know it, you are sitting on streetcar tracks with big hairy man threatening—"

"You've made your point." The last of the passengers were on the ramp. It was just Nadia, me, and a bucket of chicken left on the deck of the *Ongiara*. The next group was about to board. I glanced over at her. "How did you know about the bar thing?"

"I see it in your face. Frustration, confusion, too much anger. Is look of thirsty drunk. Right now, your addiction is somewhere doing push-ups, getting ready to take you for big night on town."

"It's not that bad," I said, but we both knew I was lying. If I let myself, I could taste vodka and lime. Tart, crisp, cold—the perfect alternative to an encounter with Ruby.

The line started slowly across the ramp. Nadia turned her head and squinted at me. "So do we take chicken to house and forgive mama, or do I move in?"

I drummed my fingers on the railing. Looked back at the Island. Thought of Grace and Jocelyn and a Getaway Swan that had nearly killed them both but would make a hell of a story one day. The only problem was that I wanted to hear that story now, while it was fresh. And I wanted to see my sister and hug her and know for myself that she was okay. And yes, I wanted to talk to Mark. Admit that I'd behaved badly and that I missed him. The only one I didn't want to talk to was Ruby.

The captain blew the horn. People kept coming across the ramp. It was getting harder and harder to see that bucket of chicken.

"Well?" Nadia asked.

"Let's go," I said, and elbowed my way to the chicken before I could change my mind. Picked up the bucket and made it back to the ramp with Nadia right behind me. We walked across together and kept on going, taking the path across the field and past the café. Neither of us speaking, just keeping a steady pace all the way to the street where I grew up, and the gate that led to our garden.

I stood back with Nadia and the chicken. The yard was full. Looked like a party was going on at the Donaldsons, complete with cake and Mary Anne's world-famous lemonade. I recognized some of the faces—Carol from across the road. Renata and Old Benny. The twins Kylie and Brianne. A guy I remembered as a deckhand on the *Ongiara*. Joe somebody. And in the middle of it all, Grace and Jocelyn, the guests of honor wrapped in blankets and sitting on lawn chairs in the sun. Laughing, talking—definitely not getting that rest they needed—while Ruby and Mark watched over them. Not hovering, just watching, even when the deckhand delivered cake to Grace and sat down beside her.

I watched Ruby smile when Mark handed her a glass of lemonade and realized something was different. She looked happy, her face calm, relaxed. *Botox?* I wondered, but she wasn't the type. No, the difference went deeper. She wasn't trying to run the show, wasn't directing every move and conversation, and she wasn't fighting Mark the way she used to. Wasn't pushing him away or brushing his hand from the small of her back. On the contrary, she was standing close, letting him love her, and letting herself love him back the way she should have all those years ago. Bravo for Ruby. And too bad for Mark. She probably would marry him after all.

I moved closer to the gate and a bird squawked in the lilac above my head. Came at us, batting its wings in our faces, trying to drive us back. "I think this is an omen," I said to Nadia just as Grace called, "Liz!" and threw back the blanket. "Wait there."

Of course everyone turned. Saw me there. Liz, the disappointment, the drunk, fighting off a bird with a bucket of chicken. Perfect.

That bird stopped attacking as soon as Grace came near. Went back up into the lilac while she opened the latch and threw her arms around me. "Liz. I'm so glad to see you."

"You too," I said, holding her hard, breathing in the scent of her hair and thinking that I probably owed Nadia one. I smiled and stepped back. "I heard you had some excitement today."

"You should have been there," she said as Ruby hurried along the path, coming straight at me.

"Liz," she said. "It's so good to see you." She pushed open the gate. Smiled at me. "Are you coming in?"

I swallowed and turned to Nadia. "If this doesn't work out, do you really need the right side of the bed?"

# GRACE

Mary Anne told me there's an old superstition for picking your wedding day. Monday for wealth, Tuesday for health, Wednesday the best day of all. Thursday for losses, Friday for crosses, and Saturday no luck at all. Of course, most people don't pay attention to old superstitions anymore and they get married on Saturday anyway. Which really does make Wednesday the best day of all, because nobody else wants the caterer or the florist or even the hairdresser. Wednesday's bride has them all to herself.

More than a week had passed since the Swan Affair, as my mother called it, and Jocelyn and I had been just fine by the second day, which was good because that meant we could help get things ready for the wedding. At last the centerpieces were done, the favors were ready, and the tent for the ceremony was set up in the baseball diamond. We spent all day yesterday decorating the clubhouse for the reception, and I didn't think we'd finish stringing lights and draping all that tulle until Christmas. But Mary Anne knew what she was doing and now the tent looked kind of like a church, and the clubhouse looked exactly like a fairyland. I couldn't wait to walk down that aisle, and I wasn't even the bride!

Even with all that decorating out of the way, we were still up bright and early on Wednesday morning because my mom wanted to go canoeing, and the florist was delivering the flowers at nine, and the caterer had to set up all her stuff at the clubhouse, and of course, the bridal party had to get ready.

My mom said it was important to keep her routine as close to normal as possible, and now that I knew about the Alzheimer's, I understood the reason for the canoeing and the notebook and the schedules. We needed to keep everything as calm as possible so that Big Al wouldn't show up at the wedding.

He hadn't been invited, that was for sure, and I made certain my mom took her meds first thing that morning, and I put her afternoon pills into my purse so she wouldn't forget to take them later. Before she left with Mark to go out on the water, I gave her a pen so she could write her daily list in her notebook: *Go caning. Grce do hair. Put drss on. Get mried.*

Sometimes her notes looked like that. Like she was sending text messages to herself. Mark told me not to say anything so I didn't, because what difference did it make? He said she'd been doing really well otherwise, and why make her feel bad about some spelling mistakes?

That made sense to me because I didn't like it when people pointed out the mistakes I'd made. And as long as I was there to give her the pills and take Mark's newspaper out of the oven now and then, the four of us would do just fine once they were married.

The ceremony wasn't until four o'clock that afternoon, but as the Official Wedding Hairdresser, I had a lot of work to do before then. So as soon as my mom and Mark went out the door with their paddles and life jackets, Jocelyn and I went over to Lori's to get my workstation officially set up and ready to go.

Four days after the Swan Affair—which also happened to be my birthday—Lori had come over with an envelope. Mark and

Jocelyn were in the kitchen icing a chocolate cake that I wasn't supposed to know about, and I was sitting in the garden with my mom, listening to my own music on the iPod that Joe brought me that morning. My mom went to help Lori fight off the mockingbird at the gate, but I wasn't about to join her. I wasn't about to turn my music off either because I couldn't imagine being interested in anything that woman had to say. It wasn't until she dropped that envelope in my lap and said, "Here's the deal," so loud that I couldn't pretend I didn't know she was there anymore, and I finally took out the earbuds and looked up at her.

"Those clients of yours are impossible," she said. "If I didn't need the business, I wouldn't care if they never came over again. But I do need them, so I'm making you an offer." She nodded at the envelope. "You'll work for me three days a week, any three you like, and you keep those witches coming back. If they stop, you're out of work. Do we understand each other?"

"You want Grace to work with witches?" my mom asked.

Lori looked at her funny so I said, "She wants me to work with Marla Cohen."

"She's a witch all right," my mom said. "So, Lori, how are things going at your spa?"

"They'll be better now," I said, and we shook hands on the agreement. Three days a week and keep the customers coming back. I could do that with my eyes closed. Happy birthday to me!

I saw Lori's place for the first time that same day. She had a sunroom that she'd converted into her spa, with big mirrors and two styling chairs, and a manicure table and even a special chair for pedicures with a soaking tub. Our old barber chair sat in a corner by the window with my workstation beside it. That would be my spot, with my very own tools right there all the time.

Lori had already told the regulars that I'd be starting at Lori's Island Spa soon, and most of them had already booked appointments. But today was my first workday, and it was all about the wedding.

I was a little nervous when Jocelyn and I walked through the door. Lori was drinking coffee and doing her books, and just watching her bent over her laptop, sighing and rubbing a hand across her face, I realized I was glad I didn't have to do all the extra work after all. I could just do the hair and go home. And if I wanted to learn how to do manicures and pedicures, Lori said I could add those to my list of services too. But right now, I was thinking about Jocelyn's new hair color.

I patted the chair and waited until she sat down. "What color do you want?"

She sighed and plucked at her stop-sign red hair with the dark roots. The color change was going to be her wedding gift to Mark and my mom. She still didn't like the idea of the marriage, but Liz had talked to her for a long time on the phone, and I don't know what she said, but it must not have been "Ruby's a bitch," because Jocelyn stopped avoiding my mom and started talking about dresses, which sure made Mark a whole lot happier. But seeing her come down the aisle with a new hair color would let him know she really was on his side again.

"I'm naturally a brunette," she said. "But can you do something more interesting?"

I laughed and threw a cape over her shoulders. "Jocelyn, I can do interesting like nobody else."

I had to admit Lori's setup was better than anything my mom and I had at Chez Ruby, with no juggling of counter space or waiting for the sink, and I had that red stripped and those foils applied in half the time it would have taken me at home. Three hours later, Jocelyn's hair was shiny, sleek, and definitely interesting, with chunky streaks of copper and gold that caught the light and made her green eyes sparkle.

"Aren't you a picture?" Mary Anne said, gliding into Lori's sunroom like a movie star in a gauzy Indian cotton skirt and matching gypsy blouse; shedding her straw hat, shoulder bag, and sandals all along the way. Watching Lori frown, I knew it was going to take her a while to get used to the old Chez Ruby bunch.

"You are positively gorgeous," Mary Anne said to Jocelyn, leaning forward for a closer look. "You must promise never to do that wretched red again."

"I promise," Jocelyn said, smiling and sneaking another glance at herself as she slid out of my chair to make room for Mary Anne. "See you at the house."

"Mark's there with Ruby," Mary Anne said. "If you want to surprise him with that hair at the wedding, you should go straight to my house and phone him. Tell him to bring Ruby over here and then start getting himself ready. Tell him it's bad luck to see the bride after noon on their wedding day. That should get him moving."

She began taking out pins, letting down all that hair while I swept up, making sure my station was orderly and neat at all times—*Job one at Lori's Spa*, so I'd been told.

When Mark arrived with my mom, she sat down in the barber's chair that used to be ours and said, "Make me beautiful, sweetheart." Then she turned to Mary Anne, and the two of them started talking about the wedding, and I took a look around and decided I was going to like working here.

When I finished with them, Mary Anne patted the flowers in her hair and smiled at my mother in the mirror. "We shall be the most beautiful wedding party ever to walk the streets of Ward's Island."

"We'll definitely be the noisiest," my mom said, applying one more layer of spray to curls that were supposed to be soft and springy. She checked both sides of her hair, demanded a mirror to see the back, and then pulled me into a hug. "Beautiful job, Grace. Thank you." She hesitated for a moment. "I should do your hair now."

Fortunately, Mary Anne took her arm. "No time for that. Lori can help her out, I'm sure."

"I'll be ready for you in just a moment," Lori said. "Have a seat at the sink and relax. You've been working hard all morning."

My mom and Mary Anne left in a swirl of pale blue Indian cotton, Lori fastened the cape around my neck, and I leaned back—closing my eyes while she washed my hair with shampoo that smelled like lavender, and neither of us said a word about my mother.

But it turned out she was right about ours being the noisiest wedding procession ever to hit the Island streets. That will happen when you have a piper and a drummer leading the way.

We were in the garden having pictures taken when we heard them coming from the ferry. We'd known there would be a piper—what Scot gets married without one?—but the drummer was a surprise. Celtic Fire, the two men called themselves, and from the moment they stepped into our garden, I couldn't stop tapping my feet and wishing Liz were there to do the Highland fling.

"That is not music," Jocelyn said, standing with Mary Anne and me by the birdbath for one more shot of the bridesmaids. The mockingbirds must have agreed because they hadn't poked their heads out of the lilac once since the pipes arrived.

The photographer held up a hand. "Smile, ladies."

"I'll bet he likes bagpipes," Jocelyn muttered, looking miffed but pretty in a short emerald green halter dress and matching flip-flops. Her bouquet was white daisies—same as mine and Mary Anne's—but she had stuck a red rose in the center of hers, just because she was Jocelyn, and no one thought to mind.

Beside her, Mary Anne looked fabulous in floor-length pink froth and I was happy with the bold tribal-print sheath Jocelyn had picked up for me and my mother had called "intriguing" when I showed it to her the first time.

"And one more shot by the stairs," the photographer called.

My mother waved a hand. "No more pictures. It's time to get this show on the road."

I don't know if it was the way the light was coming through

the trees or the way she was smiling, but my mother looked wonderful there by the roses. Not glamorous like one of those magazine brides with their big gowns and their big veils. But simply elegant, as Mary Anne had said, in an ivory silk dress with cap sleeves, ruched waist, and a tiered skirt that skimmed her calves and swirled when she danced.

She'd spent most of yesterday searching drawers and boxes for Great-Grandma Lucy's tartan sash, and now wore it draped over her left shoulder and pinned on her right hip with the same pewter broach Grandma Lucy had worn at her wedding. Instead of a veil, she had tucked a red rose into her hair, with a sprig of white heather for luck.

"You do your grandma proud," Mary Anne said, handing my mother the bouquet she kept leaving behind on chairs or the table or in someone else's hands.

"Maybe so, but Mark's going to wonder where I am." She tried to pass the flowers to Jocelyn. "Come on, you girls."

Mary Anne pressed the bouquet back into her hands. "Ruby, you're going to need this."

"And we need to go." She waved the bouquet at Jocelyn and me. "Come on, girls, there's a wedding happening someplace today."

We laughed and Celtic Fire went through the gate ahead of us, the piper already warming up for our walk to the clubhouse. Most of our neighbors were going to the wedding and were gathered on the street, all dressed up for a party.

Benny hollered, "Ruby you're a looker, just like your grandma."

My mom wiggled her hips, and everybody clapped, and we followed the piper through the narrow streets to the clubhouse.

People waiting for the ferry took pictures, and we laughed and waved. It wasn't until we were almost at the door of the tent that my mom grabbed my arm and walked beside me.

"Where's my notebook? I need my notebook."

"It's here," I said, showing her the sequined evening bag that

Mary Anne had picked out and trusted to my care. "The notebook will be in here tonight, because you don't have a pocket."

"I don't know why." She took the notebook and pen from the purse. "All dresses should have pockets."

She left the procession and ran to a picnic table by the Clubhouse Café. I waved the piper to stay where he was, and ran after her. She was already sitting down, writing in her notebook when I got there. *Thak Mark for drmer*.

"Mom, what are you doing?"

"Making a note." She frowned at the page. "I think I spelled some things wrong. Ah well, what can you do." She smiled at me and tucked everything back into the evening bag. "You'll remind me again later where that is," she said, and headed back to the tent.

I picked up her bouquet from the table and followed.

With only a few minutes left, most of the guests had gone into the tent to find a seat.

"What were you thinking?" Mary Anne asked, dusting the back of my mom's dress, adjusting her sash, straightening the flower in her hair. Returning her to elegant once more. Mary Anne took the bouquet from me and handed it to my mother one more time. "Do not put these down until I tell you to, okay?"

My mom smiled. "Okay." She turned to the piper. "There's a wedding happening someplace today. Do you know where?"

"You're too funny, Ruby," he said, and went ahead into the tent while we arranged ourselves into a proper line for our entrance.

Mary Anne had hired a string quartet to play for the wedding, and they were entertaining the guests with their pretty songs. But they were drowned out completely when the piper blew his opening notes and started down the aisle.

I couldn't wait, I had to peek around the curtain. All the seats were filled, the justice of the peace was at the arbor, and Mark and his friend Seth Harrison were coming in from the right, wearing short black jackets and kilts! Donaldson tartan kilts! Blue background with green and black plaid, just like Great-Grandma Lucy's sash. My mom was going to be so surprised!

The piper stopped playing when he reached the arbor and the trio started up again with Pachelbel's Canon—our signal to start walking.

"Oh my God, what's my dad wearing?" Jocelyn whispered.

"A kilt," I whispered back.

"Why?" she hissed, and stepped out.

Poor Jocelyn. I knew she was nervous, but she held her head up and her shoulders back. Cameras flashed, her three friends waved, and Mark's face lit up when he saw who was coming.

Mary Anne laughed. "That man is going to bust some buttons if he gets any prouder of that daughter of his. Okay, go," she said to me. "And Ruby, you come back here."

I took a deep breath, positioned my flowers, and I walked. Nice and slow, head up, shoulders back. Cameras flashed at me too. People smiled. Joe smiled and I could feel my face get all warm. I looked for Liz but didn't see her anywhere. Then again, she never did promise to come.

When I reached the arbor the music changed, and my mom and Mary Anne started down the aisle together. It wasn't supposed to be that way. It was supposed to be Mary Anne first and then my mom all by herself. *Nobody gives me away, Grace. I go on my own.* But she must have changed her mind, because she was holding Mary Anne's arm and walking nice and slow.

More cameras flashed, and Mark whispered to Seth, "She is so goddamn beautiful," and I was sure I heard those buttons give way as my mom came closer.

When they reached the arbor, Mary Anne went to stand beside me, and my mom stepped into her place beside Mark. My mom smiled and said, "Love the kilt."

"You better," Mark growled, and my mom laughed.

"Ladies and gentlemen," the justice of the peace said, "please be seated."

When everyone was sitting down again, the justice of the peace looked past my mom to the back door.

I turned my head to see what was happening, and there were Liz and Nadia, tiptoeing into the tent, trying to blend into the wall while they searched for a seat.

Of course every head was turned by that time and my mom finally looked over her shoulder. When she saw Liz she stopped breathing for a moment and she put a hand to her mouth. "Liz," she said softly, and looked back at Mark. "It's Liz."

There were no seats left, so two men in the back row stood up and motioned for Nadia and my sister to sit down. Liz shook her head, she didn't want to be a bother, I could see it on her face. But the men insisted and she and Nadia finally sat down, and all those heads turned right back around.

My mom's eyes had tears in them now. Mary Anne handed her a tissue, and Mark took her hand and drew her around again so they could get married.

"Ladies and gentlemen, a wedding is a time for celebration."

The JP went on about the institution of marriage and the tradition of marriage, but my mom wasn't really listening. She kept glancing back at Liz, and then at Mark, then back at Liz, and finally he took her arm and drew her to him so she had no choice but to pay attention.

"Ladies and gentlemen, the bride and groom have chosen their own vows for the exchange of rings." He motioned to Mark. "Mark Bernier, are you ready to make your vow to Ruby?"

They hadn't told each other what they were going to say because my mom wanted to be surprised. Mary Anne said that could be dangerous, but it sounded like a good idea to me.

Mark had a cue card, but he didn't need it. He just looked into my mother's eyes and started in, reciting a poem by Robbie Burns. "As fair you are, my bonnie lass, so deep in love am I. And I will love you still, my Dear, till all the seas go dry. Till all the seas go dry, my Dear, and rocks melt with the sun. I will love you still, my Dear, while the sands of life shall run."

He took her hand and slid the ring onto her finger. My mom looked at it and said, "Oh my," and raised the tissue again.

"He did well," Mary Anne whispered, and used a tissue herself. "Very well."

Mark turned to the JP and shrugged. "I hope that's enough because it's all I've got."

The guests laughed and the justice smiled. "That will do just fine." He turned to my mom. "Ruby Donaldson, are you ready to make your vow to Mark?"

"I am." She smiled up at Mark. "But I'm definitely going to need my notes."

The guests laughed again and Mary Anne handed her an index card. "Seems I have a poem too," she said. And people laughed again and someone said, "That Ruby is such a card." But they all went quiet when she lifted her eyes to Mark and started to speak.

"If ever two were one, then surely we. If ever man were loved by wife, then thee. If ever wife was happy in a man, compare with me, all you women, if you can. For this is the crown and blessing of my life. The much-loved husband of a happy wife. To him whose constant passion found the art, to win a stubborn and ungrateful heart."

She slid the ring onto his finger and Mark didn't wait to be invited. He wrapped his arms around my mom and kissed her then and there. The JP shrugged and said, "By the power vested in me by this province, I now pronounce you husband and wife."

Everyone cheered and clapped, and Mary Anne cried, and I cried, and Jocelyn didn't want to cry, but she did. Then she said, "I get it now. He loves her."

The reception started right after the ceremony with waiters offering hors d'oeuvres and the photographer hurrying to take as many pictures as he could before the caterer announced that dinner was served.

"Where's Liz?" my mom asked. "I want her in the pictures too."

"She is here," Nadia called, holding up a hand. "And she is coming." Nadia shoved my sister along, smiling at the guests they passed. "She is so excited to be in picture."

"Liz," my mom said, and threw her arms around her.

For the first time in years, Liz hugged her back. Really hugged her, which made me need my tissue again.

"Family photo," my mom said, waving me, Mark, and Jocelyn over.

We stood in a huddle, smiling and sniffing. Holding our positions long enough for the photographer to snap a couple of shots. Then my mom said, "Donaldson women only." Mark and Jocelyn backed away, but my mom held out a hand to Jocelyn. "Like it or not, you're a Donaldson woman now too."

I thought Jocelyn might flip her the finger or turn her back. But she looked to her dad and said, "Is it all right?"

He laughed. "Are you kidding? I'm standing here in a skirt, for heaven's sake. You get near a Donaldson, you become one. Go, go."

The four of us stood nicely for a couple of shots, then we laughed and mugged for a few more. Then the caterer announced that dinner was served, and everyone filed into the clubhouse.

I sat at the head table beside my mom, and two places were set for Liz and Nadia at the table right in front of us with Benny and Carol and other neighbors who had known Liz since she was little. They greeted her with hugs and kisses, and shook Nadia's hand and told her to be sure to ask Liz to do the Highland fling later.

Wine was poured and Mark rose with his glass. "Ladies and gentlemen, I'd like to thank you all for being here, and I'll keep this brief. A toast, to all who have come here today to celebrate something that should have happened a long time ago."

"Here, here," more than a few people called as chairs scraped back and glasses were raised.

My mom rose to stand beside Mark.

He lifted his glass. "A toast," he said. "To all of you, our wonderful friends and neighbors."

My mom lifted a fork, watched it hover in the air in front of her. Benny saw. Carol saw. Liz saw. Nadia saw. More and more people saw. And still the fork hovered.

"I'm doing this wrong," she whispered to Mark, "but I don't know why."

"She's got the right of it, folks." He set down his glass and picked up his fork. "As Ruby says, to hell with the wine, let's eat!"

"Let's eat," Benny called and raised his fork to her. "You're a corker, Ruby Donaldson, a real corker."

People were still talking about how good the food was while they pushed back tables and chairs and made room for the DJ and dancing. I met up with my mom in the ladies room and gave her the pill in my purse. "It's late, I'm sorry."

"No worries," she said, swallowing the pill with water from the tap and wiping her mouth on the way to the door. "First dance is coming up. Wouldn't want to miss it."

At midnight, my mom threw the bouquet, Mark threw the garter, and then the bride and groom left to catch a water taxi into the city and a two-night honeymoon at the Fairmont Royal York. The caterer was serving coffee and tea with plates of wedding cake, and I was exhausted after dancing the fling with Liz, hip-hopping with Jocelyn, waltzing with Mark, and slow-dancing with Joe, who was a really good dancer.

"Have you kissed him?" Liz asked me in the bathroom.

"No." My face went warm right away. "But I'm thinking maybe tonight."

"Maybe tonight?" Liz grinned and lifted her hair from the back of her neck, trying to cool down after dancing with the drummer. "You have to tell me everything, you know that. Speaking of telling all, Mark asked me to work with him on the Swan Affair. See if we can get the police to back off on you girls."

"Good luck," I said as the bathroom door burst open, and Mary Anne grabbed my arm.

"It's your mom," she said. "You need to come now."

Liz followed us out. "I thought they left."

"They did. Shut up and keep walking. Don't let on that there's anything wrong."

The three of us went through the clubhouse, nodding to guests and refusing offers of cake. Making our way to the door as quickly as possible without raising alarms. "Where is she?" I demanded as soon as we were outside. "Where's my mother?"

"Over by the canoe club. Mark said they went back to the house to change and pick up their bags for the hotel. She was ready before him, so he told her to wait in the kitchen, but when he got down there, she was gone."

"Gone?" I asked as we hurried along the street, everything around us now black and white, and a horrible grey in the yellow glow of the streetlights.

"He went looking for her right away." She stopped us by the rack of canoes across from the club. "He found her quickly enough, but she didn't know who he was. She wouldn't let him touch her, she started to run. He was terrified she'd get lost again, so he called and asked me to get you girls and to be discreet about it." She pointed to the canoe club building. "They're back there. He won't leave her, but she won't go anywhere with him." She lowered her arm. "He's hoping you can get her to come home."

Liz and I ran around the side of the building. It was darker back there, harder to see. "She's here," Mark called, and we moved toward the shadow by a rack of canoes. He was breathing hard, raking a hand through his hair. "She doesn't know me," he said. "She doesn't know who I am."

Liz put an arm around him. "She will. I know she will."

"Grace?" my mom said, her voice shaky, soft. Like she was really afraid and going to cry. "Grace? Is that you?"

I still couldn't see her. "Yes, Mom, it's me. What are you doing in there?"

She came out from behind the canoes. "I don't know," she said, looking around. "I don't know where I am." She turned back and saw Mark standing there, as helpless, as lost as she was. "Mark?" she said.

He groaned with relief. "Ruby, you had me so worried."

She walked toward him, laid her head on his chest. "I'm so tired, Mark. I'm just so tired."

# RUBY

## SHOW ME THE ICE FLOE
### The blog for people who know what they want

By Ruby Donaldson


### Number 30 in a series. Or is it 31?

*Shhh. Big Al is sleeping again. He's been wide awake since the wedding three weeks ago, and so far I have fallen into every booby trap the bastard has set. Losing things, impatient with everyone, forgetting more than the names of celebrities, believe me.*

*But oddly enough, this feels like a good morning. Mostly clear. The fog thinner, like mist when it rises from the lake. Not enough to obscure important things, just enough to soften the edges. But it won't last. Big Al will pump up the volume on his fog machine and once again I'll be wandering around in a thick soup, bumping into that bugger at every turn.*

*Of course, Hope is still there at the corner of my mind. Telling me to have faith. Assuring me that a mircle is right around the corner. Or at least in the offing. Perhaps. If we're lucky. Okay, probably not, but that's not her point. Her point is that I must hold on because what I'm contemplating is selfish and wrong. Think about the people who love me. How will they feel if I hope on the next Ice Floe?*

*Relieved, if they're honest.*

*Since the wedding, everyone has been on Ruby Watch. Even poor Jocelyn on days when Mark and Grace have to work, and Mary Anne has meetings in the city. No one talks to me about it, but I know they're all worried about what happens in a few weeks. Fall is coming. You can feel it in the night air, bringing high school for Jocelyn and a new semester for Mary Anne. Who will babyst me then? Who will give up their life to tend to mine?*

*Let's face it. I'm a pain in the neck for everyone, including my- self. Naturally, Hope doesn't want to hear that. Hope wants me to believe there are options, but Hope lies.*

*I have been to Dr. Mistry again, and she is the only one who is not surprised by my sudden decline. It's true that some people will go on for years, the illness always chugging ahead, but more slowly than it has for me. Giving them the time that Mark and Hope have dangled in front of me like a carrot. Keep coming, Ruby, keep com- ing, you'll reach it, don't worry.*

*But I won't reach it. Unlike Hope, Big Al is honest with me. He has me in his sites and he is moving in for the kill. I know the op- tions, the choices, and they come down to this:*

*Take my life back from Al while I can or go quietly into that fog and disappear forever.*

*I don't know about you, but for me, the fog is more frightening than anything I could encounter on the Ice Floe.*

*So here I am. I know it's eight a.m. because the clock beside the bed tells me so. Outside, the sky is grey and clouds are gathering. Storm's coming, as Grandma Lucy used to say.*

*Downstairs, Mark is making coffee, making breakfast. I'm in bed alone with my laptop and the sign on my ceiling—Go canoeing—because Mark's letting me sleep in, letting me ignore the sign because I had a rough night. Nightmares, restlessness. That means he had a rough night too, but he doesn't have the option of sleeping in. He has work to do, a wife to support. A wife who is sliding downhill faster than either of us imagined possible.*

*But it's a good morning and I remember bits and pieces of the wedding. A piper. A fairyland. Mark in a kilt. What I don't remember comes to me in pictures, popping up on my lptop screen, and in the special frames that Mark bought and put all around the house. There is one on the dresser. I see Mary Anne pop into the screen, wearing more pink than any woman should ever wear, yet looking fabulous as always. And Jocelyn, so pretty in a green dress and almost normal hair. And then Grace. Beautiful Grace. Even that horrible dress can't take that away.*

*Now comes a picture of people I should recognize but don't. Guests, I suppose. The important thing is that in every shot, people are smiling and happy. Enjoying the party.*

*And there's me, smiling too. I look happy. I look good. For a fifty-something bride. Where is that tartan sash now? I'd like to find that sash.*

*Now there's one of me and Mark together, under the arbor. I feel myself smiling just like I was in the picture. I like that kilt.*

*Another shot under the arbor. Mark sliding the ring onto my finger.*

*Looking down at my hand, I see it's there still. White gold, engraved on the outside instead of the inside. So I don't have to remember to take it off to see the words.* As fair you are, my bonnie lass, so deep in love am I. *A Robbie Burns poem. I've known the words by heart since I was little. Funny that Big Al hasn't stolen them away. Look, there's Liz.*

*It's a good picture. She's not so thin anymore. Not so pale. Stunning was always the word that came to mind with Liz. Stunning with her black, black hair and her dark gypsy eyes.*

*There she is again with me and Grace and Jocelyn. All the Donaldson women making faces at the camera, sucking in our cheeks, lolling our heads, definitely not proper wedding poses, and all because*

*Liz is with us I'm sure, egging us on the way she always did. I start to laugh as we must have been laughing when someone took the pcture.*

*I hear the door downstairs open and close. Mary Anne's voice. Mark going for his paper. No other voices, so the girls must be out biking or looking for birds. Did Grace and I ever get on a ferry? I don't think so. I'm sure I meant to. Mary Anne's voice again. I should get up.*

*There's Liz again, with Grace, dancing the Highalnd fling. Liz came to the wedding. And she comes to the house now too. I know because Mark writes it on the sign above my bed.* Go canoeing. *And below that is another line—*Liz has been here this many times ++++ I. *Six times.*

*Each time she visits, he puts another line on the sign. Six visits since the wedding. Six is a lot. I wish I could remember even one.*

*Mary Anne is puttering away downstairs. Puting on the kettle, making tea.*

*Time to go.*

I read over my entry. Clicked Exit. Again the box came up. *Post?* Again, I clicked No, do not post. And entry number 30 or 31 disappeared like all the others. Poof. Gone. Time to go.

Rising slowly, I stood a moment. Stretched. Despite the rough night, I felt good. Stronger than I had in a while. Perhaps because I had a goal today. Something I had to do. Go canoeing.

I changed quickly into jeans and a T-shirt then lit up one of my hidden joints and took two puffs—not because the pot was doing anything to stop Big Al, let's be frank—but because I liked the way it relaxed me, if only for a little while.

After two puffs, I stubbed out the joint, pinched the end, and shoved it into my pocket with the lighter. For later.

Grabbing my notebook, I saw Benny pop up in the picture frame. Waving to me. You old codger. What were you and my grandmother up to anyway? I'll never know. Another Donaldson mystery. Like what really happened to my mother. Did she fall or did she jump? Grandma Lucy never talked about it, never let me talk about it, but I think she jumped. I think that subway train was her Ice Floe. I'll just never know why.

Mary Anne must have heard me coming down the stairs because she was there at the bottom, smiling, wishing me good morning. Looking a little wary, not sure what mood the beast would be in. Did we start tap-dancing now, or could we have tea first?

"Good morning," I said, and smiled.

Mary Anne smiled back. "Your meds are ready."

She had them lined up on the table, a glass of pomegranate juice beside them. *There's a good girl, Ruby. Take the pills nicely.*

That was Big Al waking up. Walking around, touching things. Bastard.

"Any tea in that pot?" I asked, swallowing the meds and vitamins. No need to raise suspicions. I peeked out the window at the lilac. "Those babies flying yet?"

"Not that I saw, but Grace says they will any day now."

Too bad I wouldn't get to see them.

I glanced over at the door. The paddle was there. The life jackets were there. Mary Anne was watching me, suspicious. Or was that Big Al adding a touch of paranoia to the mist?

"Mark's gone for his paper," she said, assuming I wouldn't know. Bitch.

For God's sake, Al, could you give me a minute?

I took the mug of tea she offered. That was when I saw the hurdle—how to get out that door alone, with Mary Anne in the way. I wandered to the window. Watched the storm clouds gathering and turned back to her. "You know what I have a taste for? One of those fabulous cookies from the bakery at Sobeys."

She laughed. "White chocolate macadamia? I always have a taste for one of those."

I picked up the phone. "I should call Mark, ask him to bring home a few."

She waved a hand. "I have some in my freezer." Big Al and I were hoping she'd say that.

"I'll be right back," she said. "Don't go anywhere."

I didn't go anywhere. Merely grabbed my paddle and a life jacket. Carried them upstairs, opened the window, and let them go. Watched them fall into the bushes where they'd be easy to find later. If I was lucky.

I raced back down the stairs, reaching the kitchen just as Mary Anne came in with the cookies, her smile bright, the way it was the day she brought over the first little bag of pot.

"We shouldn't," she said as she opened the package of cookies.

"But we will," I said, and we laughed and ate them still frozen.

I finished my tea while Mary Anne chatted about the upcoming school year, the hopes she had, the disappointments she already knew were in store. Watching her fluttering fingers, her easy smile, I couldn't help thinking that men were stupid, by and large. Mary Anne was a beautiful, fascinating, intelligent woman, a catch by anyone's standard. Yet she'd been on her own for years, and for the first time, I wasn't jealous when I thought of her living next door to Mark, seeing him every day. For the first time, I hoped they did find each other, because neither one of them deserved to be alone.

I checked the clock. Ten minutes until Mark's ferry returned.

I pushed my cup aside. "I thought I was ready to get up, but I'm feeling tired all of a sudden. I think I'll go back to bed."

"Mark said you had a terrible night." She walked with me to the bottom of the stairs. "You go back and lie down. I'll let Mark know when he comes in."

I put my arms around her. Hugged her. Kissed her cheek. "You're a good friend."

She laughed. "I try. Now get up there."

Climbing the stairs, I heard her sit down at the table. Probably having a second cup of tea. Counting the seconds until Mark returned. Closing the bedroom door, I crossed to the window and opened it again. Went to the closet, reached way into the back, and took out the emergency escape ladder—the one I bought when I renovated the second floor, along with a carbon monoxide monitor/smoke detector. Funny the things the brain holds on to—or maybe Al was giving me that break.

Taking the ladder to the window, I placed the grips over the sill. Let the rest of the ladder down slowly, quietly, leaning over so the steel didn't clatter and bang against the house. My heart was beating hard and fast, pumping adrenaline and much-needed courage into my veins as I peered down the length of those metal rungs. If I fell, it probably wouldn't kill me—just put me in the hospital with broken parts, multiple restraints, and an IV drip of extra-strength antidepressants so I couldn't hurt myself again. But what was my alternative? March past Mary Anne? Body-check her if she tried to stop me? Hardly, which meant it was the ladder or nothing.

The wind had a cold edge to it now that made me shiver. Reaching over to the dresser, I grabbed Mark's sweatshirt, and pulled it on over my T-shirt. The sweatshirt was big and bulky, but warm, and the hood would be good when it started to rain. Checking to make sure no one was outside in the neighboring yards, I threw one leg over the sill, let my foot find the first rung. Gripped the handrail with trembling fingers and threw the other leg over. Found the rung and started down, slowly, looking up, not down. Breathing a sigh of relief when one foot finally touched the ground.

Gathering up the life jacket and paddle, I looked around one last time, then made a dash for the hedge that separated my backyard from Mary Anne's. Pushed through the branches and kept going, through her yard and out to the street. Turned right and broke into a run. Heading for my canoe, making my own getaway, kind of wishing I had a swan.

I heard the *Ongiara* approaching as I hauled my canoe into the lagoon. Tossing in the life jacket, I laid my paddle across the gunnels and took my place in the stern. The clouds were growing heavier, darker. The wind was coming up stronger. Out in the lake there would be white caps, but here in the lagoon, the water was calm, the paddling easy.

Sailboats were heading in, along with motorboats and aluminum runabouts. I was the only one heading out, but no one knew that. I was just a little red canoe in the lagoon—destination unknown.

The dock was deserted, the ferry already on its way when I paddled out into the bay, keeping my strokes measured, even—conserving my energy for later. With my head completely clear, I steered the canoe through the Eastern Gap, taking the route Mark and I had been following for weeks, and grateful the current was on my side.

The lake was rough and the going hard once I reached open water and I pushed myself and the paddle to the limit—wishing Big Al would pull his weight for a change. By the time I made it past the Ward's Island beach, I was already tired and hurting, but my timing was perfect. The sailors were all safely home and the threat of rain had driven the tourists away from the beach and the boardwalk. There was no one around to raise an alarm, report a lipstick-red canoe heading out farther and farther into the lake.

The storm blew in stronger and the canoe rose up on the waves and crashed down the other side. Water rushed over the bow, and she wobbled and struggled to stay upright, to follow me out where I wanted to be. The wind grew colder and the rain started falling, stinging my face, my hands. I pulled Mark's hood up over my head, and the sleeves down over my fingers. I could smell him all around me as the canoe tipped from side to side and the waves grew higher and higher.

I knew a moment of fear, of panic, and heard Big Al laugh when I turned the Queen around and started heading back. *Come on in, sweetie*, he said. *I've got the fog cranked up and a nice deep cave all ready to go. It's got your name on it, Ruby, and all your stuff's inside, keeping warm. Come on back. I'm right here, waiting.*

I stared at the shore rocking up and down in the distance. Thought of my girls. Patient Grace and wonderful wayward Liz. Thought of Jocelyn and the woman she could be, Mary Anne and the woman she was. I thought of the mockingbird with his endless love song, and Mark with his endless love for me, and I let my paddle go. That was when I started to cry.

For an instant, my bent-shaft paddle floated beside me, giving me a chance to change my mind, to turn back. But that wasn't going to happen. I was Mark's wife. His bonnie lass. And I would not let Big Al take me from him.

A wave came up, swept my paddle away. Then came another and another, lashing over the bow and across the gunnels. Soaking me, making me shiver. I closed my eyes and drew the sweatshirt closer around me. Filled my head with the scent of Mark and felt the Lipstick Queen roll.

# LIZ

Rain was already falling hard when the deckhand lowered the ramp onto the empty dock at Ward's Island. Fortunately, Nadia had shoved an umbrella into my bag as I was leaving, and I held it in front of me like a shield as I ran full out to the house, knowing I was already late.

My mother had been having a bad few weeks since the wedding, and I'd tried to help out as much as possible. Juggling my work on the Swan Affair with filling in as caregiver so Mark, Grace, and Mary Anne could go to their own jobs and Jocelyn could be a kid. Going to the protest for the first time in years because the bastards were trying to expand the airport again and the Diehards were going to need all the help they could get to fight this one. And spending more time with the woman my mother was becoming than I'd ever spent with the woman she had been and learning more about Alzheimer's than I wanted to know.

But for all the times she'd been confused and angry, there had also been long stretches when she was herself again. Being alone with her—sipping tea in the garden or sharing a joint in the kitchen—had given us a chance to just sit and talk for the first time in years. She told me all the stories about Great-Grandma Lucy—most of which I knew, but a few I'd forgotten—as well as stories of the fight to save our home, and a few about my real father that I think surprised even her.

We talked about Grace too, and William. And the more we talked, the more I realized that Nadia was right—I had nothing to fear from Ruby and nothing to gain by holding on to the past. It didn't matter that my mother wasn't going to remember much of what either of us said. All that mattered was that I had finally forgiven her, and we had both forgiven me. We were starting over. Clean slate, move on. And as an added bonus, it kept Nadia from moving into my room.

When I reached the house, I dropped my umbrella on the porch and went into the kitchen. Mark was seated at the table with his cell phone pressed to his ear, and a laptop open in front of him. "Where's Ruby?" I whispered when he looked over.

He put a hand over the phone. "In bed. Go on upstairs. She won't sleep tonight if she sleeps much longer now."

He went back to his call while I climbed the stairs. Her door was closed so I knocked once. "Ruby?" No answer so I went inside. "Ruby?" Her laptop was on the bed and the window was open. Rain blowing in. An escape ladder in place. My stomach dropped. What the hell had she imagined? A fire? The sheriff coming? Whatever it was had driven her out in a hurry.

I ran to the window and looked down, expecting the worst. Breathing a sigh of relief when all I saw were trampled bushes. But where had she gone?

"Shit." I banged the window down and ran for the stairs. "Shit, shit, shit."

"I'll call you back," Mark said when I swung around the corner into the kitchen.

"She's gone," I said. He stared at me like I was making it up.

"The window was open. She used an escape ladder. I'm telling you, she's gone."

"Impossible." He pushed past me, taking the stairs two at a time. He was closing the window again when I reached the bedroom door. "I didn't hear a thing," he said, his eyes moving from one section of the bedroom to the next, taking inventory. "I was downstairs the whole time, and I didn't hear a goddamn thing."

"She was probably determined to not be heard."

"That's what worries me." He spotted her notebook on the nightstand. "So does that." He flipped it open and I watched his face drain of color. "Ruby, what are you up to?" he whispered, and dropped the book on the bed. Headed back down the stairs.

I picked up the notebook. *I lve you* was scrawled at the top of the page.

"Her paddle is gone," he said when I caught up to him by the back door. He took a raincoat from the hook. "Her goddamn paddle is gone."

Wind drove the rain against the window. "She can't be canoeing in this," I said.

"You'd think so, wouldn't you."

I grabbed my mother's raincoat. "At least she took a life jacket."

He glanced over. "Correction. She took *my* life jacket."

He snatched Grace's binoculars off the shelf. Went down the stairs and through the gate. Heading for the beach and moving faster than I would have imagined possible.

By the time I caught up, he was knee deep in the water, binoculars to his eyes, waves pounding his legs while he scanned the lake. "There." He thrust out a hand. "She's there."

It was hard to see through the rain, and I could barely make out a tiny red dot far out in the water. "Are you sure?"

"Yes," he said, and came back to the beach. Handed me the binoculars while he wiped the water from his face. Then he took out his BlackBerry and punched in three numbers.

I stared at the dot. Lost it. Spotted it. Lost it for long seconds. Released my breath when I spotted it again.

"Goddamn useless cell phone!" he shouted, and walked back to the water with the phone. "Ruby, you bitch!" he bellowed. "Don't do this to me. Please, don't do this."

I grabbed his arm. "Mark, what is she doing? What's going on?"

He shook me off, nearly knocked me over. "She's taking herself out, just like I told you she would. She's getting on the goddamn Ice Floe."

I walked to the edge of the lake. I couldn't believe this was happening. That she'd been serious all along. The red dot was there. And gone. There. And gone. "He's right, Mom," I whispered. "Don't do this. Not now. Not yet."

His phone must have connected at last because I heard him say, "Yes, this is an emergency." And then he went quiet. Came back to the water with the phone pressed to his ear and stared out at that tiny red dot. "My mistake. Everything's fine. I'm sorry."

He pressed End.

"What are you doing?" I shouted. "There's still time. They could save her!" I tried to wrestle the phone from his hand. "Call them back, for chrissakes! Call them back!"

"No!" he roared, easily pushing me way, holding me at arm's length. "This is her choice, Liz. It's what she wants. I won't take that away from her."

He put the phone in his pocket, started back up the beach.

I launched myself at him, nearly knocking him over, landing myself hard in the sand. "You can't do this! You can't leave her out there. You're killing her as surely as she's trying to kill herself!"

"Do you think I want this? I love your mother. I want nothing more than to be here for her, to take care of her, but that's not what *she* wants, Liz. She wants this." He turned and raised a hand to the lake. "She wants this. As you said yourself a while ago, who am I to tell her she's wrong?"

He let his arm drop and looked back at me, his eyes full of

tears, his face crumbling. "If I'm killing her, if that's murder, then so be it. Whatever I do, I'll have to live with guilt. But I'd rather live with the guilt of letting her choose, than the guilt of deciding for her."

I saw the agony, the weight of the decision he was making, the love he was showing my mother. True love. Not self-serving or self-righteous. Just love for the woman she was and her right to fight the battle in her own way, as she had always done. Without judgment, without censure. Only with love.

I put my arms around him, holding this giant of a man close, feeling him brought low by this, my mother's final protest. We stood that way for a moment, then he drew in a long breath and straightened. We must not have been the only ones who spotted her out there because a marine rescue boat was on the way anyway. Slowly but relentlessly covering the distance between the shore and the place where the red dot had been.

We turned away. Walked back to the house in the pouring rain. Put on the kettle. Changed into dry clothes. My mother's track pants were too long for me, the sleeves of the jacket the same. Ruby had always been tall while I was more like my dad. A man she had loved but who had found her too difficult, leaving room in our lives for Mark. How lucky for us.

Mark pulled the ladder out of the window. Packed it away. Replaced the screen. An accident. The whole thing would be an accident. Nothing else for the Island drums to report. Her laptop was open and still turned on. Pictures of the wedding coming up on the screen, fading away, making room for another. Like the frame on the dresser, surrounding us with pictures of my mother and the people who loved her.

I touched the space bar and the pictures gave way to a document. "Show Me the Ice Floe" by Ruby Donaldson. Nothing else. Just that.

"It's her note to me," Mark said. "Letting me know we did the right thing."

He hit Exit. *Save?* He hit No. The file disappeared.

We went downstairs to make tea and wait.

An hour later, someone knocked on the door. An officer from the marine unit.

"Does Ruby Donaldson live here?" he asked. "I'm afraid I have some bad news."

# GRACE

The mockingbirds hatched just after the wedding. These last few weeks, my mom and I would sit in the yard whenever I wasn't working at Lori's, and listen to the babies calling *ce-ce-ce*, demanding food all the time it seemed like. Now the babies have feathers, and I was out in the garden this morning, trimming the roses, making sure everything was perfect for the burial, when one of them landed on the ground, plop, right at the bottom of Great-Grandma Lucy's lilac.

He sat there, blinking his big round eyes and looking around like he couldn't figure out what just happened. Then one of his parents came down and fed him something and tried to get the baby to fly, just like the robin's parents had done. Only this baby wasn't ready to work that hard yet and he kept hopping around on the grass, waiting for more food to be delivered.

I was finished with the roses when another baby poked her head out of the branches and fluttered down to join her brother. And then another and another and another until there were five of them down there, all hopping on the grass and looking around, wondering what they'd gotten themselves into.

The mockingbirds let me get close enough to take pictures of their babies and I ran back inside to show them to Liz and Mark and Jocelyn. My mom would have said, "Better watch for the cats," when she saw the pictures. And she wouldn't have been at all happy to know that once those babies were out of the nest for good, the male would start singing all over again to show the lady how much he loved her, and could they lay some more eggs, please?

But I think she would have liked watching the babies learn to fly. And I think it would have made her laugh when the first guests started to come through the gate, and the mockingbirds went at them right away.

It's been four days since the accident. Neighbors have been coming by the house nonstop ever since, bringing condolences and casseroles and more cakes than we could fit into our freezer and Mary Anne's. Which turned out okay because we served them at the memorial in the clubhouse yesterday.

The same piper who had been at the wedding was there again to play for my mom. There was no tulle and no white lights, but we put pictures around and Mary Anne made a speech about my mom and her growing up together on the Island and being best friends for life. Then Mark got up and talked about the Ruby he knew and loved, who was different in a lot of ways from the one I knew. Then we took the lids off all those casseroles and cut up all that cake. Set out an urn of coffee and pots of tea. Tapped a keg of beer and uncorked bottles of wine. And then we ate and we talked and we laughed.

And when people asked us quietly how the Swan Affair was going, Liz would say, "Grace and Jocelyn are in the clear. How that swan got there is destined to be another unsolved Island mystery." And they'd laugh again and say, "Glad to hear it, glad to hear it."

Islanders sticking together. It's what we do.

A few hours later, when people were gathering up their casserole dishes and their cake plates, we all agreed that the wake for Ruby Donaldson had been almost as much fun as her wedding. But today, standing here in the garden with Joe, waiting for our guests to arrive, I still can't believe it's real. That she went out for a paddle and never came back.

The officers from the rescue unit said it happens all too often. People go out on the lake thinking the weatherman is wrong. That they'll come right back in if the storm does come. But once the wind is up and the waves start rolling, a little canoe can get swept out too far, too fast and getting back isn't so easy anymore.

They said she had a life jacket. Mark's life jacket. She took it by mistake. They look identical and they said that happens all too often too. People take the wrong life jacket, and if the waves are strong and the water rough, sometimes it comes off. Just comes right off, and you're left out there on your own.

I know what that feels like. To be out on the water on your own, afraid, exhausted, ready to give up. Only there was no one swimming with my mom that day. No one to hold on to her and keep her head above the water and stay with her until her feet touched the sand. Help did come but too late for my mom. An accident, they said. A tragic accident. But I know the truth.

Liz and Mark told us when Jocelyn and I arrived back at the house that day. As soon as I saw Liz and Mark and Mary Anne at the kitchen table, I knew something was wrong.

"Oh, Grace," Mary Anne had said, and started to cry.

Liz got up and put an arm around me, then she reached for Jocelyn. "Come and sit down. We need to talk."

Mark sat there, staring at the empty cup in front of him. His eyes were swollen and he looked real tired, like he just wanted to climb the stairs and sleep for a year. But he took a deep breath, lifted his head, and looked at me. "You know as well as I do that your mother was never the kind to let anyone or anything decide the course of her life. She always knew what she wanted and where she was going, and nothing was going to change that. Not even Alzheimer's."

People had been curious after the wedding, wondering why she didn't come out much. Liz told Benny that my mom was just tired, and I heard him at the tennis court after that, repeating what Liz told him whenever people asked how my mom was doing. "She was tired after the wedding," he said. "Needed to spend a little extra time in bed."

Then he'd wink and they'd laugh and I figured that was exactly the way my mom would want it. Ruby Donaldson, shocking at any age.

We'd all worked hard over the last few weeks to keep Big Al a secret because during those times when she talked to me like my mom again, she'd say things like "I will not be an object of pity," and "I will not end up in a home being bathed by strangers who call me dear and wash my hair with the same stuff they use on my body. It's positively barbaric."

I told her I'd bathe her at home and use good shampoo, and she said, "Even worse, Grace. Even worse."

The day it happened, Liz set mugs of tea in front of Jocelyn and me and pushed the milk and sugar toward us. "We all know Mom had been having a bad time these last few weeks," she said as she sat down. "But it wasn't as bad as it could have been because we also knew the truth. We knew what was going on so we could help her, and help each other. And I believe we need to keep it that way. We need to be honest about everything that goes on in this family. That's why you both need to know what really happened to her."

I pulled the mug toward me, wrapped my fingers around it, suddenly cold and needing the warmth.

"Mom was good with a canoe," Liz continued. "She knew exactly what she was doing when she took a life jacket that was too big. And exactly what she was doing when she headed out onto water that was already too rough."

"The police don't know that, of course," Mark added. "They don't know she headed out after the storm started because she knew there would be no one on the break wall to see her. No one to call in an alert about a little red canoe."

"Everyone thinks she was already on the lake before the storm hit," Liz went on. "And no one in this house is ever going to say anything differently. We are Donaldsons after all. We are honest with each other, but our business is our own."

"So she did it on purpose," Jocelyn said quietly, her eyes on the tea in front of her.

Mark sighed. "It's important you understand that Ruby died the same way she lived. In her own time and in her own way. While I am brokenhearted and will miss her forever, I understand why she did it and the courage it took to go out on that water alone. And I hope you can understand too."

Four days later, I understood, and I was happy for her. But I was still sad for me.

"Is everything ready?" Mary Anne asked, coming through the hole in the hedge the way she always has, carrying two small boxes and wearing an outfit my mom would have loved and hated at the same time—silky black pants, a black floaty blouse that fluttered when she walked, and of course, a wide-brimmed black hat. She set the boxes on the patio table beside me. "Wait till you see what I have. Ruby will love it."

We were burying my mom's ashes that afternoon. In the rose garden with Great-Grandma Lucy and Grandma Rose. Only a few people were coming for this part. Mary Anne, of course, Liz's friends Brenda and Nadia, Mark's friend Seth Harrison, as well as Benny, Carol, Marla Cohen, Betty Jane Parker's daughter Chloe, the Watts twins, and Courtney. Fifteen in all. Plus Joe. He had been invited too.

"I thought of your mom the moment I saw this," Mary Anne said, lifting the lid on the box. She'd asked if she could bring the angel for my mom, and no one could think of a reason why she shouldn't.

"Your mom will love it," she said, lifting the statue out of the box and holding it in front of her like an offering—two angels leaning on their elbows, like they were talking to each other.

"Can't you just hear them?" she said. "It's like they're whispering to each other saying, 'Hey, ever hear of Ruby Donaldson? Have I got a story for you.'"

I smiled and touched the wings on each angel. "It's perfect," I said, knowing Mary Anne was right. My mom would love it.

I heard Liz say, "No, go right ahead," and turned, spotting her three doors down with Nadia and Brenda. They had paused so Brenda could take a picture and I heard her saying, "Really, Islanders love it when people take shots of their homes."

She saw me watching her over the fence and shoved a hand in front of Brenda's camera really quick. "To tell you the truth, we hate it. Let's go."

Nadia paused when they reached our gate, watching the baby birds hopping on the lawn while the parents dropped grasshoppers and other treats in front of them. "What is this?"

"A cat buffet," Liz said, and grinned at me. "Wings to go."

"Your sister is evil," Nadia said. "You should let birds get her for that."

I probably should have, but she is my sister, so I went over and opened the gate. "Don't worry. We're on the lookout for cats."

"They are kind of cute," Liz said, kissing my cheek as she went by with a big black bag over her shoulder. "Hope they make it."

"They will." More guests started arriving, so I picked up one of the babies and moved him back from the gate. "I know they will."

Joe knelt down with me as I put the baby back by the lilac. "It's amazing the parents let you do that," he said, checking over his head, not completely sure we wouldn't be attacked.

"They trust me," I said, taking his hand and letting him help me to my feet. Knowing my silly face was still turning pink even though he'd held my hand more than a few times now. And kissed me too. Here, by the gate. He'd even asked me to come to the city and meet his family. And I hoped I'd be able to do that for him one day soon. I really did.

Mark came out of the house with Jocelyn behind him, both balancing a tray of champagne flutes filled with sparkling wine and strawberries. She was wearing the green dress from the wedding. "Black is stupid," she'd said earlier, which was odd because she had so much of it in her closet. "And anyway Ruby liked this."

I wasn't going to argue with her choice. Not when I was wearing jeans and an I ❤ Iyengar T-shirt, and Liz was wearing one of her short skirts and a tank top, and Mark was wearing jeans, and all the other guests were wearing casual clothes as well.

"Yesterday was for formal dress and formal speeches," Mark had said. "Today is strictly for Ruby, and she never did like a fuss."

The kitchen door opened again and Mary Anne appeared with two bakery boxes in her hands, followed by Brenda bringing a tray of flutes with sparkling water and lime. Jocelyn and Brenda let the guests take their pick from the trays, and then we gathered by the rose garden.

I stood at the front with Liz, Jocelyn, Mark, and Mary Anne. The spot for the little pot of ashes had already been chosen, right between my two grandmas. It still made me a little sad that William wasn't there with them. Sadder still that I hadn't been to see him yet. But I would one day soon. I was sure of it.

"Ruby," Mark said. "You left us too soon, my love. But no one will ever forget you." He knelt down, put the little pot into the hole and covered it with earth, patted it down with his hands. Then Mary Anne set the angels behind the mound of earth, setting them in solidly, making sure nothing would disturb them. Then I sprinkled red rose petals all around and Jocelyn sprinkled white.

Then Liz reached into the bag by her feet, pulled out an electric-blue shoe box and held it out to me. "This is for you," she said softly, and lifted the lid.

Inside, nestled in a bed of white tissue paper, was what looked like a little green and blue cookie jar. I lifted out the pot and held it in front of me. "What is it?"

"William's ashes," Liz said, and started to speak really fast. "I couldn't let them put our baby in that place, I just couldn't. So I stole the ashes from the funeral home and kept them in my closet, hoping that one day you'd be able to put them where they belong."

"Box under suits," Nadia whispered to Brenda. "Definitely not shoes."

I stared at the jar. "These are William's ashes? They're not in the city?"

Liz shook her head and motioned to Mark. "I told Mark yesterday that I had them and he suggested I bring them today." She laid her hands over mine. "Grace, I honestly thought Mom would change her mind one day, that's why I stole them. I hope I did the right thing. I hope you're not upset."

"Upset, no." I raised my eyes to hers. "But whose ashes did she sprinkle?"

"Nobody's. They were from the woodstove of some guy I was dating." Liz shrugged and looked back at the guests. "He didn't miss them."

Brenda smiled. "That girl is something else," she whispered to Nadia.

"A real corker." Benny laughed and slapped Nadia on the back. "Just like her mother."

Mark held up a trowel. "Would you like me to do the honors?"

"Thank you." I swiped at a tear and turned back at Liz. "You brought him home."

Liz wiped tears of her own. "I don't have an angel."

"That's okay." I was laughing and crying at the same time now. "That's really okay."

Mark had William's spot ready. Right in the middle of the horseshoe formed by his Grandma Ruby, his Great-Grandma Rose, and his Great-Great-Grandma Lucy. I knelt down, lowered the jar into the hole, covered it with earth, and patted everything down. "Welcome home, little guy," I whispered. "Welcome home."

Nadia held out a small package of tissues. Jocelyn took one and sprinkled red rose petals. Liz took one and sprinkled white. Mary Anne took two and opened the bakery box. "White chocolate and macadamia nut cookies," she said between sniffs. "Ruby's favorite."

"I knew I liked her mother," I heard Nadia say to Brenda as I took a tissue for myself.

"Everybody, please raise your glasses," Mark said. "To Ruby and William Donaldson."

All glasses lifted. "To Ruby and William Donaldson."

"Good-bye to one," Benny said. "Welcome home to the other."

A blast from the horn on the *Ongiara* drew us all around. Kylie and Brianne's mom was at the gate. "You better get going," she said, batting at the mockingbirds while she hurried past the lilac. "I'll watch the babies while you're gone."

"What's going on?" I asked.

"We're going to Fran's," Liz said. "It's not a secret, it's a surprise. Like the ashes. There's a big difference."

"Hurry! Hurry!" Mary Anne said, carrying the box of cookies to the gate, making sure everyone took one on their way out. "We don't want to miss the ferry. Not today."

Liz put a hand over the box when Nadia reached for a cookie. Smiled and held out a Baggie full of carrot and celery sticks instead. "How about this," she said. "Just for today, you don't eat sweets. Tomorrow, maybe. But not today."

Nadia glowered at the vegetable sticks. "You are saying I am addict?"

"I am saying you will make yourself sick." She smacked the Baggie against Nadia's stomach. "Take this and hand over the candies in your pocket."

"You are pain," Nadia said, but took the Baggie and handed over the Werther's. Stuck a celery stick in her mouth and looked as if she might cry when Liz handed the caramels to Jocelyn.

"I do this because I am a good friend," Liz said, hurrying Nadia and Brenda through the gate before coming back for me. "Don't worry, you'll be fine," she said to me, then motioned to Joe. "Take this girl's arm and don't let go until we reach the ferry."

Sixteen people ran to the dock, arriving with stitches in their sides and cookies in their hands—except poor Nadia, who was probably going to be stuck with celery as long as Liz was watching.

The captain of the *Ongiara* blew the horn. Almost there. Just another minute to wait.

"You okay?" Joe whispered as we joined the line for the ferry.

I nodded. Wiped sweat from my upper lip. I could do this. Liz had made reservations at Fran's after all. They were holding the back of the restaurant for us. Sixteen for grilled cheese and apple pie.

"Are you going to finish that?" I heard Nadia say. "Hate to waste."

"I'm eating it," Brenda replied, and I watched her stuff the last of her cookie into her mouth, both friends working to save Nadia from herself.

"By the way," Brenda said to Liz. "My brother asked about you."

"And what did you say?"

"That you were fine. He wants to know if I can give him your number."

Liz smiled in a way I haven't seen her smile in a long time.

Then she surprised me by saying, "Not yet. I need a little more time to just be me. But tell him not to stop asking."

The ferry bumped the dock at last. The ramp slowly lowered and clunked on the ground. "It'll be okay," Joe said again, and took my hand. "It'll be okay."

I shook my head. "I'm not sure, Joe. I'm not sure."

"Excuse me," I heard Liz say. "Excuse me." She came through the crowd to where I stood. "I'm borrowing her," she said to Joe, then took my arm and pulled me over to where Jocelyn was waiting with her friends. "You," Liz said, and held out an arm to her. "Come on. All three of us are going to be first on the ferry!"

"Gotta go," Jocelyn said, looping an arm with me and moving with us to the front of the line. Finally, we stood at the head of the pack. Liz, me, and Jocelyn. Arms linked, facing forward while the deckhand slowly opened the gate.

Liz held me tighter, smiled at me. "Ready?"

I swallowed. "Ready."

"Don't look down!" Jocelyn said, and the two of them stepped forward, carrying me along. Taking me onto the ramp and all the way across, not stopping until my feet hit the deck of the *Ongiara*. I looked down, saw where I was, and the three of us whooped and cheered and kept on going, heading for the gate on the other side. Behind me I could hear our friends and family cheering me on as they came across the ramp to join us.

"Goin' to Fran's!" Jocelyn shouted.

"Goin' to Fran's!" I shouted back, and we were first in line when that ferry bumped the dock on the other side.